Dear Reader,

I did a fair amount of my growing up on a small farm in Hamilton County, Texas. When I wasn't hoeing squash or picking okra (my father and I have differing opinions as to how much of this I actually did) I was reading. Fred Gibson set his stories a couple of counties over from the very ground I worked, so *Old Yeller* and *Savage Sam* were some of the first books I read. I watched "Gunsmoke" and "The Rifleman" with my grandpa and listened to him talk about his boyhood trapping and hunting in central Texas. To me, the West was real and it was right outside my door. From my bedroom window, I could make out the ghost-white limestone markers on the neighboring ranch where a Comanche raiding party had massacred a young school teacher and her five students only a few generations before. My local librarian told me the Texas Rangers had played a large part in chasing down the renegades. So, I read everything I could get my hands on about Indians or Texas Rangers.

When it came time to choose a career, law enforcement seemed like the only choice—and early on, when I realized I wanted to write, Western stories came naturally to my pen.

When I was a young-pup detective, it was a savvy Texas Ranger who gave me some of the best advice I've ever heard—on police work and writing.

It was my first homicide investigation, and I was twenty-six years old. The victim was a pretty college coed. The poor thing's body had been dumped in a weedy ditch along a lonely gravel road, where we found her three days later. Everything I knew to do, I did twice and had a good start on a stomach ulcer by the time the Ranger pulled up in his dark blue Crown Victoria and strode over to where I stood a couple of feet upwind from the corpse. Without speaking, he hunkered down on the heels of his lizard skin boots to take a closer look.

I squatted beside him. "Billy," I pleaded. He'd have slapped me if I'd called him "Ranger" like they did in the movies. "I'm not sure what to do. You've investigated dozens of murders. Teach me."

Billy nudged the straw hat back on his head a few inches and picked at his teeth with the flat wooden toothpick he never seemed to be without. "Well, Markus," he said, fooling with the toothpick as he spoke. "Just write down everything you see . . ."

At that moment a tiny pupa, which had only recently been a wriggling critter feeding on the decaying body, hatched into a sticky, green-backed fly and flew straight into the Ranger's mouth. I looked on in horror but he never missed a beat. He picked out the fly with a thumb and forefinger, returned the toothpick to the corner of his mouth and gave me a wry smile.

"Just write down everything you see . . . and watch out for the blow flies."

Over the years, I've been fortunate enough to work with beat cops, detectives, Rangers, deputy marshals, and a whole alphabet soup of federal law enforcement agents who exemplify those standards set by the lawmen I read about as a boy. The spirit of the Old West lives in them—and most are far more interesting than any character I could ever dream up. We've had some hellacious adventures together, and through it all, I've tried to follow the Ranger's advice and keep good notes.

I'll apologize now if my comrades-at-arms find any piece of themselves reflected between these pages. You see, they may have different names, but I've had the privilege of riding with Trap, Clay, Hezekiah, and many of the others.

I only hope I can make their stories as gritty and real to you as they are to me . . . so enjoy the adventure—and watch out for the blow flies.

Respectfully,

Mark Henry
Anchorage, Alaska
May 2005

To Hell and Beyond

Mark Henry

PINNACLE BOOKS
Kensington Publishing Corp.
www.kensingtonbooks.com

PINNACLE BOOKS are published by

Kensington Publishing Corp.
119 West 40th Street
New York, NY 10018

All Kensington titles, imprints, and distributed lines are avail-
able at special quantity discounts for bulk purchases for sales
promotions, premiums, fund-raising, educational, or institu-
tional use. Special book excerpts or customized printings can
also be created to fit specific needs. For details, write or phone
the office of the Kensington sales manager: Kensington Publishing Corp., 119 West 40th Street, New York, NY 10018, attn:
Sales Department; phone 1-800-221-2647.

PINNACLE BOOKS, the Pinnacle logo, and the WWJ steer
head logo are Reg. U.S. Pat. & TM Off.

ISBN-13: 978-0-7860-4204-3
ISBN-10: 0-7860-4204-4

First printing: June 2017

10 9 8 7 6 5 4 3 2

Printed in the United States of America

First electronic edition: June 2017

ISBN-13: 978-0-7860-4205-0
ISBN-10: 0-7860-4205-2

CONTENTS

HARD ROAD
TO HEAVEN

For Ty, who provided the tinder,
And Victoria, who gave me the spark

PROLOGUE

Boston
August 1910

Angela Kenworth's mother was dead-set against her having any adventure that required the wearing of britches.

"*. . . a great Western adventure!*" her father's telegram had promised. "*. . . suggest you bring at least two pair of canvas trousers.*"

"Young lady, adventure is nothing more than the lie your memory tells you about hardship you've been forced to endure. I stand resolute on this matter."

Mother fastened the buckle on Angela's leather valise with an air of staunch finality, lest any britches find their way inside.

When Mother stood resolute on anything, it did no good to argue. "I will not permit a young woman associated with me or this family to be seen in Montana dressed like a rough boy. Pants have no place on a proper lady when it comes to adventuring."

Mother swelled up like a deviled toad when Kitty, the Irish housekeeper, quietly agreed, observing that she herself had had many fine adventures without her pants. The woman was no smarter than a stick and if she hadn't been such a gifted cook, Mother would have long since given her the sack.

"I shall always despise your father for dragging you out to that dreadful place," Mother said, driving poor Kitty from the room with a withering stare. As if the fact that she chose to live two thousand miles from her husband wasn't already enough to show how resolute she stood in her feelings for the man. "You long for adventure, Angela, but believe you me, all you will get is rough men and red savages."

"Honestly, Mother," Angela said, running an ebony brush through thick auburn hair. "It's the twentieth century. Everyone west of the Mississippi River isn't still mired in the 1800s battling Indians and dueling in the streets at high noon."

Mother waved her off with an exasperated gasp and went in search of Kitty to check on breakfast. Angela picked up her father's telegram. She had it memorized, but read it again anyway. "Mother, you'll get the vapors if you don't calm down," she sighed softly to herself. "Red savages in this day and age?"

Mother's resolution on the matter not withstanding, civilization had even come to places like Montana.

CHAPTER 1

Montana
August 18, 1910

Six days after the train groaned away from Boston's North Station, seventeen-year-old Angela Kenworth showed some resolution of her own and tossed two gray linen traveling skirts out the window of a swaying, horse-drawn coach.

Evidently, her father's idea of adventure had little to do with comfort. It was miserably hot inside the jigging vehicle that seemed to spend more time on two wheels than four. Angela leaned her head back against the smooth, maroon leather upholstery and tugged at the knees of her new canvas britches, regretting the loss of the airy skirts. The snug pants caused her to sweat profusely, confining and pinching in countless unmentionable places. Unable to do anything about it, she consoled herself with the fact that she was no longer confined to the elegant prison of her home in Boston.

Outside, what her father had described as rolling green hills of pine and hemlock had been reduced to charred rock and ruined black snags. Every few minutes the coach rolled over a scab of burned ground, some hundreds of feet across. Mountains of the Bitterroot range peeked up through a brown haze all around her, emerald isles above a sea of greasy smoke.

Her father hadn't mentioned the fires, and she had yet to see him so she could ask about them. A tall, strapping German fellow with soap-scrubbed skin had met them at the station in Saltese and introduced himself as Fritz Mueller, her father's representative. He had white-blond hair, sun-bronzed skin, and chiseled features that made Mother's representative, Betty Donahue, trip on her skirts to fawn over him.

Betty drooped beside Angela, fanning her face with a lace handkerchief. She was a fleshy woman, prone to copious sweating even in cooler weather. Beads of perspiration pasted blond curls to her high forehead and glistened over a moist upper lip. She had a dark, if somewhat alluring, smile of a stain at the scooping neckline of her robin's-egg dress. Mother considered Betty her spy, but at twenty-four the flighty woman was only a few years older than her charge and not much more mature than her five-year-old son, Shad, who sat at her knee playing with a toy wooden horse. Betty did a marvelously irreverent impersonation of Mother by plugging one nostril while she spoke.

"I despise the fact that you've dragged me out to this godforsaken wilderness." Betty's put-on whine harmonized perfectly with the chattering coach wheels. She used the hankie to dab at the sweat that sparkled like a beaded necklace and pooled into a clear jewel at the center of her abundant bosom.

"What does *despise* mean?" Shad said, wiping his forehead, without looking up from the toy horse. He had blond hair like Betty, and shared her tendency to wilt in the heat. Mother had thrown her weight in on the matter of his traveling clothes as well, and he wore an absurdly frilly white shirt with ruffled cuffs, brown knickers, and white knee socks that made him look like a sweaty little George Washington out for a visit to Montana.

Betty let her own brogue slip back while she continued to press the lace against her cleavage, though all the sweat had long since been dabbed away.

"*Despise* describes the way you feel about turnips, dear." She spoke to her son, but kept a hungry gaze on the handsome young German across from Angela. Betty's late husband had been a fisherman out of Gloucester who was lost at sea. She was heavily in the market for another, and the bosom dabbing was her not-so-subtle method of advertisement.

Shad curled his freckled nose and rolled his toy horse across the leather seat between him and the gentleman. "I despise turnips," he said.

"Mr. Mueller, how much further to my father's mining operation?" Angela asked, as much to rescue the poor man from Betty's heaving flirtations as for any desire to have a short journey.

"One half of one hour," the young man said in a clipped accent. "Please to call me . . ."

A sharp crack outside the coach cut him off, and

he cocked his head to one side, listening. Panic seized his blue eyes, and he tore his gaze away from Betty to stare down at his chest. A crimson bloom spread rapidly across the pressed fabric of his shirt.

He blinked, opened and closed his mouth like a fish out of water, gasping for air. "I am shot." A thin sheen of blood covered his perfect teeth.

Angela heard the driver's shrill whistle, and fell back against her seat as the horses leaped forward into a frantic gallop along the tilted, hillside road.

"Oh, Dear Lord!" Betty put the hankie to her open mouth and gaped, wide-eyed, at the bleeding man. Angela turned to look out her window, and got a glimpse of approaching riders emerging from a cloud of dust behind them. She heard the German groan. His cool hand yanked back surprisingly hard on her shoulder. If not for the blood and the dazed look in Mueller's pale eyes, she would have thought this was all part of her father's idea of an adventure.

"Please, don't, Miss Kenworth," Mueller said through clenched teeth. Pink spittle foamed at the corner of his tight lips.

An arrow whistled through the same window and lodged in the wall directly above Mueller with a re-verberating thud. Shrieking whoops echoed amid rifle shots and the _thwack_ of more arrows outside the coach. A shadow flew past Angela's window as the burly man riding shotgun tumbled from his perch.

The coach careened wildly as it picked up speed, bouncing over rocks and ruts. Shad clutched his toy horse, his eyes locked on the German's glistening red shirt. A crackling wheeze racked the poor man's body at each ragged breath.

Mueller pressed a hand over his wound. It seemed to help some—just enough for him to speak.

"Not much time," he groaned, risking a weary glance out his window. "These highwaymen . . . seek money . . . still dangerous. I promise . . . keep you safe. Please . . ." He held a hand out to a cowering Betty to pull her and her son across the coach, leaving the seat next to Angela vacant. Mueller's wheezing grew worse by the moment, his voice little more than a whispered croak. "Behind you . . . in seat . . . is knob. Push . . ." Mueller's eyes clouded, fluttering in a vain effort to remain conscious.

He was drowning in his own blood.

Angela's mind raced while she groped in the crease of smooth leather where the bench met the backrest. It was a tight fit, even for her small hand, and made more difficult by the jigging coach.

This was all impossible. A bone-numbing scream pierced the window as surely as any arrow and made her blood go cold.

Indians.

"I can't find anything." Angela's voice rattled with the coach. She was almost in tears. Searching frantically, her hand finally closed around a cool metal knob. She gave it a push and the leather padding next to her tilted up and forward toward Betty to reveal a hidden compartment the size of a small coffin.

Another bullet smashed into the paneling next to Mueller. Splinters of yellow wood shot across the crimson mess that covered the front of his shirt and oozed between his fingers. He didn't have enough energy to flinch.

"Your father uses . . . to hide precious cargo." Mueller rasped. "Today, you are such cargo."

Angela looked at the dark box and then up at Betty's pleading eyes. "But there's only room for one. I can't . . ."

"No time . . . to argue . . ." The German pulled a black pistol from his waistband and stared resolutely out the window. His breath was shallow, his face sickeningly pale. It seemed a struggle for the once-powerful man to hold the heavy weapon.

"They are upon us." His voice was no more than a whisper now—hardly audible above the melee. "It is your father's place . . . to decide . . ."

A volley of gunfire shattered the air. Betty flinched at each report, and Shad pressed his hands against his ears. Above them, the driver gave a muffled yelp and the coach began to slow.

A chorus of hoofbeats grew louder and drowned out the coach wheels amid the yelping shouts of approaching riders. Angela looked again at Betty's panic-stricken face.

She refused to believe this was happening. "I don't care what my fa . . ."

Mueller's head lolled forward: chin on bloody chest. He was beyond arguing.

The shooting stopped.

"Shad, honey," Angela whispered. She turned the trembling boy's face away from the gore-covered German. "I need you to lie down in here and be very quiet." Her voice was higher than normal, tight and overflowing with urgency.

Shad looked up at his mother and sucked his bottom lip. The tips of his small fingers pressed white as he clutched his toy horse.

"Hurry, sweetie," Betty said. Her eyes were awash, and her tremulous chest now heaved with terror and grief.

Harsh voices milled outside the slowing coach, mingling with the protestations and snorts of horses jerked to a stop.

Angela looked down at Shad in the compartment. "Quiet now. No matter what you hear."

The shadow of men on horseback flashed past the window. Moments later, heavy footfalls approached.

The seat snapped shut over little Shad Donahue with a resounding click at the same instant the doors flew open. Rough hands dragged the women from their seats on opposite sides of the coach. After the dimly lit interior, the blazing daylight combined with the shock of their circumstances proved blinding and Angela saw only a dark silhouette. Brutish men with stinking breath pawed at her body and threatened to yank her arms from their sockets.

She struggled against her captors, but bit her lip to keep from screaming.

Betty had no such compunction, and her mournful wails rocked the carriage between them.

CHAPTER 2

Montana
August 19

Except for the spot where the blue-eyed mare kicked him above the left knee, Trap O'Shannon woke feeling reasonably pain-free for someone who'd spent most of his forty-eight years sleeping on the ground. He pulled a thin cotton sheet up around his bare shoulders to ward off the morning chill, and tried to nestle deeper into the feather mattress. A twenty-year-old knife wound, puckered and white, decorated the tan flesh over his left shoulder. The injury had gone all the way to the bone, and it troubled him from time to time, particularly if the weather turned cold. Trap was getting to the age where he babied it a little.

Maggie had insisted on three windows in the bedroom when they built their small log home in the shadow of the Bitterroots. Ever a practical man, Trap was sure two windows would be enough, but like most times, he'd let his wife have her way. This summer had proven hotter that normal, and he'd ended up glad she'd cajoled him into that particular luxury. The night before had been so hot, they'd left all the windows open to try and catch a little of the smoky cross-breeze. It seemed a better choice to choke to death on cool, smoky air than bake in confined hot air with the smoke settled out of it.

It would be miserable again when the sun finally poked over the mountain east of O'Shannon's two-room cabin. Most of the fires had slept with the night, and though their smell still lingered, the air was slightly less congested. The cool shadows out the side window, nearest Trap, were green instead of gray, and he managed to take in a full breath of air without coughing. The day would be another scorcher, but with morning's chilly breath still lingering in the cabin, he was happy to have a warm bed and an even warmer wife to sidle up against.

Maggie was still asleep, facing away from him, her airy cotton gown bunched above her hips. Her knees were drawn up toward her belly. One bronze arm ran down in front of her, hand resting between her thighs, the other flung back above her head in careless abandon. Even as she slept, there was something feral about this woman that moved Trap like nothing else. She was still the same fierce creature he'd met when she was only fourteen—older now, with a little more meat on her bones—but just as wild.

Maggie had always been hot-natured. Even in winter conditions that left Trap's teeth chattering, she'd preferred to keep the tent wall rolled up a hair or the window cracked enough to ensure a steady draft.

Her side of the sheet was pushed down to a crumpled pile at her feet, and though the night's chill still lingered in the air, thick tresses of long, black hair sweated to the pillow ticking. She breathed the heavy breaths of exhausted sleep, belly rising and falling deeply with the slow, even rhythm of her soft purr.

They'd been up well past three in the morning playing midwife to the newest spotted mare while she gave birth to her first foal. It was a difficult delivery. Trap knew horses and he was no quitter, but twice, he'd sworn the mare was done for and started for his gun.

Maggie was a different story. A horse was not just important to the Nez Percé culture. It represented the culture itself, and saving one was worth all efforts. She'd refused to give up.

Prayers and mournful songs, helped heavenward by smoke from a bundle of burning sweetgrass from her medicine bag, had filled the dry night air.

The gods Maggie prayed to were a lot like Trap's father's God, who said somewhere or another in His Bible that a good deal of work had to be sprinkled in with your praying.

Maggie had prayed and sang and prayed some more, eventually working her small hand into the birth canal. As much communication as manipulation, whatever magic she'd done had worked.

Just before three A.M., two tiny hooves and a brown nose appeared under the mare's tail. She gave a moaning push and a dandy, spotted mule colt came sloshing out with a gush and a plop into the smoky world.

The coming of a new foal was always a magical event, and the O'Shannons had lingered for a time without talking, arm in arm, marveling at the beauty of it. Once the new baby was nursing well, they'd come inside and collapsed.

Now, Trap coughed quietly and rested a hand on the soft skin above his wife's hip where it melted into her belly. He wasn't sure of the time, but the smoke hanging lazily in the shaft of window light told him the fires were awake again. His grumbling stomach said it was late morning. He didn't care. He wasn't in the Army anymore. Wriggling closer, he nestled against the furnace of Maggie's body. His face buried in the dense tangle of her hair, Trap took a deep breath, drawing in the earthy aroma of ritual sweet-grass smoke that lingered there with the thousand other assorted Maggie-smells that held him together like glue.

He reckoned serenely to himself how retirement— or at least this change in job—had a lot of things going for it.

Maggie stirred. Though she faced away from him, Trap could tell she'd opened her eyes.

"You make coffee?" she said, the rhythm of her breath remaining slow and constant. "I can't smell any coffee."

For three decades, Maggie Sundown O'Shannon of the Wallowa Nez Percé had proven herself a devoted wife and mother, but since moving to their small homestead, Trap had spoiled her a little by making their morning coffee himself.

Trap snuggled closer and nuzzled the half-moon

bite scar on the side of her neck, just below her ear. "Why would I want coffee when I can drink in the smell of my wife?"

Maggie's lips smacked as she woke up slowly. She stretched her head back with a groan, rubbing her thick hair against Trap's cheek. Bits of hay from the ordeal with the mare the night before still hid among the strands. "This old woman's smell will not warm and wake you like some good, hot coffee."

"Oh, I don't know, old woman. I think your smells are waking me just fine." He pressed closer to her, his breath heavy against her ear.

Slowly, she rolled over to face him. "Mmm, I can tell."

She didn't bother with her gown—a fact that Trap considered a promising sign. Fully awake now, she slid a leg over the top of his, drawing him closer with the crook of her heel. Soft, familiar fingers brushed a wisp of salt-and-pepper hair out of his face. He sighed when she touched him on the end of his nose.

"It's not too hot yet." She winked. "I still want coffee, but I suppose it can wait a . . ."

Maggie stopped suddenly, and rose up on one elbow to look toward the east window.

"What is it?" Trap had learned over time to trust his wife's instincts even above his own.

"The horses," she said softly, craning her neck toward the window. She caressed Trap's shoulder over the puckered knife scar. "Our new mother is speaking."

"To who?"

"A visitor." Maggie withdrew her hand, letting it slide teasingly down his bare chest, stopping at his belly. "Someone's coming on a horse she doesn't know."

Trap threw back the sheet and gave his wife's bare rump a frustrated swat.

"It better be someone important. I hate to leave this behind."

Maggie snorted, but left the sheet where it was.

"Tell them we're not buying then, and come back to bed with me before the day heats up."

Trap heard the horses nicker, and scrambled to his feet. No matter where they went, there were always a sizable number of folks who didn't take too kindly to Indians, or him being married to one. It was a funny notion, considering his own lineage, but he had his father's thick shadow of a beard and small-ish nose. That was enough to pass for white among most folks. Nobody had said anything to him yet about Maggie, no more than a buzzing whisper or two at the store, but the feelings were there and he knew it, seething and simmering just below the surface. He'd learned over the years to take no chances when it came to uninvited visitors.

Hopping up and down, half-naked, on one foot, he tried to pull his britches up without falling back on the bed. Maggie chuckled at his little dance. The teasing sparkle of mischief in her dark eyes didn't help matters at all.

"You don't look like an old man right now." She pulled her battered Winchester off the pegs on the wall beside her while she watched. The fact she could shoot the little .44-40 better than most men had added to Trap's confidence on more than one occasion.

He winked back at his wife. He'd be hard pressed to find anything more beautiful than his stocky little bride bathed in the yellow swath of window light, holding a rifle and wearing her thin cotton gown—the hem of which had now fallen down to her knees, to Trap's chagrin. Britches finally buttoned, he abandoned the idea of a shirt and yanked up his canvas suspenders. Clopping hoofbeats passed the front door on their way to the barn. He craned his head toward the open window, listening for a moment.

"Two horses." He scooped up the long rifle that leaned against the wall on his side of the bed. Apart from the bed and a clay washbasin on a chest of drawers, the two rifles were the only furnishing in the room.

Maggie held up two fingers and nodded, agreeing with his assessment.

"I've a mind to shoot whoever I find out there," he said, giving his wife one last dispirited look before he stepped into the front room and eased open the heavy wooden door.

The bright light of morning hit Trap in the eyes like a punch in the beak, a sharp contrast to the cool atmosphere inside the cabin. He squinted to watch the tail of a tall sorrel round the corner in back of his log barn across the stump-strewn yard.

"Help you?" He kept the gun inside the shadow of the doorway, out of sight but within easy reach. There was a hard, uninviting edge to his voice. Maggie watched with her rifle through the east window of the bedroom.

It was already hot outside. So hot it seemed if a man looked at the same spot of parched grass too long, a flame would jump up to meet him. The smell of burning pine pitch hung heavy in the thickening air. Soon the cabin would be hot as well—much too hot to suit Maggie. Trap let the frustration slip out in his voice.

"What can I do for you?" he yelled toward the barn.

"Pa?" A horse snorted and the hollow thump of hooves grew louder as two riders wheeled and came trotting around the barn to the front porch. The O'Shannons' son, Blake, rode a red-freckled leopard Appaloosa they'd given him the year before. A lanky sorrel gelding followed. The sight of the man riding it brought tears to Trap's eyes.

Blake O'Shannon trotted his blocky, pink-nosed gelding up to his father and dismounted. At twenty-four, he stood ramrod straight and just under six feet tall—a trait he'd inherited from his mother's Nez Percé side of the family, along with her black-coffee eyes and the thick head of hair that he kept short, above his ears. He took off a gray, flat-brimmed hat and leather gloves to shake Trap's hand. A shiny silver star decorated the left breast of his light blue shirt. The badge was something Trap hadn't seen before. He gave his son a curious look, but didn't mention it.

"Look who I brought to see you." The young man beamed.

"Ky Roman." The elder O'Shannon shook his head and rubbed the rest of the sleep out of his twinkling eyes. "Lord have mercy, I haven't seen you since . . . How long has it been?" There was much hand-clasping and backslapping between words.

"Twelve years, give or take," the tall man said with

a wide, easy grin. He wore a brown bowler hat and a natty pinstripe suit of matching color. "It was before I left for Cuba."

"Thought you'd be surprised." Blake looked quizzically at his father. "What were you doing in the house at this time of day? You feeling sick?"

The front door to the house fairly exploded off its hinges and a barefooted Maggie ran out to give her son a crushing hug that knocked the hat out of his hands. Though they saw him several times a month, an only son could never visit enough to suit her. Once she released her son, she smiled at Ky and took his hand with both of hers, kissing him softly on the cheeks. Blake ducked his head, kicking at the dirt with the toe of his boot when he saw his mother still wore her nightgown and realized his father had no shirt on.

Roman noticed his embarrassment, and nudged the young man's shoulder. "You think this is bad, kid, you should have seen them when they were youngsters."

Maggie narrowed her eyes and shook a bronze finger at Ky. "You were a youngster yourself if I remember, Hezekiah." She sighed softly, pushing a stray lock of hair out of her face. "Is Irene with you?"

Roman shook his head. "I fear she had a lengthy list of commitments to her women's group back home. She did tell me to say hello to you, and warned me to bring back all your news."

Maggie let her head tilt to one side, her eyes glistening. "I do miss her. How is she these days?"

"Beautiful and pious as ever. She still drags me to

church every time the doors open whether I need it or not."

"I'm sure she knows what's best," Maggie said, patting the back of Roman's hand.

He chuckled. "So is she."

Maggie sighed, smoothing the front of her thin gown. "I suppose I should go and put on some clothes. Welcome to our home, Hezekiah Roman."

She turned to go back in the house, then stopped to ponder her son's face for a moment. "Something serious vexes this boy," she said over her shoulder to Trap. Her hand held Blake's cheek for a time, then slipped slowly off as she walked to the front door.

Trap watched her disappear into the cooler interior of the cabin, and hoped he was the only one who noticed the teasing wink she gave him before the door swung shut.

"How are you getting along, Ky?" O'Shannon leaned his rifle against the log wall and gave his friend a proper looking over. He'd grown a bit older in the space of twelve years. They both had.

Roman was made for the Army, with piercing gray eyes and a no-nonsense military bearing that made him look a decade older than his peers. Had he not been in command, the rest of the unit would have still respected him as their elder even though he was only five years older than Trap. The mainstay of his mystique came from the creed by which he lived.

"*When it comes to what's right, gentlemen, never pause— Proceed,*" he'd often tell his men. When the lines got fuzzy to everyone else, Captain Ky Roman always seemed able to tell the difference.

He'd trimmed back his already tame mustache so it was no more than a whisper of the one he used to wear; just a thin silver line under his hawkish nose to match the silver in his hair. The added gray and the extra pound or two around his middle only added to his natural surety, and gave him the dignified air of an honest politician—if there was such a thing. There was an aura—Maggie called it a smell—that fairly flowed from Roman's presence. He was the kind of man other men naturally trusted and followed.

"You hear Geronimo passed over last year?" Roman asked.

Trap took a deep breath and pensively toed the dirt.

"*Goyathlay.*" He whispered the warrior's Apache name reverently. Of course he'd heard about the death of their old adversary. It was big news across the entire country. Still, it came at him hard every time he thought about it. Trap had wished the ruthless, old killer dead dozens of times—cursed the ground he'd walked on. Then, he'd seen a photograph of the deflated war leader posing in some kind of Plains Indian feather getup like some sort of sideshow attraction. All the starch was completely gone from the once-proud man.

Now, each time Trap heard the name Geronimo, he could no longer think of the times they'd skirmished in the sweltering deserts and mountain country of the fierce Chiricahua. He could only ponder on the dispirited eyes of the withered old man in the photographs. It was better for some people to die in battle, but Trap tried to keep such thoughts out of his mind. He was, after all, an old warrior himself.

"Heard you got sick with the Rough Riders." Trap leaned against a rough-cut porch pillar and used it to scratch his back while he spoke. He was already beginning to sweat, even without a shirt.

Roman shrugged. "A lot of us did. Turned out to be fortuitous I went, though. Roosevelt has more energy than anyone I ever saw. Bowl right over you if you let him, but he's a friendly sort and got to know some of us quite well. It never hurts to have a friend in the White House. Old Teedie got me the marshal's appointment in Arizona after he got elected."

"I heard. Sure appreciate you helping Blake get on as a tracker with the federal boys up here. He's a good man, but with his mama and me as his breeding stock, a fellow needs a little extra boost to get a good job in these parts." Trap thumped the badge on Blake's chest with a forefinger. "What's this all about anyway? Since when they let you pin on the star?"

The fact that anyone with as much Indian blood as Blake O'Shannon would be allowed to wear a badge when he was barred from a good many establishments in Montana was a little hard for Trap to believe. Tracking for the marshals was one thing. Everyone expected an Indian to know how to track. Pinning a badge on one, that was another matter.

"I deputized him, Trap," said Roman.

O'Shannon brimmed with a thousand things he wanted to ask his old commander, but bit his tongue knowing the man would get to most of them in his precise, methodical way. Instead of quizzing the captain, he turned an eye back toward his son.

"You all right? You know your mama. If she says

you're vexed, you best just go on ahead and consider yourself vexed."

"Big things going on, Pa." Blake was not normally the fidgeting sort of person, but he twisted the stained cowhide gloves back and forth in his hands. "Think I might be in over my head here."

"Sounds serious." Trap scooped up the rifle and took a deep breath. All his life, he'd preferred to be busy while he worked important things through in his head. Digging a ditch, sharpening a knife, or feeding horses; it didn't matter. His brain worked better when it was lubricated with a fair amount of elbow grease. "Follow me, boys, and let's talk. I got a new mama out here who deserves a little grain."

While the scoop of oats hissed into a wooden feed bunk, Ky Roman put his boot on the bottom rail of the fence and leaned across the top.

"Truth is, Trap, I'd intended to come look in on you next week when my business was done in Spokane. Blake knew I was there and sent word yesterday for help. Shortly after I got his call, I received a wire from President Taft."

"*The* President Taft?" Trap bent to step between the fence rails, and began to rub the spotted mule colt while its mother munched oats. He'd met a number of important men in his life and was not easily impressed; though it was a curious thing such an important man would be calling on Ky in Spokane.

Blake said, "A girl named Angela Kenworth was kidnapped off the NPR right-of-way yesterday afternoon." He seemed to glow with nervous energy, and the spotted mare gave him an anxious snort. Blake noticed, and stepped away from the fence completely to keep from spooking the horse and agitating his father.

Trap calmed the new mother with a reassuring pat on the shoulder. He said to Blake, "Your mama was right. You are vexed at that. I feel bad about the girl, son, but you've tracked bad men before."

Blake looked at Roman, then back at his father. "From the looks of things, it was Indians that got her."

Trap let the odd news slide by. It was a modern world. Indians didn't do this sort of thing anymore. "This girl any relation to Peter Kenworth of the PK Gold and Timber Company?"

"His seventeen-year-old daughter," Roman said through his teeth, his chin on the top rail. "She was on her way to visit him from Boston where she lives with her mother. Her party was bushwhacked west of Saltese right at the junction with Goblin Creek. Most everyone else was killed and the Kenworth girl's gone missing. The kidnappers did leave behind her little finger."

"Still wearing a ruby ring," Blake added, staring blankly at the nursing colt.

"I heard there was still some renegades operating out of the Sierra Madre." Trap picked up each of the mule colt's feet, rubbing and tapping them to help gentle it for future shoeing. "We got us some deserted places up here in Montana, but none as bad as Mexico." His brow now furrowed deeply in thought. "Any place up here where a body could sell a white woman in this day and age?"

"Not that I know of." Blake shook his head. "But they only took the one. There was another woman in the party. Whoever did this used her something awful, then killed her. If they were looking to sell women, why only take one and murder the other?"

The two older men looked at each other; then Trap took a deep breath. There were certain aspects of life a father hoped he never had to pass along to the next generation. "I don't know, son. Could be a whole lot of reasons. Maybe one of them fought harder and hurt their manly pride? The Kenworth girl could be dead already somewhere else and you just haven't found the body yet." He shrugged. *"Quién sabe?"* Who knows?

Blake said, "We found a five-year-old boy hiding, but everyone else is dead. They were butchered, Pa . . ." The young lawman's eyes turned glassy for a moment. He gave his head a shake to clear his thoughts. "Anyhow, the kid hid out in a secret compartment under the seat where Kenworth hides gold he's bringing out from the mines."

Blake described the bloody scene to his father. He told him of finding the frightened blond boy, wide-eyed and catatonic, hiding in the dark box under the leather seat, the ammonia smell of urine and the buzzing drone of the green flies the only thing to give away his location.

"Looks like his mama was the woman they killed."

"Does he say it was Indians done it?" Trap straddled the mule colt and rubbed its long ears while it nuzzled the mare's flank.

"No, but there's arrows everywhere, and I counted at least two different sets of moccasin tracks along with a lot of boot prints. The bodies were carved up something fierce. Pa, when was the last time you heard of an Indian raiding party?"

Trap shrugged but said nothing.

Blake looked up toward the house to make sure his mother wasn't coming. "That's right. Nobody uses a bow anymore. I don't know much about Flathead or Blackfoot arrows or any of the Montana tribes."

He turned to focus on his father. "I could be dead wrong about this . . ." He paused, looking over at Roman.

"Blake says the arrows are made of salt cedar, which I assume doesn't grow up here," Ky said. His eyes groaned with fatigue. "I think he ought to be one who could recognize the track left by an Apache moccasin. Don't you?"

Trap stood up and climbed back through the fence, rubbing the sore spot over his knee. "How many people know about this?"

"Old Chauncey Skidmore found the bodies while he was making his deliveries."

"Everyone from here to Bozeman then." Trap bounced a closed fist on the top fence rail while he thought. The dry-goods salesman was a renowned tongue-wagger. The telephone was making a general appearance around western Montana, but there were still only two surefire ways to spread information: telegraph and tell-Chauncey.

"Since it happened on railroad right-of-way, there's been a lot of folks see it," Blake said. "Heck, they're ridin' by on flatcars to have free peeks at the show."

"True." Roman nodded. "But I doubt anybody around here could tell the difference between an Apache arrow and a quill pen."

"They don't have to." Trap chewed on the inside of his cheek while he chewed on the situation. "Most of these folks couldn't tell Geronimo and Chief Joseph apart if you stood 'em both side by side. They'll see a bunch of arrows and feel free to take their leave to exercise a hate for all Indians. They won't need to take the time to focus on any tribe in particular."

Maggie came out with three empty cups, a pot of coffee, and a sweating glass of lemonade. "I got some cold water from the springhouse for your lemonade, Ky. I'll have fry bread in a minute," she said, wearing a smile and a fresh calico dress that stopped just past her knees. Her hair was pulled back in a thick ponytail that hung to her waist.

Ky took the glass and nodded his approval.

"Clay never did get you to start drinking the hard stuff, did he?" Trap said sipping at his coffee. It was hot and black like Maggie's eyes.

"Nope." Roman winked, used to the teasing about his odd Mormon ways, and raised his glass of lemonade in salute.

"How is Kenworth weighing in on all this?" Trap wondered out loud. "I've heard tell he's got his own private army."

Roman held the cool glass up next to his temple and closed his eyes while he spoke. "He does, but most of them are out fighting fires to protect his timber investments. He's the one that called President Taft—him or his wife. She comes from old money and has a lot of connections with the party. From what I understand, she was against the girl's coming here at all." The marshal shuddered. "Lizbeth Kenworth may be a small woman, but she's as imperious as Queen Victoria. I believe I'd shoot myself if I were married to her. At any rate, the Kenworths are understandably scared. Peter knew of my service during the campaigns, and when it looked like Apaches were involved, he asked the president to have me look into it. Blake was one step ahead of him. He knew I was over in Spokane on business and eventually on my way to surprise you."

"I needed you both," said Blake. "Both the deputies are down in Billings. My marshal and Judge Straby are back in Washington, D.C., doing some politicking. Marshal Roman has the official clout I need to deal with the locals, and you're the best tracker I know. Besides that, you both know Apaches."

Trap smirked and looked over at his wife, who stood silently by his side.

"Son, I *am* Apache—half one at least. Since my dear mama was your grandma, that gives you a considerable amount of expertise on the subject yourself. And all the hazards that go along with it."

"That's why we need Mr. Roman. Kenworth doesn't trust us redskins. There's more out there," Blake said. "But I'm not sure what it all means. I think you two should have a look for yourselves." He turned to look at his mother, filling in the details she'd missed, without getting too graphic about the murders and the condition of the little Donahue boy.

"I'm worried about you out here by yourself if Papa comes with me," Blake told her. "Most men are out working on all the fires, but people with grudges are getting mighty worked up about Indians right now. I heard an old Salish man just about got himself lynched between here and Missoula last night trying to get his loose dog back from a neighbor's house. Quite a few of these folks still remember the Nez Percé war."

"So do I," Maggie said simply.

Trap snaked an arm around his wife's shoulder and gave her a squeeze. "He's right, Mag. Why don't I take you over to Trissy Bloom's place in Taft and the two of you can work on that quilt you started?"

"I'll bring my rifle." Maggie took the empty cups and strode for the house.

"Of course." O'Shannon picked up his own gun.

The men watched her walk away.

"She's pretty as ever. You remember the time. . . ?" Ky looked at Blake, who toed at the dirt again. "Never mind. I won't embarrass you, boy. You're one lucky man, O'Shannon."

"I know." Trap shook Ky's hand. "It's sure enough good to see you. Even under these circumstances. It does put me in a mind of old times."

"Me too, *Denihii*." Roman used Trap's Apache name. "Me too. All things considered, I'm glad for a chance to ride with you again."

"All right then." Trap looked at his son. "I need to get dressed and get your mama over to the Blooms' place."

"Kenworth's already greased the skids with the railroad so they'll give us all the cooperation we want," Roman said. "Just put your mule in a boxcar when you take Maggie, and then ride back from Taft to meet us after you get her settled in at her friends. You got somebody to feed your stock?"

Trap nodded. "I'll turn 'em out into the pasture and they should be set for a while. I'll stop in with

Old Man Rosenbaum on the way into town and ask him to give a look now and then in case the fires come this way. Folks around here feel pretty much the same way about him as they do about us."

"Good enough." The young deputy put his hat and gloves back on. A relaxed smile returned to his face and he breathed easier now that his father had taken up his cause. "I'm going to get Marshal Roman some better work clothes, so we should get there about the same time. I got a jailer standing guard on the place, but he's not much, so I want to hurry. Let's say three hours at Goblin Creek. It's about a mile before you start up that long hill from the valley."

Trap patted his son on the back, then gave his old captain a halfhearted salute. Roman returned it with a grin.

"That was a poor excuse for a salute, O'Shannon—but you never did stand much on protocol." The man's eyes sparkled and he took Trap's hand again. "Twelve years gives us a lot of catching up to do, my old friend."

"That it does, Captain," Trap said. "That it does."

The two visitors had mounted their horses and trotted through the jack pines by the time Trap made it from the barn to the cabin. Maggie met him as she came out the front door with a large clay bowl covered with a cup-towel.

"I got this butter out of the springhouse when I went to get Ky's lemonade. I was hoping Blake might stay for fry bread."

"Sorry, Maggie. He had to push on." Trap started

through the door, but his wife rocked sideways to block him with a hip.

"I know. This is all bad." Her face tensed. "Very bad. I was almost ready for you to go fight the fires, but now I think this trail will take you from me for a longer time. I don't like it, but I know you have to go—for Blake's sake. I see they gave him a badge now." Maggie pursed her lips, then let out a slow sigh. She held the bowl of butter against her waist and ran the fingers of her free hand along the stubble on Trap's jaw. "You're getting a little gaunt, Husband—like a hungry wolf."

Her face relaxed and her eyes became moist and bottomless. "I have grown used to having you underfoot, you know. We may be apart for a while. . . . I noticed when I got the butter that the springhouse is very cool at this time of day."

"The springhouse is always coo . . ." Trap's eyebrows shot up. "It *is* nice and cool in there, ain't it?" He looked off through the smoke where the two men had disappeared. "But we got a lot to do and I gotta meet Blake and Ky in three hours."

"Hurry then." Maggie started through the trees for the earthen cellar. She used her free hand to hike her dress up just below her bottom so she could tease Trap and move faster as she sauntered through the stump row. There was an exaggerated wiggle in her full hips. A lifetime of riding and the miles she walked in the meadows near their new home had blessed her with the firm legs of a woman half her age. Bronze calf muscles flexed as her bare feet padded their way across the dusty, pine-thatched ground.

Trap felt his mouth go dry and he swung his rifle, barrel first, over his shoulder to trot after her. He too couldn't help but think about how long he might be gone. The idea of riding with Ky again after so many years fanned a flame of adventure O'Shannon thought had long since flickered out.

Trap was proud of the man his boy had become. He knew Blake was capable; there was enough of his mother in him to see to that. Watching him work would be pure pleasure. But this business with the badge worried him. An Indian marshal investigating what people saw as an Indian killing could turn into a real powder keg.

On the other hand, women like Maggie Sundown O'Shannon only came along about every other lifetime and he'd spent enough time away from her already. He had to go; there was no question about that. It was his duty. But having to ride off from Maggie, adventure or not, left a pit in his stomach that even a romp in the springhouse wasn't likely to cure.

CHAPTER 3

Where his son was a tall spruce, Patrick "Trap" O'Shannon was more of a broad oak. Thick arms and shoulders branched from a tree-trunk chest planted squarely over stout, if somewhat stubby, legs. He was slightly bowlegged from years in the saddle, but his sure feet gripped the earth through leather moccasins with such ferocity, it seemed he was rooted to the ground. When Trap was very young, his missionary father had told him it didn't matter so much how tall he grew as long as he made certain the inches God gave him counted for something. He often wondered what his father would have thought about the way he'd turned out.

At a shade under five feet eight inches tall, O'Shannon paid special attention to the size of his mount. There had been plenty of tall, well-broke mules in the Army, and an equal number of stub-legged things with backs that could pack a four-poster bed. Hoping to save his knees from riding too long on a wide mule, he'd settled for one of medium height and narrower build. It also happened to be the most sullen beast he'd ever come across.

General Crook had seen the benefit of riding a mule. As a rule Trap agreed, finding most of the hybrids to be surer of foot, smoother to ride, and smarter. But smarter didn't necessarily mean easier to get along with.

This particular mule came to him as a two-year-old by way of what seemed at the time like a shrewd trade. Since then, it had been his companion for many a mile and the last fifteen years. Trap had heard of mules living past forty. Hashkee was too mean to die any time soon and would likely see Trap go to his grave. A wild eye seemed to say that was the plan anyway. Hashkee meant *angry* in Apache, and the mule lived up to its name on a daily basis with pinned ears and a kinked tail at every saddling.

Tomcat-mean, with lightning hooves that had lain to rest one hapless coyote, six dogs, and too many rattlesnakes to count, Hashkee had more bad habits than most of the shavetail mules Trap had dealt with in the Army. He bit and bucked and on some rides, only knew two directions: backward and straight up.

About the time Trap had decided to put a bullet behind the animal's ear, the two had come to a sort of understanding. Every day, for almost a month, Trap had saddled the sullen mule thinking he'd shoot it by nightfall. Hashkee had seemed to sense his peril, and from that point on gave no more than a half-hearted crow-hop while Trap was aboard. The mule never gave up its bloodlust for dogs, but Trap didn't consider himself much of a dog lover anyway.

What Hashkee lacked in the way of good nature,

he made up for with consistency. On one campaign, deep into Mexico, when oats were nowhere to be found, both Trap and his grumpy mount had gone almost a week on a jug of tepid water and a handful of stale tortillas. No matter the adversity, the animal did what was asked of it. Not that there wasn't a certain amount of griping. Hashkee was, after all, a mule. But he'd seen them safely out of many a bad scrape, and that was enough to make up for an ornery disposition.

There was no real love lost between man and beast, but on a mission like this one, the last thing O'Shannon wanted to worry over was his mount.

Leaving Maggie at the Blooms' place was a hard thing, the hardest thing Trap had done in a long time. He felt as if he'd tied a gut to a low limb of the sycamore tree in front of their house and slowly uncoiled his insides the further he rode from his wife. When he was younger, adventure had often curled her beckoning finger and drawn him to the trail. At each separation, the cramp in his heart grew stronger, but the urgency of each campaign pushed the melancholy back to the far reaches of his mind. Over the years, though, he'd discovered Maggie had infinitely more temptations to offer than any adventure and found, to his surprise, he enjoyed the quiet evenings with her as much as any hostile engagement.

The frolic in the springhouse had been more than enjoyable; Maggie was amazing at that sort of thing. Trap's face flushed at the memory of it. The freshness of it burned his cheeks more fiercely than the blazing sun.

He busied his mind on the task at hand and tried

not to ponder on the leaving too much, but there was no way to deny the hungry nagging that got deeper with every step the mule took. It was impossible to know how long he'd have to be gone. Once Trap cut sign, he would stay glued to it no matter where it led.

He always planned for a lengthy campaign, but he didn't need much. Three days of oat rations in a canvas nose bag straddled his saddlebags, and a wool bedroll hung across the mule's mutton-withers tied to the pommel of his Mexican-style saddle. An extra wool shirt hid between his two saddle blankets, one of which had a hole cut in it so he could use it for a serape when he had to stand watch on a chilly mountain night. His .45-70 Marlin hung comfortably under the stirrup fender on his right side, buttstock to the rear so it didn't catch the brush. On his left side, facing forward—away from the cantle of his high-backed saddle—hung a break-top Smith and Wesson Scofield in .45 caliber. There were newer pistols around, double-actions and fancy new auto-loaders, but if Trap was anything, he was faithful. If something worked, he stuck with it.

When he could, Trap eschewed a sidearm during a scrap, preferring his trusty long gun if given time to make a choice. He'd seen too many men he needed to stay down walk away from a pistol wound. Many of them died later, but in a fight, he preferred those he dispatched to go down and stay there. Good men had been killed by good-for-nothing hombres who didn't have the sense to know they were already dead. On the field of battle nothing beat the huge hunk of lead the rifle spit for assuring that sort of thing didn't happen. When the fry-pan-sized bullet hit, a person knew they were done for.

Both the rifle and pistol had their niches, but when a scrap got tight Trap preferred his knife. The blade rested in a simple leather scabbard off his right side, held in place by an antler button on a leather whang. It was relatively short as far as sheath knives went, barely nine inches overall. With a simple stag handle, it was in all ways unremarkable except for what it could do in Trap's capable hands. He'd proven more than once that his knife could work miracles in close combat, and it had the added advantage of never needing to be reloaded.

Hashkee covered the ground quickly, a jarring grudge in his normally smooth mule-gait at having to work on such a sweltering, smoky day. Standing in the flat stirrups designed to be more comfortable on his moccasined feet, Trap squinted into the hazy glare and made out two riders up the narrow valley. At a distance, at least, his eyes still worked the way they did when he was a young man. He was relatively certain it was Blake and Ky, but he hadn't survived these forty-eight years by stumbling into things on easy assumptions. Pointing Hashkee into the shadowed forest and up a steep grade alongside the train tracks, he lost only five more minutes and came in beside his two friends from a small knoll, slightly above them. The sun was to his back.

"Thought I was foolish to look for you to come up the road like a normal human being." Roman shielded his eyes as he watched mule and rider slide down the hill on low haunches among a skittering shower of dirt and pebbles. He held a hand across the pommel of his saddle as the mule came up next to him and released a low growl.

Trap shook the offered hand and shrugged. "These don't sound like normal times, Captain. Fact is, I don't think I remember ever livin' in what a man could call normal times."

"True enough." Ky nodded.

"It gets less and less normal every minute, Pa." Blake's brow creased and he twirled the end of his leather reins.

"How's that?"

"Just got a wire from Mr. Madsen. He's already in Montana and on his way to see you. Seems someone offered him a job working security for the railroad. He was up in Helena talking with them about it."

"Clay Madsen in Montana?" Trap smiled. He stood in the stirrups with a slow groan and rubbed the small of his back.

"He's on his way to see you."

"I haven't seen either of you boys for twelve years and now I get a full dose of both of you all at once," Roman told Trap, grinning, showing his teeth. "When did you two part company?"

"Almost three years ago," said Trap. "His father died and he went back to Texas to give the family ranch a go. I came north with Maggie—away from the heat." Saddle leather creaked when O'Shannon resumed his seat. He needed to do something so he could digest this new information. "I'd like to get on over to Goblin Creek and take a look if we could, Captain."

Ky tipped the wide brim of the mouse-brown hat that he'd replaced his bowler with.

"Lead on, Blake. Take us to Goblin Creek. We've got work to do." With the same ease that he'd switched hats, Roman went from a visiting guest to commander.

Jailer Joe Casey probably thought he was doing his level best to keep folks away from the bloody carnage that surrounded the stage—but he was old and there was only one of him against an endless tide of gawkers. There weren't that many automobiles in this part of Montana, but a few folks had them. Trap supposed the snaking set of tire tracks leading back down the creek-side road belonged to Peter Kenworth. Other onlookers had been coming in by the wagonload all day long, braving the smoke and heat to set eyes on what was already being called the Goblin Creek Indian Massacre.

Trap shook his head slowly while he took in the scene. No matter the brutality, someone would enjoy looking it over. He'd seen people bring picnic lunches to hangings to gnaw on chicken legs while they watched condemned men dance their last mortal steps at the end of a rope. Trap didn't have a stomach for such things. He'd taken the lives of other men, even looked them in the eye while he did, but he took no joy in it. And he certainly never stood around to admire his own handiwork.

People were softer now, protected from the harshness that used to mark the frontier. He supposed these folks had never been exposed to the real thing, so the green flies and glistening gut piles in front of them seemed more like an imagined illustration from a dime novel than the soulless carcasses of once-living, breathing human beings. Civilization might have come to Montana, but the people were no more civilized for it.

Overwhelmed by so many visitors, Casey had slipped from his role as guard to that of an informal tour guide. He kept the onlookers back a few feet from the bodies, but pointed out this wound and that, gesturing with outstretched arms to share his theories about what had happened. His gray hair blew in thin wisps on the hot breeze and the sun had severely pinked the top of his bare scalp. Trap shook his head in quiet wonderment that a man would be out on such a fiercely cloudless day without his hat.

Scarcely ten yards from the corpses, three women in plain cotton dresses stood, hands to their mouths, in front of a weathered buckboard and tired gray horse. Gaping at the scene before them, one held the hand of a curly-headed toddler, who hung disinterested at his mother's side. He wiped his runny nose on the hem of her dress. Beyond the women two boys, no older than thirteen, stared slack-jawed at the naked, mutilated bodies tied to the coach wheels.

"Get back from there, all of you," Ky growled in a righteous indignation that caused the boys to scamper up the side of the hill, where they disappeared into the jack pines. Casey began to stumble over his own feet, trying to get away himself. The three women snapped out of their stupor, and the young mother suddenly thought it necessary to cover her little boy's eyes with the palm of her hand.

Ky stopped his snorting horse upwind, a scant

twenty yards from the bodies. Dismounting, he flipped the leather reins around a scrub of buck brush. Trap and Blake followed, but remained in the saddle.

"I'm ashamed of you folks standing around here like this," Roman told the women as he would a group of small children. He meant to scold harshly, but without particular malice. "Have you no reverence for the dead? Now go on home." He nodded his head with an air of such finality, Joe Casey looked over at Blake, whom he considered his immediate superior.

"Me too, O'Shannon?" The sudden arrival of more lawmen had put Casey on edge, and his shoulders flapped up and down toward his ears with so much nervous energy when he spoke, he'd have taken flight if wings were attached. His face twitched and popped like a pot of simmering oatmeal. Trap had never met Casey, but it was easy to recognize him as the man Blake called Jiggin' Joe.

"No, you stay," Blake snapped, with a considerably harder edge than Ky had used to speak to the gawking townsfolk.

"There was too many of 'em to fend off," Casey whined. "I did the best I could." The twitching man looked ready to burst into tears.

Blake glared and raised a hand to silence him. Turning without another word, the young deputy looked over the bloodbath in front of him and closed his eyes.

Trap gave his son a nod of approval. It was the boy's second time to look at the mess the killers left behind. Trap was glad to see it disgusted him. A second helping of carnage like this shouldn't be any easier to stomach than the first.

Plumes of dust puffed up from Trap's moccasins as they hit the parched ground. What little wind there was had fallen off completely. The brooding smells of blood, death, and fear filled the void it left behind. He tied Hashkee to a twisted scrub so dry, one good pull from the mule would turn it to dust. It really didn't matter. The thin leather reins were no more than a bluff anyway when it came to keeping a one-thousand-pound animal tied. Stepping closer to the coach, Trap was careful to watch where he put his feet. He almost chuckled when he saw what the old fool Casey had done with his hat.

A stout, blond man, obviously muscled by hard work in life, hung like a flaccid doll, tied to a front wheel of the coach. His body was riddled with a half-dozen arrows. Only a trace of blood oozed around the wooden shafts at their entry points. Trap hadn't seen anyone scalped in some time, and the sight of it caused him to go hollow inside. Glistening flies, black and metallic green, crowded around the bloody edge of the white bone circle on top of the dead man's head. Flies were as bad as gawkers, and there always seemed to be some nearby to exploit such a gruesome occasion.

What was left of the man's hair lay in crusted locks against a swollen face. Long cuts ran up, down, and sideways across the puffed skin of his nude body like a scored ham. Whoever tied him to the wheel had been unwilling or unable to lift him any higher, so he sat, arms outstretched to the sides and legs straight out in front of him, like a great, bloated bird coming in for a landing. Casey's tattered hat lay across the man's lap, covering his mutilated groin.

"I kept pukin' every time I looked at what they done to him." Jiggin' Joe hung his head between bobbing shoulders.

Trap leaned over the body, careful to avoid any footprints that might remain unsullied by the curious onlookers that had visited the scene before him.

"Wound on his left side below his heart . . . bullet came out the back there, but the wagon spoke's untouched," Trap mused to himself. "Must've been killed somewhere else." A look inside the coach confirmed his theory.

"They did all this to him after he was dead, didn't they?" Blake stood a step closer to his father.

"Reckon so." Trap pointed at the arrow wounds. "All these are for show. Dead men don't bleed very much. What little bit you see there is likely from the bloating. If it was Indians that done this, they were mighty angry about somethin'. I worked the border nigh on to thirty years. Seen some mighty rough things, but this scalping business has got me puzzled." He took a small notepad and pencil stub from his shirt pocket. Touching the tip of the pencil to his tongue, he began to make sketches while he spoke.

"It's not that Apaches never scalped, mind you, but they generally did it in retaliation for something. In all those years, a lot of the meanest renegades we ever came across didn't even know how to take a scalp. Of course, the rest of this . . . I'm sad to say, I've seen this kind of thing before."

O'Shannon shook his head and groaned while he looked at the young woman tied to the back wheel. It seemed unthinkable that Casey had been moved by the butchered man enough to cover him while he'd left the poor woman so exposed.

Fleshy and pale, her skin had taken on the appearance of soap left too long in the tub. Already a day and a half under the blazing sun, she'd begun to cook. She was tied upside down, her legs lashed crudely to opposite spokes of the large coach wheel. A jagged, half-moon gash along her belly nearly cut her in half and her bowels spilled down the front of her, obscuring her face in an obscene, buzzing mass of flies and stinking entrails. She had no arrow wounds, but she'd been scalped like the man. Bruises the shape of a large hand encircled her trailing wrists. Dried blood from her scalp drenched her face and hair. The dead didn't bruise—or bleed so profusely, even from a head wound. Much of this had been done to her while she was alive.

She was lighter than the man, and her tormentors had been able to lift her a little higher on the wheel. Her head just touched the ground, and her neck bent unnaturally under the weight of her slumping body. Trap had to get down on his hands and knees to examine it more closely. A bullet behind her ear had ended her suffering. The gutting had been for show after her body was tied to the coach wheel. She'd been positioned to make a point.

The driver, apparently overlooked, had been spared from mutilation and lay undisturbed, but every bit as dead as the others, beneath the coach. A fusillade of gunfire and arrows had brought down the four horses and they lay in bloating heaps, still in their traces.

Trap closed his eyes and tried to imagine the bloody

scene as it happened. The driver shot, the groans of the butchered man, mixing with the terrified screams of the poor women, the crack of rifle fire, and the wild squeals of the horses. He could smell the gunpowder—hear the laughter of the killers—for they had surely laughed.

The men who did this took great pleasure in their work.

Hoofbeats, loud and hollow, like the thumping of a melon, drummed over the dusty ground and shook Trap from his imaginings. Five riders, dressed in starched clothes for a town visit instead of rugged travel, reined up beside the coach. The youngest of the bunch, barely old enough to coax a whimsical bit of hair from his chin and upper lip, rode a fresh horse. He had trouble controlling the animal at the smell of so much gore.

There was still enough fear in the air that Trap could smell it, even above the smell of death. The animals smelled it too, but he doubted anyone else did. The stench of fear was worse than death. Everyone died, but there were few who deserved to die afraid.

"Tom Ledbetter," Blake whispered under his breath. "I'm sure of it. Rides a big dun. He's got the reputation of a troublemaker. Been in jail a few times for letting his temper get the best of him."

"Reminds me of a scalp hunter I once knew." Trap took a step closer to his son to show some solidarity as well as protect the spot where he thought he'd have some good tracks from further defilement. "Who's he workin' for?"

"Kenworth."

Trap judged the frowning man to stand a shade under six feet tall. Thick-necked and broad-shouldered, he looked strong as a range bull. Dark eyes raged with an irrepressible anger under the brim of his high-crowned hat. He had a dangerous smell about him that made folks slink out of the way when he came toward them.

Most folks.

"We got a few tracks we need to keep undisturbed, if you don't mind, sir," Trap said, standing his ground as the burly man unhorsed himself and strode forward ahead of his four cronies.

"Well, I do mind, not that it's any of your business, Stubby." Ledbetter tugged his hat lower over angry, deep-set eyes. Muscles twitched along an angular jaw as he clenched his teeth. He continued to walk as if he expected Trap to spring to one side and clear a path. When that didn't happen, he pulled up in a blowing huff. "I'm gonna get one of them arrows for my proof when I have to hang the Indians that did this."

Blake yanked an arrow out of a dead horse and offered it to Ledbetter. "Take this one, and move on. But be careful who you hang. You could end up swinging yourself."

Ledbetter spit on the ground, narrowly missing the dusty toe of Blake's boot. "I was just about to say the same thing to you, Red Bug." This brought a chuckle from the group behind him. "Just wearing that fancy badge don't make you any more white or more of a man." Hand on his gun now, Ledbetter pressed closer.

A purple vein pulsed on the side of the man's thick neck. Molten hate hung in the dead air around him. His vehemence wasn't for show.

Blake stood his ground, but flipped the arrow so the bloody point faced Ledbetter and pressed against his gut enough to dent the tight cotton shirt. The young lawman held the arrow in his left hand and touched the butt of his pistol with his right.

"Mr. Ledbetter, I don't want this to go the way it's goin', but make no mistake, this is the scene of a crime and I'm not about to let you muck it up."

The big man wrinkled his long nose. The taut muscles in his reddened jaws flexed as he stared hard at Blake, studying him through narrow eyes. His nostrils flared and he took a step back, accepting the bloody arrow with a toss of his head.

Trap moved sideways to take up a position away from Blake. He found himself glad he'd decided to strap on the old Scofield. Ky cleared his throat, rifle in hand, on the other side of the interlopers, and Ledbetter nodded, smacking his jaws. Casey stood a few feet behind Ky with a shotgun, trying to redeem himself from his earlier foolishness. His shoulders still flapped, but not enough to keep the scattergun from providing a worry for Ledbetter and his men.

"I see how this is gonna be." Ledbetter stared daggers at Trap. "I shoulda known when I saw you wearin' the moccasins. Bein' shod like that, you got red nigger blood in you; I'd bet my life on it." He wheeled, striding defiantly over to his dun, and swung easily into the saddle for a man of his bulk. The bloody arrow was still in his hand, and his used it to drive home his point as he spoke to Blake.

"You just keep pokin' about in the blood and gut piles, boy. We'll see to catchin' the savages that did this. Mark me good, though, you best watch your own hair. I've seen Indians scalp other Indians as quick as they would a white man."

Ledbetter turned his big dun on its haunches and loped away, spanking it on the rump with the arrow. The greenhorn on the frisky mount whirled three times before he got it pointed the right direction and galloped off after his compatriots.

Blake and Trap let them leave without a word. Taunts and threats didn't do much for men like Ledbetter. He was a problem that would require seeing to sooner or later, but he'd chosen later. Neither O'Shannon saw any reason to provoke a showdown at a moment when time was of the essence.

"Got a moccasin track over here and some horse prints as well," Ky said when the riders were out of earshot. After the initial examination of the bodies, he'd moved to the perimeter, leaving the close work to Trap. Roman was a pious man and the sight of the woman's nude body troubled him. Trap was certain of that. It troubled Trap as well, but not in the same way. Roman had always been more bashful.

Trap studied the dusty ground at the base of the butchered man, then around the pile of bloating horses. Many sorts of tracks stitched the area around the bodies, most of them from Jiggin' Joe and the other onlookers; but few of them had taken time to look at the horses. A careful study of the blood-soaked dust around the bloated animals let Trap narrow the number of possible tracks to six: two moccasins and four boots. Blake had taken the time to make some decent sketches on his first trip to the site. Comparing what he had with the sketches brought the number down to five. The tracks Ky found allowed them to discard a set of hobnails that probably belonged to one of the gawking boys who'd disappeared into the trees.

"Except for the boot tracks, it sure looks like Indians are the ones behind this," Ky mused, looking across the parched hills in the direction of the hoofprints. Kenworth's place was up Goblin Creek to the north. The tracks led south. "But I suppose most Indians wear boots nowadays."

Trap grunted in agreement. "And some white men wear moccasins. But it looks like you sure hit the mark, son. The person that left this track doesn't land on his heels like a white man. Look here at the heavy toe on this one. Your grandma sewed moccasins just like this. They're Apache all right—a mite new-looking, though, to be this far from home."

"What do you make of this, Pa?" Blake squatted next to a clump of bunchgrass.

Trap found signs of struggle in the twists of yellow grass and dusty stones. A splash of blood cut a black line across a tuft of bent stem, too far away to come from the bodies beside the coach. The dry bunchgrass had been pressed into the dirt by a twisting heel.

"I'll bet one of them clipped the Kenworth girl's finger right here." Trap laid his hand across two long scuff marks in the dirt, turning so he didn't cast a shadow and obscure any sign. The dusty earth was almost too hot to touch. He made a mental note of the size and shape of the girl's track. "See where her feet went out from under her. She likely fainted."

Ky squatted down beside his friend and looked him in the eye. "I pray to God she fainted before she saw what they did to her companions."

Blake brought up an arrow he'd pulled from the coach wall and ran a finger along sparse fletching. "Trade point, salt cedar shaft. Looks like an Apache arrow to me."

"It does." Trap kept his hand on the ground, as if he were gaining information from the feel of the hot earth. "I've seen a passel of Apache arrows in my day, but I never thought I'd see one up here in Montana in nineteen and ten. Not with blood on it anyhow."

Ky took off his hat and wiped his face with a white handkerchief. "Doesn't it seem like an awfully big co-incidence that the last three members of our scout-tracker unit are all in this little part of God's vineyard at precisely the right time to track a bunch of rene-gade Apache?"

"I don't believe in coincidence and neither do you, Captain. This whole thing is a puzzlement to be sure. In the old days this is somthin' you'd pray over and I'd consult Maggie about." Trap thought of his old friend Clay and smiled. "And Madsen would seek the arms of an understanding woman to chase the whole thing out of his mind."

"We have to consider the possibility of ambush." Roman let his gaze wander along the hazy hills above them.

"I'd say we should count on it," Trap said.

"Ambush or not, the Kenworth girl's out there

and someone has to go after her," Roman said, stating the obvious.

The wind shifted a bit, giving Trap a whiff of the nearby corpses, and yanked him back to grim reality. "All right, Captain." He looked across the road at Jiggin' Joe, who stood drooling and useless, trying to hide from the hard gaze of the other three men. Trap suddenly felt the need to put as much distance as he could between himself and so much incompetence. "We should get on with it."

"Blake," the marshal said, returning the hat to his head. "Have your man lay these poor souls to rest. I doubt he'd be much use to us on the trail."

Trap grabbed the wide horn on his saddle and started to swing up, then stopped. He turned and looked at Blake, thinking. "The sign all points south, toward the Idaho line. With the captain's permission, I'd like you to go back and look in on your mama. I want her to try and talk with the boy. He survived all this and if he's got a story to tell, she's the one who can get him to tell it. If we've got an ambush ahead, it would sure help to know what he saw. You pie-aye back to us as soon as you can with Mr. Madsen. We'll leave a good solid trail for you to follow. I don't know if these renegades will stay to the mountains or not, but there are a couple of little burgs over into Idaho we should probably check."

"Yes, sir." Blake nodded. "Be careful."

"You do the same and make fast tracks. I got a feeling these killers are headed for the High Lonesome. If they do, we'll need you and Clay both to ferret them out."

Blake's Appaloosa kicked up dust as he wheeled to lope off toward Taft.

Trap turned his attention back to Ky. "Shall we go, Captain?"

"You got a fine son there, O'Shannon." A hot breath of breeze caught and tugged at Ky's gray hair. His smile seemed out of place in amidst the surrounding. "Takes after his mother."

"I hope so." Trap watched Blake disappear into the distorted waves of heat that rose up from the scorched ground. He tried not to think about the carnage thirty feet away. The possibility of ambush was almost certain, and he needed to focus all his instincts on what lay ahead.

Trap turned the mule and trotted over to take up the kidnappers' trail. From the corner of his eye, he saw Joe Casey retrieve his bloody hat from the butchered man's lap and return it to his sunburned head.

CHAPTER 4

Fire Camp

Blue smoke curled like a faded silk ribbon on the heavy green thatch of towering cedars. Giant trees slouched under the weight of the desolation they'd seen. Beneath the layer of smoke, the flint-hard odor of scorched earth pressed two dozen bleary-eyed men to the blackened ground like an unseen hand. The sharp smell of burned cedar stung their bloodshot eyes and pinched at their raw noses.

Granite Creek gurgled over clean melon-sized rocks, just a few feet away from the men. It was cool and clear in contrast to the superheated oppressiveness of the gray air, but the parched men had to rely on the warm water in their canteens for moisture. Fires in the mountains had rendered most of the smaller streams undrinkable. Flowing over the charcoaled skeletons of thousands of burned trees transformed the water into lye strong enough to make soap—or eat a hole in a man's gut.

For now, the sound of the stream was all they had to cool them. The surviving trees gave some measure of shade; the heat of an August sun ate its way through and threatened to boil the good sense out of the already blistered men. Warm water and juice from their rations of canned tomatoes were in good supply to wash down a plentiful diet of bacon and pancakes, but the heat put a tight fist around the men's stomachs and kept their appetites small.

Rather than eating, the exhausted men were content to lounge here and there on dirty blankets across from blackened snags and the few remaining cedars at the far edge of the firebreak. Many of these trees were large enough that four grown men could stand in a circle and not reach around the trunk. The last night and most of the day was spent working the wide firebreak so the ranger could set a back-burn and stop one of the largest wildfires in its tracks.

The work was much like building a road; they scraped and chopped and grubbed anything that might burn in a wide swath over a mile long. Further up the valley, Granite Creek joined a larger stream that no one seemed to know the name of and helped keep the distance manageable. Once the firebreak was completed, the men had used torches to set a back-burn ahead of the prevailing wind to burn any flammable material and starve the oncoming fire when it arrived.

It had worked, and apart from a few spots where popping embers shot across the wide break, the backfire had stayed on the far side. When the wildfire approached, it had no fuel and sputtered to a stop before it reached the break. The fire boss, Ranger Horace

Zelinski, posted fireguards for the jumping embers and they were extinguished immediately.

The blaze of the day contained, the break provided a safe haven for the beleaguered men. Most of them used the time to sleep, stretched out where they had fallen, exhausted on the dust and sand of the forest floor, blackened blankets pulled over soot-covered faces to hide them from the bright haze of light.

Four of the crew sat in the shade of one of the largest cedars, playing cards on a grimy blanket. A somber mood hung above the little group and mingled with the smoke. Their voices were a buzzing whisper, drowned out from the others by the gurgling creek.

Daniel Rainwater, a nineteen-year-old Flathead Indian with perfect white teeth, crossed his long legs under him at the edge of the dusty blanket. His poker face was a constant grin, gleaming like a crescent moon. His friend Joseph sat to his right. The same age as Rainwater, Joseph was shorter by a hand and kept his own teeth hidden behind a closed mouth. Daniel knew his friend cared little for cards, but played because *he* did.

Rainwater also knew he was taking advantage, but the knowledge that the tough-minded Joseph was nearby allowed him to push things—to take chances he wouldn't otherwise take—like playing cards with the likes of the two men across the blanket.

Ox Monroe was easily six and a half feet of mean bone, knife scar, and fire-hardened muscle. He sported two gold front teeth that snapped together like scissors when he was angry or frustrated. The giant sported a twisting green tattoo of a serpent that started at his neck and ran down the front of his filthy shirt before it crawled out and ended in a large fanged mouth on his thick forearm. Everyone assumed he'd been a sailor, but he never said anything to confirm the rumors.

Monroe's companion, Roan Taggart, was a big man in his own right, but next to Ox, he was almost dwarfed. An odd scar, pale and pinched, covered the left side of his face from chin to shriveled ear. It pulled the skin tight around a squinty left eye and ran down behind his hat before disappearing beneath the frayed collar of his dingy shirt. A remnant of a nasty burn. Premature flecks of white hair had invaded Taggart's red beard and earned him the nickname Roan at an early age. In his late forties, there was hardly any red left. A constant diet of bacon and canned tomatoes disagreed with his belly and made him prone to violent eruptions of gas that made the unscarred portion of his face go red. He blew often, and when he did, everyone else sought a safe haven upwind. Two of the crew had worked fires up on the Yellowstone, and commented on how Roan's sulfurous additions to the air reminded them of the place.

The buzz throughout the fire camp was that Monroe and Taggart had escaped from a prison in Colorado. The fire season was bad enough that every able body was needed, and if the authorities knew anything, they didn't mention it.

Both of the big men wore pistols openly on thick leather belts at their sides, but they fingered long-handled bowie knives while they played. Rainwater knew playing cards with such men was not so dangerous as winning at cards with them, but the brash young Flathead couldn't help himself.

Big Ox clicked his gold teeth in silent frustration, a sure sign he had a bad hand. Roan fiddled with the rawhide whang on his knife sheath. He wasn't holding anything worthwhile either.

Joseph had won slightly more than he'd lost, but Daniel couldn't seem to make a mistake. If he held a pair and threw in three, he'd draw a full house. If he threw back four, he'd pull back a straight or at the very least three of a kind. As the young Indian's smile spread, the mood across the blanket grew as dark as the blackened landscape across the firebreak.

Roan let go of his knife handle long enough to deal the next hand.

Monroe swept his cards up in a beefy paw. "If you ain't a son of a whore," he said, glaring across the blanket at Rainwater as if he'd been the one to give him the bad hand. His voice was rough and punctuated with a gritty cough.

Daniel shrugged, but his smile only dimmed a little. At two bits a hand, he was almost seven dollars ahead and no amount of talk could chase away his happiness. He threw back three. The white crescent of teeth was unwavering as he studied his new cards and rearranged them to his liking.

Roan drew two, passed a voluminous cloud of rotten-egg gas, and then folded. Joseph folded as well, leaving the game to Rainwater and Monroe.

Big Ox waved away Roan's addition to the smoky air and gave his cards a satisfied grunt. He smiled like he'd just swallowed someone's prize poodle and fanned three jacks on the blanket. His cards in the open, Monroe's heavy brow furrowed over seething eyes that dared the young Indian to best him. He'd stopped clicking his gold teeth, but thick fingers tapped the hilt of the long knife at his side.

Daniel shrugged, smiled, and tossed down a straight flush, queen high.

Monroe shot a withering look across the blanket. His dark eyes boiled like storm clouds that might at any moment shoot thunderbolts and consume what was left of the forest and Rainwater along with it.

"You thievin' little nit." The giant man grabbed the greasewood handle of his long knife. The blade hissed up an inch from the sheath. But he didn't draw it completely.

Joseph's hand already rested on his own blade.

Daniel Rainwater didn't move. Instead, he smiled his toothy smile. "Nothing harmed, Big Ox. We'll just play for fun."

Ox was already up on one knee, his mood as scorched as the twisted trees across the burn. "It ain't gonna be no fun what I aim to do with your hide, young buck. I ain't one to lay down and take a cheatin'." Monroe glanced down at Joseph and let loose a rumbling chuckle, which Roan Taggart joined. "You best keep that sticker hid, nigger. You'll both be stompin' your own guts before you skin it and I'll already have your hair."

Rainwater let his eyes slide sideways to his friend. Nothing moved on Joseph but his nostrils, which always flared before he did battle. The big man didn't scare him, but Rainwater's own stomach churned.

Not that he was afraid to die. He was enough of a warrior to accept that day when it came. He didn't want Joseph to die on his account—especially over a card game. Using both hands, he pushed the pile of money across the blanket, being careful not to lean so far that Monroe could reach him. Joseph would certainly strike if that happened, and Daniel wanted to prevent it if he could.

The big man jerked the blanket back toward him with a growl, upsetting the money and the cards. Most of the money was in coins, but the lone bill floated down between them in the still air. "I don't want the stinkin' money. I aim to take what's mine outta your red nigger hide."

Roan Taggart nudged his partner with an elbow and gave a sideways nod toward their grizzly bear of a fire boss, Horace Zelinski, who stood on a burnt knoll above them, giving the little group what everyone on the crew called "the eye." Beside him stood a white man in the khaki wool uniform of the United States Army. On the Army officer's right stood the thickest black man Daniel had ever seen. Dressed much the same as the white officer, the Negro trooper's muscles strained at the wool uniform blouse. If he'd taken a step sideways in front of the fire boss and the officer, the trooper would have blocked both men from view.

Zelinski was shorter than Monroe by a head, not even as tall as Taggart. Compared to the broad Negro trooper he was willow-wand skinny, but the thunderous bark that emanated from his fearless chest seemed capable of felling trees. Some of the men who'd worked with him before swore in hushed tones they'd seen Zelinski bark at a fire only to have it turn away from his wrath.

Brimming over with a puritanical work ethic, the forty-year-old forest ranger was the senior man in the newly created Nez Percé National Forest and he took his charge seriously. He held himself to a strict set of standards and didn't tolerate shirkers or trouble-makers of any sort.

Rainwater relaxed slowly when he saw this man who seemed to him to be as much a force of nature as the wind or rain, or the fire itself.

"Everything all right down there, men?"

Monroe met the ranger's icy stare and turned his head away, as a big bear might do when a bigger bear came in to challenge his territory. Zelinski had strong medicine, and even a stiff-necked man like Big Ox Monroe was smart enough to take note of it.

"Everthing's jake with us, Boss." Instead of resheath-ing his knife, Monroe snatched up a can of tomatoes and used it to punch two holes in the top, looking at Rainwater with a threatening sneer while the thick steel blade slid easily through the tin lid. Waving to the fire boss, he threw the can to his lips and sucked out the juice. The liquid cut pink ditches in the black-sooted stubble as it dribbled from the corners of Monroe's crooked mouth.

"How about it, Rainwater? Everything all right?" The fire boss had the ability to stare down several men at one time, and Daniel couldn't tell if he was focused in on him or Monroe.

"We just finished a card game, Mr. Zelinski."

"Good enough then," the ranger barked. His eyes never left Monroe while he spoke. "Rainwater, the Department of the Army has sent us reinforcements from the 25th Infantry. Would you be so kind as to show Corporal Rollins here a good place this side of the firebreak to set up their camp?" Zelinski gestured toward the black trooper who eclipsed the sky behind him.

Both Indian boys scrambled to their feet. "Yes, sir," Daniel said.

The order given and understood, Zelinski turned and walked away with the white officer.

Monroe wiped his mouth on the sleeve of his filthy shirt and belched. He kept his voice low so the huge trooper on the knoll above them couldn't hear. "If you Injuns wasn't bad enough. Now we got to sleep on the same mountainside as a bunch of . . ."

Corporal Rollins slid down the embankment toward them and held out an enormous paw. "Bandy Rollins is my name." He smiled through a row of white teeth on a face wide enough to match the rest of him.

Monroe ignored the offered hand and turned to face Rainwater. "The boss man saved your hide just now, to be sure, boy. But have a care. Even he ain't everwhere all the time." The big man cleaned his knife on the front of his thigh, then drew the gleaming blade through the air in front of his own grizzled throat. "You're a dead Injun and don't even know it. Next fire, when everyone's busy watchin' their own hides, you should be right careful. Folks can't be expected to watch over you all the time." He turned back to his can of tomatoes.

Rainwater started to walk away and Taggart put out his hand. "Leave the money." The stench that surrounded him stirred when he spoke and made the young Indian cough.

He smiled and gave the smelly, pink-faced man a nod. "I'd planned to."

"That was a close one," Rainwater said when they were across the grove and clear of Big Ox. He stuck a hand out at Corporal Bandy Rollins. "Daniel Rainwater of the Flathead Nation. This is my cousin, Joseph." Joseph shook the corporal's hand.

"I'm Bandy Rollins, Company G, 25th Infantry. The Army sent us over from Spokane. Most of us is camped over at Avery, but we been assigned to help you boys fight fires." He cast his eyes around the clearing. "Though it looks like you done got 'em licked."

Daniel chuckled and glanced at his cousin. "We got it done here, but there's always another one over the next mountain. You ever fought fires before?"

"Can't say as I have, but I'm one heck of a learner. An All Army baseball player I am. People says I'm bull-strong, racehorse-agile, and hound-dog-smart. I reckon me and my men can pick up quick enough on what needs to be done."

"You a baseball player, huh?" Daniel slapped the black trooper on his broad back. "I saw a baseball game once over in Kallispell. Looked like it would be fun enough."

"From what I just saw, you boys should take up the game so you could stay outta trouble. You liable to get in dutch playin' cards with the likes of those yay-hoos." Rollins shook his massive head and clucked to himself. "Yes, sir, boys, consortin' with those kind of men will get you kilt for certain. You best show ol' Bandy where you want us to camp. I'll look after you and teach you how to play baseball to boot. No, sir, ain't nobody gonna hurt you with somebody as bull-strong, racehorse-agile, and hound-dog-smart as Corporal Bandy Rollins around."

CHAPTER 5

Doc Bruner's modest whitewashed house doubled as his office. It was exceptionally nice for a loosely knit community like Taft, which got its name when William Howard Taft came through on a campaign tour and chastised the people at the then-unnamed railroad stop for their riotous and wicked ways. The wayward souls didn't repent, but they did name the town after their pious president.

An independent sort who enjoyed the rough-and-tumble life in a wild town like Taft, Bruner was the only doctor between Wallace and Missoula. Accustomed to living alone since his wife quit him for a life in the big city, he had the unkempt look of a bachelor who didn't have a woman to tell him it was time for a haircut, and the relaxed demeanor of a man that wasn't looking to find a woman—or a barber.

Except for the occasional whiff of antiseptic that chased back the smell of baking bread, the doctor's house had a homey feel. It made Blake feel drowsy on such a hot afternoon. He wondered how much of the massacre little Shad Donahue had seen when they'd brought him out of the coach. Blake knew what he'd be like if he'd seen his own mother butchered like the Donahue woman. The thought of it brought a tightness to his chest that threatened to crush him, and he forced himself to think on something else. He couldn't blame the boy; he'd probably go silent himself in such a situation.

A paddle fan, with great, spade-shaped blades of woven palm leaves, twisted in slow, whumping revolutions on the high ceiling. Blake slouched in a padded-leather chair across from his mother and the Donahue boy, and marveled at how cool a little breeze made the room. Doc Bruner sat a few feet away in a chair that matched Blake's. He shook his head at the progress Maggie had made in such a short time.

At first, Shad did nothing to even acknowledge the fact that there was anyone else in the room. He sat cross-legged on the floor and pushed his wooden horse back and forth on the dark hardwood along the edge of a braided-rag throw rug. Without speaking, Maggie knelt down beside him and took the leather pouch from around her neck. She began to hum a soft tune, her chest rising and falling as she breathed deeply. Ignoring the child, she continued her humming while she used a finger to sort through the soft leather bag. When she found what she wanted, she nodded, leaned back against the couch, and pushed her feet straight out in front of her, then smoothed her dress down around her thighs to make a sort of table on her lap. She dropped the pouch in the cradle of cloth and held up a small bone flute, no more than four inches long.

Blake remembered the tiny instrument from his childhood. The sight of it brought back a thousand tender memories of time spent with his mother. For a moment, he thought he could smell the pinnons and cedar smoke of his Arizona youth.

Maggie pressed the bleached white pipe to her lips and let her humming turn into a flute song that trailed softly upward, toward the whispering ceiling fan. It was a light but mournful tune. Happy and sad at the same time, it tugged at the heart and the mind all at once. Maggie had played the same tune after Blake's baby sister had died, then again when she'd prepared to celebrate his father's homecoming after a long absence. It had fit the occasion—both times.

Shad ignored her for a time, rolled his toy horse, and stared at the wooden floor—then, slowly, he began to hum the tune along with her. His fragile voice started softly, but rose gradually to match Maggie's flute song. He moved the horse more in rhythm with her playing. Then, in a flash of fluid movement that made Blake catch his breath, the boy crawled across the dark wooden floor and climbed into her lap.

Maggie's dark eyes gleamed, but her face remained stoically calm. She played on for a few more minutes, and the lonely little boy put his arms around her neck and buried his face against her soft breast. Blake had done the same thing, countless times, when he was a child in need of comfort. Gently laying the flute on the rug beside her, Maggie wrapped her arms around the boy, pressed him to her, and patted him softly on the back. The flute music gone, she resumed her humming.

"Will Mama come for me?" The boy leaned away from Maggie enough to look up at her.

"No, child, she had to go away."

"The bad men took her away, didn't they?" Shad began to whimper softly. "They killed Mr. Fritz, and made Mama and Angie cry. Then they took them away. Angie made me hide in the coach seat even though Mr. Fritz wanted her to hide there."

Blake knew better than to break the spell by speaking, and was relieved when his mother asked the questions that weighed heavy on his mind.

"Did you see the men who made your mama cry?" Maggie's voice was a soft and comforting blanket that enveloped everyone in the room. She used both thumbs to clear away the tears from the young boy's cheeks. Then she wet her finger on the tip of her tongue and rubbed away a bit of dirt from his chin. Blake recalled struggling during many such spit baths, and supposed all boys had to undergo such indignities from their mothers. Shad didn't seem to mind having someone mother him, and endured the cleaning quietly.

"I couldn't see very good," he finally said. "There was only one little crack in the wood. One of the men was bald-headed. I heard the other men call him Feet or something like that. He's the one that hurt Angie. I saw another man too. He wore a big black cover on his eye like he was blinded. He hurt Mama and dragged her off when Feet gave him permission." The boy coughed to clear a hoarse throat. "The one-eyed man was . . ."

Shad stared at Maggie's face for a moment, then reached out and touched her cheek. He was silent long enough to make Blake's stomach knot in antici-pation. Maggie remained relaxed.

Blake's gaze wandered to the ceiling. He counted the revolutions of the paddle fan above him, and got to eighteen before the boy spoke again.

"I mean the one with a patch over his eye . . ."

The boy paused again, but Maggie didn't prod him.

"He was . . . like you." Shad touched her face.

"An Indian?" Maggie's eyes opened wide in gen-uine interest. "I see. Well, you're safe with us now so you don't need to worry about him."

Shad shook his head and looked over his shoulder at Blake and Doc Bruner. He slowly blinked wide blue eyes as if seeing his surroundings for the first time.

"That's my son." Maggie kept her arms around the boy and used her chin to point to Blake. "He's an In-dian too. He's a good man and wants to help us find the men who hurt your mama."

"Can he bring Mama back?"

"No, child, he can't." Blake could see his mother looking up at him as she pulled the little boy even closer. Her eyes brimmed with tears, and she blinked them away while she tried to comfort him.

An hour later, Shad slept on the couch, still whim-pering softly with each breath, sometimes cooing the tune Maggie had played on her flute.

"The boy sounds like he could identify at least one of the men, maybe two," Blake whispered.

Maggie looked past the linen curtains on the par-lor widow.

"If the kidnappers know that, he is in danger. We

have to keep him someplace safe. I want to stay with him. He should have someone to mother him now, and I need to do something so I don't worry so much about you and your father."

Blake fell into thought for a moment, tapping his hat against his thigh. He didn't doubt his mother's ability to care for the boy—or herself for that matter. But that didn't stop him from worrying. Especially since he knew many people in the area shared General Sherman's view when he said he'd seen a good Indian once—a dead Indian. Tom Ledbetter, for instance—to him, an Indian was responsible for any sin or depravity committed by any other Indian. His own people had shared the same logic in the past . . . a lot of people had.

"Come on outta there, squaw, afore we have to come in and get you." A gruff voice crashed through the open front window like a jagged stone and punctuated Blake's worry. Murmured grumbles and demands, too muffled to understand, followed.

The sun drooped low on the horizon, and the streets in front of Doc Bruner's house danced with long orange shadows in the smoke and dust. Blake peered around the edge of the window frame to see a small band of thugs gathering beyond the doctor's sun-bleached rail fence. Some carried clubs. At least one held a pickax. No guns were visible, but Blake had no doubt pistols hid themselves in greasy waistbands.

He turned to his mother. "I think we should try to slip out the back way."

Doc Bruner stepped in from the hallway that led to his office and shook his head. His steady whisper of a voice engendered trust and soothed almost as well as Maggie's. The double-barreled coach gun in his hands helped too.

"There are two more out back to be certain you don't go that way." Bruner peered at Maggie over the top of his wire reading glasses, then at Shad, who still slept on the couch. "Both of you might as well just stay here. I can watch out for them, son. Most of those folks aren't from around here. They don't look very friendly, but I doubt they'd make a move on a doctor's office." He folded the glasses and tucked them into the pocket of his white shirt before focusing his attention on Blake. "Taft is well known around these parts for its abundance of the demon rum. I imagine these men are here fighting the fires and wandered into town for a good drunk. Tommy Ledbetter's with them, though, and that troubles me. I'm sure he's fired 'em up about your Indian mother."

Blake took a deep breath and checked the rounds in his sidearm. He slipped the old Remington back into his holster and studied his mother's passive face. She seemed completely relaxed. The way she always looked when she had walked with him in the deserts near their home back in Arizona and spoke to him of the earth. He struggled to remain calm and feel the way Maggie looked.

"Your grandfather used to say it is better to face a cougar than run from it," Maggie said. "Walk toward it, and the cat will often turn away. If you run, it will *always* give chase and strike you down from behind." Maggie rested an open hand on Blake's chest and looked up at him. "You must get to your father. Tell him what the boy said—especially the part about the

Indian with the eye patch—but I don't think we need to sneak out like mice. I only count eight people. If we face them now, we can put an end to this."

Blake cast a worried glance at the doctor. "If this goes bad, keep the boy in here and try to get a message to my father about what he told us. If we can convince them to disperse, bring the boy out to us."

Maggie patted his arm. "It will be fine. You are so much like your father. I've seen him face many men such as these."

Tom Ledbetter wheeled his tall dun and loped away without so much as a backward glance as Blake pushed open the door. Eight dour men milled around at the edge of the street and glared at Blake and Maggie through bloodshot eyes. Doc Bruner had been right. The group looked like men who'd come to fight the forest fires that had charred the mountains around them for miles. With many of the blazes now under control, the brigades were getting some time off for visits to nearby towns to wet dry throats at the local saloons and spend some of their twenty-five cents an hour on some of the fiery women of western Montana. Though they were soot-covered, bleary-eyed, and exhausted from their labors, Ledbetter had done a good job of working them into a frenzy, no doubt describing the massacre scene in graphic detail. Aggravated by the lack of women, they didn't need much to set them off. They were middle-aged men, and some of them had probably lost relatives to hostile Indians. It had been an easy job for

Ledbetter to fan their latent hatred into a terrific burn.

Blake knew these men itched for a fight. Smoldered inside for it. Sodden with whiskey after their backbreaking labor against the fires, most were no doubt frustrated by the fact that Taft and all of western Montana, for that matter, were going through not only a dry summer, but a drought of sporting women as well.

With thousands of firefighters, loggers, and miners to choose from, there just weren't enough women to go around. The sports found they could be a little fussier than normal, and the ugliest, smelliest would-be customers shared the dregs from what was an otherwise unsavory cup to begin with.

"Tell us who done it," a grizzle-faced man with a bobbing goiter shouted from the back of the group—as if Maggie had been a party to the murders.

"You men go on about your business," Blake warned, keeping his hand close to, but not touching, the butt of his revolver. "We want no quarrel with you."

"Well, you got it anyhow, son," a self-appointed leader said matter-of-factly from the front row. He was a tall, cadaverous fellow, mangy and raw from his firefighting, skinny as a fence picket, except for an alcoholic bulge at his belly that made him look as if he'd swallowed a chamber pot. The charred brim of his gray slouch hat hung across his face like an angry brow. "You got a quarrel if you want it or not unless you stand aside from that there squaw." Chamber Pot held a hickory pick handle loosely in his bony, blackened hand.

"We gotta set an example for justice," the Goiter bobbed enthusiastically in the back.

The man in the burned hat patted the pick handle against an open hand and sneered. "You ain't got nothin' against justice, have you, Sheriff?"

"It's Marshal," Blake corrected, knowing as he did that the words weren't going to make any difference. "What you're up to's got nothing to do with justice."

"First I thought you was a greaser with a badge, but you got an Injun look about you too, now that I think on it." Chamber Pot took a step forward, followed by the other men. "It's no wonder you take up with the squaw."

Blake felt his mother move a step away from him, giving both of them room to maneuver. Once he drew his pistol, there was bound to be bloodshed. Were it not for the fact his mother stood beside him, he would have welcomed it with men of this caliber. He had confidence in his abilities, but one stray bullet could spell disaster.

"Why, bless me if it ain't Maggie Sundown!" A drawling voice punched through the hazy smoke in front of an approaching rider. The southwest sun made a statuesque silhouette of him and his horse against the golden haze. Blake couldn't make out his face, but the stranger had used his mother's maiden name and there was no mistaking that booming Texas voice. It had the disconcerting effect of a cannon shot over the crowd, but just hearing it brought Blake's anxiety level down a notch.

Long shadows rode along the dusty ground in front of Clay Madsen and his muscular bay gelding.

When he came out of the sun, it was easier to see the high-crowned silver-belly hat canted rakishly to the left. A drooping mustache as dark as his bay's tail and a neatly trimmed goatee framed his smiling mouth.

"Blake, my boy, how the blazes are you?" Madsen bellowed. He ignored the gathered mob as he trotted his jigging horse through the middle of them, dismounted, and handed the reins to a dismayed man in faded overalls standing beside Chamber Pot.

"Looks like you're havin' a party and forgot to invite me." With his back to the grumbling drunks, he winked at Blake and extended his left hand, keeping both their gun sides free. After a hearty, pump-handle handshake, Clay turned to a flustered Maggie. He gathered her up with both arms and kissed her on the lips with a loud smack.

"It's been too long, Maggie my darlin'," he said, putting her down to straighten her crumpled dress. "Where is that mean little man you married? From the looks of things, these boys are having a bit of luck that he's not anywhere near these parts." The big Texan gave a swaggering smirk as he looked over the situation.

"Working." Maggie managed to regain some of her composure, but still wore an embarrassed grin and flushed cheeks, despite the fact that the men in the street wanted to see her hang.

"Working?" Madsen let his jaw drop. "Mercy, woman, I thought he retired. I'd hoped to spend a little time talking before . . ."

Chamber Pot cleared his throat. His whiskey-slurred speech quivered as he worked his confidence back to the fore. "You best be moving on, mister, if'n you know what's good for you. We got us a sworn duty to bring this Injun here to justice."

Clay frowned, letting his breath out slowly through his nose in a disgusted sigh.

"Fiery darts of the adversary!" he bellowed. "These bastards are annoying, aren't they, Maggie." Their greeting kiss had knocked his hat back some, and he used his left hand to settle it over smoldering gray eyes as he turned to address the group. His voice built like a hot wind as he spoke.

"Beat it, all of you. Mercy, I've seen meaner lynch mobs at my six-year-old niece's birthday party. These fine folks are friends of mine and I'll be go-to-hell if I'm gonna let you damnable fleas get near them." He turned back to Maggie, ignored the mob again, and tipped his hat. "Sorry about the language, dear, but that man with the funny little belly has kindled my ire."

Chamber Pot's slow simmer shot up to a full boil. He fumed, raised the hickory pick handle, and snapped, "You turn around and look at me when I'm talking to you, you high-minded son of a bitch. I can see what you're about, kissin' all over the little red whore. I'm fixin' to . . ."

Clay's long-barreled Colt hissed out of his holster as he wheeled. Advancing on the man with one quick stride, Madsen cut the threatening words short with six inches of cold steel rammed through teeth and against the back of Chamber Pot's throat. The pick handle clattered harmlessly to the dust. Chamber Pot gagged and fell back to join it with a muffled grunt, both hands grasping the gun barrel that pro-truded from the bleeding gash of his mouth.

With slow deliberation, Clay thumbed back the hammer and spoke to the men around him, his voice barely above a whisper. "You boys best sober up and be on your way. If this nice lady's husband were here, you'd all be lookin' at your innards 'bout now." He let the piercing gaze fall to his trembling victim.

"As for you, you have worse language than I do. This is a respectable woman and I believe she deserves an apology."

"Thorry, ma'am," the deflated man mumbled around a mealy pink drool of broken teeth and blood that dripped from the pistol barrel. His clenched eyes pressed tears of fear from singed lashes.

"I reckon that'll have to do," Clay said, yanking the gun barrel back so a few more teeth caught on the front sight blade on the way out. The man groaned and covered his bleeding mouth with sooty fingers. Clay held the pistol in his relaxed hand and tapped the long barrel against his thigh while he thought. "I expect you'll have revenge burning a hole in your head if I let you go."

Chamber Pot groaned and suddenly smelled as bad as he looked. He shook his head so hard, the charred hat fell off. "No, thir! No, I thwear I don't." He winced when he lisped across the broken teeth. Spittle hung in bloody threads from his grimy chin.

"Just the same," Clay said, rapping him on top of the head with the heavy gun barrel, "I think you'd better sleep on it." He stepped back to survey the rest of the crowd.

"Who's next?" He played the cocked pistol back and forth across the crowd.

No one breathed.

"That's what I thought. Now, that was just a little layin' on of hands. Make for the woods, boys, or we'll have to start havin' a real prayer meetin'."

Two of the would-be vigilantes grabbed their bleeding compatriot and dragged him by the armpits across the dust. The drunk who'd held the bay's reins silently pushed them out toward Clay, as if he wanted to get rid of them without getting too close to the formidable Texan.

Clay lowered the hammer on his sidearm and returned it to the holster. "Much obliged," he said, and smiled as if nothing had happened.

When the mob had slunk into the brown curtain of smoke up the street, Clay turned to Blake. "It's been my experience that if you apply a masterful enough ass-whippin', you can generally take care of a man's thoughts of revenge—for a while at least." He tipped his hat to Maggie again. "Pardon the plain talk, hon. Anyhow, we'd probably do well to saddle on up and scoot, in case there's a back shooter amongst that little mob. What'd you do to rile them up so bad?"

Blake filled him in, while Maggie went in to get Shad. The boy dozed against her shoulder when she brought him out. Doc Bruner stood in the open doorway with his shotgun, smiling at the entertainment he'd seen, and watched up the street for any of the men to return.

"You're right." Clay nodded, removing his hat to

let all the new information settle in his brain. "We can't leave the boy here."

"I'll stay with him." Maggie fingered the leather medicine pouch that hung around her neck. "His spirit is sick. He feels safe with me and I can help him."

Blake rubbed his face. Being a deputy was turning out to be a heck of a lot harder than being a tracker. He didn't feel right about leaving his mother. Especially not with drunken mobs roaming around trying to hang her, but he needed to get the information Shad had given them to his father.

"I'll be fine, son," Maggie said. "Really. Ask Mr. Madsen if I can't take care of myself."

"I'm sure as hell scared of her." Clay grimaced. "Sorry again, Maggie dear. If you don't count my sister—and I don't—I haven't been around a decent woman in so long I've forgotten my manners."

Blake blew out a quick breath and spoke before he could change his mind. "Let's get over to the jail. There's a room off the office you can bunk in. They've paroled near everybody in Montana to help with the fires, so it should be empty. It's built for stout, so it should keep folks out as well as in. John Loudermilk is working tonight. He's a good man. I trust him."

"What brings you all the way to Montana, Clay?" Maggie waved good-bye to the doctor. "You know Ky Roman is here as well?"

"I heard. It will be good to see him—and that little wart you call a husband. You should have married me, Maggie. You know that, don't you?"

Blake chuckled. He'd grown up around such talk,

and was used to a certain amount of harmless flirtation between his mother and Mr. Madsen. He was the only man alive who could get away with it.

"You came up to steal me away from Trap?"

"Nothing so spectacular. But it is an interesting story." The Texan looked down the street the way the mob had disappeared. "Let's head on over to the jail and I'll tell it to you."

Chapter 6

There was something familiar about the smell. Angela wanted to ask Betty about it, but she was busy over by the coach talking to one of the Indians. The sun was right in Angela's eyes, and made it so difficult to see she felt dizzy. Shad was gone or she would have asked him about the smell. He was exceptionally bright for such a young boy.

Angela needed to get to her father's mining operation and couldn't understand why they were stopped. There was really no time for this. Her head ached and she needed to use a bathroom in a bad way. She would have to talk to the driver about all this dawdling. He was an employee of her father and by association, an employee of hers. Father would be expecting them and she didn't want him to worry.

Fritz Mueller opened the coach door and leaned out, smiling widely and ignoring the fact that the Indian talking to Betty had a hand on her shoulder. The handsome young German's voice was hollow

and rattled from the dark nothingness of the doorway.

"Come back to the coach, Miss Kenworth . . . and
bring your finger with you."

Angela looked down at her feet and saw her little
finger lying on the ground. The ruby ring her father
had given her was still on it. It would never do to
leave the ring behind. Mother would be furious. Angela bent to pick up the finger and caught the smell
again.

It was a hard smell, hard enough to hold—and
smelling it made her feel heavy, like she couldn't keep
her feet. Slowly, the smell turned to a bitter taste, then
Betty screamed and the taste turned to pain. Angela
gagged and her eyes fluttered . . .

She was so hot, it was hard to breathe. Thick, putrid air closed in around her, and she realized she'd
vomited down the front of her clothes. Someone had
done a cursory job of cleaning it up, but the smell
still lingered. Pain replaced the fog in her head.
Slowly, with great effort, she willed her eyes open and
remembered where she was.

The metallic taste of blood pushed at her throat.
She'd been biting her cheek in her sleep. Sometimes,
her brain tricked her into thinking she could still
feel her little finger. She couldn't keep from checking each time she woke up from the shock-induced
naps that peppered her time in captivity with black
dots in her memory. The finger was gone each time;
nothing remaining but a tiny nubbin, no bigger than
a chicken bone, covered by a bloody, ooze-soaked scrap
of cloth. A sickening, gut-wrenching throb started
where her finger used to be and rushed up her arm,

where it threatened to blow out the top her head before ricocheting back to her arm again at every beat of her heart.

Angela couldn't remember what day it was. She felt a pressing need to use the privy, but it was not yet desperate, and she supposed from that that she'd slept through the night and into another day. She remembered the wilted woman with dirty blond hair and a large mouth taking her to the outhouse the night before. Afterward, she'd tended to Angela's finger, soaking it in salt water and whiskey, before putting on a fresh bandage. Once, Angela had torn off the bandage to be certain the finger was gone. The woman had slapped her on the hand hard enough to make her cry.

"Don't let the air get on that bone. You best keep it covered like I tell you to," the woman had whispered in a throaty, liquor-sodden voice that sounded as desperate as Angela felt. She had a humorless look and a racking cough that turned her face red when it hit her. When she wasn't coughing, she looked as if her whole body was turned down into a deflated frown.

Now, fully awake, Angela sat slumped against the wall with her eyes half open, trying to get rid of the gritty film that covered them, and looked around her dim, smoky prison. Asleep or unconscious, she'd been all but ignored, so she scanned without turning her head.

A bald man sat hunkered in a metal tub across the room, blowing noxious green smoke from a cigar as fat as his stubby fingers. Angela had never seen even the top half of a naked man before—not even her father—and she found herself wondering if it was normal for all men to have such a coarse rug of hair over their shoulders. She'd always supposed that when men went bald, they were pretty much hairless everywhere.

Angela let her head loll back against the rough plank wall. She surveyed the rest of the room to get her mind off the man's hairy back. The room was no more than fifteen feet across, and there was only one door. Beams of light cut through narrow cracks in the rough-cut timber, and Angela felt herself wondering what the cold Montana winter must be like in such a place. Next to the far wall was a sagging double bed, with a sad-looking quilt and two crumpled gray pillows. From the looks of the bedclothes, Angela thought this woman might have once had taste, but the men she entertained probably didn't take the time to care for lace and frills.

A small wooden table squatted beside the bed. A brightly bound notebook with a red linen spine lay beside a chipped porcelain pitcher and basin. She thought maybe the woman kept a diary. Angela had always kept a diary, and supposed a prostitute might find use for such a thing. The book was the only color in the room, and looked out of place in the otherwise drab surroundings. Two chairs that looked wobbly even with no one sitting in them completed the meager furnishings.

"Come see to scrubbin' my back, woman." The bald man's voice was a rough growl.

The same blond woman who'd helped Angela with her wound sat up from a tangle of quilts on the creaky bed. She wore a sweat-stained bodice, yellowed by time and washes in mineral-laden water, and a cotton petticoat of the same dingy color. Her blond curls stuck in ringlets against the perspiration on her flushed face.

As Angela's head cleared, she recognized the man in the tub as the same man who'd ordered the murder of the stagecoach driver—the same man who'd cut off her finger. She remembered the Indians had called him Feak.

The sweating woman's breasts bulged against the threadbare cotton of her soiled bodice. Angela thought of Betty, and caught a sob. It was hard in her throat like a piece of food that was too big to get down, and brought a sharp pain between her shoulder blades and tears to her eyes.

Feak blew another cloud into the air and coughed while the woman scrubbed his back. "Don't be so damned rough, Moira." He leaned forward in the tub, the white knots of his spine erupting from the hairy mat of his back like mountaintops above the tree line.

"Take off the dirt, not the hide." He spit into a rusty can on the floor beside the tub.

When Moira had pinked his back sufficiently, he leaned back and threw an obscenely pale leg over the side of the metal tub. The top of his boot had rubbed a bald spot in the thick rug of black hair halfway up his calf and made him look like a dog with a bad case of mange.

"I got to be figuring on what to do about that boy." Feak blew more smoke into the close air. "He mighta seen my face."

"He don't know you from Adam, Lucius." Moira coughed into her sleeve, then dipped her scrubbing brush into the water and worked on his shoulders— lightly, so he shut his eyes.

"Don't matter. Can't be leavin' things unfinished." Angela heard the same cruel rumble in his voice she remembered hearing just before he'd cut off her finger.

Shad was okay! At least for the time being. If that were not the case, Feak wouldn't be worried about him. This fact alone filled Angela with a new sense of hope, and she felt the pain in between her shoulders ease some. Even the throb in her hand quieted with the news.

The door opened and a baby-faced white man sauntered in with the two Indians. He held a half-empty bottle of whiskey by the neck in one hand and a rifle in the other. Feak and the woman must have been used to such intrusions because Angela was the only one who jumped. His name was Scudder, she remembered that much.

"Look who's awake," Scudder slurred, staggering across the room to prod Angela's foot with the toe of his boot. His pouting mouth was turned up into a sickly grin. The few dark hairs that tried to be a mustache were pasted across his pale, carplike lips in stark contrast and made them look like a badly infected wound sewn together with catgut. "She don't look like she's worth ten thousand dollars."

Feak didn't look up from his bath. "Well, she is, so leave her be for now."

Angela sighed quietly when Scudder walked away. He was a young man—maybe four or five years older than her—not too tall, but big around the belly from lots of drinking and with a cruel look in his puffy eyes. Angela had seen the look before in her neighbor's cat when it was toying with a wounded bird. He enjoyed other people's torment. He didn't look too awfully strong, merely mean-hearted. His look was the only thing sharp about him.

A horse snorted outside, then pawed at the ground. The sound of muffled voices carried through the cracked window on the smoky outside air. The door probably led to a back alley so Moira's patrons could come and go unnoticed by their neighbors unless they happened to pass one another in the alley, in which case they were likely to keep such things between themselves. Bumping into someone in an alley behind a prostitute's house is not the kind of thing a person brags about. In any case, Angela knew rescue from this place was unlikely. The Indians or Scudder would be on her before she made it to the door. She felt weak, hardly able to even get to her feet, and knew she wouldn't make it far without collapsing if she did get outside.

Angela tried to sit up to ease the pain in her back and make herself a little more comfortable on the rough pallet of blankets, but realized the need to use the privy was becoming more urgent. The woman had offered her some warm soup earlier, but the smell of it had made her gag. Now she felt hungry, but she was afraid if she had anything to eat, it would only make her situation more critical. At first she'd been glad she was wearing britches instead of a skirt. It made her feel more modest when they'd dragged her around. But now there was no way to accomplish what she had to without taking down her pants, something she would put off as long as she could around these men.

Billy Scudder flopped down backward on one of the two rickety chairs and rested his arms along the backrest. "Turns out you heard right, Feak. There was a kid," he said, yawning wide enough to show a mouth full of whiskey-rotten teeth. "From what I can tell, they got him over at the jail in Taft. Some Injun woman's with him. "

"What they want with a Injun woman?" Feak sat straight up in the tub and stared intently at Scudder. For a moment, Angela feared he would stand up.

"She's lookin' after him, I guess. Funny, I ain't never heard of no Injun with an Irish name. Maggie O'Somethin' or other. They got her tryin' to get the boy to talk." Scudder chuckled into his folded arms and nodded toward the two Indians, who idled by the wall. "I reckon me and the boys scared the water right outta him with our doin's yesterday." He spoke as if they had done no more than a harmless prank. He looked across his arms at Angela and chuckled. "Too bad you conked out and missed all the fun."

Angela felt bile rise up in her throat at the thought of what they'd done to Betty.

"See to the screamer," Feak had said. But Scudder and the Indians had argued, reminding their boss he'd promised they could have some fun with her before they rubbed her out. Angela turned her head and tried to vomit on the floor, but her stomach had already voided itself of everything but anger and pain. So much pain. It hit her in the back of the head like a hammer. She drew her wounded hand to her belly, curled up in her filthy quilt, and sobbed.

"What? You got no stomach for such talk?" Billy

Scudder sneered. "Neither did your chubby little friend . . ."

Feak snorted. "Shut up, Billy, before you scare her to death. The boss wants her alive."

Moira slumped back on the edge of the bed, her scrub brush dripping suds and dirty water on the sheets. If she cared, she didn't look like it.

"Maggie O'Shannon," Moira droned. "I've heard of her."

The older of the two Indians glared at the far wall intently with his good eye as if he were remembering something from his past. A mottled burn scar furrowed the left side of his face from jawline to forehead. The string of his black felt eye patch ran across a twisted nub of skin where his ear used to be.

"Maggie Sundown of the Wallowa." His voice was pinched and he spit the words more than said them. "Strong medicine, that one. She is the wife of *Denihii*, friend to the one who did this to me." He gestured to his eye and the scaring on his face. "Her power is all that kept me from killing Roman those years ago. She is an evil witch. If she were among my people, we would torture her and hang her from a cottonwood tree for the buzzards. I would very much like to cut out her filthy heart."

"Mercy, Juan Caesar, you got it in bad for that woman." Feak chuckled, then rubbed his face in thought with a wet hand. Moira slouched and let the scrub brush drip more gray suds onto her bed.

Scudder sat upright at the mention of the word *witch*.

"I need you to be ridin' back to Taft tonight, Billy.

We gotta do somethin' about this boy, big medicine or no."

"T-t-tonight? Me?" The sneer bled from Scudder's mouth. "Why, come on, Lucius, you just now heard Juan Caesar allow as how he wants to be the one to carve her heart out."

"If Billy is afraid of this witch, then I'll go. I have no fear of an old woman and a pitiful child." The younger of the two Apaches smirked.

Juan Caesar looked at his young companion and shrugged. "Her medicine is real. It is no joke. But she does have a weakness. She keeps her charms in a leather bag around her neck. I believe if she was caught without the bag she would not be as powerful."

Bill Scudder's eyes darted around the room, searching for some way, any way out of this assignment. "I . . . I don't want to go after no witch. I . . . think maybe I should stay here with you. What if someone comes to try and rescue the girl?"

"The A-patch will stay and help me with that."

"Send them to kill the kid." Billy's voice was high and tight as a guitar string. "They know more about this Injun woman anyhow."

Feak's mood went as dark as the cloud of his cigar smoke. "Come here, Billy, so I can be sure you're hearin' me proper."

Slowly, Scudder skulked up to the edge of the tub, a dog waiting, knowing it's about to get kicked, but too afraid or stupid to do anything else.

Without warning, Feak's hand shot out from the tub like a viper curling between Scudder's legs and behind his left thigh so the young man straddled his crooked arm. Billy's eyes went pie-pan round and he swallowed hard, standing perfectly still. The Indians grinned openly.

"It ain't safe for the A-patch to be seen too much." Feak's voice was a whisper, slow and even. "The boss wants us to keep them out of sight. I'm tellin' you to go and take care of the kid. If you can do it without comin' up against this fierce Injun witch, so much the better. Hell, kill her too, I don't care. Cut her heart out so Juan Caesar can chop it into little pieces. Take her medicine pouch and burn it if you have to, cut it off with her Injun neck. But . . . whatever you do, you best be takin' care of that kid so he don't ever talk again."

Feak paused, staring hard at the man, who towered over him while he sat in the tub. "Understand, Billy?"

Scudder nodded. His belly trembled and his breath came in short gasps. He was almost whimpering.

"Thought you would." Feak withdrew his hand slowly, and Angela was able to see the long skinning knife. A dark trickle of blood mixed with the soapsuds and water along the razor-sharp edge of the blade.

Angela slumped as far as she could to the floor. What chance could she possibly have to survive if these people were bent on hurting each other?

CHAPTER 7

"Ten thousand dollars is a hell of a lot of money." Peter Kenworth slammed a ream of yellow stock certificates on the flat of his desk. The shiny red of his well-fed jowls reflected in the polished cherrywood finish. Kenworth always sounded pinched when he talked about money. One didn't get to be rich by buying other people's lunch at every meal and Peter Kenworth was very rich. Cattle wearing the PK brand ranged over most of five sections of rolling foothills above the Bitterroot Valley. Most years the grass covered these hills and the cattle were fat as ticks, but the spring of 1910 brought unusually hot weather, and what little snow that fell in the high country melted early. Not a drop of rain fell through May, June, or July. August brought only more searing heat—and fire.

Already, acre after acre of PK land had been consumed by the spot fires that dotted the dry, brown hillsides and sent plumes of dark gray smoke up into the darkened sky, only to settle back to turn the once-picturesque Bitterroot Valley into a haze-filled mess of charred stumps, bloated dead cattle, and black, skeletal husks of what used to be his buildings.

As strange as it seemed to some, Peter Kenworth didn't care about the cattle or the vast ranches. He hated the loss of his profit, but mining was his first love. While others enjoyed the wide-open spaces and tree-covered hills, Kenworth longed for the darkness of the mines, the cool breeze that blew from a side shaft when it connected him with the heart of the earth herself. When he went below, Peter felt connected, part of something larger than himself. On top of the ground, with all the big sky in the world above him, he often felt untethered, as if he might float away.

Even with the fires, Kenworth mines near the St. Joe and holdings near Anaconda still brought him a steady income. Not as much as they had in the beginning, but steady nonetheless. A good deal of that he sent to his wife back in Boston. Not that there was any love lost between him and Lizbeth. If circumstances had not conspired against him back at his humble beginnings, he'd have divorced the dictatorial woman long before. As far as he could see, she had only ever given him two things of any value in the twenty-year span of their miserable acquaintance—a grubstake, which he'd paid dearly for over the years, and a daughter, who she'd kept from him and held over his head at every turn. Lizbeth had always hated tight places, and Peter often wondered if his own love for the mines signified something about his strong desire to be as far away from her as possible.

She'd not been able to get through to him on the

telephone, but her wire had been bad enough. She was unforgiving and vindictive after he'd informed her of the kidnapping.

"Get her back quickly. Stop. When you do, send her home at once. Stop. My fault for trusting you. Stop. No foolishness will be tolerated. Stop. Lizbeth "

Peter knew it was sheer foolishness with Lizbeth on a dark, humid night in Boston so many years ago that had led to Angela's arrival, but that didn't keep him from doting on his daughter at every opportunity. Lizbeth had tried to keep them apart, but the girl was too much like him—too full of spirit, goaded by her sense of adventure to try out new things. No matter what his wife did, she'd never been able to keep him from getting to know his own daughter.

Now he even doubted himself. He'd vomited when he saw what had happened to the poor Donahue woman. His whole body ached at the thought that they would find Angela somewhere in the nearby woods—his poor, beautiful daughter, disemboweled and naked. Strangely, it was a comfort when one of his men found her finger with the ruby ring still on it. It seemed like a sign that she'd been taken alive. Peter had wrapped the precious little finger in his handkerchief and tucked it safely inside his vest pocket. Even now, the pitiful thing rested in a small wooden box in the lap drawer of his desk.

Tom Ledbetter stood across the spacious wood-paneled room. He held his hat in one hand and an arrow in the other. "We didn't see who shot it, Mr. Kenworth. I have men out now looking for a trail. We plan to track whoever it was at first light."

Kenworth held the rolled note that had been tied around the arrow up to the gaslight again. "I'd gladly pay ten thousand dollars if I knew she was still alive. I'd pay ten times that if I could only be certain."

Ledbetter's face glowed red. He hung his head as if he was about to cry. "I feel downright awful, sir. I know it was my idea to send Mueller to pick the young lady up in the coach. I can't help but think if I'd been the one to go . . . maybe met her myself . . ."

"Then you'd be dead as well and I'd have no one to rely on right now. Stop blaming yourself, Tom. All I care about now is getting her back, not what we all should have or could have done."

"The note seems like the only chance, sir. We take the money to the crossroads and they'll have the girl there. There's not much of a choice for now." Ledbetter shrugged. "They picked a perfect spot. Open land all around so they don't have to fear we'll ambush them. If they're telling the truth, I'll have your daughter back by tomorrow night."

Kenworth collapsed back in the padded chair and rubbed his beleaguered eyes with both hands. The man meant well but, dammit, it wasn't *his* daughter out there with a mutilated finger and who knows what other kind of humiliations. He should never have gone and seen what they'd done to the poor Donahue girl. Now he couldn't close his eyes without envisioning the same treatment for Angela. He spoke into clenched fists—more to himself than to Ledbetter. "And if they aren't?"

Ledbetter's eyes grew dark. His long lips pressed together. He nodded slowly to his employer. "I will take care of this myself, sir. One way or another, I plan to track down these redskins and kill them all whether they bring back your daughter or not. I promise you, they won't have the money for long."

Ledbetter made an imposing figure in the dancing gaslights. Kenworth felt a little better to have such a capable man on his side. "Are you so certain Indians did this?"

Ledbetter held up the arrow and snapped the wooden shaft in half with a beefy thumb. "I'd say this is proof enough."

"I don't know, Tom. It's all just too pat. Indians may be cruel, son, but they're not stupid. Why use an arrow unless they wanted us to know they were Indians?"

Ledbetter's jaws convulsed as he ground his teeth together. His vehement hatred for all things Indian was common knowledge in western Montana, but few knew why. "Hell, I don't know what was going through their sick minds. But everything about this massacre stinks of red sweat and treachery."

"Just the same," Kenworth said with a weary sigh, "I think we should talk to that Donahue boy, see what he has to say about it. He had to have seen something."

Ledbetter shrugged. He suddenly seemed preoccupied with something outside the window. "If you say so, Boss. I don't mean no disrespect by this, but it's a waste of time. They say he's not doing much talking."

"You know the lawmen guarding him?" Kenworth snatched a pen from the gray marble holder on the desk and began to scribble a note.

"I do." Ledbetter took a step toward the desk. His eyes twitched and he looked into the gaslight instead of at Kenworth. The muscles along his jaw clenched again as if he were chewing through a difficult thought. "I know you're worried about your daughter, sir, but I hate for you to get your hopes up about this boy. It won't do no good to talk to him. Even if he talks, he's gone crazy. After what he seen them savages do . . . anybody would."

"Nevertheless, I want to talk to him." Kenworth blew on the paper to dry the ink, then folded it lengthwise before sliding it into a tan envelope he produced from the lap drawer. He handed the letter to Ledbetter and rested his elbows on the desk, leaning his chin against his hands. "You take that to the deputy and then bring the boy here tonight. I want to talk to him as soon as possible."

Ledbetter nodded, a soft sigh escaping his narrow lips. "They say there's an Indian woman with him. She may not be so eager for us to talk to him if she thinks we can find out the truth."

Kenworth kept his chin against his hands, but let his tired eyes float up to meet Ledbetter. His voice creaked with the weariness of a man twice his age. "Arrange to bring me the boy, Tom. Nobody but the people who have Angela will care if I talk to him or not. There's something not quite right about all this Indian business. How would Indians know my daughter was to be on that coach?" He sighed and closed his eyes. "I just don't buy into it yet."

"What about the things they did to those poor people? You can't believe a white man would do such things as that."

"Oh, Tom, my boy." Kenworth leaned back in his stuffed chair and tried to stretch forty years of tension out of his weary spine. "You shouldn't underestimate what one white man could do to another. Indians don't have the corner on the atrocity market."

CHAPTER 8

The other firefighters looked like woodchucks far below Daniel Rainwater as he swayed in the smoky wind 120 feet up in the lonely top of a ponderosa pine. It had been an easy climb, and Daniel had the best eyesight of anyone he had ever met. He felt a strange need to make the fire boss proud of him, and volunteering as a spotter seemed a good way to make that happen.

Even with the thick haze, Daniel could see for miles. Jagged peaks stuck up from a blotchy patchwork of parched brown and singed black. Rivers of smoke ran in thick streams along the low-lying valleys. Plumes of gunmetal smoke billowed up every mile or so in all directions as far as the eye could see. So many fires burned, he couldn't count them. Taking a deep breath of the relatively cooler air before he clambered back down the swaying tree, Daniel took one last look around. He was supposed to give a report to Mr. Zelinski with the location of the nearest fire so they could march to it. From his vantage point, it didn't look like finding a fire to fight would be a problem. Any direction they walked would give them ample opportunity to do battle with any number of blazes. They were surrounded by fire.

While locating a place to work would be easy, surviving the night might pose a bit of a problem.

After shinnying back down the tree, Daniel let himself drop from a high branch about eight feet off the ground. He landed in a crouch a few feet from his friend Joseph. Zelinski was nowhere in sight, but a dozen other men pressed in closer to hear what Daniel had seen. Big Ox Monroe towered in front of the group. He sneered and clicked his gold teeth when Rainwater looked at him. Roan Taggart leaned against a tree beside him and stared across his pink nose.

"What did you see?" a tall man with soot-streaked blond hair asked. He wasn't much older than Daniel.

Corporal Rollins stood to one side with his oak-tree arms folded across a massive chest. The rest of his men were working a line about half a mile away. There had already been two brawls between colored troops and men egged on by Monroe and Taggart, so Rollins preferred to keep his men working as far away as possible but still get the job done. He watched, but said nothing.

"Where's the boss?" Daniel looked at Joseph. "I need to see him."

"Talking to White," Joseph said.

"Come on," the blond man, whose name was Peterson, pleaded. "How many fires did you see?"

"Who says he saw anything at all," Ox Monroe said

from his leaning spot at a nearby tamarack. Though
Roan Taggart stank to high heaven from his farting,
the air around Ox felt dead as a corpse. "He's probably up there sendin' signals to his red devil friends so
they know where to slip in and cut all our throats. I
say we send somebody up we can trust and dump the
skinny little buck and his friend in the creek where
they belong."

A nervous chuckle rolled through the small group.
They cast bleary, bloodshot eyes back and forth as if
looking for guidance. It didn't pay to ignore Monroe's jokes completely.

"How many fires, Daniel?" Corporal Rollins unfolded massive arms and let a relaxed hand rest on
the upright handle of a pickax beside him. He spoke
to Rainwater, but sent a pointed smile at Ox Monroe.
"Don't listen to Mr. Ox there. He just foolin' with you,
I'm sure of it. Ain't you, Mr. Ox?"

Monroe grunted and spit on the ground, but he
didn't answer.

"I hope you was just funnin', Mr. Ox." Rollins
flipped the pick around and around in a hand the
size of a shovel blade the way a smaller man might
toss a hammer, catching it by the end of the handle
on each full rotation. "I think you and me, we gonna
have to wrestle one of these days, Mr. Ox. I think
you'd get a kick outta that." He beamed and shook
his head slowly back and forth while he spoke. His
eyes never left Monroe. "Yes, sir, I just love to wrestle."

"Why don't you wrestle your own self, you ignart
tar baby, I got no truck with you." Monroe didn't
know it, but Roan Taggart who was always stuck so
close he seemed like another appendage, looked

around for a place to hide and took a half a step back at the last remark.

Rollins caught the pick by the handle and held it out in front of him as if it were no more than a light twig.

Daniel sighed. His ever-present smile faded away. "I need to talk to the boss, boys. There's too many burns to count. The whole country's on fire and we're in the middle of it."

"Why don't you do that, young buck?" Monroe said with a swagger, his eyes still locked on Rollins.

The corporal nodded slowly, flipping the pick again in one hand. "Yeah, Daniel, why don't you go ahead and tell Mr. Zelinski what you saw while me and Mr. Ox decide the rules to our wrestlin' match."

Monroe scoffed. "Why you always takin' up for the Injun? You're too stupid to see what's goin' on here, ain't you. They must call you niggers buffalo soldiers 'cause you're so thick-skulled."

Rollins let the pick fall to the dust and slowly popped his powerful neck from side to side. His head bowed like a bull on the fight as he spoke. His quiet words cut the air. "I don't know about them others, but the name suits me 'cause I'm 'bout to trample your mangy ass."

The fire boss's thunderous voice rolled through the trees. "Rainwater, get over here and look at this map."

Daniel looked back and forth at the two giants, poised for a fight. Monroe's hand hung above the handle of his knife. Rollins stood with empty hands, his big chest heaving, eyes narrowed.

"Ask Corporal Rollins to come along," Zelinski yelled. "I need to see him as well."

"You best run along like you're told, soldier man." Ox Monroe smirked. "I reckon we'll have to put off this match until later."

"Oh, we'll get to it, Monroe," Rollins said. The relaxed smile returned to his broad jowls. "I'll make certain of that."

Horace Zelinski rubbed at a five-day growth of black beard and stared at a square map held down by four stones on the flat stump in front of him. An enormous gray wolfhound with a head the size of a small horse's head rested on the ground to his right, its shaggy face cocked quizzically to one side. The dog had appeared in camp the week before, wandering in to steal or beg whatever it could find in the way of scraps and fresh water. It was a little gaunt, but other than a singed coat, it looked in excellent health. It couldn't have been roaming the hills for too long. Several men, lonely for their own families, tried to coax the animal over to them with bits of bacon or ham, but it remained aloof to everyone but the fire boss. The dog seemed to sense the leader of the group, and after sniffing the air around the camp padded straight to Horace Zelinski. Ever alert to the moods of its new master, from the time it first went to him the shaggy wolfhound never strayed far from the ranger's side.

The fire boss scratched his own head and then the dog's before he pitched a small book, its pages curled and worn from much reading under the elements, on top of the map. When he stopped scratching to rub his weary, smoke-reddened eyes, the wolfhound whined and nosed at an elbow until he resumed his attentions.

"George," Zelinski sighed, his voice gravelly from shouting orders over countless roaring fires. "We are up against something the patent-leathered bean stackers back in Washington didn't think on when they wrote our little handbook."

George White, Zelinski's second in command, took a swig of water from the canteen on his belt and wiped his mouth with the back of his blackened forearm. At just over thirty years old, his thick hair had gone prematurely gray. Some said it was from trying to live up to the expectations of his mentor and superior in the Forest Service. If it was stress-related, it didn't show in the rest of his demeanor. Where Zelinski's gaze was sharp and hard as fire-tempered steel, White's sky-blue eyes always held a spark of mischief and pure glee. The bulk of the fire crews followed both men out of sheer devotion and respect.

White chuckled. "I used the last few pages in my little book earlier this morning at my constitutional." He winked at young Rainwater, who returned the kind look with a smile.

The Use Book that was intended to guide each forest ranger on his roving patrol over what sometimes amounted to millions of acres was not much use for anything besides kindling backfires.

"Ride as far as the Almighty will let you and get control of the forest fire situation in as much of the mountain country as possible," the handbook taught. *"And as to what*

you should do first, well, just get up there as soon as possible and put them out."

By way of strategy, Zelinski and his men were on their own. Luckily for the crew, Zelinski was a man of action who needed little direction from his superiors. Though the Washington bureaucrats who wrote the Use Book gave men like him little in the way of practical instruction, Congress had made fire bosses arguably the most powerful men in the government's employ in 1908 when they passed a law permitting deficit spending to fight fires. Who else could hire as many men as he wanted, requisition as much equipment as he needed, and never worry about the cost? Not even the Army had that kind of authority.

Consequently, the Washington bureaucrats put a great deal of time and forethought into the type of men they hired for such positions. They needed men of high moral character, men who could be trusted with the lives of other men as well as the taxpayers' dollar. They needed men of action. They needed men like Horace Zelinski. The son of a Lutheran minister and Wyoming schoolteacher, Horace was as at home in the woods as he was in front of a congregation. He'd never missed a day of work in his life due to illness, and the word "shirk" was not in his vocabulary. He pushed himself beyond the limits of human endurance, and expected those in his employ to do the same. Firefighting was, after all, just that: a fight. It was a battle against the most destructive force in nature. A devil incarnate sent to destroy his beloved woodlands.

Snow in the high country the previous winter had been sparse, so the streams and rivers flowed at half their usual rate. Every blade of grass and twig was dried to the point of combustion at the tiniest notion of a spark. So dry, the swish of a pretty girl's petticoat walking by might ignite them.

No one knew what started the first fire—summer lightning, sparks from a passing train, a stray cigarette from a wandering cowboy. There were so many separate fires now, all were likely to blame. Hundreds of men had been hired or pressed into service in fighting the fires: from rich cattle barons down to a trainload of vagrants brought in from Spokane. Almost everyone with a backbone was enlisted, not only to save the forests, but to save their towns and their own homes as well.

"What did you see up there, lad?" Zelinski waved Rainwater over to the stump table.

"Too many fires to count, sir. Thirteen plumes of smoke coming up in this valley alone. All the really bad ones look like they're to the south of us." Daniel looked down at the map and tapped it with his finger. "Two big fires over along the back side of Bear Mountain—here." He pointed to a deep, narrow valley running from the high country and spilling into a wide plain that swept down above the tiny railroad town of Grand Forks, Idaho.

Zelinski's head snapped toward White, then back at the Indian boy. "Did you say there are two separate fires back there? That's a mighty narrow valley."

Rainwater gave a single nod. "I saw two plumes of smoke, one near the mouth of the valley and another north, closer to the headwaters of this little creek here."

The wolfhound gave a startled jerk when Zelinski pounded his fist against the stump. "I've got men down there, George." His voice echoed across the parched clearing. He turned to Rollins. "Corporal, has the Army got any troops nearby that can go assist them?"

Rollins shook his head. "No, sir, not that I know of. Want me to take some of my men and look in on them?"

"No." Zelinski glared across the shadowed camp toward the base of a huge white pine where Ox Monroe sat napping, his huge paws across his belly. "I'm afraid I need you here for the time being." The fire boss turned to George White.

"Pete Seaver and his boys are down there, maybe trapped between two fires. George, I need you to take two men with you and get a signal to them. The fires should lay down tonight. Pete might have sent up scouts, but he's young and inexperienced. I should never have sent him over there in charge of such a young crew. Let's just pray you can get to them in time." Zelinski picked up the map and held it closer to study in the failing light. "It's just over four miles, but you have two sizable mountains to hump before you get there." He traced a line on the map with a blistered finger. "If you cut down here toward the trail to Grand Forks, you should be able to make it well before morning."

George White studied the map for a moment before he handed it back to his boss. "I'll get to him, H. I'll take McGowan and Baker. Be nothing but a short stroll for us."

Zelinski rolled the map and slid it back into a

leather tube. "Thank you, gentlemen," he said, buckling the end cap. "Oh, one more thing. Corporal Rollins, you have my permission to stage a wrestling match whenever you see fit. I think it might be good for the morale of the men."

Rollins slapped his great hands together with such relish, Monroe jumped in his sleep clear across the camp.

Firefighting was a war all right, but Horace Zelinski aimed to win it without any casualties. He waved George White on his way, confident he'd picked the correct men to make the journey. Ninety-nine times out of a hundred, White made the same decisions Zelinski would have made himself. The other one percent of the time, it was a coin toss as to who was right.

The big wolfhound nosed at his master's thigh and let out a low, mournful whine, sniffing the air. The ranger scratched his companion on the shaggy head and raised his own face to the smoky breeze.

The wind was shifting around to come in from the south. The dusty green fronds of the great cedar trees seemed to shake with anticipation of things to come. The dog noticed it, as did Zelinski.

Almost imperceptibly, the wind began to build.

CHAPTER 9

"I'm askin' with all due respect." Blake O'Shannon rode abreast of his father's best friend. Clay Madsen had been a fixture in the O'Shannon home for as long as he could remember, and Blake thought of the brash Texan as a much-revered uncle. "All I ever heard you talk about to my father was how you wanted to get back to Texas and work your father's ranch someday."

The trail before them was a bold one, so they kept the horses at an easy dogtrot and tried to eat up ground as fast as they could.

"I did say that. Hell, I even thought it was a fact until I went back and started in doing it." Clay turned up his nose and shrugged. "Found out that the ranchin' way of life is pretty much like bein' a farmer. It's every rancher's dirty little secret. Seems like I was on the ground doing something or another with the hay fields or fences more than I was in the saddle working cattle. Reckon I always wanted to be a cowboy more than a rancher anyhow. A rancher can't afford to be as lazy as I am."

Madsen's bay had a smooth trot, and he carried on the conversation like he was sitting around the stove swapping stories. The Texan had a kind of easy, hat-thrown-back, feet-up personality and his zest for life jingled as loudly as his spurs.

He leaned across the space between the two horses as if to confide a secret matter to Blake. "Truth be known, I reckon I don't really have the gumption for that kind of hard work. Once you get a taste for man-huntin', everything else is bland as empty piecrust. When the railroad called and said I'd come highly recommended, well, it seemed like my ticket off the ranch." Madsen shrugged. "My sis wanted it all for herself and those mean-hearted little whelps of hers anyhow. She always did resent me coming back to take it over, what with me being the prodigal and all."

"And they didn't say who recommended you to them? The railroad, I mean." Blake was still having a hard time chewing over the fact that arguably the three best trackers in the nation just happened to be in the right spot when marauding Apaches carried away a Boston girl.

"Nope. Just said they needed someone to head up security for the railroad and wanted to offer me the job if I'd come up to Helena. We ain't got one of those telephones out on the ranch yet, so all our correspondence was by letter or telegram."

Madsen let out a rumbling chuckle that caused his horse to cock an ear back and throw him a wary eye. "I should have known something was up when the letter said I came highly recommended. I ain't been highly recommended for anything in my life except maybe a whippin' back in grade school when I popped the gawky kid who called himself a teacher in the ass with a piece of broken quirt." He saw Trap and Ky on the road ahead of them and stood in the saddle, urging his horse a little faster at the sight of his friends. Before letting the bay break into an easy lope, Clay looked over and winked at Blake. "The bully son of a bitch had it comin'. The whippin' was well worth what I paid for it."

It was impossible not to like Clay Madsen.

Ky Roman sat, arms folded loosely across the saddle horn on his lanky sorrel, keeping an eye on the horizon while Trap studied the ground. Both figures seemed to dance in the heat waves that drifted up from the blackened landscape. A scar of burned buffalo grass cut a swath a half mile wide as far as the eye could see to the east, and culminated in a huge gray-white plume of smoke that billowed up from behind a scorched ridge to the west where the fire devoured a stand of lodgepole pine.

Madsen coughed as he reined in the bay next to Trap and Ky. He spit to clear his throat. "I thought Texas was hot. If it weren't for all these pretty mountains, I'd figure you were about to welcome me to Beelzebub's doorstep."

"Not quite yet, but I imagine you know the way." Roman extended his hand with a grin. "Good to see you, Clay. You're looking well."

Madsen tipped his hat. "So are you, Hezekiah. Or, it's Marshal now, isn't it? I hear from young Blake here congratulations are in order."

"Thank you, but it's got nothing to do with me; it's my wife and her good politics."

"Well, whatever it is, they ought to pay you marshals a little more so you can afford the rest of that mustache you're trying to grow. I remember your face hair being a lot more robust than that little shadow of a thing you're wearin' now."

Trap groaned from his stooping and took a step toward his old friend. "I'm glad you're here, Clay Madsen," he said with a genuine grin that turned up not only the corners of his mouth, but caused the apples of his cheeks to glow and his brown eyes to sparkle with more life than Blake had seen in them in a long while. "We could use another good set of eyes on these tracks."

Aside from Clay, none of the men were given to much foofaraw or wordiness. After a quick exchange of pleasantries at their reunion, they were content to let him do the lion's share of the talking.

After a short scout, Trap regained the killers' track on the far side of the burn. The trail headed straight for Grand Forks, a little nubbin of a town not far across the Idaho line through the railroad tunnel and less than a mile away to the southwest. Blake watched the way his father smiled while he studied the trail and listened to his friend go on and on. He thought of the times when it was probably just so—his father watching the ground, Captain Hezekiah Roman scanning for ambush, and Clay Madsen providing the entertainment with his lusty yarns and general love for life on the trail.

After hearing what the others knew about Angela and the massacre, Clay filled them all in on his life in

Texas, his father's death, and the telegram from one Mr. Elwood R. Pasqual III, Esquire, of the Northern Pacific Railroad that had asked for his services as a railroad detective.

"I figured it would be a good excuse to take a trip up here to look in on that beautiful wife of yours." Clay twirled his reins while he spoke. "Needed to see if she was ready to get shed of you yet and take up with someone of greater substance and charm."

Trap beamed and shook his head at Blake, like he was just so proud to be back in the company of such a good friend. Another man might have earned a bullet for the same kind of talk, but Blake knew Madsen was more devoted to his father than any man alive.

The Texan slowed his horse along with the rest of the men and looked across the trail at Blake, scratching his goatee. "What the hell kind of a name is Pasqual anyhow?"

Ky stopped his sorrel at a broken water trough by a dried-up spring where dusty trail turned into rutted wagon track. Most anything that would burn looked as if it already had. Everything else had been hewn down with a vengeance in a wide swath along the edge of the tumbled excuse for a town. The dry ground was tilled in such a way that the ramshackle tents and buildings looked as though they were surrounded by a parched, unproductive garden two hundred feet wide. A scorched wooden sign made out of a broken barn door proclaimed in white letters a foot high: FIREFIGHTERS WELCOME AT THE SNAKE PIT.

"They got a constable of sorts here," Blake said.

"Least he used to be a constable over in Missoula—he's a railroad agent for the Northern Pacific now. Think he migrated here to make it a little easier to booze on duty." He pointed to the assortment of yellowed canvas tents and shacks of rough-cut timber that made up the settlement of Grand Forks, Idaho. It lay jumbled in the rocky crook of a mountain valley like a pile of unwanted lumber, and was likely filled with the same sorts of vermin, poisonous spiders and snakes. "He's gettin' along in years," Blake went on.

"You mean old, like your pa," Clay offered.

Blake nodded. "A mite older."

"Looks like a fire swept through here not long ago," Trap said, shaking off the comment on his age.

Blake crossed his hands on the saddle horn. "Back in July, the whole town near went up in flames. A local sportin' woman robbed one of her patrons and ended up killing him to shut him up. She decided to burn the body to cover her crime and by the time she was done, she'd torched the whole town for good measure."

Madsen whistled low under his breath. "You gotta watch those mean ones. What'd they do to her?"

"This one got away. No one cared much for the victim, but a lot of good whiskey went up in smoke, so they were prepared to hang her for that. I still got a wanted poster for her back at the office."

"So all this has been rebuilt since July by the good citizens of Grand Forks," Ky said.

"That's a fact." Blake pointed to an odd, boxlike structure high amid the branches of five white pines. The little copse of trees had somehow escaped the July fire. "A few of the local sports put themselves up a new crib up yonder in that tree house. They been doin' a right smart business from what I understand."

Clay slapped his knee and squealed enough to startle his bay. He gazed up at the treetop brothel. "Well, that would be a first for me."

"I doubt that," Ky replied. "We better get on about our business before Madsen goes to climbing trees."

Clay shook his head back and forth mocking the marshal, grinning. If he was offended, he didn't show it.

"I know Constable Steese," Blake offered to the group. "I can go talk to him and see if he's seen or heard of anything."

"Couldn't hurt," Ky said, working out all the possibilities of confrontation in his mind. "Better if we don't ride in all together anyhow."

"True enough," said Clay. "You two badge-toters go and talk to your lawman friend while me and ol' Trap saunter on over to do a little reconnoiter at the Snake Pit." He made an X with a hand across his chest. "I promise I won't go swingin' from the branches while you're away, Hezekiah."

Ky looked at Trap, who shrugged.

"It might be worth a try, Captain," O'Shannon said. "If there's a woman there, she's liable to tell him all she knows."

"And some she doesn't," Ky agreed. "One thing you two need to know before you go." He held out a gloved hand toward Blake, who'd ridden his Appy up beside him. The young deputy reached in his shirt pocket and produced a folded leather envelope. He passed it to Roman.

Ky cleared his throat. "By the authority vested in me . . ."

"Ain't this nice." Clay threw an arm around Trap's shoulders as they sat stirrup to stirrup. "He's gonna marry us."

Trap knew what his old captain was up to, and shrugged off his friend's arm.

Ky rolled his eyes and sighed, cutting to the meat of the matter. "I'm making you both my deputies. This isn't my district, so I'm deputizing you for the Judicial District of Arizona. As long as we're here and Blake needs the help, I think it best we're all official. I'm certain President Taft would approve."

Railroad agent and constable when it suited him, Fred Steese was only four days away from his seventy-first birthday. He was out cold in a drunken stupor, and Blake thought the old man might be dead when they first found him sprawled across a sagging cot in the small office next to the whistle stop. When they finally did rouse the old man, they found him stricken with such a bad case of the wheezing croup, it was difficult to understand a word he said.

The thick smoke that hung in the air like dirty quilt batting was hard on the old man. Each time Steese drew a breath to speak had him red-faced and sputtering to catch his breath. The two lawmen thought he might suffocate or burst a blood vessel at every word.

"Lucius," he coughed. "Snake Pit," he spewed. "Bald-faced killers."

The old man pointed a bony finger out the greasy window in the direction of the Snake Pit roadhouse, and broke into a riotous fit of coughing that caused him to pound his fist on the edge of the mattress, and then collapse back on his pillow. His forehead was drenched in beads of sweat.

"Amazing how nothing else matters when you can't get air," Ky said when he put his hat back on outside the constable's makeshift office. The marshal's voice was strained, and it was plain he wanted to get over and check on his friends. "Don't like the sound of this, son. Let's go see what our two partners have gotten themselves into."

CHAPTER 10

The new slab-wood door still oozed sticky amber sap in the heat of the evening. A long wooden frame covered with a canvas roof made up the building called the Snake Pit. Most of the lumber had been fresh cut no more than a few weeks before and thrown together with no time to cure. Every piece warped its own peculiar way, and this gave the frame a twisted, drunken appearance.

Anyone who wanted to get into the place bad enough could just cut through the canvas over the six-foot wooden walls. Several long rows of stitching showed that someone impatient for whiskey had done exactly that. Consequently, management didn't spend too much of its profit on fancy doors. An establishment like the Snake Pit drew a rowdy clientele that could put them through three broken doors a week.

A crumpled drunk lay slumped in the canvas breezeway, propping open the sticky door. Spraddle-legged and drooling, the man sat with his mouth agape, exposing both of his two bottom teeth. A greasy pall of smoke drifted out on a shaft of yellow light, and mixed above the drunk's head with the brown haze of smoke from the forest fires.

Trap tied his mule to a rusty iron ring on a stump beside Madsen's bay. He had to step around the sprawling man to get through the door. It galled him that he had to go out of his way to get somewhere he didn't particularly want to be in the first place.

His rifle nestled in the crook of his arm, Trap looked over at Clay as they crossed the threshold into the dingy bar. "As you get older do you have more trouble—"

"Peein'?" Clay finished. "Why, yes, I do now that you mention it. I reckon it's just something we have to live with as we get on in our years."

Trap shot a glance back to the entrance, remembering how a conversation with Clay was liable to lead any which direction if it wasn't headed off quickly. "I was going to say with malingerers like that gump there in the doorway. Seems like I have less and less patience with lazy folks."

Clay clapped a hand on his friend's back. "Then go easy on me, my friend, because lest you forget, I'm likely the worst one of that sort you ever came across." Madsen's eyes sparkled in the dim lantern light of the bar. "Now Trap, I aim to order two beers, one for me and another for me. You don't go drinkin' anything. You get mighty mean when you drink."

"I haven't had a drink in years, you know that," Trap said, his eyes trying to adjust to the smoky tavern.

Inside, the Snake Pit was just what the name implied: full of venomous creatures. In the long, thrown-together structure, there was just enough room to get one row of four tables down the left wall. Split pine slabs lay across squat barrels along the other wall. This served double duty as a bar and as a hiding place for the poisonous-looking man wiping dirty glasses with an even dirtier rag. The barkeep recoiled at the new arrivals and eyed them carefully. He stared hard under bushy black brows, and gave the odd assortment of greasy whiskey glasses a squeaky rub.

A short, stout woman with matted red hair, the color of a cigar coal, leaned on both elbows against the table across from the glaring man. A green summer dress clung heavily to a round rump as if she'd sweated through it. Her solid legs were set slightly apart over bare feet, roughened from life on a hard-packed dirt floor. Trap was a tracker. He noticed feet.

A glass, two times as large as the ones served to patrons, sat half-full of whiskey on the bar in front of the woman. If it weren't for the hard-knock life she led, she might have been considered pretty by some—Clay surely would have chosen her in his early years. Trap smiled inside himself when he remembered how his partner used to describe his favorite woman.

"A fine woman is like a fine horse," Madsen was fond of saying. "Fiery of spirit, round of hip, and pretty of face."

This one met at least the first two criteria, and in a dim bar after a couple of drinks, Clay had been known to overlook some things.

The barkeep's head swayed menacingly on the end of a long neck as the woman pushed up from her leaning position over the poor excuse for a bar. He tongued a fleck of something black out of his front teeth and muttered a spate of hissing, unintelligible words. It didn't matter what he did; Clay had his eyes on the woman, and no foolish mumbling from an uppity barkeep was about to make him change his course.

The two had already begun the quiet eye-to-eye dance some folks came by naturally. Trap was never quite at ease around much of anyone, let alone women, and had never been able to muster such communication with anyone but Maggie. Clay was at ease with just about everyone, particularly this sort of woman. Trap had always known him to be fiercely faithful during his married years, but between wives, he'd been at ease with women of varied shapes, sizes, and moralities.

At the far end of the narrow room, three men in soot-covered shirts and ragged britches hunkered around a heavy table of split logs. The moth-eaten head of a mule deer buck hung just behind them on an upright support post. Dusty cobwebs draped from the antler forks to the nappy forehead, and one of the ears was burned to little more than a singed nubbin. If you didn't count the woman in the green dress, the dead deer was the only decoration in the bar.

Under this lone bit of barroom décor, the men sat bleary-eyed and exhausted, going through the motions of a card game. One looked up to give Trap a cursory glance; the others ignored him completely. They seemed no threat, though they might know some useful information.

Trap approached them surely, not quite as forcefully as a lawman might, but his words were direct for an inquisitive stranger.

"Looking for a girl," he said while the men dealt a new hand.

One of the gamblers, an older fellow with an overbite and huge mustache to enhance it, looked up at Trap and nodded, before spitting on the floor. "There's one over yonder, but I wouldn't wait around for her if I was you. Franco, the barkeep, was about to have a go with her when you two came in. He's wicked jealous for a man who runs a sport. Now that your friend's laid claim on her, it's liable to be a little wait. And that's if there ain't a fight."

Trap nodded when he saw the woman had resumed her position leaning against the bar. Clay stood sidled up next to her, elbow to elbow. Franco stood a few feet away, eyeing Clay with dart eyes and a deadly look.

"I meant a particular girl," Trap said.

All three of the men snickered. The bucktoothed spokesman arranged the cards in his hand and spit again. "Well, Cora ain't particular. That's for damn sure." He winked at his friends.

Trap held his breath and chewed on the inside of his cheek. It had been so long since he talked to anyone at length besides Maggie, and much of their communication was unspoken. He felt out of his element with so many words coming out of his mouth. "Have you seen any other girls around here? Maybe earlier today?"

"Sorry, friend." The old man stared at his cards. "We only snuck in from the fires not more than an

hour ago. Fact is, we just had time to have a few minutes each with old Cora there and get this game
goin' before you came in. Ain't seen nobody but you
fellers."

Trap's stomach did a flip at the thought of Cora
entertaining all the men in turn. He was grateful
Clay was the one doing the talking to her. Convinced
the three cardplayers had no useful information, he
busied himself studying the cobwebs on the deer
head to give Clay time to see what Cora knew. For a
time, the two talked in hushed tones. Clay listened
intently with his hat thrown back in that boyish way
of his, every few moments giving an understanding
nod. After a few dragging minutes, he counted some
bills out on the bar before a wide-eyed Cora. Trap
couldn't hear the conversation, but he saw Franco
throw his dirty towel down in disgust. Cora began to
cry. Clay patted her on the back and then tilted her
head up with his index finger so he could look her in
the face. He dabbed at her eyes with his bandanna,
kissed the round little woman on the end of her nose.
She sniffed, took his bandanna, and kept talking,
pointing out the back door. Clay stood up straight at
whatever it was she told him and shot an excited look
at Trap.

Clay kissed her again, this time on her forehead.
He took something from his vest pocket and placed
it in her hand, curling her fingers around it and
holding her fist in both his beefy hands. She looked
up at him, blinking with the wide eyes of a lapdog.
Gently releasing her, he turned and shook a finger at
the sullen bartender before rejoining Trap.

"Our man's name is Lucius Feak. According to

our new friend, he's not above cutting the fingers off a woman." Clay cast a nod over his shoulder as he started for the door. For the first time, Trap saw Cora was waving her good-byes minus the ring and little finger on her right hand.

"She allowed as how Mr. Feak got tired of her a few months ago. He's taken up with a new woman named Moira Gumm—stays with her when he's in town. She's got a little shack a couple of stumps around the mountain, over behind what used to be the old Anheuser Hotel. Her place is one of the few that didn't burn in July." Clay shoved open the rickety door and nodded into the darkness behind the little tavern. "Cora was kind enough to give us directions. I didn't get the impression she likes Miss Moira very much."

Trap looked over his shoulder one last time before stepping into the smoky air. Compared to inside the Snake Pit, it seemed fresh as spring. "Looked to me like you gave her some money, then made her cry."

Clay shrugged, absent his usual chuckle. "She's dumber than a boot sole, Trap. Been used something awful—too many times. I gave her a little tortoise-shell comb I picked up down in Dallas a while back. You'd a thought I gave the poor girl a diamond, the way she looked at me so. Reckon no one ever gave her much but a hard time." Madsen sniffed. "Whenever I meet a woman like her, I can't help but ponder on what she'd be like if I'd found her before she was pushed so hard by whatever it was that pushed her and damaged her so. You ever wonder about things such as that?"

O'Shannon strained to see his old partner in the darkness. "Sorry, Clay, but my mind just don't work that way." Trap could see the big Texan's eyes sparkled with tears in what little light sifted through the cracks in the dry lumber walls and amber tent fabric.

Clay wiped his nose and coughed to clear his throat. "The mean-eyed booger behind the bar was about to help himself to her when we showed up. If I'd had more time, I'd have knocked his head down into his shoulders. Instead, I bought her services for the rest of the night and told him to leave her be. If we have time tonight after we kill Feak and get the Kenworth girl back, I think I'll stop in and check on his behavior. I might have an opportunity to swat him yet."

"I hope we have the chance to get our hands on this Feak character and his men as soon as all that," Trap whispered as they weaved in and out of the charred stump row. The entire settlement of Grand Forks was nothing more than a pile of tents and shacks nestled in the crook of a rock-strewn mountain.

"We'll find out shortly." Clay pointed with an open hand. "From Cora's description, I believe that's Moira's place yonder."

"I'm a little quieter than you in my moccasins. I'll see if I can get up close enough to see how many there are."

Clay nodded and wiped his nose with the back of his hand. "Sorry about that nonsense there. Didn't mean to go all blubbery on you. I reckon I'm gettin' a little emotional in my old age, especially when it comes to the womenfolk."

Trap rested a sure hand on the Texan's shoulder

and gave him a wide smile. "You were always emotional when it came to womenfolk. That's why my wife loves you enough to make me crazy."

Clay opened his mouth to say more, but bit his lip instead. He took a deep breath and got back to business. "There's a crack in that south wall a body could throw a cat through. You should be able to get a good look from there. Hopefully, Ky and Blake will see our horses out in front of the Snake Pit. Cora said she'd send them this way." Clay had his pistol out in a relaxed hand.

Trap stooped to a crouch and glided off toward the cobwebs of light spilling out from the cracked walls of the tiny shack Moira Gumm called home. He kept his rifle low, even with his belt, but ready for action. Feak and his men faced hanging for what they did, and were sure to put up a fight.

The cabin walls were thin, and Trap heard muffled voices by the time he was twenty feet away. He couldn't make out words, but there was definitely a man inside and he sounded mighty unhappy.

CHAPTER 11

In front of the Snake Pit, Blake patted Clay Madsen's bay on the shoulder as he dismounted. He tied his own animal to the same hitching ring. The horses groaned quietly and the stout Appaloosa cocked a hind leg up to rest it. Roman stepped down next to him and froze in his tracks. Both men listened intently to the inside of the rough saloon.

The sound of breaking glass chattered through the canvas walls. A pitiful yelp cut the thickness of the night air and caused Blake to shudder. Ky's eyes narrowed at the sound of another whimpering scream. Hackles up, his long neck bowed like a horse ready to charge, the marshal set his jaw.

"One thing is certain," Roman said, striding with deadly purpose toward the open saloon door. "Your father and Madsen aren't alive if they're in there. No woman would cry like that twice if they were." The tall lawman hopped nimbly over the drunken body of the man in the threshold and shoved the door hard enough to loose it from its top hinge.

Blake followed closely on his heels, startled by the thought that something might have happened to his father. What he saw inside stopped him as surely as a stone wall.

Shards of broken glass mingled with puddles of spilled whiskey on the filthy floor. Two men, their yellowed teeth gleaming in the amber glow of coal-oil lamps, held a sobbing woman by each arm, face-down across a low wooden bar. Most of her ragged green skirt had been ripped away, and what was left was hiked up in a crumpled wad above her waist. A third man, with dark, raccoonlike circles under his eyes and a bartender's apron, administered cruel blows to the bare skin of her buttocks with a leather razor strop.

The poor woman's face was toward the door, and Blake could see her eyes clenched shut in fear and anticipation of the next blow.

The bartender stopped when he saw the two new-comers. His dark eyes blazed and the veins in his forehead bulged as he screamed at them in a high-pitched gurgle. The thick strop hung poised in the air. His face was flushed from the exertion from his beating. "Go out of here or you will be the next." He had a thick Italian accent.

A maniacal growl erupted from somewhere deep within Hezekiah Roman, and he scooped up a tall wooden stool from beside the bar. Advancing on the team of men holding the woman, he never looked around.

The only other man in the place sat with his chair tipped back watching the show. Blake drew his pistol and gave him an eye to get an idea of his intentions.

The grizzled man raised his hands and smiled. For him, one show was as good as another.

And Ky Roman gave him one.

Slamming the flat wooden seat of the stool into the face of one of the grimy men who held the woman, he grabbed the other by the ear with his free hand and yanked hard. The ear ripped half away from the screaming man's skull and propelled him back to Blake, who finished him off with a rap on the head with the butt of his pistol. The ne'er-do-well Ky had smacked with the stool lay in a heap on the floor—either unconscious or sensible enough to stay down and out of the path of the seething fury that was Hezikiah Roman.

The dark-eyed bartender stared in disbelief as Roman dragged the sobbing, half-naked woman off the table and passed her back to Blake before bringing the stool crashing down on the wooden bar between them. The bulk of the stool broke away and left two feet of splintered pine the size of a short bat. Without pausing, the marshal kicked the bar over with a mighty shove of his boot, trapping the bartender between it and the short wall. Before the dazed man could form a plan, Roman was on top of him, smashing the wooden baton across the arm that held the strop.

The wounded man squealed out in pain. A gush of tears quenched the fire in his eyes and he dropped the leather. "She is only a whore, *patrone*."

Ky growled again from low in his chest. He clubbed the blubbering barkeep across the shoulders, and sent him sprawling against the overturned bar. The stick shattered at the blow, and Ky dropped what was left to the ground as if he'd expected it to happen that way. The lawman took up the strop without pausing and he looked up at the woman in Blake's arms.

"Some things you don't even do to a whore," Roman spit through clenched teeth, and laid the wide leather across the man's back and buttocks. When he tried to rise, the marshal pushed him down with the sole of his boot and struck him again and again. Ky whipped until his hat fell off and sweat dripped from the end of his nose. When it was apparent the bartender was unconscious, Roman toed him over with his boot. He was still alive, but long past feeling the effects of the beating. When he came to, he would feel them for quite a while.

Roman regained his hat and tipped it to the woman. She'd found her composure despite the fact that most of her pink bottom still poked out the back of her shredded dress.

"They call me Cora," she said through a sniffle. Extending a hand toward the marshal, she smiled through a tear-streaked face. "If I had to guess, I'd say you were Clay's friends."

Blake's head snapped around. "You know Clay Madsen."

Cora smiled and patted Blake's elbow. "Why, yes, honey boy, we're old friends as of twenty minutes ago." She brushed a wilted lock of red hair out of her eyes. "Really, he's the first man to treat me nice in a long time." Her eyes shone in the lamplight. "You two are the second and third."

"Did Clay say where he was going?" Blake felt Madsen and his father must have been onto something since they were already gone from the saloon.

"Sure did." Cora let her head loll dreamily and sighed. "He paid for a whole night with me. Hell, more than that—what he paid could have had me for a month—and that's if I decided to charge a handsome gentleman like him. Then he told Franco to keep off me for the night. Said he'd be back to look in on me, but Franco didn't believe him." She sniffled and wiped a tear from her eye with the heel of her hand. "After Clay left, the bastard took my money and whipped me for bein' nice. As if that ain't what he pays me to do anyhow."

It suddenly occurred to Cora that Franco still had her money. She trotted over and rolled him over to get at his pockets. The bartender's body arched back across the demolished bar rubble like he was trying to do a backflip. She squatted beside him, the tattered cloth of her dress falling between her fleshy pale thighs like a flimsy green loincloth. She searched around under his whiskey-stained apron until she came up with a wad of cash the size of her fist. Money in hand, she rose and stared down at the man who moments before had beaten her without mercy. Rearing back on one leg, she gave him three solid kicks with her bare foot to his unprotected groin. Cora was built low to the ground and had powerful legs. Franco's eyes fluttered but stayed closed, and his lips parted in a mournful moan as he drew himself into a tight ball like a dead spider. Even through the veil of his unconscious stupor, Franco could feel some pain.

Blake winced within himself. He hoped he never passed out in front of a woman who hated him that much.

Ky leaned over and whispered, "He's lucky. Your mama would have used a knife."

Cora looked up at the two lawmen. "Please tell Clay thank you for me. I need to get gone before Franco comes to his senses and shoots me—or worse."

"I'd be happy to tell Mr. Madsen whatever you want me to, ma'am, if you'd be so kind as to point us in the right direction." Roman still breathed heavily. He kept his head tilted back to keep from looking at the stout pink hips that peeked between the rags of Cora's dress.

Her hand shot to her mouth and she giggled. "I'm so sorry. I never did tell you, did I? Him and his friend was looking for Lucius Feak, so I sent 'em over to Moira Gumm's place. Feak used to take a fancy to me." Cora held up her nubby fingers and sneered. "Til he decided I wasn't his style. Moira ain't got the sense God gave a gopher. She's hoein' the same row, so she's in for the same treatment sooner or later."

Cora gave the men directions, and started to shuffle off toward her small room sectioned off in the back of the tent. Franco's cruel beating was still evident on her bottom and in her gait.

Ky started to leave, then turned. "Ma'am," he said, clearing his throat. Now that the excitement was over, he had a hard time even looking her in the eye. He took some bills out of his wallet and offered them to her. "Do you have anywhere to go?"

She took the money and gave him a coy wink. "I'm still young, sir. A gal like me will have places to go for a few more years anyway. With all the boys in the fire camps around these parts, I'm sure I can be of some service out there somewheres."

Roman's shoulders drooped. "But you could take this money along with what Clay gave you and make a new start for yourself—away from men like that." He pointed to the heap that was Franco.

"Doin' what?" Cora smiled, but a tear rolled down her pudgy cheek. "Listen, mister, I don't know how to sew and I don't aim to learn now. I can't cook worth a damn and even if I could, the way I been livin' no good man like you or Clay would ever take up with me. You see, I already got it figured that I ain't never gonna see no heaven on earth. I'm just hopin' to sock enough away while I got somethin' to offer that I don't have to live in Hell all the time—till after I'm dead."

She sniffed and rubbed her eyes with both fists. "You best go find your friends. If it's Lucius Feak you're huntin', they'll need the help."

CHAPTER 12

Billy Scudder was mad enough to choke a cat to death with his bare hands. Who did that son of a bitch Feak think he was anyhow, ordering him around like that in front of the A-patch and all? Billy had a good mind to stand up to him next time and show him Mama Scudder hadn't raised no sucky baby. No, sir! Not by a long shot she hadn't. Billy was tough as any man around and he knew it.

The whiskey he'd shared with the Indians earlier that evening had clouded his thinking, and he couldn't seem to come up with as many curse words as usual. He compensated by using the same ones over and over as he urged his gaunt pony into the deserted back alleys of Taft and cussed the mortal soul of Lucius Feak.

Killing the boy would be no problem—if it weren't for the witch. Mama Scudder had taught Billy much more than how to kill a person. She'd also taught him to have enough good sense to be scared of witches. Once, when he left the curtain open after dark with the lantern lit in the front room of their house, she'd nearly caved in his head with a stick of stove wood. "Them Mexican *brujas* are out there watchin' for fools liken you," she'd said. "Fools who leave their curtains open in the night so they can slip in on their spirits and give you the *mal ojo*—the evil eye—or suck the life's breath right out of you so's they can raise their dead sweethearts or some such thing."

Mama'd seen it done, she said. Mama knew about things like that.

Billy wished the sheriff back in Santa Fe wouldn't have hung Mama. She could have given him some good advice about this particular witch. She would surely know what to do.

The jail was near now, only half a block away. Scudder got off his horse and tied it to a short vine maple growing along the alley. In the distance, a hound sent up a mournful howl. The shiver going up Billy's spine met a trickle of sweat rolling down it. He belched up a particularly harsh whiskey burp that burned his throat and brought tears to his eyes.

He coughed and spit to clear his mouth. Billy seemed to remember Mama saying witches liked to steer clear of crosses. Not having such a thing handy, he bent to the dusty street and stirred his spitball into a muddy cake. He smeared the greasy mixture between his fingers and held it up close to his face so he could get a good look at it in the darkness. Satisfied it would mark him sufficiently, he smeared the sticky goo in the shape of a jagged cross on his forehead. If Mama was right, he would be safe from any witch trying to suck out his life's breath to raise her dead sweetheart—or any such thing.

He checked the rounds in his Colt, then slid it back into the holster that rode high on his hip. The deputy would be no problem; few men were as quick or as eager to kill as Billy Scudder. He tapped the wood handle of the large bowie knife on the other side of his belt. He'd use the blade to kill them all if the Indian witch didn't get in the way. A knife would be quieter—bloody, but not so much fuss as a pistol barkin' in the night.

Scudder touched the rough mark on his forehead where the muddy spot was beginning to dry. He started into the darkness, down the alley toward the jail. The dog howled again, and Scudder felt his bowels go loose like something broke inside him. That was the last thing he needed. He needed to concentrate on protecting himself from the witch and her *mal ojo*, not worrying that he might crap his pants. He paused to relieve himself under a clothesline full of long underwear behind a quiet shack along the alley.

"Mama," he whispered into the black night air while he plucked a cotton sock off the line to clean himself. "I sure hope you told me right about witches." Even as he questioned his dead mother, he ducked slightly, anticipating the piece of stove wood that inevitably landed somewhere on his head or shoulders when he'd shown any sign of doubt in her word. When nothing happened, Billy Scudder pulled up his britches, screwed up his courage, and walked toward the back of the jail. The bowie knife gleamed in the moonlight, and the sparkle of a plan that would take care of the deputy, the boy, and the witch began to form in his mind.

* * *

Shad hadn't let go of Maggie's skirt since he woke from his sleep at Dr. Bruner's office. The poor boy had seen enough misery to last him a lifetime, and though he was beginning to come out of his stupor, his eyes still held a wistful, faraway look. He held onto her as if she were the only anchor that kept him from drifting away. Though Shad refused to leave Maggie's side, he had been taken with Madsen. The big, swaggering Texan made faces and clowned with the boy enough to coax out a smile or two. Clay had always had an endearing way with women and small children. Women wanted to mother him and children considered him a playmate.

John Loudermilk puttered around with his coffee grinder in the front office, whistling some song Maggie had never heard before but that seemed to be his favorite. The deputy had wanted to lock Shad and Maggie in a cell for their own protection, but she wouldn't hear of it. In the end, he'd put her in a storeroom behind the office alongside the two ten-by-ten cells. The small room, no more than a third cell without the bars, had two cots, a pile of wool blankets, and a barrel of drinking water.

All the prisoners had been released on their own recognizance to help fight the forest fires. Apart from Maggie, Shad, and Deputy Loudermilk, the jail was empty.

"I'm hot, Miss Maggie," Shad said, lying on a cot with his head in her lap.

"Me too." She tousled the little boy's blond hair. "My husband says I'm always hot unless it's snowing." Her thoughts drifted to Trap while she patted Shad's cheek. "I'll show you something my mother taught me when I was a little girl."

Shad sat up and rubbed his eyes. It was late, but he'd slept away much of the day and was wide awake now. Maggie had taken off the absurd little jacket and knee socks he'd been wearing, and cut the knickers into a much cooler pair of shorts. A heavy woolen blanket covered the open barred window high above the cot. The covering kept anyone from looking in, but held off any breeze as well.

"You come sit over here for a minute and watch me." The window was over six feet off the ground, but Maggie didn't want Shad anywhere near it when she took down the blanket. He would be an easy target for someone outside with a ladder.

Using a wooden bucket, she dipped enough water from the barrel to completely submerge the woolen window covering. She carried the bucket to the window, and then used the cot as a stepladder to replace the dripping blanket on its nails in front of the iron bars. Water streamed from the bottom. Another blanket, rolled into a long tube and placed along the floor, caught the drizzling runoff.

"Sit here." She pointed to the cot beneath the window and stepped to the door.

Loudermilk still shuffled in the other room with his grinder.

"Now," Maggie said, her hand on the knob. "Watch what happens when I open the door and give the air a place to go." She cracked the door a few inches, and watched the blanket over the window billow out as a breath of wind blew against it from outside.

"That's nice," Shad said, leaning his head back to

feel the cool air cascade down from the wet blanket over his head. His feet stuck straight out in front of him on the wide cot. "Mama was always hot too. She would have . . ."

Maggie cocked her head to one side and trained her ears toward the cracked door. The boy kept talking, but she didn't hear what he said. For as long as she could remember, Maggie had felt a peculiar tickle when things weren't quite right—as if her heart had walked through a spiderweb. Her mother said it was a gift from the spirits. Trap's father said it was a spiritual gift.

"What would you say to some Indian tea to help you sleep?" Maggie took the medicine bag from her neck and held it up in front of her. She smiled to keep from frightening him. "It's one of the special things I keep in my bag here."

"All right. Will it taste funny?"

Maggie strained to hear Loudermilk's movements. Nothing. "You'll like it. It's sweet—like licorice. I need to get some hot water from the front. Be right back."

Shad scooted to the edge of the cot and hopped to the floor. "I'll come with you."

Maggie raised her hand. "No, you stay here. I'll only be a minute." Her voice was sharper than she intended, and his eyes went wide. Pointing to the cot, she put a finger to her lips and motioned him back there. The boy obeyed, but his breathing grew shallow and his eyes lost their focus. He was slipping back into his stupor. It couldn't be helped. Maggie couldn't afford to have him clinging to her if her fears were realized. He was safer back here.

The door yawned open a crack, and Maggie peeked into the hall. The front office was quiet. Light from the lamp spilled down past the cells and cast a spiked shadow from the key ring on the wall.

Shad sat back under the window, tight-chinned, like he might break down at any moment. It broke her heart to leave him.

"Be right back." She grabbed her rifle, hoping Shad didn't notice, and pulled the door shut behind her. The door leading to the back alley lay off to her left. It was still closed and barred from the inside. In front of her lay a small corridor with the two cells. It ended at a second door to the deputy's office. To her right, a funnel of light at the end of a short hall lead into the same room.

In the front office, John Loudermilk's coffee grinder lay in pieces on the wooden floor. One of the double-barrel shotguns was missing from the rack behind a cluttered desk, but the deputy was nowhere to be found. Maggie stepped to the front door. The bolt was locked, but there were scuff marks on the floor in front of it and the thick timber bar that should have been in brackets leaned against the wall.

The tickling feeling grew stronger in her chest, and Maggie fought the urge to run blindly back to Shad. With the rifle in both hands, she peeked around the open door that connected to the small alcove in front of the two cells. It was dark and hot. The smell of human sweat and boredom from the recent prisoners' confinement hung in the stale air. A tawny rat moved across the far wall of the closest cell, its claws clicking against the wooden floor. Maggie shuddered, but rats were the least of her fears.

"John," she whispered, holding the rifle out in front of her.

Nothing. Nothing, but the prickling web pulling across her heart.

Heavy footfalls echoed off the walkway outside the front door. The bolt rattled while someone gave it a shake. Maggie considered replacing the thick cross-beam, but decided against it when she realized she'd have to put down her rifle to lift the heavy timber. Only then, as she stepped away from the doorway, did she notice the boot heel jutting from behind the cluttered office desk. It was John Loudermilk. His shotgun lay beside him along with a half-dozen errant wanted posters in a growing pool of blood. Maggie knew enough of death to see there was nothing she could do for the poor deputy.

A pitiful scream from the storeroom rent the night.

Shad.

Straining to hear another sound from the back room, she began to move toward the boy. She rounded the corner and ran headlong into a shadowed figure in the darkness. As she crashed into him, the rifle slipped from her hands and clattered to the floor. Face-to-face, close enough to feel his sour breath against her forehead, Maggie could smell blood on his clothes. She shoved as hard as she could with both hands. At the same instant the intruder lashed out with a knife.

Shad opened the door behind them, bathing the hallway in light. The man with the knife froze like a cockroach caught in the flare of a newly lit lamp. His eyes wide as silver dollars, he looked Maggie in the face and screamed.

He wheeled, stumbling on his own feet, and ran out the back door, slamming it behind him.

Breathing heavily, Maggie scooped up her rifle and peeked cautiously inside the storage room door, scanning for danger. She'd seen Shad out of the corner of her eye when he opened the door, but the piercing screech from her would-be killer had sent him back into the little room. Maggie scanned for other intruders. Trap had taught her an old saying he used many times to save his own life when it came to attackers—*see one, think two.* Luckily, it seemed this killer was alone.

The boy stood in front of the cot, tears streaming down his face.

"I heard a noise," Shad sobbed. "Sorry I hollered, but I couldn't hide again while they killed you too Miss Maggie."

The blanket above him still billowed in the breeze. Maggie bolted the door solidly behind her, then took Shad in her arms and held him.

"It's all right now. He's gone."

When she backed away, Maggie saw the front of Shad's shirt was covered in blood. She frantically searched for wounds on his chest. He sniffed and pointed to her.

"It's not me, Miss Maggie. It's you."

She looked down. The front of her dress, across her breast, had been slashed by the man's razor-sharp blade. She'd been able to push away fast enough that the cut was only superficial, but blood oozed from the long gash that ran almost from armpit to armpit. Shad looked at her in growing horror.

"Are you going to die?"

"I'm fine," she assured him. "It's only a scra . . ."

The sound was faint at first, just a creaking of wood barely audible above Maggie's breath. The creak grew louder directly outside the door. Maggie trained her rifle on the threshold. She chided herself for not barring the front entry when she'd had the chance. A toss of her head told Shad to get back behind her on the cot.

Seconds ticked by, and she realized her forehead was dripping with sweat. She sat motionless as a loud rapping bowed the storeroom door. Expecting someone to burst through it at any moment, she let her finger tighten on the trigger.

The knocking stopped.

Maggie risked a glance over her shoulder at Shad, who still sat unmoving on the cot. A coarse chuckle came in under the door, along with a peculiar crackling sound she couldn't quite place.

Then she smelled it. Smoke. The jail was on fire.

Maggie put her shoulder to the door and shoved. It didn't budge. Someone had boarded it shut from the outside. Whoever killed John Loudermilk planned to burn them all alive. She would have to move quickly if they were to survive.

Looking back at Shad, she prayed for guidance. Instinctively, she reached for the leather bag around her neck. Moist blood covered her chest.

The medicine bag was gone.

* * *

Taft's volunteer bucket brigade turned out with amazing speed at the first sign of flames from the jail. No one cared so much about who might be inside, especially the lawman. They were more interested in getting the blaze put out before it could jump to the nearby Berryman Tavern and its large supply of whiskey. The mere mention of a spark could reduce any of the nearby buildings to ashes.

Billy Scudder sat panting in the shadows at the end of the train platform, a block away. The Indian witch's medicine bag rested in the palm of his hand. He must have cut it off when he lashed out at her in the dark. He felt foolish for screaming, but that wasn't the worst of it. When the door had opened and light spilled out into the hallway, the woman before him had borne an uncanny resemblance to his mama. The same mama the sheriff in New Mexico had hung by her neck until she was good and dead. The same mama that had a fair aim with a stick of stove wood when she got riled. The sight of her rattled Billy's bones and scared him so bad he'd wet his britches.

After he ran outside, Billy realized the witch had beguiled him. She'd turned herself into his mama to save her skin. The fact that he'd lost control of his bladder infuriated the trembling outlaw. There was fresh blood on his knife along with the darker stain from the dead lawman. He knew he'd cut her, but he didn't know how bad. Feak would be furious if the witch showed up alive, so he had to make sure.

The boy still needed killing. Billy had started to go back in and finish the job, but made it only as far as the front office. The chance he might run headlong into his mama again hit him like a shovel in the face.

That's when he came up with the idea to burn the whole building down. No one would ever suspect arson. There were fires all over the mountains; a stray spark could have blown in from anywhere. He'd been able to scrounge up some nails and a hammer from the deputy's desk. The rest was easy.

From his hiding place by the train station, Scudder watched the flames lick away at the heavy, stacked timbers of the wooden jail and nodded to himself. That would teach the damn witch to take on Mama's visage.

A long line of people, some still in their nightclothes, formed a bucket line from a water trough to the building, but they weren't doing much good. Most of their efforts went toward the Berryman Tavern.

Scudder rubbed his sparse mustache and drew a ragged breath, trying to rid himself of some of the tension he had from meeting the witch face-to-face. By now, he hoped his mama was giving her a good welcoming to Hell.

Billy clambered to his feet and caught a whiff of himself. It wouldn't do to go back to Feak and the A-patch smelling like he'd pissed himself. He remembered the clothesline he'd passed on his way to the jail, and headed in that direction. The same looseness he'd felt in his bowels came back to haunt him again, and he picked up his pace.

Even from over a block away, Scudder could feel the fire against his back. The witch and the boy were both dead by now; they had to be.

CHAPTER 13

"Couldn't get a good look, but I think there's only one man in there with her. He's kind of a grump." Trap used his .45-70 to point at the shack. Moonlight glinted lazily off the octagonal barrel in the hazy blue darkness. "She called him Sam."

"A customer?" Clay rubbed a thumb and forefinger down his drooping mustache.

"That's what I'm thinkin'. I'd like to have a look around for tracks out back. There's a privy beyond that stump row there from the door. Should be a whole load of tracks going back and forth. As far as I can tell, it's the only way in or out."

"A whore's door nearly always leads to the back," Clay whispered. The rough catch still lingered in his voice. He had a way of taking on strays. Given time, Cora would become his project for redemption whether she was willing or not.

Clay looked intently at the shack for a moment, then waved his pistol toward it. "Shall we go interrupt poor Sam's riotous evening?" His voice smoothed out at the prospect of adventure. All but a hint of the melancholy that had filled him fled by the time they reached the door. The shine of tears that moistened his eyes only moments before was replaced by the glint of mischief as he rapped on the wood with the edge of a closed fist.

"Later." A tired voice barely made it through the thin walls. If a voice could have a hue, this one was drab.

"Can't wait." Clay stood to the right of the door while he knocked again. Harder this time; a persistent knock that bowed the door in on its hinges and left no doubt that the one knocking was there to stay. Trap took up a position oblique to Clay's, a few feet back with his rifle trained on the threshold—just in case they were wrong and it was Feak who was inside.

"Be gone, damn you." This time it was a man's voice, thin and brittle as cheap glass. More whining plea than threat, it was hard to take as an order. "Can't you see she's got the book in the window?"

Clay looked back at Trap, who bobbed his head at an ornately bound book with a red cloth spine, resting inside the cloudy window on the edge of the sill. A small circle of dust and grime was rubbed away to make the book visible through the otherwise opaque glass.

"Must be her sign that she's otherwise occupied," Clay said, loud enough for everyone within a block to hear. A few shanties down, a dog began to bark at the disturbance.

"You're damn right that's what it is," the voice whined from inside.

"Open the door, Sammy." Clay's mouth was a wide grin. He was enjoying this far too much.

"Now, you look, mister. I was here first. Off with you." Sam's voice took on an edge now. It was louder, and close to the door.

Trap withdrew another step into the shadows as the door creaked open an inch. A metal belt buckle jingled inside, and the black barrel of a pistol nosed its way out at chest level.

"I said get outta here. You're a slow learner who-ever . . ." The intense heat of his preoccupation with Moira had imbued Sam with a little too much counterfeit bravery.

Clay grabbed the pistol easily and shouldered his way in through the door.

"Wh . . . wha . . . what do you think you're doin'?" Sam was even thinner than his voice, with a long craning neck that seemed too narrow to hold his lolling head upright. He wore no shirt, and hadn't had the time to get his suspenders up over bony shoulders. A bony hand held up the bunched front of his sagging britches.

As soon as Clay breeched the door, Trap moved up and peeked in. A sallow woman, with lifeless hair the color of sun-bleached wood, slumped in a rumpled pile of sheets on a sagging bed along the side wall. Beads of sweat covered her forehead. Knobby bare legs hung like sticks, akimbo from under the frayed hem of a dingy sheet. Jutting collarbones peeked out from above. It seemed absurd that such a woman would pretend any sort of modesty under the circumstances. Even Trap found it hard to believe anyone could pick a woman like this over the robust and smiling Cora.

Inside the shack, the tight air had the dank, sour

odor of an illness. If not for the welcome scent of wood smoke that came through the open door, Trap felt he might get sick to his stomach.

Clay shook his head at the gangly man in front of him. "You know, friend, women are worse than whiskey for giving a man a swelled-up view of his own abilities." He emptied the offending revolver, shell by shell.

Sam's eyes twitched as if he'd been shot each time one of the heavy bullets clattered to the wooden floor. He hitched up his pants, looked back over a bony shoulder at Moira, and attempted to hitch up his courage.

"Now see here." The raw whine caught in his throat, but he plowed ahead in a stutter. "I d . . . done p . . . paid."

Clay took a deep breath, swelling his already puffed chest, and advanced on the quaking man. "Mister, I got the only two reasons I need to put a boot in your ass. I'm mad and you're handy. Now, you best git while I'm in the mood to let you."

Sam's head sunk on the end of his long neck and settled in the hollow of his chest, which looked like it was made for it. Deflated, he picked up his shirt and slinked to the door.

"I'll come back later," he said to Moira. "You still owe me."

She shrugged and ignored him, apparently more concerned now with the new men in her life. Trap stepped in as Sam disappeared through the doorway. A muffled yelp came through the door behind him, and Ky stepped in following Trap.

"I believe you let one get away," Roman observed.

Blake came in next and winked at his father. The two new men finally got a reaction from the sullen woman when she realized she wasn't dealing with customers.

"Now, what could you all want with me?" Moira groaned, raising her arms above her head to slither into a threadbare yellow dress. She squinted through rheumy eyes, as if she were looking into the sun, though the lamp globe was so covered with lampblack it hardly gave off any light.

Clay pulled up a wobbly wooden chair and flipped it around so he could sit and lean forward across the backrest while he spoke. He sat only a few feet from the bed.

"We're lookin' for a man you're familiar with."

"I'm familiar with a whole passel of men." There was a sense of gloom about her as heavy and squalid as the room. Without warning, she launched into a coughing fit that added some color to her face for a moment. It made the vein on the side of her neck bulge with effort. Spittle pooled in frothy bits at the corners of her mouth. When she regained her composure and her face had returned to its normal pallid hue, Clay began again.

"This one likes to cut the fingers off of young girls."

"Did Cora send you? That little whore, I'll tear her heart out for this." Moira's words came hard and vehement from an impassive face, like fire from the cold steel barrel of a gun.

Trap thought it funny how a woman like this could call another woman a whore and consider it an insult. He let his eyes play around the small room, as much to give them something to look at besides Moira as anything. "Blake, take a look at those quilts." He pointed his rifle at a pile of blankets against the far wall.

Clay rested his chin on his hands along the back of the chair and closed his eyes. "Listen, hon, you got a dark future ahead of you. As things stand now, the only thing that'll save you from the gallows is if the vigilantes get to you first and hang you from a tree."

Moira sat forward and cocked her head to one side. Only the slightest bit of animation perked the corners of her otherwise lifeless eyes. Her voice was as gray and lifeless as the faded pillows behind her. A peculiar rattle gurgled in her lungs when she spoke. "I don't know what you're talkin' about. I ain't done nothin' worth anybody hangin' me over."

Clay nodded. "Consortin' with murderous men . . ."

She snorted, coughed again, and spit something thick and putrid into a rusty can by the bed. "If consortin' was enough, my neck woulda been stretched long ago. Hell, you'd have to hang all the sports in this little burg."

"And going along with a kidnapping." Blake squatted on the rough floor beside a pile of soiled quilts. "The Kenworth girl was here. Looks like they made her sleep on the floor." The young lawman used the barrel of his pistol to poke through the dirty blankets. A louse scurried down the front sight and he shook it off in disgust. "There're some bloody rags here. Looks like they came off a bandaged finger."

Clay turned his attention back to Moira, opening both palms in front of him. "There's nothin' we can do for you if the Kenworth girl dies."

Ky moved up beside him. "If that girl dies, young

lady, I'll come back and hang you myself." Roman stared hard across his hooked nose. He was not a man to make idle threats. If Roman said you were about to hang, you'd best start in with your praying.

Moira threw up her hands. "Look, fellas. She was alive when she left here. What did you want me to do? Slip off and report this to the old fart of a railroad agent? He's got the croup so fierce, Lucius woulda killed him before he got halfway up the street. I'm only one woman. What was I supposed to do?"

Clay looked at her and nodded slowly. The other three men were content to let him do the talking. "I see what you mean. But chew on this for a second, kiddo. What you do from now on can make a big difference in your future." He paused for a moment, staring at the hardened face. "Did Feak say where he planned to take the girl?"

Moira's head twitched slightly. "I know they were taking her to meet somebody else. This wasn't all Lucius's idea, you know."

"Who?" Ky couldn't help but chime in. "Who are they supposed to meet?"

"Didn't say." Moira shrugged. "I'd tell you if I knew. When he mentioned it, Lucius just called him the boss."

"Did Lucius say which way they were goin'?" Clay looked at Ky while he spoke.

"Nope. But I'm pretty sure they were headed deeper into the mountains. Whoever they're meetin' was a private sort of fella. Didn't want to be seen around here."

"When is this meeting supposed to take place?" Ky asked as Blake joined the men beside the bed.

"Look, gents." Moira lay back on the sagging bed and covered her face with a forearm. "I told you what I know and I know that ain't much. Lucius keeps important matters between hisself and the Apaches. He don't even tell that stupid kid, Scudder."

Clay glanced back at Trap and Blake. "The Indians with Feak are Apaches then?"

Moira nodded behind her arm.

"How many?"

"Two. A youngster, about the age of that young buck here with you." She peered over her forearm at Blake. "And an older one with a scarred-up face. He wears an eye patch, but he's got enough meanness in him that one lonesome eye will melt you for sure."

Trap looked over at Ky, who met his gaze with a nod.

"Did Lucius ever call these Apaches by their names?" Ky touched his pistol absentmindedly as he spoke.

"Not so as I would remember. I called 'em Ugly and Uglier. Most of the time they was off somewhere and Lucius had me . . . otherwise occupied, if you know what I mean."

"What about this Scudder kid?" Clay reached out with his boot toe and kicked at the bed to keep Moira focused. "Tell us about him."

"Billy Scudder. He's a mean one, he is. Gets his jollies by threatenin' me, but he's too scared of Lucius to take it any further than that."

"When did they go?" Clay stood and hitched his belt like he was ready to leave. Leaving seemed like a good idea to Trap. The closeness of the room and the sour smell of the woman worked hard against his churning stomach. Even with the cracks in the walls, there didn't seem to be enough air in the tiny room for everyone.

"Just after sundown—about a half hour before old Sam came by." Moira suddenly swung her legs over the edge of the bed and sat upright. "Listen, boys, are you about to take me to jail or what? The night is still young and I got appointments to keep if you ain't."

"I reckon that's up to you," Clay said. He took a half step backward and almost bumped into Ky. Even he was surprised by the woman's sudden boldness.

Her face suddenly took on the hardened edge of a flint knife. "Well, don't you think you're scarin' me with all your talk of hangin' and vigilante booger-men. I know Lucius Feak. I been a witness to what he's capable of. He's just as likely to come back and kill me if I talk to you or if I don't—it don't make no difference. My life ain't worth a pinch anyhow and I know it. I don't reckon I'll make it past this coming winter no matter what happens." She coughed again, as if to illustrate her point, and wiped her mouth with the back of a filthy sleeve.

"So go ahead and hang me if you're of a mind to. The way I see it, you can stay on here and pester me or you can go on and catch Lucius and his bunch."

Clay shook his head and followed the others out the door without another word.

Outside in the alley, Clay leaned back against a table-sized stump and spit at the dirt. "I've never felt like I needed a bath as bad as I do now—and I mean a good scrubbin' too, not just a soak-and-ponder bath."

"I know what you mean," Ky said before he turned to Trap. "Any one of you ever heard of this Lucius Feak character?"

All the men shook their heads.

"What about the Apache with the eye patch?" Blake said to his father. "I caught the way you three looked at each other when she mentioned him."

"Maybe somebody from a long time ago, son." Trap shot a quick glance at Roman.

"A very long time ago. And if it's who I think it is, he doesn't think too much of me," Ky said.

"Come on, boys," Clay groaned. "Explain it all to the youngster after we've gone to roost. My old bones are sore and it's too dark to track for a few hours yet. I've got a hankerin' for a thick beefsteak. I'll lay odds our pretty Miss Cora can rustle us up some before she shows me a soft bed while you make your hard, miserable camp." Without waiting for a reply, Clay began to pick his way around the stumps and downed trees toward the back of the Snake Pit.

Ky gave a tentative cough. "Madsen, there's been a bit of a change in developments since you last visited Miss Cora. . . ."

CHAPTER 14

Angela's horse was a poor, puddin'-footed thing with feet as big as frying pans and thick ribs that jutted from black slab sides like slats on a hay bin. It was old to boot and prone to stumbling even on the flat. The broken mountain ground was murder, and the horse spent more time down on both knees than it did on its four large feet. Both hands tied together in front of her, Angela had to claw at the saddle horn to keep from falling off into the darkness over the side of the steep trail. The jagged nub of her little finger pained her past the point of hysteria, and even the cruel rawhide gag the older Apache had tied around her mouth did little to take her mind off the stomach-churning ache in her hand.

Angela knew how to ride. There were two fine stables not far from her house in Boston. But now, tied, weakened, and injured, she found it impossible to keep her seat. Each plodding misstep of the lumbering horse jammed or jostled the shard of bone. Her teeth slammed against the stiff gag. Tears poured from her eyes and ran in muddy lines down her filthy cheeks.

Feak led the way on his big sorrel horse, almost out of sight in the darkness. The younger Apache followed him, just ahead of Angela. Juan Caesar brought up the rear. She knew he was back there, but didn't dare turn around to see. It seemed to infuriate him when she looked at him, as if her mere glance was an insult to his scarred face. If she slowed or moved her head to look back, he jabbed at her cruelly with a long cedar branch he'd carved to a rough point and carried for the sole purpose of punishing her.

They'd left Moira's shortly after sunset, keeping to rough mountain trails well away from the railroad. The wilted prostitute had shown a tiny shred of decency when she'd offered to take Angela to the privy before they left. Feak agreed, but threatened to cut off both their noses if Angela made a run for it. He sent the young Apache to stand guard.

Breathing open-mouthed around the gag parched and dried Angela's throat, but she was afraid to drink any more for fear she'd have to go to the bathroom again. It didn't really matter because no one offered her any water anyway.

Apart from the groan of clambering horses, the creak of saddle leather, and the occasional scuff of a horseshoe against sharp rocks, the group moved in a silent parade. The air grew noticeably cooler as they gained elevation. Smoke still permeated the surroundings, and once in a while she could even see the far-off orange glow of a smoldering fire. But now and then, the telltale hint of cedar or spiced scent of

Grande fir kicked up on a gentle breeze. The crisp air soothed Angela like a sip of springwater and for the first time in two days, she felt like she could breathe.

The trail, such as it was, snaked back and forth in a zigzag pattern, working its way up the black mountains before them. Angela's stomach flew into her mouth as her clumsy horse tripped over a root or river rock when they crossed one of the numerous little creeks and gullies that wrinkled the hillside. She gripped the saddle horn like a madwoman for fear of falling off and receiving a severe beating from the stick-wielding Juan Caesar, and somehow managed to keep her seat on the ungainly horse as it clambered up the other side. The effort brought more tears to her eyes and shot spasms of light through her head as bright as a fireworks show over Boston Harbor.

In the darkness, she heard her mother's nasal voice chiding her about wearing pants around such men. Her brain was fevered, and she shook her head to clear it. Deep voices drifted across a small switchback on the trail above her. She'd been hearing mutterings of one kind or another for the past several hours, and she tried to ignore them. But lights danced in the darkness along with the new voices. Lantern lights— and singing men.

Angela shut her eyes and held her breath. She dared not hold out hope for a rescue. When she opened them again, Javi, who'd been in front of her, was gone. She risked a glance behind her, and saw Juan Caesar had dissolved into the inky darkness as well.

"Pete, is that you?" a jovial voice hallooed from a junction in the trail above them. Small rocks skittered down the mountain as men milled about in one spot in the darkness. The glow from three lanterns cast huge shadows among the trees.

"Who's askin'?" Feak yelled tentatively.

"Pete? It's George White. The old man sent me to look after you. Fires looked like they might pen you down." The voice from the blackness was more cautious now. "Am I talkin' to Pete Seaver?"

Lucius Feak cursed under his breath and drew his pistol.

Firemen.

Angela's breath quickened. From the lanterns it looked like there were at least three of them, maybe more. They might stand a chance against her captors if she could warn them. She looked behind her again to make certain Juan Caesar wasn't about to smack her with a stick. She craned her neck in an effort to stretch the leather gag and give her more room. It cut at the corners of her chapped mouth and she tasted blood on her cracked lips. She wouldn't be able to make herself understood, but she could definitely scream.

And scream she did. A loud, wailing cry that summed up all the trials and torments of her last two days as it curdled the cool night air. She tried to lunge her horse up the mountain past Feak, to the firefighters who meant her safety and freedom. The outlaw turned and glared at her.

She'd misjudged how narrow the trail was as well as her stupid horse's desire to expend no more energy than necessary to make it up the hill. Feak wheeled his mount in one smooth motion and clouted her smartly in the temple with the fist that held his pistol.

Angela kept screaming when he hit her, but reeled as blue and yellow lights exploded behind her eyes. Miraculously, she kept her seat in the saddle. When the pain dulled enough for her vision to clear, she saw Feak pointing the gun at her belly.

"You best be keepin' quiet," he hissed though the blackness. "I'll kill you slow after I let the A-patch have a go at you if you don't shut your gob."

"Who's out there?" All three lantern lights flickered out at once. The voice above them was less than fifty feet away. "What's going on here? Identify yourselves."

Feak held the gun barrel to his lips to remind Angela to keep quiet. "We're just out here for the fires same as you," he yelled up the mountain.

"Who screamed?" George White demanded through the darkness, his voice firm as wrought iron. He spoke more quietly to his men, but it was clearly audible filtering through the trees. "McGowan! Baker! Spread out and stay quiet!" Again, he spoke with authority. "Listen, whoever you are. Identify yourselves. I am a duly appointed agent with the federal government and until I am satisfied as to what's going on around here, you should consider yourselves under arrest."

Feak scoffed at such talk. "Come on down here and we'll talk."

"Come up and show your . . ."

Gunfire split the darkness on a bald knob above them. An odd moan, like the air hissing out of an India-rubber balloon, caused Angela to cringe in pity. There was a clatter in the rocks above them and something heavy slid down the mountain. A chilling scream followed off to the right, and she knew another man had died.

"McGowan? Baker?" The demanding tone bled from White's voice with every syllable. "Are you all right? Who's out there?"

Feak chuckled in the darkness. "I reckon they just be busy arrestin' a couple of my men."

"Now see here. We're firefighters in the employ of the U.S. Forest Ser . . ." White's voice trailed off into silence.

A short moment later, a low loon-whistle wafted down through the trees. Feak reholstered his sidearm and twisted in his saddle to face Angela. Little moonlight filtered down through the smoke and thick canopy of branches, but Feak's yellow sneer was plainly visible in the darkness.

"It's all over now, little britches. Go ahead and scream if you feel a mind to, but you best follow me up the trail. Them A-patch wouldn't want me to be losin' their little treasure just yet."

Juan Caesar was busy pulling the scalp off a dead man with silver-white hair when they arrived at the site of the massacre. He used his foot to brace himself against the dead man's shoulder while he pulled. The popping sound the small circle of flesh made when it tore away from the bone caused Angela's stomach to lurch and she vomited around her leather gag.

Slumping in the saddle, she turned away only to see Javi walking out of the underbrush holding a lit lantern in one hand and two bloody scalps in the other. He smiled and offered the tangled masses of hair to Angela. When she shook her head, he shrugged and grabbed one of the scalps in his teeth as if he were about to bite off a piece.

"Suit yourself," he said around the morsel of flesh, "but it's good grub."

Angela heaved again, tasting the bitterness already in her mouth. She had never been in a spot where things were so desperate, where there seemed no escape—no relief, no comfort. With each passing moment, the realization formed more clearly in her fevered mind. Sooner or later, she would end up like one of these poor dead souls—murdered and mutilated only to have her defiled body become an object of entertainment and derision for these savage men. Three more men were dead now, for no reason but that they got in the way. Bitter tears of complete despair caught in Angela's throat at the thought that she might have prevented their deaths—had she only been braver and ignored Feak's threat. Her screaming might have given them a chance.

Feak walked up beside her and put a rough hand on her thigh. He spoke quietly as he stroked her above the knee, his voice a scornful hiss in her ear.

"Quit your blubberin', little britches. This is the last pee break you'll be gettin' for a while, so you best take advantage of it. The A-patch will be busy for a minute or two butcherin' up the bodies so as to make things look real Injun-like. If I was you, I'd be droppin' my drawers while they was otherwise occupied. I got my orders to deliver you unsullied, but that Juan Caesar, he hates whites. I seen what he can do to a pale woman like you, and it ain't at all a pretty picture. If he was to get an opportunity . . ." Feak licked his lips. "I don't know as I could even slow him down, let alone stop him."

Even in the darkness, Angela could see a glistening sheen of whiskey-dull lust in his black eyes. It didn't matter anymore. If he wanted to rape her he would. If he decided to hack off another piece of her, just for entertainment, he would. There was absolutely nothing she could do about it except fight and prolong the inevitable. She knew she would fight when the moment came—but for now, she needed to go to the bathroom.

A few feet away, in a ghostly pool of yellow lantern light, the two Apaches stooped over the lifeless corpse of George White. Engrossed in their own brutal actions, they paid no attention to Angela.

She looked down at Feak and nodded weakly, straining her jaw against the filthy leather gag. Her lips and mouth were cracked and raw from the constant rubbing of the wide strap. She'd been able to chew the corners down somewhat, but it still kept her from closing her mouth completely. Drool and dried blood matted the tangled strands of her once-beautiful auburn hair to her cheeks.

Feak helped her down from the horse and chuckled to himself when she said "Thank you" out of habit. "You really don't belong out here. Do you, little britches?" He gave her a rough shove in the behind and hissed at her again, all humor draining from his ice-cold voice, "Don't you be thankin' me just yet. Hurry and get your squattin' done. If you try to run, I'll cut your nose off and feed it to Javi. He's right partial to woman nose. Eats 'em like candy."

Angela bit down hard on the gag to keep from

screaming again. She felt insane for thanking the man who only hours before had brutally hacked off her finger. He would likely be the one to kill her—or at the very least order her death—in the not-too-distant future.

Stepping behind a nearby cedar tree, she fumbled with the buttons on her britches, careful to keep from bumping the inflamed shard of bone where her little finger used to be. She knew Feak was watching her from the darkness, and found she didn't care. For some unexplainable reason, she began to laugh softly to herself. She thought of how Mother would be able to say, "I told you so." Boston seemed so far away. For as long as Angela could remember now, her world had been nothing but rough men and savage Indians.

When Angela was finished and buttoned up her pants, she couldn't help but chuckle, even though the action hurt her mouth. She wondered how Mother would handle such men—or how such men would handle Mother.

If Lucius Feak had known the big sorrel possessed such a tendency to hold air, he never would have stolen it in the first place. The outlaw heard the noise in the thick brush behind him while he was busy tightening his cinch. A crackling rustle of branches rubbing together.

The forest at night held so many sounds, he ignored the noise at first, but it came again, more tentative than before. Most animals didn't creep around at night; they either walked along like they didn't have a care in the world or ran off, crashing wildly through the underbrush. A cougar might creep, or even a bear if it was hunting—but men, they most always went sneaking around when they were in the woods.

Another dry branch snapped in the shadows. Feak heard someone catch their breath. He looked up at the Apaches, who were still busy dragging the bodies of their victims out onto the trail so they would be easily discovered.

This whole plan set Feak's nerves on end. He'd never gone out and done so many bad things and then left so much sign on purpose. It went against his instincts to leave so many things undone. Killing was one thing, but leaving the bodies in the open where any lawman with half a brain could find them, that was just plum crazy.

Another rattle of a branch jostled the darkness behind him, followed by the swish of a limb against clothing. Feak let the loose end of the latigo drop, and slowly reached for the near rein with his left hand while his right slid down to his pistol. The stupid girl sat moaning in her saddle on the other side of him. Feak eased his horse around, putting himself on the ground between both animals, the girl to his back. If things turned sour, Feak could easily jump on his horse and slip off into the darkness.

Training his revolver across the seat of his saddle, the outlaw yelled into the darkness—as much to warn Juan Caesar and Javier of approaching danger as to evoke an answer.

"Get out here so we can see you!" Lucius's voice was a fierce growl, and his horse threw its head and snorted with a start. Steel bits jingled in the still night, and the girl caught her breath behind him. Both Apaches vanished into the blackness.

"Hey, hey, hey!" came a tentative voice from the dark line of mottled shadows at the edge of the trail. "Don't shoot. It's only us."

Lucius relaxed when he heard the voice. The Indians heard it too, and reappeared from the shadows to resume their grizzly fun.

Holstering his gun, Feak finished tightening his cinch. When the two men moved in closer, he spoke to them without looking up.

"You two are liable to get your throats cut—sneakin' up like a couple of Papago Injuns. Get your horses and let's get movin'. We got a little ways to go yet before we meet the big boss."

Billy Scudder held up a leather bag. The white elk ivories adorning the outside caught the nearby lantern light and seemed to glow in his hand.

"She be dead then?" Feak trained his eyes on the young outlaw.

Scudder grunted. "Cut her guts out with my own knife. Boy's too. They won't cause you no more trouble."

Javier walked in from the darkness, chewing on something. He looked at the decorated bag dangling in Scudder's hand. "There are those among my people that believe the owner's ghost inhabits their medicine bag after they die. They say if you hang onto one that belongs to someone else, pieces of you start to rot off. Bad medicine." The young Apache stared into Scudder's eyes. "I always bury or burn them after I'm through with my business."

Billy looked down at his hand, his eyes wide in horror as if the rotting process might have already begun. He held it out to his companion, who spun the leather drawstring back and forth around a thick forefinger. "Billy, you're a slobberin' idiot," the new man said, shaking his head. "That Apache buck is just tryin' to make a fool of you, and I'd say he's doin' a good job of it."

Javier shrugged, fishing something from his back teeth with the tip of his tongue. He turned to walk back to where he'd tied his horse in the trees. "Suit yourself," he said over his shoulder. "When pieces of you begin to stink and turn black, there will be nothing you can do."

"You don't scare me, you thievin' red bastard."

Juan Caesar perked up at the insult, and moved like quicksilver from his place in the shadows to beside the other Apache.

Feak began to panic. "Hold on here, boys. Everybody be simmerin' down now. The boss wouldn't take kindly to us killin' each other before the job's done. Let's us all just play nice for a little longer. We got some money now, but we got a chance at a hell of a lot more if we just see this through."

The two Indians eyed the other men for a long minute. Feak didn't know about Scudder and the newcomer, but the Apaches scared him, and he didn't mind saying so. Controlling them was like trying to eat a soup sandwich. They did as they pleased when it pleased them. He wasn't sure the money meant much to them, and suspected they only came along with hot revenge burning a hole in their brains.

Everyone jerked, including Feak's horse, when Juan

Caesar wheeled and walk away into the darkness. Feak
let out the half lung of air he'd been holding.

"I wish you could be keepin' your fool mouth shut
till all this is over," Lucius said. "I think it would be
wise for you to remember what them A-patch done to
that old boy back at Goblin Creek." Lucius climbed
into the saddle and spit, his nervous grimace a blue-
gray gash across his face. "After you're mounted, you
be ridin' up here by me. I got a little plan. Think we
might need to do a little changin' out on our horses."

The newcomer dangled the medicine bag in front
of Scudder's face. He curled his own ring finger
down so it looked like it had already fallen off. "You
want this back, Billy?"

Scudder tried to put on a brave face, but he wouldn't
get near the bag. "Naw, you go ahead and hang onto
it. Maybe it'll bring you some luck."

Chapter 15

Maggie rolled a wet blanket lengthwise and stuffed it under the door to keep out as much of the smoke as she could. It was difficult to move with Shad dogging her every move, but she didn't have the heart to tell him to sit down. She could hear the crackling of burning timbers outside mingled with the shouts of men working to put out the fire. Already, smoke poured in through cracks in the storeroom walls like fingers on a ghostly apparition, and threatened to suffocate them before the fire actually got to them. Maggie had a fleeting thought that it would likely be better to pass out from smoke than be burned alive. But it wasn't in her nature to give up. She was no quitter.

The temperature in the stuffy room was already rising. Maggie put her hand on the door. It was hot enough to the touch that she couldn't keep her hand on it for more than a second or two. Shad put his hand next to hers, and immediately jerked it away.

He yelped and looked at her. "I don't want to hide anymore. I'd rather just die out here with you. Are we going to die, Miss Maggie?"

"I don't know," she said with an honest shrug that appeared more relaxed than she really was. "I'm not ready to die quite yet. I'd like to see some grandchildren and watch you grow up." Her mind raced while she spoke.

The crackling outside the door grew louder, and the blanket she'd stuffed under the door began to smolder. Sticky black pitch boiled out of seams in the thick wooden door.

Maggie cast her eyes back and forth around the room, struggling to figure out what to do. Jumping up on the cot, she yanked at the iron bars that blocked the window above her head. She'd hoped one might be loose enough to get Shad out, even if she was doomed.

More men's voices buzzed past the window and she cried out.

"Help us! There's a child in here with me!" The roar of flames and snapping of timbers combined with the general hubbub of the bucket crew and covered any pleas for help.

One of the five bars in the window did wiggle in her hand a bit. If she could just get one out, Shad might be able to get though.

"Shad, honey." She glanced over her shoulder at the boy while she continued to work at the bar. "I need you to do me a favor."

"No, please, Miss Maggie. I can't. I can't hide and let you get killed." He was racked with a series of violent sobbing coughs.

"I'm not asking you to hide, child. I need you to get my rifle. I may be able to shoot this bar loose so you . . . we can climb out through here."

He slowed his crying and handed her the gun, plugging his ears with the palms of both hands after she took it.

Maggie figured it would be better to shoot at the wood that held the thick iron than the bars themselves. She set the muzzle where she thought it would do the most good, then turned her head before she pulled the trigger to keep from getting flying splinters in her eyes. It was becoming more and more difficult to breathe. The entire door smoked as if it were ready to burst into flames.

"Shad!" she barked after she shot, and levered another shell into her rifle. "Can you throw that bucket of water against the door?"

The boy jumped off the cot and did as he was told. The water hit the superheated wood with a great hiss of steam, turning the room into a sauna.

"Good job," Maggie said between pulling the trigger. "Keep doing that and we may be able to get out of here."

Someone outside screamed for everyone to get away from the burning building, warning that the ammunition inside was cooking off in the fire.

Six deafening shots later, she leaned the gun against the wall. Wrapping both hands around the loose iron bar, she bore down against it with a mighty heave. It didn't move. If anything, the stubborn bar seemed more solid than before.

She still had four rounds left, but was loath to shoot the gun dry. Even if she did succeed in getting the boy out, someone out there still wanted to kill him. Trap had always told her to leave an extra round or two. She'd learned better than to empty her weapon back with her own people when she was only thirteen, during the Battle of Big Hole, but she chose to let Trap believe he was the one to teach her.

"There's not much water left, Miss Maggie," Shad said, splashing another bucket against the steaming door.

The situation looked hopeless. For her entire life, Maggie Sundown O'Shannon had been a great believer in hope. Now, there seemed to be no avenue of escape, no Trap O'Shannon there to help her save herself from the evil things of the world. He was busy on the trail as he'd been so many times before, depending on her to take care of herself.

He would not—could not come. No one would.

Maggie slumped down on the cot and motioned Shad to her with a flick of her hand. The smoke and steam were thick now, and she could hardly see him. It would only be a matter of seconds before the door ignited and flames rushed into the room. She tried to say something to comfort the boy, but found a hard knot in her throat so she couldn't speak. She tried to sing the song she'd used to comfort him at Dr. Bruner's office, but sobs gripped her chest and she began to cry.

Shad leaned against her, coughing. "It's all right, Miss Maggie. I only said I wouldn't hide. Why don't you hide this time?"

Maggie rubbed her eyes and looked at the boy through the thickening smoke. "Why all this talk of hiding?"

"It was awful dark in that box, and I could hear Mama screaming . . . I don't want to go in there again."

"That was on the coach, child," Maggie said, pulling the poor boy's head closer to her breast. "You won't have to go in there anymore, I promise."

Shad wriggled away from her grip. "I know that. I'm talking about the one under the bed."

"What?"

"There's another hole under the bed. I was going to hide in it when you went out and the man cut you, but it was too dark. I'm scared, but you . . ."

Maggie lifted the boy up and slid the bed to one side. Along the floor was a trapdoor. With no time to lose, she yanked on the metal ring and found it opened easily. It was indeed dark down the square hole, but the air was remarkably cool and free from smoke.

"Come with me, Shad." Maggie coughed, grabbing her rifle off the cot and hiking up her dress so she could step down on the wooden ladder she could just make out in the blackness.

"No, it's too dark," said Shad.

She took his hand. "I need you to protect me."

The door burst into flames.

"Hurry, Shad, we need to go now. We'll protect each other."

The boy looked at the flaming door, then down at the black cavern below him. He took a step toward her, and Maggie pulled him in before he could change his mind.

Once they were inside the narrow crawl space, it was relatively easy to work their way to the latticework vent at the side of the building. Shadows and light from the fire reflecting off the hotel cast eerie orange shapes along the dirt floor. Spiders and rat droppings littered the ground, but Maggie was happy to be away from the fire and didn't care. Shad hung onto the hem of her dress while she crawled on her hands and knees to the louvered wooden vent.

People milled about outside. They'd suspended their bucket work, now only watching for stray sparks that threatened the nearby hotel.

Maggie used the butt of her rifle to break the brittle wood away from the vent. It was almost too hot to breathe around the opening, but it was the only way out and she was overjoyed to have it.

A man in striped bib overalls and no shirt stared in shock and dropped his empty bucket as she pushed a wriggling Shad through the small opening and squirmed out with her rifle directly on his heels.

A group of volunteers, including the man in overalls, ran forward to brave the flames and grabbed the two scorched survivors and dragged them to safety. Doc Bruner was in the crowd. He herded them away quickly before any of the local townsfolk could recover from the shock of seeing them escape from the belly of such a fiery beast.

When they were a half block away, the doctor looked at them and whistled under his breath at the wound across Maggie's chest.

"I should put some ointment on that. You've been through it, young lady. Looks like you may need stitches."

Maggie chuckled in spite of her appearance at the thought of anyone calling her young. "May we stay for a while at your place? It might put you in danger."

The doctor shook his head in amazement. "Of course, of course. I wouldn't have it any other way. I wish my wife would have had your pluck."

Pluck. Maggie knew she had many qualities, but she'd never been told she had pluck. She'd have to tell Trap about that one.

Turning to get a last look at the fire that had almost beaten her, Maggie froze in her tracks.

Well away from the blaze, at the fringe of the bucket brigade, stood a man from the past—a man she was certain had been dead for over twenty years.

CHAPTER 16

August 20, early morning

Trap O'Shannon woke before the fires with the dream of Maggie's breath like a warm breeze in his ear. His back and shoulders ached from the packed earthen bed. Clay stirred when he heard Trap roll out, and threw his arms back in a long, yawning stretch. It was just after four in the morning, and dawn was only beginning to gather up her orange skirts behind the eastern mountains.

"Blast this cold, hard ground for a mattress," Madsen said through his yawn. "If you boys wouldn't have trounced that bartender, Franco, so soundly, I might have been able to spend the night with Cora on a real bed in that little room of hers."

Blake sat up in his bedroll and rubbed a hand through his mussed black hair. Ky was already standing and making water a few yards away. His shirttail hung loose with leather suspenders around his britches. He looked over his shoulder at Clay.

"Sure you would. I only gave the man a severe thrashing. I do believe you would have killed him had you come back and found your rotund Miss Cora in the same position we found her."

Madsen stumbled to one knee and pushed himself up, still cussing the ground. "Indeed I would have, sir. That is a plain fact, but I might point out that if Franco was dead, I would still have had a bed to sleep in. As it stands now, with the job half done, Cora's sought a place to roost her bones elsewhere and I am forced to spend my repose against the cold, unfeeling bosom of Mother Earth." He glanced over at Blake.

"You don't know Roman. He don't get angry, he gets indignant. Believe me, that's much worse. When you're full of righteous indignation like he gets, he believes the Good Lord is on his side. That's when he gets hard to stop. Spit in his face, he'll wipe it off and walk away. Mistreat an innocent—even an innocent whore—and you best watch yourself 'cause you're about to receive one of Captain Roman's famous layin' on of hands."

Once on his feet, Clay put both hands on his knees and pushed himself to a semi-upright position. Still hunched forward like a man twice his age, he hobbled to the edge of the woods to relieve himself. Trap watched him walk back and stoop slowly to retrieve his blankets.

"What are you looking at, O'Shannon?" Madsen smiled at his friend. "I don't see you up and boundin' about like a prairie dog either. I reckon my bladder wakes up a mite quicker than my old back does—too many rank horses and fistfights in my time."

Trap nodded. He was every bit as sore and bent as Clay, and it took him as long to get up in the morning; he just did it without all the moans and groans. Trap had never possessed his friend's flair for the dramatic.

After wolfing down a quick breakfast of coffee—except for Ky, who stuck with water—and cold lamb and tortillas compliments of Maggie, the four lawmen took to their saddles. Trap settled into the lead. He had a general idea of the kidnappers' direction of travel after they'd left Moira Gumm's place. First light was always his preference for tracking. In a few minutes the sun would be low and bright on the horizon, its long shadow casting over the parched ground to make all kinds of sign virtually jump out at the eye.

The outlaws had traveled in single file. Someone had ridden a clumsy, big-footed horse that stumbled back and forth along the trail without any guidance from its rider—likely the Kenworth girl. All four sets of tracks led along the rough road toward the mountains to the west—into the High and Lonesome. A glow of pink and orange already tinged the hazy fog that clung to the highest peaks. Smoke from a dozen spot fires billowed straight up from the dark green forests in giant plumes, shooting skyward, then flattening out as it cooled on the chilly pillow of morning air.

The kidnappers' trail led directly into the fires.

Clay jabbered quietly while they rode, intent on imparting some of his wisdom to Blake whether he wanted to hear it or not.

"You know why the Nez Percé rode Appaloosas

into battle?" Clay gave Blake's spotted horse the once-over from under the brim of his hat.

Blake shook his head.

"On accounta they wanted to be good and mad when they got there." Clay slapped his leg and guffawed at his own joke. "Your mama used to threaten to skin me alive the way I picked on her favorite ponies so much."

Trap rolled his eyes and winked at his son. "Don't let him get started, boy. Take it from me. He'll wear you out if you let him."

"You just pay attention to the trail, O'Shannon." Clay waved off his old friend. "This here conversation doesn't concern you. How old are you now, Blake?"

"Twenty-four."

"You know, my daddy once told me a man couldn't call hisself a man till he was past thirty. Well, sir, I hit thirty-one and paid the old man a visit. He looked me over and up and down and says to me, 'Son, it takes some men a mite longer that others.'"

Trap slid out of his saddle and squatted beside the jumble of tracks in the dust. He studied them for a while, touching the ground with his ungloved hand. Hashkee stood by stoically, ears pinned back and grumpy, but otherwise obedient. At length, Trap stood, took off his hat, and scanned their back trail. He had a habit of chewing on the inside of his cheek when something troubled him.

"Blake, come check my eyes, son, and tell me how many tracks you count," he said, rescuing the boy from Clay's tutelage.

The younger O'Shannon spurred his Appaloosa up next to his father and dismounted. He looked at the ground, studying it for a moment, and then scanned the valley behind them.

"Four?"

"That's the way I figured it."

Ky and Clay rode up to take a look.

Though none of them would ever admit it, deep down they all gave at least a pinch of credence to the notion that tracking expertise was a gift at which Indians—especially those with Apache blood—excelled. Expert trackers in their own right, either Roman or Madsen could follow bandits across bare stone if pressed. But if Trap was around, they always yielded to that extra sense of his that no one ever even tried to explain.

"So we're short by one?" Ky rubbed his chin, ruminating on the new information.

"That we are, Captain," Trap said. "There were five sets of tracks leaving the site of the massacre: the four bandits and the girl's. Looks to me like they put the girl on this plow horse." He poked the leather tip of Hashkee's reins at the huge tracks that meandered along the narrow road.

"She wouldn't be able to outrun anyone on that beast," Clay said, perusing the large impressions. "I think I dated a gal with feet that big once—she had a pretty face, though, and a butt like a barmaid. Come to think of it, she never did go lame on me."

Roman rolled his eyes. "So one of them's split off. Blake, you make it your job to watch our back trail for a piece while your pa concentrates on the tracking. Clay and I will keep our eyes peeled to the sides."

It was the way they'd traveled in the old days. Trap on and off his horse, studying the ground, setting the pace, while the others in the squad watched for ambush. Once in a while, if the trail became forthright and relatively simple to follow, Trap might ask for a break to ease the strain on his eyes, but more often than not, the break turned into a teaching session with Trap as the headmaster, pointing out this subtle nuance or that about whatever tracks they followed. There were so many things a footprint could tell a person, if he just listened.

Trap was fairly certain by the overlay of the tracks that he knew which horse Feak was riding. It had a loose front shoe on the left side and it stayed pretty much to the trail. It was obviously the lead horse, and many of its tracks were partially obscured by those left by the puddin'-foot. When it stopped, the horse always pranced on its front feet; an action likely caused by someone heavy-handed on the bits. Considering what he'd been up to, Trap didn't figure Feak to be a man with a light touch when it came to horses—or anything else for that matter. The other two sets of tracks were more precise, moving in straight lines, one in front of the puddin'-foot and one behind it, sometimes fanning out in opposite directions but always returning to their spots in line. These he picked for the two Apache mounts.

As time passed, Trap began to learn even more about them. The rear horse was most likely ridden by the older Indian because the lead fanned out on slightly more scouting trips while the rear horse stayed in place. A younger Apache would usually defer to his elder and generally do more of the work in the lit-

tle group. Trap studied each set of tracks for the
slight differences in hoof angle, drag, shoe and nail
type, and gait so he could tell them apart as individu-
als in case another member of the group split off for
any length of time. He used his pencil stub to scratch
out some notes in his little book. Time was he'd kept
all such information in his head—but those times
were gone.

The kidnappers stayed to the trail and tracking
them was no more of a job than following—a fact
that gnawed at the men's craws considerably. In the
old days, it hadn't been uncommon to follow the trail
of a person who wanted to be followed, but when they
did, it always meant an ambush.

By eight in the morning, the sun was full up and
blazing down through the thick brown haze that was
so full of sap it stung the nose and eyes and left a
sticky film on clothes and skin. Even the horses began
to be bothered by it, and became more agitated with
every mile. Hashkee in particular had a kink in his
tail. No matter how hard he coaxed, Trap couldn't
soothe him. Though the animal never hesitated, every
step was a growling, pin-eared reminder of how unhappy he was with the situation. Clay had observed
once that Hashkee was the type of mule who'd walk
off a cliff with you if you pointed him that way, then
cuss you all the way to the bottom and kick you in the
afterlife.

Blake, with his younger eyes, was the first to notice
the crows and magpies flitting and fighting through
smoke and yellow pine up the mountain switchback
a scant hundred yards ahead of them.

"Think something might be dead up there?" He stood in his saddle to get a better look.

The older O'Shannon shook his head and put out an overturned hand. "Don't stand up like that, son. Men standing tall sometimes get shot off their mounts."

Blake dropped back to his seat immediately with a sheepish look.

"Don't look so glum, boy," Clay said, trotting up next to him. "Me and your pa learned that lesson the hard way. Lucky for us, the guy who taught us was a poor marksman and only winged me." Clay rolled his shoulder to illustrate the wound.

"I think Blake's right." Ky squinted against the cool layer of smoke that flowed downhill like a pungent river. "Something's not right up there. Could be an animal, but we'd best not take that chance. Trap, that mule of yours still climb?"

O'Shannon nodded and touched a knuckle to his forehead in a sloppy salute.

"Good. You and Blake spread out to either side and go poke around up ahead. Clay and I will take up positions back here with rifles and watch for any movement at your approach." The Arizona marshal turned to look at Madsen. "That is, if you're not feeling too old and stove up from all your life's escapades."

Clay scoffed. "Scoot on up yon hill, O'Shannon boys." He slipped his rifle, boot and all, off the saddle and threw a leg over the horn to hop nimbly off his horse. "I still got some sass left in me." He held his rifle in one hand, and took off his hat to squint up at the direction of the screeching birds. "Can't see too well that far off, but we'll do our best not to hit either of you."

The Texan grinned at Blake and gave him a conspiratorial wink. "Now, don't you worry, sonny. Time was I could shoot the *cojones* off a horsefly at a hundred yards. Old as I am now, I just have to aim for the whole bug."

Trap sighed and then motioned up the trail with his chin. "You go to the north, son. Don't be afraid to sing out if you see anything. If it's an ambush, they already know we're here."

Ten minutes later found Trap on a panting Hashkee overlooking the birds from a shadowed copse of tamarack on a little knoll above them. He called out to ·Blake and the men below, then let out the little extra bit of air he always kept back in his lungs when he was ghosting around on half breaths in what Madsen called his panther mode.

"More dead," Trap sighed to himself. He stole a moment to let himself worry about Maggie. She was a capable woman who'd proven herself in pitched battle more than once. But the missing track nagged at him. One of these raw killers was unaccounted for, and that fact alone was enough to leave his mind in a constant whirl of worry.

Blake and his Appaloosa appeared out of some floppy-topped hemlock trees along the trail to the north of the bodies. He waved up at his father, who had already pointed his mule down the hillside and was half-sliding, half-riding toward him.

"I got a track here I've not seen before," Blake said. "It's got a hooked shoe on the back right."

Trapped smiled inside himself at how well his boy

was doing. It didn't surprise him—Maggie was his mother after all—but he couldn't help but be pleased.

"Looks like these three unfortunate souls bumped into our killers during the night," Ky said, his hat in hand when he and Clay made it up the switchback.

All three of the dead were positioned across the narrow trail. Each had an exposed circle of white skull where they'd been scalped. They had been killed with a knife, all from behind. A white-haired man, young but obviously the oldest of the three, had defensive wounds on his hands where it looked like he'd been able to put up a fight at least. All were stripped of their clothes and mutilated in the same manner as the blond man at the stage massacre site.

Clay spit vehemently into the dust. "I'm sure looking forward to the time I meet up with these folks."

"Blake found a new track over here, Captain," Trap said from up the trail. "Looks like two new riders have joined up."

"Sure they're not from the firefighters' horses?"

Blake motioned back to the woods with his rifle. "I think the dead men were on foot. I came across a mess of tracks back there where one of them was killed. Didn't see any hoofprints."

Trap stood and walked up the path. "One of these belongs to our missing rider from yesterday; more than likely it's Billy Scudder. The other track looks familiar, but I can't place where I've seen it." He perused the ground as he walked. "Yep, the two newcomers came out of the brush here, leading their horses."

He poked around in the trees for a few moments, then whistled softly under his breath. "The girl was still alive last night. She made water here behind this tree. All the tracks join up again up the trail."

Clay rode in alongside Ky. "Moira said Feak was supposed to meet someone he called the boss."

Ky nodded and tapped his saddle horn. He bowed his head in one of the little prayers he was wont to say from time to time. Everyone stood silently until he was finished.

"We best get some rocks over these poor souls to keep the magpies off them till we can notify someone to come get the bodies." Returning his hat to his head, Roman dismounted and looked around at the clouds of smoke coming up from behind the mountains. "I imagine there are fire crews all over up here. Somebody's bound to be wondering about them."

CHAPTER 17

Horace Zelinski slung a faded canvas rucksack over his back and tapped the canteen at his belt to make sure it had water in it. He constantly warned the men to drink. It reminded Daniel Rainwater of his own mother, the way the man took care of everyone over whom he had stewardship. When Zelinski was nearby, Big Ox and Taggart kept to themselves, unwilling to do anything in front of him. Now that he was preparing to leave, both men glared at the two Indian boys with open hostility.

The fire boss gathered the crew around him in a little green glade of hemlock and cedars to explain his plan. "You men can obviously tell there's a big fire brewing over that mountain to the southwest. It's uncommonly dark for this early in the day, and the wind has an edge to it that puts some fear in me, I don't mind saying."

Daniel and Joseph looked at each other, then up at the huge cloud of smoke that billowed up behind the black mountain five miles away. It rose into the hazy blue, its top knocked queerly to one side like the pompadour on a Nez Percé warrior. The Flathead elders had warned them about the late summer winds before they left to volunteer.

Dry wind and fire always spelled disaster.

Zelinski continued his speech. "I'm going to do some scouting and see just how big the fire is. I'm leaving McGill in charge. He knows exactly where we are and I'm sure the two Indian boys do as well. I should be back before nightfall, but if you get into something you can't handle, follow them to safety." He stooped to rub the shaggy head of the wolfhound at his side. "In the meantime, work on a firebreak along this creek. If the fire makes it over that mountain, we can stop it here." He stomped a foot and pointed to the ground before him. "Right here, lads. This is where we stop it."

Even with the air of bravado in his voice, Daniel knew the fire boss was more than concerned about what lay in wait for him on the other side of the mountain.

Before Zelinski was out of sight, McGill tightened the blue bandanna over his balding head and hoisted his ax. Without saying a word to the rest of the men, he walked toward the small creek and began to work on the firebreak. He was a good man and a hard worker, but possessed none of the charismatic leadership qualities of Zelinski or George White. Rather than giving orders, McGill seemed to hope he would inspire the men to work because he did—a tactic that might be successful with some of the group—but not Monroe and Taggart.

Daniel Rainwater shouldered his ax and threw a

grubbing hoe to Joseph. Zelinski was still visible making his way up the mountain trail on the far side of the trees. It wouldn't be long before he'd be out of the sound range of a gunshot.

Big Ox swaggered up to the two boys with Roan Taggart at his heels. "He's about gone, young 'uns." Monroe shook his head and sniffed, wiping his nose on the back of his forearm. "I reckon it's only a matter of time before you niggers get what's comin' to you."

The big man was close enough that Daniel could smell the acid odor of canned tomatoes on his foul breath. "Just get to work, Ox," said one of the men, an older fellow everyone called Swede, slapping Monroe heartily on the back. "Don't you go scaring the children."

"You ready for our wrestlin' match?" Bandy Rollins had a way of materializing out of nowhere. It was an odd skill for a man who took up so much space wherever he stood.

Big Ox coughed. "You heard Zelinski. Why don't you get to work and mind your own business?"

"Oh, he wouldn't mind. He told me I was welcome to fight whenever I pleased."

"Go ahead and fight yourself then. I'm goin' to work." Monroe turned his back just as a tall black trooper in a sweat-soaked uniform ran up and whispered urgently in the corporal's ear.

Rollins suddenly became animated, gesturing up and down with his huge hands before dismissing the other trooper with a curt nod. When he turned to face Rainwater and Joseph, his face was set and tense.

"You boys gotta look after your own selves for a

while. Company G's bein' recalled back to Avery. Seems like they got 'em a bad fire and they evacuatin' the whole town by train." The trooper suddenly brightened and slapped his leg. "Why don't you boys come and go with me. I can get you out on the trains. It sure enough ain't safe for you here."

"Mr. Zelinski told us to stay here in case the fire comes this way," Daniel said with more commitment than he actually felt.

Rollins nodded his great head slowly, his eyes shut for a moment while he came to a decision. "All right then. I'll likely hang, but I reckon I should go on over there right now then and shoot Mr. Ox between the eyes before I go." The corporal hitched up his pants and started for the tree line.

Joseph broke his customary silence. "Don't worry about us, Bandy. We can take care of Monroe and his stinking partner."

Rollins turned back with a shrug. "Suit yourself then. I'll be back as quick as I can." He leaned in to the two Indian boys and took on a solemn tone. "You listen good to ol' Bandy now. If either one of those two comes near you, kill 'em quick. Don't pussyfoot around or they'll get you for sure. You can't trust none of these yayhoos 'cept maybe McGill, so slip away right off."

The corporal winked. "When I come back I'll wrestle the son of a bitch and save the world a bullet."

CHAPTER 18

"You remember ol' Go Go Gomez?" Clay let his boots hang out of the stirrups while he rode to rest his knees. "What was his first name?"

"Enrique," Roman said. He'd always made it a point to know the given names of every trooper under his command.

Clay nodded. "That's right, Enrique Gomez. Damn, that boy could run. I wonder whatever happened to ol' Go Go."

"Died," Roman offered, his eyes on the horizon.

"In Cuba with you and the Rough Riders?"

"Nope, just died. Late last year. Stomach something or other, I heard."

Clay stared at his saddle horn and shook his head. "Damn. He was younger than me." He looked up at Trap. "You ever think about gettin' old?"

The trail was clear enough that Trap could read it from atop Hashkee. He kept his head down, but glanced up from under his hat brim at Clay's question. "I reckon I do now and again. But I don't feel all that old."

Clay slowed his bay and pointed hard at Trap to emphasize his words. "Well, I read that in these United States the average man don't live to see fifty. In fact they don't even live to see forty-nine."

Trap scratched his chin and studied the tracks. He was glad Blake had faded back to be a rear guard and was spared such depressing talk. "I don't plan on dyin' anytime in the next year."

Clay slapped his thigh with a leather glove. "Well, I don't neither, but that's the point. You just never know."

"I hope you boys aren't thinking you're too dog-gone ancient," Ky said from his mount, a few yards through the buck brush to Trap's right. "Since I'm considerably older than either one of you."

"Yeah." Clay shook his head back and forth with an undisguised smirk. "But you look old. Hell, you and Trap both look like you could be grandpas. You two make me afeard to get too near a mirror on account of what I might find lookin' back at me."

"It might surprise you at that. I noticed you wear your hat a lot more than you used to," Ky mused. "Is that because that great mop of yours is thinning a bit?"

"I don't believe it is," Madsen said, snugging his hat down tighter on his head. "But even it was, the ladies would just want to rub it all the more."

Trap leaned back slightly in the saddle and lifted his reins. Saying nothing, he stared down at the trail for a full minute, shaking his head slowly from side to side. He waved Blake up and groaned.

"What is it, Trap?" Ky urged his lanky horse over next to the trail. "Looks like the trail splits here."

"Indeed it does, Captain." Trap pointed up the dust-blown path that was wide enough for three riders abreast. "Four went that way and two—our hook-shoed newcomer and the puddin'-footed nag—went west up this old wagon track that runs along an old Nez Percé trail—dead into the High Lonesome."

"What lies down that trail?" Ky nodded south after the four sets of tracks.

Trap looked at Blake. "I don't rightly know," Trap said.

The young O'Shannon took off his hat and rubbed the sweat out of his eyes with a blue bandanna. "I'm not certain. I never been this far out, but I've heard tell of an old placer outfit that used to work off Old Man Creek. I'm thinking there would apt to be some buildings and such there, but the gold played out long ago. I reckon they're mostly abandoned."

Roman crossed his arms across the pommel of his saddle and looked up into the old Nez Percé Corridor. His gray eyes squinted as if he was trying to penetrate the smoke haze that permeated the dense undergrowth of the jack pine forest.

"You say the puddin'-foot went deeper into the High Lonesome?"

"It did," Trap said, "but I can't be certain the girl's still sittin' the same horse."

Clay nodded in agreement. "It's a pretty moldy old trick to switch horses to throw us off the trail."

"I don't see anywhere they changed, but they could have done it without getting off the horses." Blake rode down the back trail a ways and searched the dust for clues. "They did a lot of milling around back here."

Ky gazed up the mountain slope again, his brow creased in thought. "And that way leads directly into the midst of all the fires."

The three other trackers sat quietly in their saddles and studied the ground, looking up every few seconds and scanning their surroundings, but always returning to the ground with their eyes so as to give Marshal Roman plenty of time to make a decision regarding their plan of action.

"Denihii," Ky said at length, using O'Shannon's Apache moniker. He drew a slow steady breath through his hawkish nose—a sure sign he'd come to a conclusion. "Can you tell me how long ago the riders passed this way?"

Trap nodded. "Half a day—if that. We're close."

"Let me tell you how I see it then, boys," Roman said. "And remember, this isn't the Army so feel free to question me. With all these fires, we're apt to be cut off from either trail at any time. I'm not familiar enough with this country to know what kind of a game these people are up to, but I'm not prepared to leave here without the Kenworth girl. I am loath to split our forces, but I propose taking Blake with me for a reconnoiter of the mine area by Old Man Creek while you two slip up this old wagon track toward the fires as quick as you safely can and see what sign you can cut. If you find anything that leads you to believe they've taken the girl in that direction, or you find the group has reunited somehow by means of a side trail, one of you watch while the other scoots back to get us. We'll follow the same counsel if we see anything of the girl our direction."

"If we have the chance, we'll just take her back when we come on 'em." Clay wasn't much for a lot of waiting when his quarry was in sight and everyone knew it.

"*If* you can do it safely." Roman narrowed an eye and stared hard enough at his old subordinate to make most men look away. "I trust your judgment."

Clay grinned. "No, you don't, Captain. You can't help but like me, but you never did learn to trust me to be anything but a hothead. Trap'll be along to lord it over me and you trust *his* judgment, so I guess that'll have to do." He took off his hat and made a wide, sweeping gesture toward the High and Lonesome. "After you, partner. Let's go give the captain something to fret over."

CHAPTER 19

The side trip to the ghost town was not part of the plan and never had been. Lucius Feak had thought that up all by himself. The more he pondered on his decision to deviate from the original arrangements, the more frightened he got—and Feak was not an easy man to scare. Even now, it wasn't the kind of skin-crawling, trembling, piss-your-pants kind of fear he saw in other people's eyes.

This was deeper. Much deeper. It was as if he knew he was finished, like the final seconds of realization a condemned man must feel in the moment before the rope tightens around his throat and snaps his neck—a kind of broken-bone ache that seeped through his entire body like the smoke in the air round him.

Maybe the boss would agree with him about the place. Anything was possible, although from what he'd seen of the boss, he wasn't a man who liked anyone changing his plans.

The abandoned house where Feak chose to hole

up was still in decent shape considering it hadn't been lived in for over five years. Dust and cobwebs covered the inside of the small single room. There was porcupine damage to some of the wood, and the lone window on the west wall had been pried out, presumably by the place's frugal former inhabitants who thought they could put the glass panes to good use elsewhere. Apart from the window, the previous owners had not taken much. There was still a small wood stove in the corner, complete with a dust-covered pile of split kindling. A rusted coffeepot sat on top of the old stove, and two sets of matching plates lay abandoned on the table. The more Lucius chewed on it, the more he thought the cabin probably never had a window in the first place and the oil-paper covering had likely just rotted away. It didn't matter, and Lucius Feak wasn't the type of man to spend too much time pondering over one subject.

The sight of the plates and stove reminded him he was hungry.

He struck a match on the sole of his worn leather boot and held the fire to the half-burned stub of a cigar. He puffed for a minute to get it going, reasoning that with all the smoke in the air, he might as well not put off any more of his guilty pleasures than he needed to. Though the cigar tasted good, it didn't do much for his parched throat and grumbling stomach.

"What I really want is a hot beefsteak, a bottle of whiskey, and a soft woman."

Juan Caesar looked up from where he squatted with his partner, playing cards on a piece of red cloth. "We got a woman and Javi's deer haunch."

They'd seen numerous animals fleeing the fires throughout the day, and the younger Apache had shot a fleeing doe with his bow. Leaving most of the animal to rot, he'd cut out the tender back-straps and one of the hams and slung them over his saddle.

"Well, we ain't got no whiskey, and that's what I really need." Feak rubbed his cracked lips and puffed on the cigar. "There's so much smoke, I don't reckon it would hurt to get a little fire goin' in that stove and rustle us up some of that deer meat."

Javier looked up from his cards long enough to sneer. "I'm not cooking when there's a woman here to do it. You won't let us use her for anything else— she should have to cook."

The young Apache chuckled and threw his hand down on the red cloth next to a small pile of money. Juan Caesar swore an unintelligible oath and threw down his own cards. Rising, he glared at Feak and then down at the girl, who lay feverish and pale in the back corner away from the window hole on a pallet of filthy saddle blankets. His already scarred face was twisted in anger at losing to his younger companion, and he looked ready to take it out on someone. Feak was his paymaster, so Angela was the obvious choice.

Prodding her in the thigh with his toe, he glowered over her. "You cook us some grub." His voice was sharp and cruel as a bloody knife.

Angela drew her knees to her chest and turned away from him, moaning quietly.

The one-eyed Apache let fly a vehement string of Spanish oaths since his own language was scarce on such terms. Squatting next to the pitiful girl, he grabbed her knee and rolled her roughly back to face him. She cowered there, sobbing around the leather gag that was still in her mouth, her injured hand drawn up to her chest to protect it.

The Apache's good eye flashed like black obsidian and he licked his lips. His hand still rested on the girl's knee.

Feak could see where this was going, and it only added to the sickening fear that piled up inside him. He was a mean hombre and he knew it, but in a fight against these two Apache, it would be touch and go who would emerge the victor. It put him in a real quandary.

The boss had given strict orders about what not to do with the girl. But the Apache were friends of the boss, and the only way to stop them if they got their blood up was to kill them—something the boss wouldn't take too kindly to either.

Lucius was in a pure fix. He leaned the rickety wooden chair back against the wall and blew a smoke ring into the already close air. When backed against a wall with an impossible decision, it was customary for him to do the thing that required the least effort— and that usually meant making no decision at all.

Angela decided early into her abduction she would fight, no matter the odds, the moment any of the men tried to rape her. It was not part of her internal makeup to lay back and take such things, even if it might keep her alive for a few more hours. Her face hurt from the harsh rawhide gag and her hand had swollen up to the elbow. Even through her fever, she had enough of a grasp on reality to know she would likely lose her hand, if not her whole arm—if she made it out of this at all.

The one-eyed Apache pushed at her knees, and she pulled them up as if to shield her chest, grateful, at least for the moment, that she had defied her mother and worn britches. From the corner of her eye, she could see Javier towering above her, waiting his turn. She understood the futility of fighting, had even played it over and over in her mind while she rode the night before. But fight she would, hopefully angering the men enough they would strike out in haste and kill her quickly.

Perhaps Feak would end it with a bullet or one of the Apache would finish her with a knife. She didn't care. As long as she could make them do it quickly, death would be a welcome respite from her constant pain.

Thinking her half-unconscious, Juan Caesar leaned in closer, ripping at the brass buttons in front of her britches. She knew she should wait, but the way she was curled put his forearm next to her face and almost out of instinctive reaction, Angela sank her teeth into the sinewy bronze flesh.

The Indian jerked away and covered the gushing wound with his other hand. Instead of killing her instantly as she had hoped, he only glared at her harder. After a moment, he turned to his grinning young partner and said something in quick Apache. Angela couldn't understand the words, but she caught the meaning.

You go first.

Javier nodded smugly and slowly drew his knife.

Feak, who'd been Angela's protector of sorts, did nothing but sit and watch.

"I'm going to cut off your clothes," the young Apache said. "The more you fight, the better—and the more of your skin comes off with your drawers. It will make a fine snack."

Angela started to scream, but the rickety slat door flew open and slammed against the wall. The scream caught in her throat.

Feak and both Apaches looked toward the noise, and Angela pulled herself up so her back was to the wall and hugged her knees.

Though the outside light was sparse, it was still brighter than the dismal interior of the cabin and the figure at the door stood backlit in the doorway, filling the space with his enormous dark silhouette. The stranger wore a flat-brimmed hat tipped low over a shadowed face and carried some kind of sack in his left hand. A long-barreled dragoon pistol occupied the right.

His voice carried in on the smoke like a hoarse whisper, though it was easy enough to hear. All three men jumped when they heard it.

"What in Hell's blazes is happening here?"

"Be careful!" Angela screamed, fearing the newcomer would be killed like the firefighters as soon as the Apaches regained their senses. "These men are killers—scoundrels holding me prisoner." It felt good to say it out loud.

The figure turned to study her for a moment, then looked back at Feak, ignoring her altogether. The gun still hung, poised like the head of a rattler, in his right hand.

"I asked you a question." The voice was cold and rasped enough to take off skin. Angela realized a man with such a voice was not likely to be any salvation.

Feak squirmed and dropped his cigar on the ground. He stomped it out nervously. "The bitch took a hunk outta Juan's arm. Javi was just about to teach her some manners and tie her up so she couldn't hurt no one."

The dark figure stood there motionless for a full minute, his shoulders moving up and down slowly as he breathed. When he spoke again, Feak yelped softly as if he'd been shot.

"If anyone needs a lesson in manners, I'll be the one to do the teaching." The man heaved the cloth sack he'd carried into the center of the room. It hit the packed earth with a dull thud, and the severed head of Billy Scudder rolled out to face Angela.

Three days before, such a horrific sight might have caused Angela to faint, but now she could hardly work up a shudder. Though she'd wished him dead for the cruelty he'd meted out to Betty, she bowed her head to her knees to escape the hollow dead eyes and hideous gash of a mouth that seemed not to have changed much between life and death.

"Young William and I already had our lesson for the day," the man said matter-of-factly as he stepped through the doorway. He holstered the pistol, but the tensions of the other men remained taut enough that anyone could snap. "Seems he went back and tried to kill that boy along with O'Shannon's wife."

"He mighta been able to identify us," Feak said

weakly, unable to tear his eyes away from Billy Scudder's head.

"So?" The newcomer took off his hat and ran a freckled hand through thinning, sandy-colored hair. Every move he made evoked a twitch or jerk from Feak. "We want them to catch us or the plan doesn't work. If O'Shannon learns of a plan to kill Maggie, he'll quit the trail immediately. I know him, you imbecile. That's why I make the plans. The man loves his wife above all else." The man drew a deep breath and let it out again through a bulbous nose, webbed with tiny red veins from too much hard liquor. "If Trap O'Shannon turns back now and misses our rendezvous, Mr. Feak, I'm holding you personally accountable. Young William there is just a lesson." He smiled. "I told you I'd be the teacher."

Lucius nodded weakly.

"All right then. Get the girl ready to move. As I said before—nothing should happen to her yet." He glared at the Apaches with narrow, slate-gray eyes. "I want her untouched for the time being. Do you understand?"

Both men grunted, and Javier finally put away his knife.

The newcomer offered a friendly smile and opened his hands in peace. "I don't care about the reward money. You men can keep all of it. My business is with O'Shannon and his friends. Bring the girl where we planned." He pulled his hat on again and turned before stepping out the door.

"And don't cross me again."

CHAPTER 20

There were five men in all. Running like a wronged woman was after them with a meat cleaver.

Zelinski stopped at the crest of a bald knob, blew off some steam, and took off his hat while the gaggle of men scrambled up the loose scree on hands and knees. Mopping the sweat from his forehead, he let his gaze shift to the blossoming cloud of gray and white smoke coming from the low mountains behind them. When the men got closer, he recognized the leader as Joe Voss, a forest supervisor from Missoula.

The fire boss took a swig from his canteen and handed it to Voss as the men took the ridgetop beside him.

"Horace," Voss said, taking a long pull of water. "You're going the wrong way." He was a tall man with watery, noncommitting eyes, befitting the vaporous politics that had helped him rise to his lofty position within the Forest Service. Certain Voss wouldn't know which end of the ax to hit the tree with, Zelinski was surprised to find him leading a group through the Clearwater.

"Fancy that." Zelinski nodded. "Looks like I'm goin' the right direction if you boys are running from a fire. That's what you pay me for, isn't it?"

"Not this fire, Horace. Get your men and get out of here. I understand there are evacuation trains headed for Avery. The colored boys from the Army have been called in from the field to help with the move."

"What?" Zelinski felt the dry, superheated wind whip across his face. The news hit him hard.

A stub of a man with round spectacles that kept sliding off the end of his chopped-off little nose reached out for the canteen from Voss. "Milton Brandice, Bureau of Entomology." He pushed up his glasses again and raised the canteen toward Zelinski. "Do you mind?"

"Go ahead. Bureau of . . . what did you say?"

When Brandice had drunk his fill, he pushed the canteen toward Zelinski, who motioned to the other men. "If you go easy, you might each get enough to wash the ash out of your gullets."

"Bureau of Entomology," Brandice replied, using his forefinger to push the glasses back into his squint. Zelinski couldn't help but think if the man would just relax his face, they might stay put. "I'm a beetle specialist. Three of us are. The Secretary sent us out here to study beetle-killed trees and their causal relationship to forest fires."

Brandice was what the field folks in the Service called a patent-leather man. Someone who stayed at his desk back East, read books, and wore fancy shoes. Zelinski shook his head. "I can't believe it, Voss. I beg for more men to fight fires and you folks send people with bug specialties."

"Shut up, Horace. Look back there." The forest superintendent took off his hat and used it to gesture toward a greasy yellow haze that all but blotted out the sun. A huge black and gray cloud boiled up five miles distant. Zelinski knew the mountains in front of the smoke rose at least 2500 feet from the valleys behind them. The smoke towered over three times as high as the mountains—more than a mile—before being sheered off at the top by a high-altitude wind. "It won't matter how many men you have once that rolls over you."

"We used to have horses," a forlorn-looking bug specialist Zelinski hadn't noticed before said, shaking his ruddy face sadly. "Fire took them all, so now we run, walk, and crawl. It doesn't matter, it'll catch us no matter what we do. I'm sure of it."

Brandice handed the man the canteen. "Calm down, Prescott. It's not as bad as all that. Avery's mostly downhill from here." He looked at Zelinski. "Right?"

"Sort of. Down, then up again a time or two, but you're not far off the mark. What's this you say about your horses, Voss?"

The superintendent continued to stare at the smoke. "That's what I'm trying to tell you. It's an inferno back there. We'd tied our pack stock and riding horses up next to a small stream that runs through Ruby Canyon. Brandice wanted to climb up and check on a bunch of beetle kill along the ridgeline above us. The going was rocky and I'm not much of a horseman, so I thought we'd give the animals a rest. If we'd been down in that canyon . . ." Voss trailed off and shook his head. His moist eyes narrow and rimmed in red, he turned to look Zelinski full in the face. "There was a wind, H. A wind like I've never seen in the mountains. When we got to the top of the ridgeline, I could see a small fire smoldering about half a mile from the horses on the other side of the creek. One instant it was a small fire, barely putting off a piddle of smoke; the next there was a horrible belch of wind and fire and the whole valley was a wall of flames, rushing below us. It all happened so fast the horses just disappeared in a river of fire. I don't think they even looked up from their grazing.

"The fire raced down the valley. I thought it would stop when it got to Boulder Canyon, but it just jumped half a mile of rock and kept going. The only thing that saved us was we were beside it and not in its path."

"What the deuce is that?" Brandice shaded his squinting eyes and looking up at the hazy sky.

All around them, tiny glowing embers the size of stickpins whirled on the wind. The air seemed alive with millions of orange lights.

"Pine needles," Zelinski whispered, more to himself than to the bug specialist. "Another ten minutes and it will be brands as big as your arm." He nodded to Voss. "You were right, Joe. I was going the wrong way."

The fire boss shouldered his rucksack and started down the backside of the hill at a lope, knowing the others would follow. His boys were a good enough lot, but they would never be able to make it out of this. George White had not returned, and if the 25th had been recalled to Avery, then they were all on their own.

The time for scouting was over. It was time to retreat.

CHAPTER 21

A furious wind shook the dry spruce along the ridgeline the way a dog might shake a snake. A heavy pall of resinous smoke rode the wind through the whipping trees and stung the trackers' eyes and noses. Blake had his bandanna pulled up over his face to help filter out some of the smoke, but it did little good. Ky had the lead and ducked his head against the wind, the brim of his hat folding down over his eyes from the force of it.

Dropping off the lee side of the ridgeline, he followed the trail down and away from the brunt of the wind before reining his sorrel to a halt beside a charred twist of lightning-killed ponderosa. The mountain fell away abruptly, and the trail began to wind through a park of white pine. A ground fire had already swept through the area and cleaned out all the debris and snags beneath the huge trees without doing anything to them but blacken their skirts. The thin trickle of a mountain waterfall beside the debris and tailings of an old mine was barely visible through the haze on the rocky cliffs a half mile distant. The fan of green grass and shrubs that followed the only water in the area gave the bleak gray dress of the rocks a green apron.

"There's the mine you were talking about." Roman spoke above the wind that folded the brim of his hat down over his forehead.

Blake nodded. "There are some old shacks down in the bottom. If we move up a little, we should be able to have a good view of them from up here without getting too close."

Ky nodded, holding his hat down with a gloved hand against a sudden gust. Unbuckling his pommel bag, he produced a small brass telescope. "Bring your rifle and let's go see what we're up against."

Blake slid his .45-70, a twin of his father's Marlin, out of the saddle boot and followed the marshal up the trail. He could see why his father and Clay had had no trouble following such a man. Roman listened to what the situation dictated and acted. Always moving forward, Ky Roman seemed an icon of action in a profession where politicians were the rule and preferred to send others to implement their plans. He himself was a doer, and led from the front rather than a desk.

Once inside the dim forest, they made their way to a small outcropping that overlooked the narrow valley some two hundred feet below. A towering ponderosa pine sat squarely in the middle of the outcropping. Its girth was too big for Ky and Blake to both get their arms around, and made a perfect spot for them to hide behind and study the three tumbledown buildings that made up the old placer mine.

A sun-bleached outhouse had been blown over by the wind—recently from the look of it—and the lonely wooden seat stood out in the open, a few yards from what had been the main house. A chicken coop with a tar-paper roof sat abandoned and caving in on the far side next to a small stream that led from the waterfall.

"Not too wise to put the chickens that close to the water supply," Ky mused, taking off his hat and lying down next to the pine tree.

Blake took up a position with his rifle next to him, scanning the scene. At first, he saw nothing. Then, a flash of movement caught his eye through the broken window of the shack. He pointed it out to Roman.

"I see. Someone's in there all right," the marshal said, letting his spyglass swing slowly in a wide arc across the valley. "The horse tracks lead over to that thick stand of fir to the left there. I can just make out the outline of a horse in the shadows." Roman lowered the glass and rubbed his eyes with a bandanna. "If it weren't for the smoke, I'd be able to make out how many there are."

He gave the telescope to Blake. "See if you can tell."

Blake looked, then shook his head. "I can't make out the horses." He moved the glass back to the broken window and jumped when he saw more movement. An Indian walked past the window, holding something in his hand. Blake fiddled with the telescope, drawing it in and out to focus on the dark recesses of the shack's interior.

"I can't be sure," he said, squinting with his other eye. "But I think I see the Kenworth girl. She's leaning up against the other wall." He coughed and dabbed at his eyes again, blinked to clear them from smoke, then adjusted the telescope some more. "Yep, it's her." Blake felt a wave of exhilaration wash over him.

"We got 'em." Roman took the glass back and studied the area for another full minute before he said anything. Even as he spoke, he kept his eyes on the dilapidated shack.

"Remember, we're chasing four horses. That means three in there with her—and that's if the others didn't swing around and join up. They must have known we would follow them, and yet they chose a place out in the middle of the valley where we were sure to find them. It makes for a rough approach, but it also leaves them little room for an escape. If not for the girl, I'd say you and I just sit here and wait them out. I'm not happy about her chances if we rush them with just two of us. We'd take them, but the girl might perish in the endeavor. Bad odds all around." Roman shook his head while he spoke around the telescope. Blake had to roll right up next to him to hear him over the rising wind.

"I'll stay here and keep watch." Ky lowered the glass. "Looks like they got a little fire going, so I expect they'll stay here for a while. You rush back up the trail and tell your pa and Clay to come runnin'. With all of us in on this, we'll have the girl back home by nightfall."

Almost immediately after Blake disappeared into the swirling smoke, Juan Caesar stepped out of the shack. Roman watched him walk out of the wind beside the chicken coop and make water. Seeing the

Apache after so many years made Ky's mind swim. He had assumed the old outlaw was long dead, his thieving, murdering ways having overtaken him somewhere along the way. He watched the prowling way his old enemy moved when he walked, the slow way he swung his head back and forth to compensate for the lack of vision in his bad eye.

Ky Roman was not a man prone to bad dreams, but memories of Juan Caesar had been responsible for many a sleepless night over the past twenty-five years. The fact that the Apache had once been a trusted soldier made matters even worse. Roman had handpicked him as a scout. When Juan Caesar went renegade and began to wreak havoc outside the reservation, the young lieutenant had taken it as a personal insult.

Watching the man he'd once trusted took Ky back to Arizona. For a moment, he felt the desert heat and sandstone beneath him instead of Rocky Mountain granite. He could hear the screams of the women on the wind. The memory of the carnage he'd witnessed made him wish he'd not been so hasty to send Blake back. If Juan Caesar had his way, the Kenworth girl was in a very poor state indeed. The man had almost cost Roman his life. In return he'd taken the Apache's eye. . . .

Ky drifted back to the fight that had almost killed him. The way Irene had been proud that he'd been strong and brave, but deeply troubled that he, Hezekiah Roman, the man she knew as a gentle, God-fearing father, could be so brutal as to beat another human so badly it would cost him his sight in one eye . . .

The smoke-filled wind whirred against Ky's ears. He was focused on Juan Caesar, and failed to hear the crunching of twigs behind him. When he did notice a small rock roll across the ground beside his elbow, he assumed it was Blake returning with some news. After all, his quarry was before him, in the valley.

"Run into a fire?" he said without looking up.

"It's good to see you, Hezekiah."

The voice, almost lost on the wind, made Ky's blood run cold. After hearing of the Apaches with Feak, he'd been able to prepare himself for an eventual meeting with Juan Caesar.

Nothing had prepared him for this.

He lowered the telescope and stood, turning slowly with his back against the huge orange pine tree. Before him stood a ghost from his past.

"How have you been, Captain?" The man was smaller than Ky remembered. Age could do that. But every bit as dangerous. The same wan smile across a ruddy face, the same nose that signified the unhealthy love for hard drink he'd developed toward the end. The fire of pure hate still burned in the darkness behind the man's green eyes.

"Did you make out ol' Caesar down there?"

Ky nodded, still unable to believe his own eyes. "I'm surprised to see either one of you."

"Thought I was dead, didn't you, Hezekiah? Everybody did." The man smiled. "You'd be surprised at the things a dead man can get away with. I even checked in on Irene while you were up in Spokane."

The air rushed out of Ky's lungs. "You what?"

The apparition raised a gloved hand. "She's all right. She didn't even know I was around. I just wanted to have a look at her for old times sake. I wanted to see all of you." His green eyes narrowed and flared in intensity. "Especially our little half-breed friend. How is he these days?"

"He's well, considering." Ky chided himself for his position. The ghost had moved to less than an arm's length away. Ky had nowhere to retreat with the tree at his back. He felt for his pistol.

"Don't do that, Captain. The one I want is O'Shannon. My quarrel is with him alone. The rest of you are dross. Whatever happens in all this, I had no part in hurting Maggie. That was never part of the plan."

"What do you mean? Now look here, Jo . . ."

The long steel blade went completely through Ky, pinning him to the pine. The voice was quiet but sharp, as the ghost pushed the knife home and held it in place against Ky's struggles.

"No! You look here, you arrogant wretch." The voice strained as the man held Roman in place with a forearm across his chest, just above the blade. "I am sick to here with you people thinking you know so much more than everyone else. O'Shannon thought he could play God with my life. Now it's my turn to play God with him. I've done a pretty fair job, don't you think?"

Ky shuddered and tried to get a breath. He tasted the salt of blood and felt the strength leave his legs. The man withdrew the knife and slipped Roman's pistol out of the holster and tossed it to one side. The strength bled from Ky's legs and he slid to a crouch at the base of the tree.

The cruel ghost squatted beside him and smiled. He was close enough, Ky could make out the sour smell of whiskey and meat. "I didn't harm Irene. Not yet anyway. Who knows, I may go back and let her convert me to that church of hers like she did you. That seemed to work her into a lather, didn't it? A few words from the Good Book is all it takes to get her going, if I remember correctly."

Ky could only gasp. He heard a gurgling noise and realized it was his puny effort at trying to talk. "Jo . . . Maggie?"

The man shook his head and snorted. "That's just like you, Roman. You're done for and you know it, but still you check on that miserable half-breed's woman." He wiped Ky's blood off the knife on his pants leg. "She's fine for now. Not that they didn't try, the fools. I'll have to look in on her myself after I'm done with our little Trapper."

The redheaded man patted Ky on the shoulder—softly, as if to reassure him. "I've got to go now. You shouldn't linger too long. Look at this as a blessing. You'll know soon if all the philosophy you've studied over these years has any truth to it."

Alone with the wind and smoke, Ky pressed both hands against his abdomen, trying to staunch the flow of blood that poured from his belly and covered his shirt and trousers.

He'd lost all track of time, but knew Blake would be back with the others soon. He had to hold on until then. His killer had been right—he was done for. But he had to warn the others of the danger.

He had to stay alive long enough to tell them who he'd seen.

CHAPTER 22

Blake slid off his horse and led him in so as to stay undetected by the outlaws in the valley below. Behind him, Trap smelled blood on the wind and knew something was wrong before he saw Ky leaning against the pine tree. All three men ran to his side. Blake kept a wary eye toward the mine. Ky saw him and shook his head feebly.

"Gone," he groaned. "After you left . . . took the girl . . . could . . . only watch . . ." A solitary tear rolled down from the corner of one eye.

Trap stooped down beside his friend and tried to check the wound. Thick blood oozed, dark as oil, between Roman's clenched fingers. His teeth were clenched and his breathing labored. When Trap tried to look under his bloody hands, Ky shook his head again and smiled up at him.

"Leave it . . . no use."

Clay's face teetered between sorrow and murderous rage. "Who did this to you, Ky?"

Mark Henry

The wounded man tried to speak. Leaning his head back against the tree and staring up at the sky, he seemed to be gathering all his strength. He opened his mouth, and then swallowed against a spasm of pain.

"Johannes," he groaned.

Trap looked over at Clay, who came up next to the two men and knelt beside them.

"Hold on there, Ky." Clay touched his friend's shoulder. "Stay with us. You'll be seeing Johannes soon enough."

Roman smiled weakly and struggled through three quick, shallow breaths. "Johannes . . . alive . . . Trap!" He let go of his stomach and grabbed O'Shannon by the sleeve with a bloody hand. Blood began to flow from the wound in earnest, and Ky's already ashen face took on a blue-green hue. His voice was a tight whisper, and the others had to lean in close to hear him over the howling wind.

"Maggie's . . . safe . . . now . . . but watch out . . . Johannes is alive . . ." His eyes fluttered and closed for a moment while he labored though another series of breaths. His body seemed to relax and the twisted grimace of pain lines fled his face.

"Adios, boys," he said, almost in his old voice, only weaker. "Look after Irene for me. Tell her . . . I'll be waitin'." He looked up at Clay and grinned. "I thought you . . . might like to know, Madsen, . . . this . . . doesn't hurt like we thought it would."

Roman's face went slack. Trap put an open hand gently over his eyes, closing them and feeling the last bit of warmth before his friend's body grew cold.

"Son of a bitch!" Clay screamed ferociously over

the roar of the wind, his hat a crumpled wad of felt in his clenched fist.

Trap stood and put a hand out to hush him. "They'll hear you."

Clay jerked away. He turned toward the valley and spread his brawny arms out to the sides. "Bring 'em on!" he shouted. "Let them come and try to kill us and see where it lands 'em. Juan Caesar, you one-eyed bastard, come on up and see what I got for your other eye!"

Blake looked nervously toward his father at Madsen's outburst. Trap shook his head slowly and held up a palm to keep Blake back. He knew Clay well enough to know the more vocal portion of the anger would blow over like a hailstorm, while the quieter, more dangerous part would seethe and smolder inside of him until it exploded out on whoever was responsible for Ky's death—or anyone else who got in between him and revenge.

"What do you think he meant by talkin' about Johannes?" Clay said while he knelt and used his small hand shovel to scrape out a makeshift grave until they could get back and move Ky to a proper gravesite back in Arizona, nearer his wife. The ground was baked hard, and he did little except scratch at the pine needles and forest litter a few inches deep. "Ky said Johannes was still alive."

Trap chewed on the inside of his cheek and shrugged. "Do you think he could be?"

Clay paused in his digging and looked up at Trap. "We never did find no body, but there's no way he could have lived through that explosion. It would have torn him to pieces."

"Or buried him alive," Trap said, staring into space, thinking about the past.

"Who's Johannes?" Blake stood by, alternately checking the trail behind them and the valley floor below.

Clay threw the shovel down in disgust and pushed himself to his feet. Tears dripped off the end of his nose. "This is bullshit. I can't dig in this rock." His voice was gravely from his screaming fit into the wind. "We'll have to take the captain down and leave him in that shack and hope the birds leave him be till we get back."

Clay put a hand on Blake's shoulder and sniffed. "Johannes Webber served in the same unit as your pa and me under the command of our good captain here. He died when you were a baby—at least we thought he did."

"Why would he want to kill Marshal Roman?"

"That's a good question, son," Trap said. "He had a pretty good reason to hate me, but the captain and him were always on good terms. It's a story that takes too long to tell for now. We should settle the captain and get on the trail. That's where the answers are."

Clay took off his hat again and folded his hands in front of him. "I wonder if we should say any special words seein' as how he was a Mormon and all."

Trap removed his hat, as did Blake.

"I don't really know," Trap said. He wished Maggie was there, or his father. Either would know infinitely more on the matters of religion than he did. "I suppose we should just make our own peace with it, in our own way—that's what we always done when he was alive and we were buryin' someone else."

Clay nodded, his head moving up and down slowly while his eyes blazed.

"Peace!" he finally spit. "I can't make no peace. But I will say this. If Johannes Webber is still alive, Ky Roman won't be seein' him in Heaven anytime soon 'cause I aim to send him to Hell the next time I run across him."

Both Trap and Blake looked at each other, then replaced their hats.

"Amen," they said at the same time.

After they wrapped Ky in his own bedroll, they loaded him across the back of his lanky sorrel and started wearily down the steep trail for the abandoned mine shack. Trap took the lead and Blake and Clay followed, leading Roman's horse.

"Can I ask you something, Mr. Madsen?" Blake knew his father was well out of earshot because of the blowing wind.

"What is it, lad?" Clay looked straight ahead, but urged his mount forward to match stride with Blake's Appaloosa.

"What did my pa mean when he said Johannes Webber had reason to hate him?"

Clay reined up and let his hands rest across the pommel of his saddle. He looked straight at Blake, and sighed. "It's a story best left to your father to tell. But suffice it to say, Webber is insane. Always has been, if you ask me. I never did have much use for him—thought he had a bad smell about him—but your pa and the captain, they took him in like the stray dog he was. He is a smart one, though . . . and he firmly believes your pa had a hand in killin' his woman."

CHAPTER 23

Big Ox Monroe grabbed Joseph from behind, pinning his arms to his side and lifting his feet off the ground while he squeezed the life out of him. Daniel Rainwater looked up from felling a tangled hemlock snag just in time to see it happen. He raised the ax in protest, but before he could move, he felt a sickening blow on the back of his head.

Reeling in pain and nausea, the boy slumped to his knees, and then fainted.

Rainwater came to his senses a few moments later with Roan Taggart sitting heavy on his back and pulling his hands together with rough cord that the food rations came wrapped in. It cut deeply into his wrists, and Daniel bit his lip to steel himself against the pain. When Taggart rolled him over, he saw Joseph, also tied with his hands behind his back, sitting, slumped against the downed hemlock snag a few feet away.

A man Daniel had never seen before sat on a muscular dun horse at the edge of the little glade. He was a big man, with a barrel chest and a head of thick gray hair combed straight back like a wood duck. His face was red, as if he were exerting himself at some heavy task instead of merely sitting in the saddle, and he breathed through his nose in loud puffs and snorts like a train getting ready to pull away from the platform.

". . . do it the way I tell you and you can be rid of the thievin' nits and stay out of trouble to boot. Get the rest of the crew over here and put the question to them. Ask 'em what should be done with redskins who would steal from their own fellow workmen," the man on the horse said to Big Ox, who nodded like a schoolboy getting instructions.

"Right, none of them will take to a cardsharp," Monroe replied.

The red-faced man shook his head. His huffing grew even more intense. "Not cheatin' at cards, you moron, stealing from your kit. Put some of the money and things from your outfit in their pockets. When the others see that, most of 'em will side with you right off. I'll step in as a disinterested third party and back up your story. That should even convince any nigger-lovers you got in the group."

When he'd pulled the knots tight behind Daniel's back, Roan Taggart stood up and kicked him between the shoulder blades, sending him headlong onto his face. The Indian boy rolled onto his side, curling into a ball to protect himself from another blow. Instead of kicking him again, Taggart chuckled and looked up at Monroe.

"He ain't so cocky once his wings is clipped." He raised one leg and let out a ripping fart.

"Leave him be, you imbecile." The man on the dun shook his head in disgust, his nostrils flaring like an angry horse. "I don't care what you do with 'em once the others decide to hang 'em. The fires are movin' this way. Once they're hung, we can leave 'em to burn."

Ox Monroe had the remaining fire crew rounded up beside the hemlock snag in less than ten minutes. Each small group of men came in cautiously from their respective duties, eyeing the prisoners as they gathered around. Monroe had already primed the pump with stories of their treachery.

Zelinski had left Cyrus McGill holding the reins of the small outfit of firefighters in his absence. McGill was a young man, not yet in his thirties, with a tendency toward premature baldness and hands that looked slightly too large for his sinewy arms. Though he was a strong and capable woodsman, McGill didn't have much of a hold on the men, and Daniel didn't expect he would do much to intercede where Big Ox was involved.

Taggart worked on getting the ropes ready to hang the boys while Monroe produced the evidence of their misconduct: a wad of folded bills and a silver watch that he said belonged to his departed uncle.

Joseph sat silently across from Daniel at the base of the hemlock, his dark eyes locked on the crowd. Daniel thought it funny that Joseph could look so unrepentant for something he didn't do. It actually made him look guilty.

"What have they got to say for themselves?" McGill did show a little backbone at least.

The newcomer on the dun horse stepped down at this and strode forward, huffing and puffing like he might run down anyone who got in his way.

"My name's Tom Ledbetter," he said. "I don't know how many of you folks know about this because of your service up here with the fires, but there's been a bad killin' back down in the Bitterroot. A pretty young gal's gone missin' and another was butchered up somethin' awful. Two men massacred as well." Ledbetter stopped to let his words seep in to the smoky crowd. "It was Injuns just like these that did it. I'm on their trail now."

McGill rubbed his thinning, mouse-colored hair. "Well, I hate to hear about that, but these here Indians been with us for over a week. I doubt they had anything to do with it."

Ledbetter sneered. "I'm not sayin' they had anything to do with it. I'm just sayin it's natural for an Injun to be up to no good. Your own boys here got the evidence that they been up to just that." He turned to the rest of the murmuring group, ignoring McGill as if he were no more than a flyspeck. "I ask you men, what kind of people would steal from their own troop? Are you to trust a sneak thief with your life? It's dangerous enough out here with all these fires. I heard two men already died up at Moon Pass. It could just as easily have been two of you, especially if you can't even trust those who work alongside you."

The murmur swept through the crowd again. An

old Swedish fellow in the back suggested they banish the boys to their own fate among the fires.

Ledbetter threw back his head as if in horrible pain.

"I ain't talkin' about sending these redskins off so they can hurt someone else. Didn't Ox tell you that sullen one there tried to stab him when he caught 'em stealin'?"

Monroe's head snapped up at that information, but the crowd was so focused on the two boys now, Daniel doubted anyone noticed. Stealing was one thing; trying to kill someone was a different thing altogether. None of the men would be able to work if they thought they might get a knife in the back as soon as it was turned.

The old Swede bowed his head at the revelation. "Well, we have to do somethin' about that then." His voice was low, just loud enough for Daniel to hear.

"That's what I'm tellin' you. These two are a threat to the whole group. You should get rid of 'em like you would a rabid dog before more people get hurt."

The muttering of the fire crew swelled as they whispered among themselves. McGill had his back to Daniel, and it was impossible to hear the conversation. From the hard looks on the soot-covered faces, it was easy to tell things weren't looking good.

At length, the men began to nod. Some, including the old Swede, took off their hats and stared with long, solemn faces at the two boys.

McGill shook his head violently while the two ropes Taggart had prepared were thrown over a slanting tamarack that had fallen into the crook of another, above and slightly behind the hemlock snag. Neither boy struggled when they were dragged to their feet and placed on the scarred black stump of the snag. Taggart placed rough pack-rope nooses around their necks and stepped back, grinning openly.

McGill waved his hands back and forth, and stepped in front of the boys so they could lean their knees against his shoulders.

"This is all wrong. We should wait till the boss gets back. We got no right to do this."

"You got no right to stop it now that everyone's decided," Ledbetter said with a matter-of-fact nod. "It was a jury of their peers."

"I ain't letting you do this, mister." McGill drew his sheath knife to cut the boys' hands free.

"Step aside, damn you." Ledbetter put a hand on his pistol. "Can't you get it through your thick skull . . ."

"Hello the camp!" A roaring voice that rivaled Horace Zelinski's rattled the trees and caused Ledbetter to slump. Daniel turned with the rest of the fire crew and watched three men ride in through the smoky trees. The men weren't smiling.

Ledbetter's twisted face tightened when he looked up, the muscles in his red cheeks clenching above his jaw. He was only a few feet from Daniel, his hand still resting on his gun. Big Ox and Roan Taggart stood to his right. All three men looked as if they'd been caught rustling cattle.

"You know these folks?" Monroe fidgeted with his knife handle and clicked his gold teeth.

Ledbetter nodded. "I do. They're the lawmen lookin' for the Injuns who done the massacre I told you about. Two of 'em are Injuns themselves." His clenched voice was low and breathy. "They picked a hell of a poor time to show up."

Daniel Rainwater leaned his knees against McGill's shoulders and watched the lawmen ride in slowly, like panthers sniffing the air. A large white man with a great curling mustache took the lead atop a muscular bay horse. A young Indian who looked to Daniel like a Nez Percé followed with an older man who could have been Indian. Each man had hard, unflinching eyes that appeared to drink in all around them at one long look. They had stern, hard-put faces that looked as if they'd seen much sadness lately. There was an air of decisiveness about them that frightened Daniel. He hoped these men didn't want to see them hang, for if they did, he knew he surely would.

"What do you reckon they want?" Big Ox's brown eyes widened and darted back and forth between the new arrivals and Mr. Ledbetter.

Ledbetter stood planted for a long moment, then shrugged and turned away. "How am I supposed to know? Don't let 'em stop you from your hangin', though. You've come too far to turn back now. Push the nits off and let 'em swing before anyone stops you."

"What do you mean *my* hangin'? You was the one to think of all this." Big Ox's huge head kept swinging back and forth between Ledbetter and the newcomers.

Taggart, unnerved at his compatriot's hesitation, raised a singed, roan-colored eyebrow and loosed a squeaky fart.

CHAPTER 24

"Looks like you boys are havin' yourselves a little party," Clay Madsen said. He reined up a few feet from the two Flathead boys, who teetered precariously on top of the hemlock snag. Though it was just after noon, the heavy forest and thick smoke made it seem like dusk. Clay had to lean forward to give the crowd a glimpse of the marshal's badge Ky had given him. The balding man who propped up the two guests of honor gave him a smile of relief a mile wide. He looked as if he might cry with pure, unabashed gratitude when he saw the badge.

"These Injuns stoled from my kit and were plannin' to kill me," a filthy, soot-covered giant said, stepping forward. Tom Ledbetter stood back and looked on but said nothing.

"What's your name, sir?" Clay stared down at the man with gold teeth. On top of his horse, it didn't matter how tall the giant was. Clay was taller and had the psychological advantage.

"Ox Monroe. Folks call me Big Ox."

"Well, Mr. Monroe, it looks like we got us a ticklish situation here," Clay said, leaning back and stretching his neck to one side. Trap and Blake both had their rifles handy across their laps. "I do believe it would be better if these boys stepped down from there for a minute while we sort this all out."

Blake stepped down from his Appaloosa and moved to the makeshift gallows to help the bald man. Trap let his finger slide across the trigger of his Marlin.

"Look here now." Monroe raised a hand, his eyes flashing. "You men got no cause to stop this hangin'. We're out here fightin' these fires for the federal government and we got no time to lollygag with any more of a trial. We need swift justice so's we can get on with our work."

Blake pulled the knife from the scabbard on his belt and cut the ropes binding the two Indian boys' hands. He didn't even look at Monroe. "You make a move to stop me, sir, and swift justice is exactly what you're gonna get."

Trap smiled inside at the grit he saw in his son. He was indeed Maggie's boy. The only two men worth worrying over were Big Ox and Ledbetter. Everyone else looked to be followers, blown like dandelion fuzz by whichever wind was strongest. And all appeared to be smart enough to see the prevailing wind was against the blustering giant. Clay and Blake could easily handle a blowhard like Monroe. Ledbetter never did anything but stand on the sidelines and egg others into doing the dirty work.

The fact that they were there to stop the hanging at all was just pure luck for the boys. It was a track that led them to the fire camp—the track with the hooked back right shoe. It had split off from the others a quarter mile back at the edge of a wide fire-break. Trap had heard voices through the trees, and after a short vote they decided any man who'd been riding with the kidnappers was worth talking to, especially if he'd had anything to do with Ky's death.

The little fire brigade possessed only a motley-looking trio of worn-out pack mules who stood forlorn and singed in a small rope corral at the edge of the glade beside a muddy wallow of hoofprints that had once been a poor excuse for a stream that angled off of Granite Creek. As far as Trap could see, there was only one saddle horse—Ledbetter's big dun. Unless he missed his guess, it had a hooked shoe on its right hind foot. Ledbetter had tethered the animal at the far edge of camp, and it was difficult to see through the drifting smoke and dusky shadows.

Trap slid his rifle back into its scabbard. Throwing a leg over the saddle, he hopped to the ground, leaving Hashkee ground tied and grumpy. Considering Ledbetter's past behavior, Trap was looking forward to a little face-to-face discussion about why he happened to be riding with known killers.

The crowd of dirty, tired men milled about in a loose group and watched Clay explain the facts of life to Monroe. Unwilling to lose face in front of all his peers, the big oaf stood defiantly in front of the Texan's horse, touching the hilt of the long knife that hung from his belt.

"These niggers was found guilty by all the men here—even the cue ball." He nodded his big head toward McGill. "He don't have the guts to see it through, but he was in on the decision. You got no right to stop us."

Clay groaned and slid off his gelding so he could look Monroe in the eyes. He was a half a hat shorter, but that didn't matter. Standing brim to brim, Clay tapped the silver badge on his chest. "I don't even need this to stop an illegal hangin', but I got it just the same and you can count your blessings I do, 'cause if I didn't I'd plant you here and now."

Ox stared hard with coal-black eyes, but he took a half a step back as if to steady himself. "You can go to hell, mister. We ain't scared of no law."

Clay closed the distance between them and sneered.

"I don't know what you mean by *we*, big'un. Your partner there's shakin' like a puppy passin' a peach pit. It's just me and you."

Monroe waved Clay off. "Go on then. Take your red nigger friends and get out of here then if you love 'em so much."

"No, sir," Clay said smugly. "Don't believe I will. You'll be the one doin' the leavin'. Real easy now, drop your knife and that rusty old hog-leg on the ground." Madsen turned his attention to Taggart, who stood with both hands raised high in the air. "You too, stinky. Weapons in the dirt."

Taggart complied, but Monroe blustered.

"What makes you think you can just blow in here like this and start givin' orders like you own the place? You so cocksure I won't best you?"

Clay rubbed his goatee with his left hand. His twinkling eyes never left his opponent. "Oh, I reckon there's always that possibility." He chuckled. "I suppose there's a chance I could have a heart seizure because you're puttin' so much fear in me—but it ain't likely." Madsen's face clouded over. "I'm sick of messin' with you, Ox. Throw down your gun or pull it; makes no never-mind to me."

Monroe let out a deep breath, deflating so he looked like he shrunk a good six inches. He studied his own boots while he slowly lowered his pistol and bowie knife to the ground.

Trap truly enjoyed seeing his old friend work. He normally would have stood by and watched, but Ledbetter had eased back through the smoky shadows to climb back on his horse.

"Hold on there, Mr. Ledbetter." Trap stepped in front of the dun as Ledbetter tried to slip out past the crowd.

The right rear track of the horse hooked noticeably.

"You step aside, runt," said Ledbetter. "I stopped for you once. I'll be damned if I'm gonna do it again. If you and your friends are more interested in savin' Injuns than catchin' the ones responsible for the massacre, then I'll have to go do it myself." The muscles in Ledbetter's beet-colored jaws bunched and clenched after he spoke. His mouth pulled back into a tight grimace as the skin on his thick neck tightened in hatred. Ledbetter jerked back on the dun's reins. The horse pranced sideways, fighting the bit.

O'Shannon's eyes widened as the big animal came to a halt broadside to him. Hanging from the saddle horn of Ledbetter's dun was a finely crafted leather bag with elk ivory and porcupine quillwork. Trap felt as if he'd been kicked in the stomach, and he had to steady himself to keep from dropping to his knees.

It was Maggie's medicine bag.

Trap looked at it in horror and imagined all the terrible things a man like Ledbetter would do with an Indian woman if given the chance. He should never have left her—not the way things were. Not with folks feeling so worked up.

Trap felt a sickening ache fill the void that occurred when he first saw the small leather pouch—as if all the joy had gushed from him like water from a broken pitcher. She would never have lost the bag. It held the things that were important to her, locks of her children's hair, spiritual things she was never far from—it would have to be taken from her by force . . .

Ledbetter mistook Trap's unsteadiness for fear and lowered his reins to goad him a bit. "What do you think of my new saddle ornament?" He'd obviously figured out Trap was an Indian, and couldn't seem to resist the opportunity to gloat over the fact he'd gotten the better of another redskin, even if it happened to be a woman. It was a deadly error on his part.

"It looks right nice on my saddle. Don't you think? I heard tell the squaw it belonged to was a witch." Ledbetter smirked and patted the bag. "There's all sorts of goodies in here. Maybe they'll bring me some luck. That damn old coyote bitch don't need it anymore."

Trap struck like a rattlesnake, stepping on Ledbetter's boot toe to vault into the saddle facing him, just back of the horn. His left hand grasped the loose muslin of the bigger man's shirt while his right drew the bone-handled knife from his belt as he moved.

Ledbetter had time to give a startled grunt as he was joined in the saddle by 160 pounds of furious Apache. "What the . . . ?" He was able to get his revolver out of the holster, but Trap's arm snaked around his elbow, locking the arm out straight in front of them. There was the glint of a knife blade between the two men. Ledbetter growled in surprise and pain. He struggled to turn the gun toward Trap, but the little tracker yanked up hard on the man's elbow with a mighty heave.

Ledbetter cried out in pain and his finger convulsed on the trigger. A horrific boom rocked the smoky glade and the poor dun horse collapsed under the two grappling men, a forty-five slug through the back of its head.

Trap used his forehead to butt Ledbetter in the nose as they rolled off the dead horse, but kept his grip on the arm to keep from getting shot himself.

Ledbetter was no weakling, and once the initial shock of Trap's surprise attack passed, he wasted no time in returning Trap's head butt with one of his own. Pulling in tight, face to sweating face, Ledbetter slowly began to wrench his gun arm free from Trap's grip.

"That was my horse, you stupid son of a bitch," he grunted through clenched teeth.

Trap could feel Ledbetter's arm bending—slipping free. The pistol began to move across his back. The tracker drove his knee hard into the big man's groin and sank his teeth into a bulbous nose. Before Ledbetter could recover, Trap's knife found its way between his ribs. He worked it back and forth with two quick flicks, severing Ledbetter's heart. He felt the man go weak beside him, heard the gun clatter to the earth.

Trap spit out the bloody mess that had been Ledbetter's nose and staggered slowly to his feet. Kicking the gun away, he gently lifted the medicine bag off the saddle horn atop the dead horse.

O'Shannon stared down at the dying man and tried to catch his breath as he smelled the soft leather pouch.

"That was my wife."

CHAPTER 25

Everyone in the glade, including Ox Monroe, stood in silent wonderment at the outcome of the fight. Tom Ledbetter had been a force to be reckoned with and though Trap O'Shannon was obviously no slouch, without knowing about the medicine bag, few would have guessed he could prove to be so deadly.

"I've never seen him like that," Blake whispered. The speed with which his father had dispatched Ledbetter gave pause to everyone in the group. For a moment, even the wind seemed to lull. "It was like an execution."

Clay leaned in next to the boy and slowly shook his head.

"There's a mighty big difference in the way you and your pa view things." The Texan chewed on the corner of his mustache in thought. "Your pa ever tell you our unit's motto?"

Blake nodded, unable to take his eyes off his father. "*Sanguis Frigitus.* He told me it means *calm in the face of danger.*"

"That it does . . . in a way. But it more literally describes your pa. It means *Cold Blood*. You look at this little escapade as a law-enforcement matter where a civilized legal system can make everything right and proper. If you have to arrest someone or even kill them in the line of duty, then it's well and good—but it's always a last resort. Your pa, well, he sees this as war, a kill-or-be-killed kind of thing where the battle lines are clear as a slap in the yap."

"How do *you* see it?" Blake still watched his father as he spoke.

"Like your pa, I reckon. Though it wasn't always that way. Trap O'Shannon was born a warrior. I was sort of formed into one in his image."

Across the clearing, Trap grabbed the saddle horn with both hands and swung up on Hashkee. His chest still heaved from the battle and his eyes glowed with an intensity Blake had never seen. He dug his heels into the mule's flanks and bolted the short yards between him and the others.

"I'm going to check on your mother." Trap reined up next to his son and held up the medicine bag. "You keep the trail with Clay. He'll look out for you."

Madsen stepped in close to Trap and grabbed a handful of saddle string. He patted his friend on the knee in an effort to calm him.

"I know what you're thinkin', Trapper, and it just ain't so. She's fine. I know Maggie, and it would take more than some blowhard to bring her down."

"That's what I always thought about the captain." Trap stared into the wind.

"I hear you, but even the captain said Maggie was all right. Johannes told him so."

O'Shannon shook his head. "Let go of my saddle, Clay. I've got to go. You know it and so does my son."

Blake gave a somber nod. He felt the same anxiety his father did, the same hollow dread at the thought of his mother in the hands of a person who blamed every problem they had on Indians. He wanted to go check on her himself, but at the same time he'd always believed he shared a deep spiritual connection with her and his father both.

"Pa," Blake said, his voice halting. "I . . . I'm as scared as you are. But don't you think we'd know—feel it if anything happened to her? When I was a little boy, she used to tell me you two were connected that way."

Trap didn't speak, but looked down at Clay, who held his saddle strings. His eyes still blazed with barely controlled fury.

Clay stepped back, holding his hat down against the rising wind. "I'll back your play, partner, you know that—whatever you decide to do."

With a brisk nod, Trap wheeled his mule and trotted off to the east without another word.

"This don't bode well," Clay said to no one in particular.

"Guess we should get on the trail then," Blake said. He felt a little dizzy after his father's quick departure, and it took him a minute to get his feet back under him.

Clay chewed on the curl of his mustache and gave

him a wink. "A couple of sharp-eyed hunters like you and me, we'll bring the girl back all right." He surveyed the rest of the fire crew, who stood staring in shocked disbelief. The two Indian boys still had the rough nooses around their necks where Blake had cut them down from the snag.

"You boys might as well take those neckties off," Clay said. "I think enough folks have died for the time bein'. These men seem to have lost their appetite for a hangin'. Ain't that a fact, Mr. Big Ox Monroe?"

Monroe nodded, his eyes still glued to Ledbetter's body and his dead horse. "Sure thing."

"Good enough," Clay groaned when he climbed aboard his bay. "Y'all behave yourselves 'cause I aim to come back and check.

"Now, Blake, I've worked with your daddy on the finer points of philosophy for lo, these many years and he ain't learned a blessed thing. Let's see if I can do a little better with . . ."

"You men get what food and water you can carry and follow me!" Horace Zelinski's voice roared over the howling wind. The fire crew all looked as if the cavalry had arrived when they caught sight of their boss. They huddled around him as he strode into camp, enveloping the gaggle of wide-eyed men who accompanied him. To Blake's surprise, his father rode slowly behind the procession, veering off to join him and Clay.

"We've got about a half an hour," the fire boss yelled over the whirling melee of dust and wind. "Maybe a little longer before this whole area is smack in the middle of a firestorm."

Taggart, who stood a few feet from Blake, gave the fire boss a naively mournful look. "What does he mean firestorm?"

"The wind," the Indian boy with the smiling eyes said solemnly. "It's the wind blowing the fires together like a blacksmith's forge."

As if Zelinski had struck a match and set them on fire himself, the entire camp became a rush of furious activity as everyone gathered canteens, blankets, and what tins of canned ham and tomatoes they could cram in their pockets and pokes. Zelinski supervised, issuing orders and keeping things running as smoothly as they could for men who were running for their very lives.

The intensity of the wind grew with each passing minute and by the time the men were ready, the flurry of glowing needles had reached them.

"Any minute now," Zelinski screamed over the wind, holding his hat down with the flat of his hand. "Any minute now, we'll see spot fires spring up from all this falling debris that's being driven before the fire. Don't stop to put them out, it won't matter. Our only chance is to make it to an old mine adit I know about two miles from here."

Trap reined up beside Clay.

"Fire's got the whole landscape to the east and south cut off. I got to go around and up over the mountains to circle back down to Taft."

Clay smoothed his mustache and nodded. "What's keeping you then?"

"That fire boss said he saw some settlers headed up the mountains to the northwest between here and Avery—over Porcupine Pass. Two Indians, two white men, and a girl."

"You aim to tell me and Blake so we can go after them?" Clay stood in his stirrups and rocked back and forth with anticipation.

"I'm going too," Trap grunted. "It's on the way."

CHAPTER 26

A steady drizzle of sweat poured down Lucius Feak's spine despite the driving wind that whipped at his loose cotton shirt. Without any hair to help keep it on, his hat had blown off miles before, and gone rolling on its side through the buck brush and dry bear grass like it wanted to flee as badly as Lucius did. Horrible luck to have hat come off in the wind.

Webber had made him cut the gag off the girl, but she still rode along in silence with her mouth half open, looking at him with a kind of catatonic out-of-her-head stare that made his flesh crawl like it was festering. If it were up to him, he'd have killed her long ago, but he didn't care to end up like the witless Billy Scudder.

Even the Apaches had the jitters, and old Juan Caesar kept checking his back trail as if the devil himself was behind them. Lucius smiled at such a thought—Apaches believing in the devil, that would be something. That was like the devil believing in his own self. Feak found himself wondering if the devil might be just a little bit scared of Apaches—until Johannes Webber's voice, flat and crisp above the wind, yanked him out of his thoughts.

"You must leave O'Shannon alive. Kill the others. Make him watch those he cares about vanish from him. But be watchful. The Scout Trackers are nothing to be trifled with. They are excellent marksmen, and Trap is as brutal as Juan Caesar in his own way. Split them up, pick them off one by one, but leave Trap O'Shannon to me."

Johannes glared at Caesar, who kept looking over his shoulder.

"This is not like you, my friend, to be so afraid of another man," Johannes said.

The one-eyed Apache turned to face the group and scoffed, a murderous scowl across his scarred face.

"It is no man I fear." He gestured over his shoulder with his chin. "It is the fire. We cannot fight against that. It's grown too large even to outrun, I think."

"Focus on the task at hand," Webber said, his face not quite concealing the utter contempt he had for anyone who might stand in the way of his planned destiny.

"Once you have killed O'Shannon's only son, then take from him his dearest friend." Webber grabbed the reins of Angela's horse and gigged his own gelding cruelly in the ribs, leading her away from the other men. "Leave Trap to me, and don't worry, the fires will be the least of your problems."

* * *

Angela couldn't tell if it was the fever or merely the hot wind that made her feel as if her face was on fire. Her lips were badly cracked and bleeding, but any moisture in her mouth had long since dried up from breathing around the rawhide gag. Her tongue felt foreign to her own mouth, as if it she'd bitten off a piece of meat too big to swallow. Her jaw ached as bad as her injured finger, and she found it difficult to keep her eyes open. If only she could have a sip of water, that might ease the swelling in her tongue and ease the pain in her face.

Webber slowed his horse and urged her stumbling mount up next to him with the reins. Smiling at her softly as if he were a favorite uncle, he shook his head and clucked.

"Feak and his ilk are heathen scum, Miss Kenworth. I apologize for their rough treatment of you." He drew a long sheath knife from his belt and used it to cut the bands that held her wrists. She saw blood on the blade, and found herself wondering if it was the same knife he'd used to cut off Billy Scudder's head. Once her hands were free, he offered her his canteen.

Angela drank greedily, the cool water running down both sides of her blood-encrusted lips and spilling onto the saddle horn. It cooled her throat and gave her the energy to cry.

"Don't fret yourself, my dear," Webber said. He took the canteen back and hung it across his saddle horn. "They won't harm you again. My old friends will make short work of them. I'm certain of that."

Angela wondered if she were hearing things.

"I thought you wanted them to kill your old friends."

Her voice was hoarse and raw and her mouth didn't work quite right from the long hours in the gag. But Webber understood.

"If things go as I have planned, they will, but I'm sure some, if not all of them, will die as well."

"What about me?" Angela sniffed, rubbing her eyes with the heel of her good hand.

"What about you?" Webber's lips pulled back in a flat grin—almost a grimace. "You are the bait that brings O'Shannon to me. You will be fine, my dear. Just fine."

Angela slumped in the saddle. Although she was no longer tied, she was still being led just the same to a certain death, if not by the cruel men who'd had her before, then by the madman who had her now. She sniffed the air and watched a flurry of glowing sparks dance on the wind before they landed on the dry grass.

Maybe it wouldn't be the men who killed her at all.

CHAPTER 27

"Have to say, I don't like it one bit," Madsen said amid a cloud of whirling ash and cinders. "I feel like a goose in the middle of a cookstove."

The others rode along in silence, Trap watching the ground while Blake scanned the trees around them.

"And another thing." Clay used the tip of his reins to point at Trap. "I don't like the way that Zelinski character said we should head toward some 'distant valley.' That sounds too much like the afterlife if you ask me."

The wind howled through a thick stand of paper birch that had miraculously escaped a previous fire. The white-barked trees stood out in stark contrast to the surrounding black landscape.

"I ain't never seen anything like this in all my life." Clay whistled above the moan of wind that surged through the gray haze of the birch forest.

A black bear sow with two white-collared cubs the size of feeder pigs hustled past him in the trees.

Scarcely half a minute behind the bruins, a small herd of whitetail deer trotted through, only a few feet away from the horses. A fresh young doe, her sides heaving from panic and exertion, froze in mid-step when she noticed the men. Snorting, she stomped a slender foreleg and blinked huge brown eyes—as if in wondering awe that anything would be so foolish as to amble before the approaching flames. She was close enough that the men could see the wind ruffle her soft brown undercoat of hair.

Clay tipped his hat, and the doe seemed to vaporize into a flash of snow-white tail and a blur of tawny brown. When she had vanished along with her friends, Clay shook his head and stared after them.

"It's like the deer are chasin' after the bear. Just don't seem proper."

"They're likely the only ones with any sense," Trap said, chewing on the inside of his cheek. The specter of what might have happened to Maggie hung over him heavier than the thick billows of smoke and ash that swirled by with the wind. His gut told him she was all right, but he'd never rest until he was certain. If he had really believed she was dead, he would have turned around and let the fire overtake him, for without Maggie, life would be totally void of worth or flavor. He cursed himself for leaving her in the first place, with all the danger that was in the air.

He knew better. That's why he'd stayed alive for so many years living the kind of life he'd lived.

The three trackers rode as quickly as they could and still keep a reasonable trail. They traveled over a fresh ground burn, and step-by-step tracking, though possible, was painfully slow. Instead, they followed the natural lines of drift. With a general direction of travel from the last known set of tracks and the description of the area where Zelinski had seen the group, Trap decided to follow the flow of the land. Unless they were pushed, people as well as animals tended to follow natural contours and drainages. In the forests there were only so many routes a horse could take with all the blowdown and tangled snags.

The drainage they searched now was a maze of scorched, moss-covered logs and shallow creek beds that resembled a great green quilt bunched together in a fan of wrinkles. Head-sized chunks of granite littered the low washes and wreaked havoc on the horses' footing.

The wind blasted every bit of debris out from among the trees and ditches. Hundreds of animals, including elk and moose, had already followed the same natural routes of escape, so finding a decent identifiable track without inching along was next to impossible.

His eyes to the ground, deafened by the whir of wind in his ears, Trap traveled on for several minutes before he glanced up and realized he couldn't see Blake. Clay, quiet for an unnaturally long spell, was off to his left, flanking him and keeping a sharp eye ahead. With the fire, there wasn't much chance of anyone sneaking up behind them.

Trap turned in his saddle and scanned every direction. Blake was nowhere to be found. The way the land rippled, he could have been below the lip of a wash twenty feet away and still been out of sight, and so Trap didn't worry at first. Instead, he gave a shrill whistle like the call of a hawk. He received no answer, so he tried again, cupping his hands in front of his face to focus the sound to his right and then his left.

Nothing.

Alarmed now, he waved at Clay, who was already picking his way around a knee-high blow down to ride up next to him.

"Where's Blake?" Clay leaned in close and yelled above the wind.

"That's what I was going to ask you." Trap began to get the feeling he knew he would feel if anything happened to Maggie or Blake—a sickness down to his center that spread like palsy over his entire body—a deep, broken-bone sort of ache that made it hard to catch a breath.

Something was terribly wrong.

Blake O'Shannon was off his horse when he realized someone was watching him. He couldn't see anyone, and the wind moaned so mournfully that the idea of hearing anything above it was unthinkable. A shudder up his spine and a prickling along the short hairs on the back of his neck told him eyes were on him. He chanced a look to his left, where his father and Clay should have been. He saw nothing but a tangle of wilted hemlock trees, devil's club, and smoke.

The young deputy chided himself for straying too far away from his companions. He knew better than to venture out on his own, and had been happy to follow such knowledgeable men as his father, Ky Roman, and Clay Madsen. Maybe Madsen had been right about not being a real man until you were thirty. Blake was not the type to panic, but he was smart enough to realize the chances of survival on his own in the midst of hostile forces and a rapidly approaching fire were less than poor.

He got the prickly feeling on his neck again, even reached up to touch it, hoping he was wrong, hoping it was just the wind hitting him above the collar.

The rattlesnakelike thrum of wilted huckleberry shrubs gave him the warning. Alerted by the familiar noise off to the right, Blake's Appaloosa gelding expected a snake and jerked against the reins. Blake fell backward and stumbled on the uneven terrain of the mossy wash where he stood.

The arrow whistled by him and lodged in the red bark of an alder, now naked of all its leaves before the driving wind. It missed the startled lawman by scant inches.

The wind had saved his life.

Blake fell to the ground so quickly, an onlooker would have thought the arrow hit him. He pressed himself flat against the forest floor and tried to make himself as small a target as possible. It was a little less smoky in the small hollow, and he could smell a hint of the huckleberries above him, fragrant even amid the fires. The line of bushes that had warned him of danger formed a thick barrier along a three-foot hummock of moss and deadfall to his immediate right. This flimsy bulwark was all that stood between him and whoever shot the arrow.

He thought of calling out for his father or Clay, but didn't want to get them shot because of his stupidity.

He couldn't just lay there forever, though, and he

knew his father. It wouldn't be long before he'd come to check on him, especially being so worried about his mother.

A sudden tingle ran up Blake's spine, and he steeled himself when he heard a change in the wind above him. Danger was near now. He rolled onto his back.

The one-eyed Apache stood above him, a long knife in his hand, coming up to check and see if he was dead. He didn't have a bow, and was likely covered by someone who did from a safer vantage point. The attackers obviously didn't want to risk alerting Trap or Clay by using a gun.

Juan Caesar sprang as soon as Blake turned. The Apache was surprisingly agile for a man of his age. He landed on Blake with his knees, hard enough to take the wind from the boy's lungs and crack at least two ribs. Blake was just able to catch the arm that held the knife. He pushed it off to the side so the knife landed in the duff only inches from his neck.

Clawing at the one-eyed Apache's back, Blake kneed him in the groin, trying to push him off before he could regain control of the knife. Caesar's grip loosened enough for Blake to get a foot up and deliver a terrific blow to the Indian's exposed belly with the flat of his boot. Caesar flew backward, staggering from the impact, and coughing as he tried to catch his breath in the thick smoke.

The knife disappeared into the thick huckleberry shrubs. When the renegade chanced a look for it, Blake sprang on him. Juan Caesar was strong, but without a blade in his hands he was no match for Blake's youth and stamina. Trap and his friends had

wrestled with the boy since he was no more than a
sprout. Man or not, Blake knew about hand-to-hand
combat.

Feinting with his left hand, Blake drove a crushing
right hook into his opponent's temple, capitalizing
on his lack of vision. The Apache reeled, staggered
by the blow. Blake's right fist shot out again, catching
Juan Caesar low in the jaw and spinning him around
in the loose duff and pine needles. Worried about
the second Apache, Blake grabbed the disoriented
renegade in a choke hold from behind and drew him
close. He continued his struggles and Blake tightened his forearm, stopping the circulation in the
man's neck.

Blake looked right, then left, dragging Juan Caesar with him. The Apache was still conscious, but just
barely. It was impossible to see more than a few feet
in the thick smoke, and the gathering wind made
hearing anyone approach impossible. He strained
his ears and thought he heard his father's whistle,
but couldn't be sure. It could just as easily have been
the other renegade or Feak.

Blake coughed from his exertions. The sticky
smoke stung the back of his throat. Sweat ran into his
eyes. He closed them and pressed his face against the
back of Juan Caesar's greasy hair to gain some relief.
It smelled of grease and spoiled meat.

Blake's mind raced while he tried to think of a way
out of his situation. If he let the renegade go, he'd
revive in a few minutes and the fight would start all
over again. Blake drew his revolver with his free
hand, holding the Apache close with his left arm. He
knew what his father would do in this situation. This

was war. There was no time to take a prisoner who would not hesitate to put a bullet in him the next time they met.

The shrill whistle came again, high and piercing over the wind. It was impossible to tell from which direction in the wind and whipping, moaning trees, but it was close. A crash in the brush made him spin to the right, his revolver at the ready. Two cow elk blew by on the wind, nothing but tan-rumped blurs. The noise of their passing was drowned out almost immediately by the forest that seemed to be alive with wind.

Bits of limbs, needles, and leaves began to separate from the trees and be driven before the wind. Grit and sand, picked up in the rush, flew into Blake's eyes, and he rubbed them with the back of his gun hand in an effort to keep them clear. His arm began to cramp from the constant effort of holding it around Juan Caesar's neck.

He felt the familiar tingling in his neck that his mother had taught him to recognize as a sign of danger. He dragged the unconscious Apache with him to get his back against the thick trunk of a ponderosa pine a few yards away. He heard movement, saw a shadow ghost through the frenzied green and yellow shadows of smoke and wind-whipped trees.

Someone was out there, circling him.

The brush was too thick to stay on horseback. Trap had to lead Hashkee over or around the numerous deadfall and blowdown snags that cluttered the thick forest. The mule was a better jumper than Madsen's bay gelding, and Trap made good time while he studied the ground looking for any sign that might tell him he'd intersected his son's trail. He looked mainly for horse tracks, knowing Blake's big-footed Appy would leave infinitely more sign than moccasin or even boot prints.

He knew Clay followed only yards behind, keeping a sharp eye through the smoke for anything "with teeth" as he would say. They were moving in a general direction away from the fire, a fact that made it easier to get both animals' cooperation.

The whine of a pistol shot above the wind brought Trap up short. He froze, straining to hear any other sign of danger. Hearing nothing but the wind, he dropped Hashkee's reins and slid his Marlin out of the saddle boot before bounding off in the direction of the shot in a half crouch.

Clay caught up to him at Blake's Appaloosa, whose reins had tangled around the snaking branches of a vine maple. He carried his pistol, and led Trap's mule and his own gelding with his left hand. The bay nickered at the sight of the other horse, and Hashkee gave a tedious groan, showing a white eye at having to work so hard jumping all the deadfall. Apart from being agitated over the wind and his natural aversion to the scent of fire, the Appy was in good shape—no blood or injury that Trap could find.

Trap surveyed the ground at the horse's feet. Few tracks remained on the windswept surface beyond the prancing circle the horse had dug around the vine maple. Another shot echoed through the trees.

Trap looked at his friend.

"Sounded like the boyo's Remington to me, bud. That's a good sign."

Trap nodded, his jaw set in grim determination, his eyes narrow.

"Watch yourself," he said above the wind.

"Lead on." Clay pointed in the direction of the shot with his pistol. "I'm right behind you."

Clay tied the two animals so they'd be around if they were needed, but would still be able to break free if they pulled hard enough and escape the fire if things took a turn for the worse.

Blake felt Javier's presence before he heard him, and spun Juan Caesar around a fraction of a second before the shot.

The older Apache stiffened. For a moment, Blake thought he was waking up, and attempted to apply more pressure with the V of his bicep and forearm. Suddenly weak on his feet, Blake stumbled, letting Juan Caesar slide to the ground in front of him in a dead heap.

A young Apache stood before him only a few yards away, his stringy black hair whipping across his cruel face in the wind. A blue steel revolver still pointed directly at Blake.

Blake tried to raise his own pistol, but found himself curiously weak, as if he were mired in the middle of a nightmare where someone was shooting at him and he could only move in slow motion.

The young lawman willed his gun hand up to face the threat, but no matter how hard he tried, he couldn't make it move. The Apache gave a crooked grin when the pistol fired harmlessly into the ground, then fell harmlessly out of Blake's hand.

Blake swayed on his feet, squinting to make out the form of the man who was about to kill him. The salty, copper taste of blood rose in his throat. The mere act of standing against the furious battering of wind suddenly seemed more of a chore than he could manage. He stumbled backward, grabbing for a handful of flimsy huckleberry brush as he fell.

Javier walked slowly toward him, seemingly unperturbed that he'd killed his own confederate only moments before. It was enough to him that the same bullet had passed through and through to hit the lawman.

"Caesar told me your white blood would make you weak," the Apache sneered.

Blake started to speak, but decided against it. Talking to a maniac like the one before him was pointless. His own pistol had landed less than two feet from where he sat heaving, his back against a rotting log. Blake tried not to look at it, knowing he would be dead in the short time it took him to get to it the way the other man covered him.

The young Apache squinted against the wind and looked down in disdain. He slid his long-barreled Colt back into the flap holster on his belt and drew a long skinning knife. It was obvious he no longer considered Blake a threat worthy of a bullet.

Blake pressed a hand against the jagged hole in his thigh. It didn't seem to be bleeding as badly as he thought it would be considering his sudden weakness. Javier took a slow step toward him. Blake eyed the revolver again and steeled himself for the attack he knew was about to come. He couldn't just sit still and let himself be carved up. His mind raced back to the men he'd seen butchered already by this man and his friends. No, he'd die fighting, no matter how weak he was. Even the thought of it made him stronger.

The fire was closer now, the pungent smell of wood smoke heavier on the wind. Even the young Apache looked up to take note. Blake had shifted his weight to make a rolling move for his pistol when he heard another shot, this time from behind him, beyond the rattling huckleberry brush.

Javier's face twisted in angry surprise. He dropped to one knee and put a hand to his side. Up again in an instant, the young renegade bolted for a nearby line of fir trees and disappeared into the shadows.

Blake clenched his eyes shut in relief and leaned his head back against the snag, expecting to see his father or Mr. Madsen at any moment. Instead he heard a bawling voice he'd never heard before carry through the whirling.

"Everthing all right over there?"

Blake froze, fearing it was Feak. Shooting their own didn't seem to bother anyone in the murderous group of kidnapers.

"This here's Corporal Bandy Rollins, United States Army," the voice yelled above the wind. It was tentative but friendly. "I'd be obliged to find out whose life it is I just saved."

Blake knew there was an Army presence in woods because of the fires. He raised his left hand from behind the snag and waved so Rollins could see where he was.

* * *

A beefy colored man in filthy military khakis knelt over Blake when Trap came into the clearing. A rifle leaned against a nearby tree, out of the black man's reach, but Trap leveled his Marlin to be on the safe side.

Blake raised his hand in a feeble gesture. There was enough grin on his face to let Trap relax a measure.

"This mountain saved my life, Pa."

Bandy Rollins looked up grimly from where he attempted to dress the wound in Blake's thigh. The soldier introduced himself without getting up.

"I don't know for certain if I saved his life yet or not."

Trap handed his rifle to Clay and knelt beside his son and the corporal. Blake's britches were cut away to reveal a thumb-size hole in the front of his thigh. Bandy rolled him slightly so they could have a look at the back side of his leg. Bits of flesh hung in tatters, crusted with pine needles and dirt. Blood poured into a growing pool on the dirt.

"I'm thinkin' they nicked an artery, maybe even clipped the bone." Rollins pressed his broad hand over the wound. He looked back in the direction of the wind. "We got to move him soon, though. He'd sure enough die if we stay here. We all will."

"I don't think I can outrun this, Pa. I can't even stand up."

"Nonsense." Trap put a hand on his son's forehead. "Your mama wouldn't be very pleased with me if we let that handsome Nez Percé hair of yours get all singed."

Blake chuckled weakly, and then winced. "So you're willing to admit she's still alive."

Trap nodded. "I'm too scared of her not to. Now let's get you on your horse and around this mountain to go with the fire crew. That ranger seems to know his business."

"You mean Mr. Zelinski?" Rollins's face brightened.

"You know him?" Clay toed Juan Caesar. Gave him a swift boot to the temple to make sure he wasn't playing possum.

"Yessir, I know him. My company was workin' right alongside him till they got called back to Avery. There was two Indian boys with him. I'm worried somethin' awful about 'em. I just know that Monroe character is up to no good. That's why I'm here. I got permission to come back and tell them about the relief trains. I wanted to check up on my two friends."

"Mercy, Rollins." Clay grinned. "You talk as much as I do." He filled the corporal in quickly on the attempted lynching.

"He's takin' the boys to a mine?"

Trap put the finishing touches on a tight bandage around Blake's thigh. "A place called the Ruby Creek Adit. Said they'd be safe there."

"I know the place," Rollins said. "Let's get this boy there. He needs to get somewhere fast so the bleedin' will stop. The people are like ants, just running outta these hills for their lives. Seen a man and young woman as foolish as me, ridin' back in towards the fire. Most likely they forgot somethin' or another they consider more important than their own mortal lives."

Blake winced and looked up, blinking. "What did the man and woman look like?"

"What are you talkin' about, son?" Rollins patted Blake's shoulder. "Hush now. Let's get you up on a horse."

Blake reeled when he got to his feet. His face was set in a tense mask as he tried to disguise his agony. "With this leg, I don't think I can fork a horse."

"Where did you see this man and woman riding back towards the fire?" Clay asked.

"They were ridin' along just below a hogback ridgeline 'bout two drainages over. Why?"

Clay explained their pursuit.

"Poor girl." Rollins's already sad expression took on a wilted look. "That fella she's with must have taken leave of all his senses. I seen a huge plume of smoke risin' up over that biggest batch of mountains to the south. What with the wind a-whippin' so, it'll be right on top of 'em in no time. If he don't bring her out, she's good as dead."

Trap took a deep breath. It went against his grain to leave the care of someone he loved to anyone else, but he didn't know the way to the adit. Corporal Rollins, as sharp as he was, would be no match for Johannes Webber's cruel intellect.

"Corporal, could you take my boy to the adit and see that he's safe?"

Bandy raised an eyebrow, but gave a nodding shrug. "I'll carry him. It would be easier on him than riding, but not much."

"Clay, could you go with them?" Trap looked at his friend.

Madsen let his head loll back and forth. "I could,

but I won't. This mountainous corporal here will have no trouble seein' to Blake's safety. I don't think it would be a good idea for him and me to be together very long. I'd have to compete too much for talkin' time. Besides, I got as much of a score to settle with Webber as you do. Ky Roman was a good friend of mine if you'll recall." He winked at Blake. "Not to mention the fact that Maggie would never forgive me if I didn't look after your sorry little hide."

Corporal Rollins took a sniff of the wind and shook his head in disbelief that anyone would willingly go back into the fire.

"I say you all done flipped your wigs." His hangdog eyes squinted into the smoke. "But I reckon it don't really matter much. We all apt to get cooked anyhow."

CHAPTER 28

"I hope you got some idea of where you're takin' us, Trapper," Clay groaned a few yards behind as they forded an ash-choked stream. It was littered with the white bellies of dead trout, killed by rising lye levels in the water. His voice was loud, but Trap could only just hear it above the howling wind. Both men had long since given up wearing their hats and lashed them down firmly behind their saddles.

In point of fact, Trap was only guessing at the route, following natural lines of drift from the ridgeline where Rollins had seen the man and woman. He was haunted by the recurring notion that they were following a couple of settlers gone back to get a milk cow, and not Johannes Webber and Angela Kenworth at all. Tracking over the wind-driven ground was slow and tedious, but he was heartened when he stumbled over a fresh set of horse tracks in a section of bear grass burned over from an earlier fire.

The area had been logged, and dozens of smoking stumps dotted the gently sloping hillside like short quills on a black porcupine. Above the hill was an apron of loose gray talus fanning out from a large mountain to the north. Turned earth in a line to the west of the talus rock, along with the depressions of tents and a split-rail eating table, showed the remains of a fire camp. The fire had swept through only hours before, burning itself out against the rocky bulwark of the mountain. It had been a small blaze compared to the one behind them.

Trap twisted in the saddle to look southwest, and shuddered in spite of himself. An enormous gray-black cloud billowed thousands of feet above the tumble of mountains north of the St. Joe River. Ghostly orange gasses churned inside the cloud, casting menacing shadows as the whole mass rolled toward them at an incredible pace.

"Oh, my Lord!" Trap heard Clay over his shoulder, and turned back to see him dismount and stoop next to a smoldering stump.

O'Shannon urged Hashkee forward to see what had Clay so distraught. When he drew closer, he realized it was no stump but a badly burned body.

Blackened beyond recognition by the searing heat of the previous ground fire, it resembled the stumps around it more than a human being.

"The poor thing's feet are completely gone," Clay moaned. "I ain't certain, but I think it's a woman."

Trap slid off his mule and took a deep breath before he got too near the corpse. The body was face-down, its hands drawn up underneath in a sort of fetal position. The head was turned back, as if to watch the fire that killed it.

"Think it could be Angela Kenworth?" Clay let out

a deep breath and looked up at his friend, his eyes already glassy with tears.

"Let's turn her over and see if she's missing a finger." Trap scanned the surrounding trees and rocks. He expected to see Johannes looking down at them with a rifle. This would be just like him.

"Oh, no. No, no, no not her . . ." Clay said as they rolled the body over as gently as they could. "Poor sweet, pitiful thing."

The body was missing not one, but two fingers. Though her face was badly deformed and twisted into a grimace by the fire, the turtle-shell comb Clay had given her earlier and the swatch of green taffeta dress revealed too plainly it was Cora, Clay's new friend from the Snake Pit bar.

"Why did she have to come up here, Trap? Why couldn't she . . ." Clay caught himself, breathing heavily. He stood to untie the leather strings that held his bedroll. "Ground's too hard to bury her. You mind helpin' me get her rolled into a blanket and leaned up against one of these stumps?"

Trap put a hand on his friend's shoulder. "That fire's gonna drive through here again, Clay. It'll turn what's left of this place to dust."

Madsen shrugged. "I know it, Trap. But supposing it doesn't. We can't just leave her layin' here for the coyotes and crows."

Clay spread the blanket out beside Cora's body, his back to the wind so it didn't fight him. He muttered to himself as he worked, sniffing and shaking his head. Trap couldn't make out everything he said, but he knew the gist of it.

"Poor thing just couldn't get a break, could you? I

hope you had you some happy times in your life, darlin'." Madsen suddenly looked up at Trap. "You think she ever had any good happen to her at all?"

"She met you. That appeared to make her smile."

"You reckon life is just that, sadness with a tiny sprinkle of good only once in a great while?"

"What do you mean?" Trap was sorry as soon as he spoke. Asking such a question was like pulling the cork out of Clay Madsen, and only *he* knew when his ramblings would stop pouring out. Luckily, he kept working as he spoke.

"If you think back on it, can you ever think of a time when everything fit just right—as if the Good Lord might have intended you to be happy once in a while and not just livin in one degree of misery or another?"

"I reckon I been happy enough," Trap said, helping hold the rolled blanket at Cora's feet so Clay could tie it with a length of leather cord from his saddle kit.

"I ain't talking about just not bein' sad." Clay snorted and gave an exasperated shrug. "I mean truly, sublimely happy. That moment of perfection when there's no wind and the sights and the sounds and the company all bundle up together like . . . I don't know. . . ."

Trap knew better than to get in front of Clay when he was heading off on a philosophical gallop.

"I never thought on it that way, but I guess I been happy like that with my Maggie."

"Yeah, but what you and Maggie have ain't even normal. I think that's what galls Johannes so awful. He always thought he should be the one of us who found that sublime sort of partnership with a woman."

Trap scratched his head at all the talk of awe-inspiring relationships. His marriage to Maggie was what it was and that was it. Talking about it made him feel uncomfortable, almost naked.

"I know you've been happy, Clay." Trap focused the talk back on Madsen. "I've seen you laugh your head off on more than one occasion, if I recall correctly."

"Laughing don't necessarily mean you're happy." Clay stroked the crown of Cora's charred head with the tip of his finger. "She laughed. I seen her. But I'd bet you the ranch she wasn't very happy."

"Yeah, but you've been happy."

"A few times, I reckon. I could likely count them without too much effort, though." Clay sniffed. "Two come to mind. One was when I was married to Inez and we took that little trip out to Sedona. There was this evenin' thunderstorm followed by the prettiest sunset you ever saw, all bright and yellow orange across the desert—but my Inez, she was even brighter." Clay wiped his nose with the back of a gloved hand. "I know a man shouldn't pick a favorite. Inez wasn't the handsomest woman I married, but she had a way about her that made me feel like I was drownin' when I wasn't around her. She was salve to my soul—like Maggie is to you." Clay rubbed his eyes and blinked to clear them. "Your wife is still alive, you know."

Trap nodded, fighting back the gnawing ache in his stomach. They situated the blanket roll that held Cora's body in a seated position next to a smoldering tree stump a few feet away.

"When was the other time?" O'Shannon stretched his back.

Clay was lost in thought, gazing up at the gray jumble of horse-sized rocks on the talus slope above them. "Huh?"

"You said there was another time that came to your mind when your were happy."

"I did at that." Clay nodded and turned to face his partner. There was a look of grim determination in his furrowed brow. His eyes sparkled the way they did when a battle was about to be joined. It was as if he'd suddenly been imbued with a double dose of swagger. He motioned toward the horses with a slight nod. Trap followed.

"If you take a gander over my left shoulder, you'll see a man workin' his way across the rocks up yonder. He's carryin' a long gun, but I'm bettin' he won't be close enough to have us in range for a little spell yet."

Trap looked up the slope. He could just make out a dark form slipping down through the jumble of rocks, a rifle in hand.

"I don't think I ever introduced you to my newest sweetheart," Clay said, sliding a long, bolt-action rifle out of the sheepskin leather boot on the off side of his saddle. Trap recognized the Mauser-style bolt action, but hadn't paid attention to what type of rifle Clay carried. While O'Shannon was perfectly happy with his 1881 Marlin—even loyal to it, any new firearm to hit the military or civilian market was likely to steal Clay Madsen's eye.

"She's what the U.S. government calls a 'Ball Cartridge, Caliber 30, Model of 19 Aught 6.'" Madsen smiled casually and rubbed his hand across the smooth steel barrel as if there were no sniper a few hundred yards away, possibly sighting in at that very moment. "Thirty-aught-six, for short. I just call her Ramona."

A bullet whined into the charred dust twenty yards in front of the horses. A short moment later, the report of the rifle popped in the distance, barely audible above the wind.

Clay shook his head. "He's trying to walk it into us, but in this storm, he's got a better chance of shooting himself. I bet he's still using an antique like you." Madsen nodded toward a downed tree and a small hummock of burned ground big enough for two men to hide behind if they lay flat. "Just the same, we best hunker down in case he gets lucky."

"Why Ramona?" Trap hesitated to ask, but he was too good a friend not to allow Clay time to make the explanation he sorely wanted to give. Madsen had had a habit of naming his firearms from the day Trap met him, and some of the reasons proved interesting.

"Remember that little Mexican whore down in Nogales?" Clay squinted down the barrel, then closed his eyes, feeling the wind. Both men were on their bellies. Trap acted as a spotter, watching the target while Clay worked out his aim. "She had that darlin' spot of a mole above her upper lip?" His words muffled into the polished wood of the rifle.

Trap grunted, though he didn't keep a catalog of whores in his brain like Clay did. If he said he didn't remember, Clay was liable to give him more of a description than he was up for.

"Well." Clay pressed his cheek against the walnut stock. "I heard tell Bill Cody named his Springfield needle-gun after Lucretia Borgia on account of her bein' so beautiful and deadly. Well, that Mexican whore, Ramona, was by far the most handsome thing I ever did see—and the most deadly—just like my aught-six here." Madsen aimed in earnest now. More reports echoed down from the rocks above, but the rounds still fell harmlessly, yards away.

"He don't have the patience it takes to get a good shot off," Trap observed when a bullet drove up a dust cloud ten yards in front of them. It was carried away immediately by the wind.

"Or the gun," Clay said, squeezing off a crisp shot from Ramona. He worked the bolt and rolled half up on his side, a wry smile parting his lips. "Unless I miss my guess, Ramona just gave him a 150-grain lead kiss about where his left hand used to be. If it's Mr. Feak up there, I reckon that will be a lesson to him about cuttin' fingers and such off poor folks. What do you say we go talk to him before he bleeds to death?"

The two trackers approached through the rocks cautiously since Clay figured the sniper might still retain the use of his gun hand.

They needn't have worried.

Though still alive, Feak was a mess when they found him. Ramona's kiss had torn away the top two thirds of his left hand where he'd been holding the forearm of his rifle. Ironically, only his little finger was left, dangling by a bloody thread of flesh. Bits of wood from the demolished weapon had lodged in the outlaw's face and arms, flecking him with blood. Feak lay on his back behind a large rock, panting and staring up at the smoky sky. Bright swatches of blood marred the rocks where he'd thrashed about after the shot—until he'd grown so weak he could do nothing but lay back and wait to die.

Though he would have lost his hand and maybe part of the arm, the wound hadn't been a mortal one. A quick wrap of a tourniquet would have stemmed the flow of blood. But Feak was shot, and to some people being shot was as good as being dead. Trap was glad Blake didn't share the same thoughts on the matter. Trap himself had been shot several times, once not even realizing it for several minutes until he noticed a hole in his britches leg.

"Johannes Webber be damned to Hell," Feak groaned, a pallid sweat forming across his bald head.

Clay kicked Feak's pistol aside, just to be sure he didn't get a sudden burst of energy, and looked down at the dying man. "Funny you should say that, mister. You're readin' my mind. Did Mr. Webber say where he might be headed?"

Feak snorted, then winced. He squeezed above his shattered wrist with his right hand. His voice was pointed but weak. "You must be Madsen. He said you would be the mouthy one. It ain't really you he's after." Feak lifted his head to get a good look at Trap, then let it fall back to the rock. "It's O'Shannon he be lookin' for. He never told me why he had it in for you so bad. Just said it was personal." Feak's eyes fluttered and a wan smile crossed his fat lips. The pain was easing. He wouldn't last much longer.

Trap stooped down next to the outlaw to hear him more clearly. "Did Webber say where he was going, what he had planned?"

Feak shook his head. A small tear formed in the

corner of his eye, then dried in the wind before it fell. "He plans to kill you—make you see those you care about die in front of your eyes—then kill you."

"Is the Kenworth girl still alive?" Trap didn't like thinking about the grudge Johannes still held for him. Too much guilt still festered in his heart about what had happened all those years ago.

"Last I saw of her she was. Damned little coyote nearly bit ol' Juan Caesar's arm off." Feak tried to chuckle, but the effort was too much for him. "Webber will be waitin' for you." The killer coughed like he'd been lung-shot. "He's a smart one, that Johannes is. I doubt you can take him."

"Where?" Trap raised his voice to get Lucius back on track. "Where's he taking the girl?"

"A canyon . . . west of here." Feak stammered pitifully, "You boys don't have any water, do you?"

Clay shook his head. "It's down with the horses. Which canyon?"

"Stone Canyon. It ain't far—he wants you to find him—all part of his plan." He clutched at Clay's arm with his blood-smeared right hand. "I'm dyin'."

Clay jerked away in disgust. "Feak, you blasted boob. There ain't no reason for you to die just yet unless you have a mind to. Show some backbone for pity's sake."

Trap rose. He now possessed the information he needed about Webber's whereabouts, and saw no further reason to listen to the dying outlaw's self-pity.

"I'll be meetin' my maker soon, boys." Feak seemed to be talking to someone who wasn't there. His eyes fluttered. His face and scalp grew pale. "I ain't long for this world now."

Clay shook his head and stood. "Well if you're bound and determined, go ahead on to Hell then. We'll be sendin' Johannes your way shortly."

"When was the other time?" Trap asked as they mounted to move off down the trail again together.

"What do you mean?"

"You said there were two times that came to your mind when you were truly happy."

Clay smiled and twirled the thin leather reins in his hands. "I was just bein' a bawl baby."

"All right. If you don't want to talk about it." Trap knew there wasn't much chance of that.

Ten feet down the trail, Clay broke the short silence.

"It was when I saw you and Hezekiah on the road there yesterday and we was all back together again. I reckon most of the times back when we was younger, trackin' bandits and chasin' outlaws was the finest hours a man could ask for. I was just too young and knot-headed to realize it at the time.

"Hell, I'm even looking forward to burnin' to death along with Johannes. To tell the truth, I reckon I'm as happy as I can be right now."

CHAPTER 29

With a raging fire behind them and a bright smear of blood on the alder leaves ahead, Zelinski paused and held up an open hand to slow the column of men sloshing down ash-choked Ruby Creek in the narrow ravine. Something the trackers had told him earlier tugged at the corners of his mind. He'd been so concerned about the death of his friend George White and his crew that he hadn't taken the time to listen like he should have. The big Texan had said there were renegade Apache involved.

"Renegade Apache my hind end," the fire boss said under his breath as he drew his forty-four. For Horace Zelinski, a veteran of the Spanish American War and many furious battles with fire, to be faced with renegade Indians of any sort in 1910 seemed an outlandish notion and he didn't have time to fool with it.

"Ranger!" the familiar voice of Corporal Bandy Rollins hailed from a thick stand of alder bushes off a fork in Ruby Creek. "I brought you a lost sheep. Don't you be shootin' us now."

Zelinski let out his breath and watched as the gigantic soldier walked out of the gray cloud of smoke that poured out of the side ravine as thick as the plume from the top of a steam engine. The ranger recognized the wounded lawman.

"What happened to you? Renegade Apache?" Zelinski chuckled holstering his revolver.

Blake nodded and the ranger's smile vanished. "Corporal Rollins winged him, but he slipped away."

Zelinski gave the boy a once-over and shook his head. "Can you walk?"

Blake nodded. "With help."

"Good," the ranger said, waiving his ragtag troop of men forward. "We don't have the time for all this." He looked at Rollins and then at Daniel Rainwater. Worried about more trouble with Ox Monroe, Zelinski had entrusted the young Flathead with his rifle. "If either of you see a wounded Apache and he so much as looks cross-eyed at you, shoot him."

Both men nodded. The face of Brandice the beetleman creased in worry, and it looked as if he might lose control of his bowels.

"There were two others with you," Zelinski panted to Blake as he half-trotted beside Rollins. It amazed him how the soldier could carry the wounded deputy at such a fast pace that some of the men were having trouble keeping up.

"Yes, sir, my father and Mr. Madsen. They went south after the missing girl." Blake spoke through clenched teeth from the jarring gate and Rollin's big arm around his middle.

Horace slowed enough at that news that Brandice, horrified at the prospect of being left behind, almost crashed into him.

"They went toward the fire?" Zelinski said.

Corporal Rollins's eyes caught Zelinski's and he nodded knowingly. "I tried to stop 'em, but they wouldn't pay me no heed at all. The little tracker just asked me to save his son here, so that's what I'm doin'."

The group had to slow to pass single file around a lumbering porcupine that scurried as fast as it could down the same drainage—fleeing the oncoming fire.

"Even the whistle-pigs are smart enough to run from this," Zelinski said to no one in particular. He turned to look back at his collection of panting, mud-soaked, bone-weary men.

Few of the others knew what was about to happen. All had seen fire from a distance. They'd fought it and pushed it back, moved when it got too near or jumped the breaks—even Voss's group, who'd watched it devour their pack train, had no inkling of what was going to occur.

First the smoke would thicken, get so hot they might not be able to see more than a few inches. Then the crown fires would tear through the tops of the trees. Running before the wind and raining down flames, these horrible, screeching demons would suck up all the usable oxygen. What little useless air was left would be superheated enough to blind them and sear their lungs closed at every attempted breath. Even if they found a way to survive all that, the ground fire would bring up the rear, eating up the thick underbrush—an unstoppable, unquenchable fury consuming everything in its path.

"We're here, boys," Zelinski cried over the storm of dust and flying ash when they arrived at the tiny entrance to the mine adit. "Wet your blankets in the creek as best you can and move with speed into the tunnel."

"Mercy, would you look at that!" someone cried from the rear of the party. "It's dark enough the bats have come out." Indeed, the tiny black creatures flitted in and out of view in the swirling clouds of dark smoke. Some of them, confused or overwhelmed, flew directly into trees to be thrown to the group's feet by the wind.

The ravine opened up to about two hundred feet wide before them. The slanting walls rose over two hundred more on either side covered with thick stands of white pine.

A horrendous moan like the roar of a furious ocean storm tore down the ravine toward them. It grew too dark to see more than a dozen yards.

"I ain't goin' in there," Roan Taggart yelled over the wind. He stared at the yawning six-by-six mouth of the mine adit.

Brandice rushed past the red-bearded firefighter, happy to find some relative safety from the encroaching flames. Other men followed, their sodden wool blankets flapping wildly in the wind.

"Monroe!" Zelinski barked into the dark hole. "Get out here and get your friend into that mine shaft!"

As big as he was, Monroe poked his head out the adit entrance but would come no further. He looked back and forth from Taggart to the now-glowing ravine, but he dodged Zelinski's eye.

Flaming brands, as big as a man's arm, began to fall in earnest and a blast of superheated wind blew in behind them, taking Zelinski's breath away. He fought to keep his footing. He had everyone in now except Taggart.

Zelinski grabbed at his shoulder, but Roan tore away and turned to run at the oncoming fire. A monstrous orange glow ripped through the tree crowns on either side of the ravine high above, snapping and cracking like gunfire as it was pushed by the faster winds. Trees fifty to seventy feet tall snapped like matchsticks and spun in the whirling gale. Flaming brands two and three feet long exploded into showers of sparks as they collided with the ground. Countless fires sprang up along the mountainsides, ahead of the main blaze.

"Get back here!" Zelinski screamed above the melee. Taggart paid no attention. He seemed transfixed, staring at the orange glow up the steaming creek bed while fiery sparks spun around him like a swarm of angry wasps.

Then, with slow deliberation, as trees flew past and the whole world seemed to melt around him, Roan Taggart pulled the revolver from his belt and shot himself in the head.

With no time to mourn the man, Zelinski dove into the tunnel as a wave of flame engulfed the entire gorge.

Corporal Rollins handed him a waterlogged blanket and helped him beat at the support timbers around the door as they began to catch fire.

"Taggart . . ." Zelinski said, shaking his head.

"I saw." Rollins tried to hold his blanket up to block the door. Steam rose from the wet cloth and a flame caught along the bottom edge.

Men coughed and choked in the cramped, steaming darkness. Someone in the back whimpered for his mother. Others chattered nervously like children. Cyrus McGill, with his fine tenor voice, began to sing "Abide With Me" at the top of his lungs.

Thick smoke poured into the tunnel as the air rushed out.

Horace Zelinski saw the world outside the opening turn bright orange.

Then, everything went black.

CHAPTER 30

Angela pressed her back against the rough bark of the jack pine and cast her eyes back and forth looking for a way to run. The red dirt trail behind her led almost straight uphill. Above it marched the huge column of smoke and flame that would surely kill her. Webber was off his horse, cutting some sort of mark on the smooth red bark of an alder.

They were heading into a circular valley surrounded on all sides by high walls of rock and towering trees. It was difficult to see what awaited them on the valley floor, for smoke poured over the cliffs filling it like a deep bowl of smoky soup. The wind stirred it some, and Angela thought she could make out the thin trickle of a small stream amid the huge boulders and thick groves of dark green trees and scrub.

There was nowhere to go, nowhere to run without getting burned or killed. Still, it was not in Angela's nature to march quietly to her death.

Webber turned from his business with the knife

and walked toward her. He didn't resheath the bone-handled knife. The long blade reflected dully in the dusky haze, and Angela could see blood on the brass finger guard.

"O'Shannon should find us soon." He held the knife between them, staring at the blade, but didn't threaten her with it. In fact, his tone was civil, almost friendly. His eyes were a different matter. They blazed with a fury Angela had never seen. She knew Webber had no more against her than the fire did, but it didn't matter in either case. Both would destroy her if she got in the way—without even a hint of remorse.

Trying to survive had overwhelmed Angela's thought processes since she'd been abducted. She'd always assumed it was about a ransom. She'd read stories about men who kidnapped rich people's children for money. But none of this made sense.

Sensing she was doomed no matter what, Angela was suddenly consumed by an overpowering urge to understand.

"Why?" Her voice still croaked from breathing around the rawhide gag. She wondered if it would ever come back—if she lived at all.

Webber smiled and drew the blade of the knife across the palm of his hand. He let the blood drip down on the stirrup fender of Angela's horse, then on the ground.

"Why indeed." He returned his knife to the sheath at his belt and wrapped a strip of cloth around his hand when he seemed satisfied with the amount of blood he'd left. "I suppose you are deserving of, if not entitled to, a few answers, my dear." He looked back to the west. "It looks like we have a moment." He looped the puddin'-footed horse's lead around the low branch and beckoned Angela to follow on foot with a flick of his hand.

It was not a request.

"The men that are following us are the best at what they do." Webber walked along without keeping to any sort of trail, expecting her to follow. Bunch-grass whipped in the wind at Angela's feet, and she stumbled to keep up.

"I used to work with them, called them my friends— until I was betrayed."

Webber stopped talking and Angela coaxed him. "How? What did they do to you to make you hate them so much?"

The madman stopped in his tracks and nodded, letting his head bob up and down while he took several deep breaths. "It was the little half-breed, O'Shan-non. He's the one who's to blame. It was his fault, but the others backed him up. They were there and thus they bear some of the responsibility—but the bulk of the burden, the bulk of the guilt falls on Trap O'Shannon. I will show him he cannot play God with other people's lives."

"Why me? Why now?"

Johannes chuckled, his gaze softening some as he looked at her. "Because, my dear, you were handy. I'd not counted on this cursed fire, but it makes little difference. I didn't give myself much of a chance of survival anyway."

"What do you mean, I was handy?" Angela wanted to strangle him for not getting to the point.

"It was my nephew's idea really. Tom Ledbetter. I

don't know if you ever got the chance to meet him, but he works for your father. The poor boy hid under the porch while he watched my dear sister butchered by a band of Cheyenne dog soldiers. He was nine. Had what you might call a thirst for Indian blood since that time . . . and who can blame the boy?"

Webber resumed his walking, brusquely, as if he had a particular destination in mind and it was not too far away.

"Poor Tom knew about the debt I owed O'Shannon. When it seemed your politically connected father was having you out west for a visit, we knew he would call on the best trackers around to find you. It was Tom's idea to have you ride in the coach and give you the 'Western experience' rather than your father's model T.

"All I really had to do was start things in motion. Natural momentum took care of the rest. You see, I know these men. I ate, drank, worked—and killed alongside them for years. A telegram here, a phone call there, it was really all too easy."

"How can you be sure this Trap O'Shannon won't kill you first, if he's as good as you say?"

"He's got to save you." Johannes shrugged, as if the fact was obvious. "You see, he feels enormous guilt."

Angela wanted to scream. She struggled to keep up through the brush-choked trail. "If he feels guilty, then why do you still want to see him dead?"

Johannes stopped and turned to face her. Leafy alder limbs whipped back and forth around him, adding their whispering whoosh to the moan of wind. "Guilt is not enough," he said through clenched teeth. "I feel guilt. O'Shannon has to atone for what he did. I know him, Miss Kenworth. He'll come for me in order to save you. No fire will be able to stop him from trying."

"Then you plan to kill me. You want him to fail." Angela felt strangely calm to know her ordeal was almost at an end, one way or another.

Webber smile serenely. "Don't think so much, Angela. It's not good for you." He turned and motioned for her to follow.

The trail flattened out into a wide valley of birch and towering cottonwood. Angela kept her head down and trudged along behind. She wondered how her end would come—a fire or at the hand of this lunatic? There were times the pain in her hand was so intense, she felt she would welcome death.

Webber suddenly stopped in the trail ahead of her and drew his knife. Angela had just enough time to make out the figures of two men through the smoke and swaying trees before he spun her around and locked her arm behind her back. He took an iron grip on her bad hand. Searing pain shot up through her elbow at the rough treatment. She didn't have the energy to resist.

A thick cottonwood tree stood between them and the two other men. Webber put the blade to Angela's throat and used his shoulder to pin her to the rough bark of the tree.

"Be still," he whispered. The wind was loud enough he could have yelled and the trackers would have had trouble hearing him.

One cheek pressed against the rough bark of the tree, Angela was able to catch glimpses of her would-be rescuers. There were two of them, leading animals across a small stream not thirty feet away.

"That's right, my old friend. Keep coming," Webber whispered as the two men moved cautiously in their direction. Angela could feel his muscles quiver with anticipation.

He tightened his grip around her and jammed her harder against the tree. His breath was hot against her neck. "Now," he hissed. "Go ahead and scream."

So this was it, Angela thought, and drew in a lungful of air. Before she could make a sound, the trackers stopped in mid-stream. The shorter of the two cocked his head to one side and looked hard in her direction. He dropped the reins of his mule and let his hand fall down to his pistol. The burly man next to him followed suit. He looked directly at her.

CHAPTER 31

"I can't even hear myself think over this damned wind," Clay barked as he sloshed into the ankle-deep stream. The bay gelding pulled at the reins behind him, trying to get enough slack to take a drink. Clay jerked its head up. "Stop it, you fool horse. This water'd kill you deader than a nail keg. You're gonna force me to ride a jackrabbit like O'Shannon if you don't watch yourself."

Hashkee, with plenty of slack, bent to sniff at the water, but refused to drink any.

Trap studied the shoreline on the far edge of the creek. White-barked birch trees whipped in the wind, their limber trunks bending in great arcs with each dynamic gust. In the towering cottonwoods, leafy canopies as large as houses swished and sang on the shrieking gale. It was too dark to see into the trees more than a few yards.

Trap caught a familiar smell on the wind and stopped in his tracks. It was an odor he recognized from the massacre site: the smell of fear.

He looked at Clay, who for all his jabbering noticed it too and strained his eyes forward, searching the tree line.

"There!" Clay spit. "I see him." He started for the shore again, but Trap stopped him with a quick hand on his arm.

"Don't make it so easy for him," Trap said, stepping back behind his mule. "Let's settle in to this."

A shrill laugh carried toward them on the wind. "Go ahead, Clay. You can leave," Webber shouted. "I only want Trap today. You're free to go if you like."

"I'd only circle around from behind and kill you, Johnny. You know that." The wind was in his face and Clay had to yell to be heard.

"Together again, eh?"

"Yup," Clay said, not caring if Webber heard him or not.

"Madsen, you imbecile. You're still playing Damon to his Pythias—too foolish to realize you are the better man. You two were always much too close for your own good."

"Whatever you say, Johnny." Clay moved slowly toward his horse. "But the fact remains that I'm stayin'. I'd much rather look you in the face when I kill you than go sneakin' around like that boob Feak you counted on to take care of me."

The winds from the firestorm blew in such a fury, it was impossible to know if Johannes heard anything Madsen said. Trees groaned against the stress. Ash and dust choked the air, and caused Trap to squint as he strained to see Johannes through the whirling torrents of smoke and debris. Clay pulled something out of his saddlebags and turned, a wide smile pulling back the tight corners of his mouth.

"What have you got in mind?" Trap asked, risking a quick glance away from Webber. His jaw dropped at what he saw.

Amid a virtual tornado of fire and sparks, Clay Madsen held three sticks of Dupont dynamite. The Texan winked. "Thought this might come in handy someday, so I borrowed it from the jail when I was lookin' in on Maggie. I was thinking of usin' it to blast Johannes to Hell."

Trap swallowed hard. "You mean to tell me I been riding beside you through these fires and all this time you've been sittin' on a sack of explosive?"

Clay shrugged off the danger. "Dynamite don't explode unless you put a fuse to it. It just burns. You know that."

Trap tilted his head toward the sticks in Madsen's hand. "Those have got fuses in them already, in case you haven't noticed."

"I'll be damned." Clay chuckled. "I guess they do at that."

"Come get what you came for," Johannes shrieked. He threw the Kenworth girl to the ground in front of him. She landed on her knees at the base of the huge, swaying tree. "You and I have an appointment to keep, O'Shannon. Come to me and I'll let her go to Madsen."

Clay tucked the dynamite in his hip pocket. Both he and Trap started for the tree line—and Johannes.

"Both of you stop," Webber screamed. He dragged the sobbing girl back to her feet and put the point of his knife to her throat. "One more step, Madsen, and

I kill her here and now. There is only one way for her to live through this."

Flames ate away at the trees behind Johannes. The furious wind howling ahead of the fire sent small rocks skittering across the scoured ground. The surface of the shallow creek rolled back from the force of it at the trackers' feet.

"He'll kill her anyway," Clay groaned to Trap. "I'm sick of playin' around. Pardon me while I go . . ."

A horrific groan from high above caused all the men to look up. Webber moved the knife a fraction of an inch and the girl fell away, just as a fearsome wind grabbed the towering cottonwood and slammed it to the ground. The tree landed with a reverberating crack, its huge branches snapping under its own weight.

For a moment both Webber and Angela were hidden from view by the leafy crown. Trap and Clay seized the opportunity and leapt forward. Angela crawled out of the branches to meet them.

The fire up the canyon swept through the trees toward them with the screaming cries of a banshee. It was less than a mile away now, and they had nowhere to run but the tiny creek behind them.

"Does Webber have a gun?" Trap yelled above the melee as Clay dragged the weakened girl into the shallow water between Hashkee and the gelding.

"I think so," she whimpered. Her words came on jagged breaths. "He . . . I . . . think the tree fell on him."

"Johannes, you all right?" Trap yelled toward the downed tree. There was no answer.

"We're still in the open if Johnny's got his gun

handy." Clay gazed back in awe at the approaching firestorm. "But I reckon it won't make any difference for any of us in a minute or two," Orange and yellow flames surged on all sides of the valley now, pushed through the trees by the angry gale. The Texan pulled the trembling girl to his chest and patted her softly on the back to sooth her. "We got her back from Johannes, Trap, but a lot of good that does her now." He ducked his head toward the fire, squinting at the brightness and heat of it. "This sorry little pissant creek ain't gonna be no help at all."

Trap looked down at the shallow stream. Only inches deep, it barely covered Hashkee's fetlocks. "Maybe there's a hole further down." He grabbed the mule's reins and motioned for Clay to follow with Angela. "We have to try."

Madsen put out a hand to stop him and motioned up the canyon. "It's too late, old buddy. We gave it our best, but that blaze will be on us momentarily. I feel good about what we've done. At least we can rest easy knowing these fearsome winds will blast Johannes on to Hell in a . . ."

"How many sticks of dynamite do you have?" Trap dropped the mule's reins.

"Six, but I don't . . . wait a minute." Clay looked down at Angela and gave her an excited squeeze. "I think my little friend is gettin' one of his famous last-minute ideas."

"Six should be enough—I hope. Don't have much experience with this sort of thing." Trap slapped Hashkee on the rump to herd him out to the stream away from the approaching firestorm. "Give me all six and get the girl back behind those rocks."

Clay dug the rest of the dynamite out of his saddle-bags and gave it all to O'Shannon.

"How long will fuses like this burn?" Trap yelled as Clay sloshed out of the creek with Angela.

Clay gave him a sheepish look. "I don't know, maybe a minute or so," he screamed back, though he was still only fifteen feet away. "They came that way."

A minute or so—Trap looked back at the approaching flames. He cringed at the growing intensity of the heat. Steam rose from the edge of the tiny stream. Falling brands sang and hissed as they flew into the water like flaming arrows. Two minutes and they'd all be cooked.

Trap estimated as best he could, and used his knife to cut the fuses in half.

Behind him, the branches of the downed cottonwood began to burst into flame—and Johannes Webber began to scream. Trap winced at the thought of the man, even one as bent on evil as Webber, trapped under the huge tree, burning alive. Grateful for a loud wind, he tried to push the sounds out of his mind as he worked to find a place to put the explosive. O'Shannon glanced for a moment in the direction of the screaming, but saw nothing. He was certain Johannes posed him little danger now.

Wasting precious seconds on a search, Trap finally found a small pile of rocks the size of musk melons located roughly in the center of the shallow current. Water swirled around the dynamite, but the fuses stayed dry, inches above the water. He kicked at the gravel bed, hoping it was loose enough for his plan to work.

Small fires burned everywhere, and it was no problem to find something to light the fuse with. Trap grabbed a burning length of pine at the water's edge and sloshed quickly back to the dynamite. He had to bend over and protect the fuses from the wind to get the fire to catch. When it did, he dropped the torch and ran, slogging for the rocks where Clay hid with Angela and the animals.

CHAPTER 32

The explosion knocked Trap off his feet as he stumbled behind the protection of the rocks. A muddy slurry of gravel and sand rained down in all directions. Rocks the size of his head slammed into the bank up and down the creek. Miraculously, none fell on the huddled group.

Clay helped him up and gave him an exuberant kiss on the top of his head. "You're a genius, O'Shannon."

"Is it working?" Trap mumbled to himself. Even his own voice was a muffled grunt inside his head. He couldn't hear a thing.

Clay chanced a peek around the boulders and slapped his friend on the back. O'Shannon looked up to read his lips. "Water's flowin' into your brand-new pond."

The ringing in Trap's ears quieted some by the time the trio waded into the rising water. He estimated it would be four feet deep by the time it was full. He hoped that was deep enough.

"Throw this over you," Trap heard Clay cry above

a rush of fiery wind as they led the animals into the water beside them. He was happy to see the creek already lapped at the mule's belly. Trap took the water-logged blanket and ducked into the water beside his friend and the girl. He thought he could still hear Webber's screams as the molten gases engulfed the world around him.

Clay laughed as he sloshed out of the creek, the girl in his arms. His teeth chattered from almost an hour in the chilly, lifesaving water. "Ain't it amazing how things change? I never thought I'd look for another fire again as long as I lived when that demon was bearin' down on us like that. Now, I fear we'll all freeze to death if we don't get warm."

Trap looked at the smoldering remains of the huge cottonwood that had fallen on Johannes. The world was eerily quiet, with no more than the gurgle of the nearby creek and the telltale snap of burning embers. If not for Madsen's constant jabbering, Trap would have thought he was still deaf.

"You think he suffered bad?" The little tracker stood staring at the tree.

"He's been sufferin' a lot of years, Trap. Gone plumb loco—outta his mind."

"I guess we should still bury what's left of him," Trap muttered, his eyes locked on the pulsing embers along the thick cottonwood trunk.

Clay shook his head. "You stay here with Angela. I'll take care of that."

Moments later, Clay called out from the other side of the smoldering tree. "You're gonna want to see this."

Despite his fatigue, Trap trotted around the cotton-wood. Angela, unwilling to be left alone, followed.

Johannes was gone. Madsen put his arm around a trembling Angela Kenworth and toed a shallow depression in the dirt. He shook his head and laughed out loud. "The son of a bitch cut his own arm off to get away."

A chill ran up O'Shannon's spine. He looked around at the blackened, ghostlike trees. The underbrush had been burned away for miles. There was no place to hide.

In the dirt, half hidden by the huge tree trunk, was a charred arm, the bone crushed, the flesh cut away just below the elbow. Beside the arm, in a small depression of earth, Trap found a gold pocket watch. It was still hot, and he used his bandanna to pick it up. He chewed on the inside of his cheek as he pushed the button to open the timepiece so he could look at the inscription.

He already knew what it said.

CHAPTER 33

"The boss is dead," Horace Zelinski heard a muffled voice say. The ranger couldn't move his arms or legs, but he felt the pistol, clutched in his hand, and assumed that if he truly had crossed over, the Good Lord would have had him check his firearm on the other side.

He had a splitting headache, and the longer he lay still, the more he became aware of the pain in his blistered hands and forearms. He reckoned the pain was a good sign, since it attested to the fact that he was alive.

"He died valiantly." Horace felt the gentle prod of a boot toe and heard the pinched nasal voice of Milton Brandice. "He gave his life to save the rest of us."

"I'm not dead yet, you patent-leather idiot!"

The beetle specialist squealed and jumped backward as Zelinski groaned and pushed himself upright.

Bandy Rollins gave a hearty laugh and yanked the ranger to his feet.

"Easy now, Corporal. You're gonna tear my wings off. I fear my flesh is a bit on the tender side after the fire."

"Forgive me, Mr. Z. I'm just tickled to count you among the livin'." Rollins pressed a damp rag to Zelinski's forehead. It dripped with cool water. "Hold that up against you there. It'll make you feel some better."

The moist rag helped immensely. As the pain in his head subsided, Horace slowly became aware of the men around him. Some lay on scorched ground around the tunnel opening, nursing their wounds and gasping for air like landed fish. Some wept with the relief of knowing they were alive. Daniel Rainwater sat against the mountainside with his cousin. Both of the Indian boys grinned openly when Zelinski looked at them.

"Did we lose anyone?"

Corporal Rollins cast his eyes at the ground. "You already know about Taggart."

"I remember that. Anyone else?"

"The Swede and Ox Monroe," Rollins said in one exhalation of breath.

Zelinski eyed the black trooper under a crooked brow.

Rollins raised his thick arms and shook his head. "Don't be so quick to jump, Mr. Z. I was busy lookin' after the wounded deputy. I didn't have time to do no wrestlin'. Turned out I didn't need to kill the fool anyway. Seems he was so all fired bent on savin' his own skin, he bullied his way to the back and passed out in a seep. He drowned right there in no more than a three-inch trickle of water oozin' in from the guts of the mountain."

It was easy for Zelinski to accept Monroe bullying himself to death. "And what about Peterson?"

"Don't know for certain," Bandy said. "Heart seizure maybe. All of us was breathin' the same amount of smoke. That's for sure."

"How did the O'Shannon boy fare?"

"He's fine. Bleedin's stopped and he's restin' peaceful. He'll be up chasin' outlaws and gals in no time. I hope not in that order."

"Well and good then." Zelinski was ready to move on. The odds of any one of them surviving such a firestorm had been long in the first place. To lose only three men was nothing short of a miracle. He tossed the damp rag back to Rollins and turned to the survivors of his tired crew. "I don't know about the rest of you, but I'm ready to get into town for a meal and a bath."

A general buzz of excitement ran through the men.

"And," Horace added, a small tear in his eye, relief flooding his emotions, "if anyone is still alive down there to serve us, supper is on me."

CHAPTER 34

August 27

Clay let the pocket watch twirl in front of him, twisting and untwisting on the long golden chain. The weather had turned cooler and brought enough rain to stop the fires. An afternoon drizzle had beaten the dust back down, and the sun now shone bright yellow on the crest of the western mountains. The light reflected beautifully off the spinning watch.

Trap stood in the corral, rubbing the mule colt's ears but looking at his son, who sat on a stump, his leg in a splint courtesy of Doc Bruner. "Isn't it about time you filled me in on everything?" Blake asked. "I was a part of it, if you both care to recall."

"I'd be happy to, if I understood it myself, son." Trap shrugged and turned his attention back to the colt.

"He sure twisted off on us, didn't he, Trap?" Clay seemed hypnotized by the watch. "I mean, he put that young Kenworth girl through hell just to get back at you. That seems too wicked even for Johannes."

"His mind was gone, eaten up by revenge," Trap mused. "How's the girl doing?"

"Pretty well, considering what she's been through," Blake offered from the stump. He seemed more outspoken now that the ordeal was over, as if he'd passed some test of manhood and was now allowed to be a larger part of the conversation. "Telegraph and telephone lines are all down, so her mother can't get through to make her come home. She and her daddy are gettin' reacquainted. Old Man Kenworth told me he was startin' to think about bucking his wife and having the girl stay out here permanent. I don't know if he'll ever pay to get the lines fixed."

Clay cocked an eyebrow at Blake. "So, you been out to the Kenworth place checkin' in on the girl, have you? Good boy. You remind me of me."

Blake smirked. "I took her on a buggy ride yesterday evening, but all she could talk about was how handsome and brave that Mr. Madsen was." He threw a pine cone at Clay. "It's like you weren't even there, Pa. I don't know how you put up with that all these years."

"Wouldn't have bothered him unless your mama was involved." Clay let the watch twirl around his finger while he spoke. "And she never was, to my utter dismay."

"You think he's still out there?" Blake leaned forward on the stump, steadying himself on his homemade cane. He looked hard at both men.

"I don't know." Trap shrugged, dropping the colt's rear foot to stand up straight and face his son.

"Well, I know." Clay caught the watch in his palm and held it. "I know and so do you. Johannes ain't dead, and that's a fact. Any man bullheaded enough to dog after you all these years, patient enough to put together a plan like that, and tough enough to hack off his own arm to get away, didn't die in the fire. No, sir, I don't know how he escaped from that inferno, but I do know this: He damn sure didn't die."

"So." Blake leaned back again. He scanned the trees around him, as if a singed, one-armed Johannes Webber might come running out at any moment. "He's still out there somewhere, making another plan."

"Reckon so," Trap conceded. He bent to step through the fence rail to join Maggie, who'd come out of the house with a plate of fry bread and butter. He put his arm around her shoulders. The cooler weather over the last few days had made him a lot easier to get along with. One morning, they'd even awakened to an early dusting of snow. Maggie had been pleased. Trap had been ecstatic.

"Well, then." Blake looked at his mother while he spoke. "If Johannes Webber is still out there, just biding his time until he can try and kill you again, someone had better tell me the whole story."

"It's hard to understand," Trap said, repeating his earlier misgiving.

"Still." Clay held the watch out to Trap. "The boy's right. Johannes is bound and determined to hurt you, and by hurtin' you, he's likely to hurt all of us. Hard to understand or not, we got to try to figure out what's goin' on in that sick head of his. I say let's find the son of a bitch wherever he is and take the fight to him." The Texan grimaced and turned to Maggie. "Forgive the language, darlin'."

Maggie smiled and tapped the watch that was now in her husband's hand. "I think Blake is right. He needs to know what happened. We have to think about the future. Sometimes, the best way to do that is to rediscover the past. To understand Johannes, stop thinking about him as an enemy. Perhaps if you would reflect on the time when you gave him this gift, you could better understand his thoughts."

Trap depressed the golden stem at the top of the timepiece. The round face flicked open with a whisper.

"To: Johannes, a trusted companion," the inscription read. *"From: Trap, Ky, and Clay, 1881."*

Maggie closed the watch and Trap's fist in her own hands. "To catch this killer, you must remember when he was your friend."

EPILOGUE

The firestorm raged on through August 22nd, finally destroying over three million acres in Idaho and Montana alone. Entire mountainsides were reduced to ash. On the 23rd, much-needed rain, and later snow, finally slowed its relentless advance.

Scars from the fires are still visible today.

The towns of St. Regis, Saltese, DeBorgia, and Taft, Montana, along with Grand Forks, Idaho, were actual locations. All but St. Regis are now just dots on a map, destroyed by the great fires residents later came to call The Big Blowup.

AUTHOR'S NOTE

Every Boy Scout knows that with a little fuel, a little heat, and a little air you can have yourself a little fire. In the summer of 1910, the Rocky Mountain West saw giant helpings of all three ingredients—and a devastating inferno that destroyed three million acres in Montana and Idaho alone.

The United States Forest Service, still a fledgling agency, enlisted the aid of every able-bodied man they could find to join the battle against over 1500 fires that threatened to destroy western Montana, Idaho, and southern Canada. Loggers, skid-row bums, Native Americans, miners, and Army soldiers all united in the fight.

By mid-August, many of the fires appeared to be under control. Then, a low-pressure system moved into the West from the Pacific Ocean, spawning hurricane-force winds in the rolling grasslands of southeastern Washington. By late afternoon of August 20th, sustained gales of over seventy miles an hour roared into the northern Rocky Mountains.

Fanned by these fierce winds, sleeping fires sprang to life. Separate blazes rushed together engulfing each other and melding into a huge firestorm.

Some five hundred miles away, in Billings, the sun

was completely obscured. At five P.M., eight hundred miles distant, a forty-two-mile-an-hour gale ripped through Denver, Colorado, bringing with it a swirling amber cloud of thick smoke that engulfed the entire city. The temperature fell by nineteen degrees in ten minutes. The next day, the sky was dark enough in the eastern United States that streetlights in Watertown, New York, stayed on all day.

Hundreds of settlers were blinded or permanently maimed. Official records show eighty-five—including seventy-nine firefighters—lost their lives in the inferno. No one truly knows the actual number of dead.

The characters here are works of fiction, and while they move in a historical setting, their adventures spring purely from my imagination. Though based on real locations, beyond the main roads and towns the geography is also fictionalized—out of respect for the brave souls who died along the various ridgetops, valleys, and creeks doing battle with the fires on August 20, 1910.

ACKNOWLEDGMENTS

Many thanks to mentors Henry Chappell and Jimmy Butts for their critique and comment; and to Tyson Bundy for reading just because he wanted to see what happened next.

I am indebted to my agent, Robin Rue for her tireless work on my behalf and Gary Goldstein—an editor who understands the written word and the West.

Most especially, I'd like to thank my fellow guntoters and trackers—all of whom added in one way or another to this story.

THE HELL
RIDERS

As always, for Victoria

PROLOGUE

October 5, 1877
Montana
Alikos Pah—The Place of Dung Fires
Thirty miles south of the Canadian border

Looking Glass was dead. Ollokut, Poker Joe—most of the young warriors were dead or dying in the freezing mud.

Maggie Sundown, of the Wallowa Nez Percé, struggled against the stiff rope that bound her wrists and ankles and wished she was dead as well.

The once-beautiful fourteen-year-old was covered in mud, her fingernails blackened past the quick from frantic digging in the soggy prairie muck in advance of Colonel Miles's unrelenting army. Dirt and bits of grass matted her waist-length hair into a tangled nest.

Only hours before, she'd been reloading rifles for Broad Hand in a hastily dug pit, while he poured fire down on the blue-coats. Now, the blood of her childhood friend mingled with the grime on the side of her face.

In the ghost-gray fog of early morning, a group of soldiers had flanked their position and shot her brave friend in the eye with a big-bore rifle. He was only fifteen.

Maggie had taken up one of Broad Hand's Sharps to continue the battle. Tiny crystals of snow spit against the barrel, sizzling and evaporating on contact from the heat brought on by heavy fire. She fully expected to be shot at any moment. Instead, a blond soldier with freckles across his nose like the spots on an Appaloosa pony leapt into the sodden hole. He clubbed her in the head with his pistol before she could turn the big gun back toward him.

When she awoke, Maggie found herself bound hand and foot with rough hemp, slumped against the wheel of a supply ambulance. A searing pain, made worse by the earlier blasting of the soldiers' artillery, roared in her head. The copper taste of blood cloyed, hard and bitter, in the back of her throat.

The battle had fallen off to a lull of sporadic pops and hollow shouts of distant skirmishers. Yellow-tinged gun smoke drifted like soiled cotton across the rolling plain and hung in blurred layers. Dead horses and fighters from both sides, corpses tight from the cold, littered the frosted grass. Gossamer flakes of snow drifted down through the haze in serene indifference to the murderous landscape.

Dozens of soldiers milled about in small groups. Phlegmatic coughs rattled their chests and they stomped their feet against the chill. Some wore capes; others pulled wool blankets tight around their whiskered necks.

Maggie thought little of the cold. She felt nothing but a hot, seething anger—tight in her breast—a fist around her heart. All around her, the air was filled with the drawn-out twang of the white men's chatter. The foreign whine of it bit at her nerves like a swarm of mosquitoes in her ears.

The Nimi'ipuu—her people—were silent.

A Crow Army scout with a pockmarked face and a mean scar from chin to ear squatted on his haunches beside her, leering with rheumy, black eyes and a cocked head. He touched himself lewdly, then licked his lips and reached out for the hem of her muddy calico skirt.

A swift kick from the freckle-nosed soldier sent him sprawling. It was Broad Hand's killer.

"Get from here, you heathen cur." The blond soldier drew his pistol and thumbed back the hammer. His pale fingers were blackened from putting the gun to much use during recent hours. "Do you understand me, you miserable wretch? Touch her again and you'll not leave this place alive."

The Crow gave a sullen shrug and padded off out of pistol range in search of an unguarded prisoner.

"You understand English?" Maggie's savior took the Indian scout's place and squatted beside her, only inches away from her knee. She held her breath, not knowing what to expect from the young soldier. He had a yellow bar on his shoulder. She knew enough of the military to know this meant he was one of the leaders. There seemed to be a lot of men with such decorations. Joseph said that was the trouble with the whites—they had too many chiefs who didn't know what the others were up to.

Leader or not, Maggie planned to bite the nose off of any man who touched her again. This one kept his hands to himself. He wasn't too many years older than her. Not yet past twenty-five.

"Lieutenant Peter Grant." He pointed to himself as if she couldn't understand him, then wrapped his arms around his own shoulders and pretended to be shivering. "You need to warm up, child; you're soaked to the skin."

He disappeared into the gray mist for a moment before trotting back through the muddy grass with a wool blanket. Squatting, he moved to drape it over her.

"I'm not cold," Maggie grunted, focusing on the falling snow. She'd learned English from the Christian missionaries in Oregon who'd been intent on converting her people.

The lieutenant grinned when she spoke and clapped his hands together like a happy child. His eyes played over her in silence for a time as if he were coming to some decision. He opened his mouth, but a commotion behind him caught his attention.

"It's him," he whispered, rising to his feet. "Joseph himself, under a truce flag. Thank the Good Lord in heaven. I reckon it's finally over."

Maggie stared at the ground. At first it was pleasant to hear the words pour out in her own tongue, but the longer Joseph spoke, the more those words cut her spirit. Another soldier translated for Howard, the one-armed Bible General who had pursued her people almost two thousand miles—and for the colonel, who had finally caught them.

A tremor beset Joseph's voice as he spoke from the back of his tired pony. ". . . *I want to have time to look for my children and see how many I can find. Maybe I shall find them among the dead. Hear me, my chiefs. My heart is sick and sad. . . .*"

The once-proud leader dismounted and with a nod from the Bible General, gave his rifle to Colonel Miles. Then, in shame, he pulled his blanket across his face.

A single tear, the first Maggie had shed since leaving her homeland in the Wallowa Valley, creased her dirty cheek.

Lieutenant Grant turned his attention back to her. He gave a thin smile. "Don't you worry," he said. "This is all for the best."

Whose best? Maggie thought, but she didn't say it. "Will you let my people return to their homes?" She refused to look at this soldier, refused to let him see her cry.

Lieutenant Grant remained silent, watching her. At length he shrugged. "I don't have any say in such matters. To tell you the truth, I'm not sure the general does either. I'm sure he'll try if he says he will."

He knelt down next to her again. His saber scabbard rattled when he pushed it behind him. "No matter what happens," he said, "I'll personally see to it that you're well taken care of."

Maggie was young, but she'd celebrated her womanhood a year before. She knew what it meant when a soldier said he would *take care* of an Indian girl. The old women often told bawdy stories of such things while they gathered camas bulbs in the spring.

The pale lieutenant's boyish face suddenly grew somber, a serenely benevolent look in his water-blue eyes. "There's too much sickness on the rez. You're so very beautiful . . . or at least you could be." He had the condescending look of piety about him, as if he were about to give money to a beggar. "My uncle sits on the board of a Presbyterian Indian school down Missouri way. They can help you there—teach you to be a proper Christian American. Help you become civilized." His wide eyes brimmed with youthful dreams. He spoke slowly so she would understand him. "I've cleared it with the colonel so you have nothing to worry about."

She shuddered when he put a gentle hand on her shoulder.

"Listen to me, now," he said. "I know this is hard. But take my word for it. The folks at the school are good, solid people. It'll be a darn sight more tolerable than any reservation." He smiled and took her hand in his. Rather than pull away, she let it sag.

"I'll be up for a promotion to first lieutenant in three months." He spoke to her as though he was convinced she must share whatever dreams he held for their future. "I'll look in on you then when things settle down some. Would you mind that? If I came to visit you, I mean."

Maggie sat still. She could think of nothing but Chief Joseph's words and her defeated people.

The lieutenant pressed on with his objective. "I know a good number of men who made happy homes with Indian women. Met a squaw man once down in Kansas who appeared to be a right happy fellow."

Grant gazed at her for a moment—locked in a daydream—then shook his head as if to cast off the thought. He put both hands on his knees and pushed himself to his feet with the groan of a much older man.

"I just realized—I don't even know your name." Maggie nodded, but didn't speak.

Grant smiled. "It's all right, I guess. We've got plenty of time to get to know each other." He let his eyes play over the pitiful groups of Nez Percé dragging in from the low hills and brushy draws along Snake Creek.

"Poor souls," he whispered. "I wish I could send them all to school." His pink face glistened in the flat light.

Maggie had seen the look before, back in Oregon. The lieutenant was a missionary in a uniform, a man with an unbending surety of his own beliefs and righteous purpose.

He had the clear eyes of a man with no guile. His heart was good—but at that moment, if given the means, Maggie Sundown would have gladly cut it out of his chest.

"There are worse futures than marrying an officer in the United States Army." The freckled nose wrinkled when he smiled. His eyes twinkled. "Don't you fret now." His mind made up regarding his future wife, other more immediate duties called him away.

Perhaps, Maggie thought, he should go wash the blood of her people off his hands before he takes me to his bed.

He turned to smile at her as he walked away. "They'll take good care of you at the school," he said softly. "I'll be there to get you soon enough. I promise."

PART ONE

CHAPTER 1

November 1910
Montana

The nine A.M. Great Northern train out of St. Regis rarely pulled away from the station before a quarter to ten. That gave Deputy U.S. Marshal Blake O'Shannon a little over an hour to make the trip that normally took twenty minutes. But normally, he didn't have to plow through stirrup-deep snow.

O'Shannon urged his stout leopard Appaloosa forward, into the bone-numbing cold. A fierce wind burned the exposed areas of his face above his wool scarf. Important news weighed heavy on his shoulders and pressed him into the saddle. He groaned within himself and prayed the train would be late in leaving—not so much of a stretch as far as prayers went, considering the rank weather.

Driving snow lent teeth to the air and gave the sky the gunmetal face of a stone-cold killer. The young deputy stretched his aching leg in the stirrup. He'd only been able to walk without a crutch for a few weeks. If not for the message he carried, a message his father needed to hear, he never would have attempted a ride in such frigid conditions.

"What's a hot-blooded Apache like you doin' up here in all this white stuff?" he mumbled. A bitter wind tore the words away from his lips. He often talked to himself on lone rides, letting the three aspects of his heritage argue over whatever problem he happened to be chewing on at the time.

His gelding trudged doggedly on, but cocked a speckled ear back at the one-sided conversation.

Blake pulled his sheepskin coat tighter around his throat. "Better not let your Nez Percé mama hear you talk like that about her precious mountains," he chided himself. White vapor plumed out around his face as he spoke. He wished he'd inherited his mother's love—or at least her tolerance—for the cold.

A weak sun made a feeble attempt at burning through the clouds over the mountains to the east, but the gathering light only added to the sense of urgency welling up inside Blake's gut. He had a train to catch.

He came upon the stranded wagon suddenly in a blinding sliver swirl of snow at the edge of a mountain shadow.

The driver, a sour man named Edward Cooksey, worked with a broken shovel to free the front wheel from a drift as deep as his waist. A flea-bitten gray slouched in the traces with a drooping lower lip. The horse was almost invisible amid the ghostlike curtains of blowing snow.

Blake reined up and sighed. St. Regis was less than

a mile away to the west. He took a gold watch from
his pocket and fumbled with a gloved had to open it.
He was cutting it close.

Cooksey had a half-dozen arrests under his belt
for being drunk and disorderly. Each time he'd gone
in only after an all-out kicking and gouging fight.

Blake didn't have time for this. Still, he couldn't very
well ride by and leave someone to freeze to death—not
even someone as ill-tempered as Ed Cooksey.

The deputy cleared his throat with a cough. "Hitch
up my horse alongside yours and we'll pull you outta
that mess." Wind moaned through snow-bent jack
pines along the road and Blake strained to be heard.

Cooksey had a moth-eaten red scarf tied over his
head that pulled the brim of his torn hat down over
his ears against the cold. He wore two tattered coats
that together did only a slightly passable job of keeping out the winter air. Stubby, chapped fingers poked
out of frayed holes in his homespun woolen gloves.
The man was no wealthier than he was pleasant.

"Damned horse bowed a tendon on me. She ain't
worth a bucket of frozen spit for pullin' anyhow," he
grunted against the wheel. When he looked up from
his labor, his craggy face fell into a foul grimace as if
he'd just eaten a piece of rotten fruit. "Push on," he
spit.

"You don't want my help?" Blake was relieved but
not surprised.

Cooksey leaned against the wheel and wiped a
drip of moisture off the red end of his swollen nose.
He brandished the broken shovel. "I'd rather drown,
freeze plumb to death, or be poked with Lucifer's
own scaldin' fork than to take assistance from a red

nigger Injun—'specially one who's high-toned enough to pin on a lawman's badge."

Blake caught the sent of whiskey, sharp as shattered glass on the frigid air.

"Suit yourself then." He lifted his reins to go.

"Twenty years ago, boy," Cooksey snarled, "you and me woulda been tryin' to cut each other's guts out."

"Twenty years ago, I was four years old."

Cooksey gave a cruel grin. "I reckon that woulda just made my job all the easier."

The Appaloosa pawed impatiently at the snow with a forefoot, feeling Blake's agitation through his gloves and the thick leather reins.

"I doubt that," the deputy said.

"I tell you what." Cooksey sucked on his top lip, an easy chore since there were no teeth there to get in the way. "I don't need any of your help, but I will take that horse off your hands."

"I said I'd be glad to hitch up the horse and pull you out."

"I don't want you to hitch the damned thing up." Cooksey's gloved hand came out of his coat pocket, wrapped around an ugly black derringer. "I want you to get your red nigger tail out of that saddle and let me ride back into town."

Like most derringers, Cooksey's hideout pistol was a large caliber, capable of doing tremendous damage in the unlikely event it happened to hit anything. Blake was less than ten feet away. At that distance, even the bleary-eyed drunk might get lucky.

"Think again, Cooksey." Blake gritted his teeth,

racking his brain for a way out of this predicament. "You're not getting my horse." He'd had enough sense to strap his Remington pistol outside the heavy winter coat, but wearing gloves and sitting in the saddle made him awkward at best. Cooksey definitely had the advantage.

"Hell, you probably stole it from some honest white man anyhow," Cooksey sneered. "To my way of thinkin', that makes it more mine than it is yours."

A fat raven perched in the shadows of a ponderosa pine directly behind the gunman, hopped to a lower limb, and sent a silent cascade of snow though the dark branches. The bird turned a round eye toward the two men.

Blake's Nez Percé mother said the raven was a trickster. She'd often told him the story of how one had saved her life. He began to work out an idea that would have made her proud.

"Brother Raven," he said, in his best how-the-white-man-thinks-all-Indians-talk voice. "I am glad you could come visit on this cold day."

Cooksey's eyes narrowed. He raised the derringer higher. "What in the hell are you talkin' about?"

Blake pressed on, keeping his voice relaxed. "I need a favor, my brother. Would you fly over here and tell Ed Cooksey he cannot have my horse?" Blake gave a tired shrug for effect. "I already told him, but he doesn't believe me. It would help me a lot if you would make him understand."

"Shut up and clamber down off that horse before I blow you outta the saddle."

The raven winged its way over to the tree directly

behind Cooksey. Wind whooshed off its great wings, and it began to make a series of loud gurgling noises like water dripping into a full bucket.

The would-be gunman's bloodshot eyes went wide. When he snapped his head around to look, Blake put the spurs to his Appaloosa and ran smack over the top of him.

Cooksey let out a muffled screech and fell back to disappear in the deep snow. The derringer fired once, echoing through the snow-clad evergreens. Blake was off the horse with his hand around the gun in less than a heartbeat.

O'Shannon was a powerful man, tall and well muscled. Even with his healing leg, he had no trouble with the half-frozen drunk. Three swift kicks to the ribs loosened Cooksey's grip on the little pistol and diminished his appetite for a fight.

Blake snatched up the derringer and took a step back, plowing snow as he went. Snapping the pug barrels forward, he tugged the spent casing and the remaining live round into the snow. He flung the empty pistol as far as he could into the tree line. His hat had come off in the fight. A silver line of frost had already formed along his short black hair. He bent to pick the hat up, panting softly.

"You can come back and look for that in the spring," the deputy said. Huge clouds of fog erupted into the cold air as he spoke. "Wish I had time to arrest you, but I figure you'll give me all kinds of opportunity later. You're too mean-hearted to do everybody a favor and freeze to death."

Cooksey moaned and tried to push himself up on an unsteady arm. He held the other hand to his chest. "You broke my ribs. . . ." His breath came in ragged gasps. "You redskin bastard."

"Better'n you had planned for me." O'Shannon caught his Appy and climbed back into the saddle, sweating from the exertion in all his heavy clothes. He winced at the pain in his injured leg. "I gotta move on." He shook his head and grinned. "I can't believe you fell for that Indian-who-talks-to-the-raven trick."

Wheeling his horse in a complete circle, he looked down at the sullen man who still lay heaving and helpless in a trampled depression in the snow. "My mother's the only one I know who can talk to ravens."

Blake turned into the wind again and urged the horse into a shuffling trot through the deep snow. He wanted to put as much distance as he could between himself and Edward Cooksey. Twenty yards up the trail he passed the raven, who'd taken up a perch in another pine after the shot. The huge bird fluffed black feathers against the chill. Its head turned slowly and an ebony eye followed the horse as they rode by.

"Many thanks, my brother." The young deputy winked and tipped his hat. "I owe you one."

It was a quarter to ten when Blake O'Shannon finally pushed into the outskirts of St. Regis. The wind had let up, but snow fell in huge, popcorn-sized clumps.

The train, and his parents along with it, was gone, shallow furrows in the snow the only sign it was ever there.

He slumped in the saddle, the news he bore for his father still heavy on his mind.

"Pulled out on time for once," a man with narrow shoulders and mussed gray hair said from a green wooden bench along the depot platform. He'd pushed the snow to one side to give himself room to sit and it formed a white armrest alongside his elbow. A light woolen shirt was all that separated him from the cold. Frost ringed his silver mustache and Van Dyke beard. "All the lines are down so I can't get word to Coeur d' Alene or Spokane to stop 'em." He wrung his hands and shook his head slowly as he spoke. "I assume you're looking for the train."

Blake grunted and slid down from his horse to work the kinks out of his sore leg. The snow came well over his boot tops. "Yessir, I was hopin' to get here before it left." He gazed down the deserted track and added under his breath: "Pa, I guess your news will have to keep."

"You have loved ones aboard?" The way the man said it caused Blake to go hollow inside.

"Both my parents. Why do you ask?"

"I tried to get here myself, you know," the man moaned in a brittle voice. "I'd have made it if that Bjornstead woman hadn't decided to have her baby at dawn. I have so many patients, you see. Especially since the fires."

"You're a doctor?"

"I am. Dr. Holier." The man suddenly stiffened and looked straight at Blake. "It's a providence you happened along when you did, son."

Blake shook his head. "And just why is that?" He

realized he was squeezing the reins tight enough to cut off the circulation in his hand.

"Four cases this morning—miners at a camp east of town." The doctor groaned. "I'm ashamed at being so late . . . afraid one has made it on board . . ." He looked wide-eyed at Blake, as if struck by a sudden revelation. "It's imperative that you stop that train."

"Cases? Stop the train?" Blake dropped the Appaloosa's reins. All this talking in circles made his head ache. "Get to the point, man. What are you talking about?"

The doctor bit the silver whiskers on a trembling bottom lip.

"Pox," he said.

Chapter 2

Birdie Baker had a nose for things that were out of place. It was a hooked nose, perched on a wedgelike face, perfectly suited to horn in on other people's business. Born with a keen sense of order, she took it upon herself to set things right when she observed them to be otherwise—liquor where there should be temperance, wanton women where there should be fidelity, and most of all, Indians where there should be only God-fearing white people.

No one, least of all Birdie, knew the exact reason she hated Indians with such a passion. But hate them she did, and she made it one of her many missions in life to be certain the hotels, restaurants, and trains in western Montana were properly segregated.

Her husband, Leo, shared her feelings if not her zeal and generally backed her up—in a sullen, simmering sort of way. Birdie swung her husband's title like an ax, as if he was a general or Japanese warlord instead of the postmaster of Dillon, Montana.

Where she was tall with big hands and sharp, accusing eyes, Leo was more of a thick-necked stump. His wire-rimmed spectacles looked absurdly small on his wide face. Deep furrows creased his forehead and frown lines decorated the corners of his nose and down-turned mouth. People often wondered if it was the constant squint through the tiny glasses or the day-to-day burden of living with Birdie that gave Leo his permanent scowl. Those who were familiar with the family knew his eyesight wasn't all that bad.

Birdie stood on the wide train platform and sniffed the cold air around her, testing it for nearby improprieties. She stomped snow from her highly polished boots and stared down at the balding top of her husband's head.

"Leo," she barked. "What have you done with your hat?" He was taking her to a postmasters' convention in Phoenix. The last thing she needed was for him to take ill and muck up all her vacation plans.

He tugged at a cart piled high with her luggage and his single leather valise. A chilly wind blew back his wool topcoat and revealed a short-barreled pistol with pearl bird's-head grips in a leather shoulder holster. He looked up at his wife and shrugged off her comment with a scowl.

Birdie was not one to be ignored. "Leo Baker! Your hat?"

"The damned thing blew off while I had my hands full with your blasted steamer trunks," he grunted. "You know, woman, this is a three-week trip, not an expedition to the Fertile Crescent. I see no reason to bring along your entire wardrobe."

"Get the bags on board and meet me in the dining car," Birdie said in her usual imperious manner. The porter standing beside Leo blinked his eyes at every word as if he were facing into a strong wind.

"I, for one, am hungry," Birdie blew on. "I want to make certain the railroad carries the things I eat before we pull out of the station."

Leo grunted around his scowl and passed the luggage up to the waiting attendant. "Wyoming has ruined it for us all," Leo muttered. "We'll be damned fools if the rest of us give women the vote."

Birdie watched for a moment before she stepped onto the train. The porter was a young black man, a bit on the scrawny side for handling such heavy bags, to Birdie's way of thinking. She supposed riding on a train with a Negro was acceptable, so long as he was one of the servants.

Looking after a body—even the body of a friend— was enough to give Trap O'Shannon a case of the jumps. Though he'd sent a fair number of people to meet their Maker in the course of his forty-eight years, he'd never been one to hover too long near the dead. But Hezekiah Roman had been not only his commander; he'd been his friend—and Trap had never had more friends than he had fingers on his gun hand. If Captain Roman wished to be buried in Arizona, then that's the way it would be. Even if it did mean days on board the same train as a corpse.

O'Shannon pulled the collar of his mackinaw up close around his neck and blew a cloud of white vapor out in front of him. Ice crystals formed on the brim of his black felt hat. His ears burned from the cold and he could hardly feel his feet. He kept both hands thrust inside the folds of the heavy wool coat. Leaning toward gaunt, he had very little fat to keep him warm.

A dull blue light spilled across the muted landscape. Up and down the tracks the snow was peppered with a wide swath of black cinders belched from the coal-fired steam engine.

O'Shannon's Nez Percé wife, Maggie, stood beside him on the cramped walkway that linked the dining car and the passenger compartments of the train. She wore only a thin pair of doeskin gloves and a light suede jacket with beadwork on the breast and sleeves she'd done herself. Her long hair was pulled back into a loose ponytail, kept together with a colorful, porcupine-quill comb her cousin from Lapwai had given her. The cold air pinked her full cheeks. Moisture glistened in dark brown eyes. She was virtually unaffected by the chill, and even appeared to thrive in it.

"Thought Blake might come see us off back in St. Regis." Her voice was husky-despondent.

Trap crossed his arms over his chest and stomped his feet to get some feeling back. "You know how it is in the lawman business. He was likely busy with some outlaw or another."

Maggie looked up at her husband and touched his cheek with a gloved hand. She never had been the brooding type. When she got sad, she got over it quickly, wasting no time fretting over things out of her control. "You about ready to go inside?" she said. "You got an icicle hangin' off your chin."

"Don't know why." O'Shannon's teeth chattered. "It's only fifteen degrees. Hardly what a body c-could call c-cold."

The smiling Indian woman let her finger slide to the tip of her husband's nose. "Let's go in." She winked. Her black coffee eyes held more than a hint of mischief. "I'll scoot up real close. That'll warm your bones."

Trap let her herd him through the narrow accordion entryway. The pink flesh on his hands and arms was still tender and tight from the devastating fires only months before. Maggie hadn't fared much better. She'd singed almost a foot off the waist-length hair she was so proud of, and the right side of her face still looked like it had a bad sunburn.

She'd stayed so close to him in the weeks after his return from the fires that for a time, Trap thought their healing bodies might grow together and become one person.

He didn't complain.

The warm air of the dining car hit Trap full in the face. The aroma of hot coffee and bread tugged him toward a table just inside the door. Maggie chuckled behind him, low in her belly, and leaned against his shoulder blades with her head, pushing him to the chairs. He helped her with her coat, and then took off his own before he sat across from her.

"You don't want to sit beside me?" Maggie raised an eyebrow and pretended to pout.

"I want to look at you for a while when my eyeballs thaw out." He also wanted to keep his eyes on the far door.

A big-boned woman two tables away was the only other occupant in the car. Given a bronze breast plate and a horned helmet, she could have passed for an opera singer. Trap attempted a smile, but she eyed him malignantly over a hooked nose. He reckoned her to be in her fifties—a few years older than him maybe—but she had so many frown lines around her deep-set eyes, it was difficult to tell for certain.

Maggie peeled off her gloves and laid them on the table, taking Trap's hands in hers. Her face was passive. "She's looking at me, isn't she?"

Trap nodded. "Giving us both the once-over like we might have the plague. People like her have a way of getting my blood up."

"Don't let her bother you, husband. I'm fine, no matter what she does. The important thing is for us to get Hezekiah back to Irene. It's only right he should be buried where she can visit him from time to time. I would want to visit *you*."

O'Shannon sighed. It was just like his wife to think about others when someone was about to impugn her heritage. They traveled little and this was the reason.

Maggie rubbed his hands gently between her palms to warm them. "I'm a tough, old bird, husband. She can't say anything I haven't heard before."

Trap grunted. The fact Maggie had touched him in public seemed to send the woman into a purple rage. "She's about to bust her brain trying to get a handle on me," he said. "Probably sniff out an Indian from a mile away. Wonder if she'll be able to figure out I'm half of that wild breed of Apache who would have had her guts for garters just a decade or two ago."

Maggie gave the relaxed belly laugh that made him love her so much. "Garters?"

Trap rolled his eyes. "It's something Madsen always says."

"Where did he run off to?" Maggie toyed with the leather medicine bag around her neck. "I saw him talking to a handsome woman before we boarded. Surprising to see him flirt with someone his own age."

The train began to speed up, slowly at first, the car rocking enough to sway the draping edges on the white table-cloths.

"I'm sure he's back getting her settled in her compartment," Trap said. "Her name's Hanna something or another—a schoolteacher, I think he said. He's been seein' her for a few weeks now. Says they're really hitting it off."

"Every female I ever met hits it off with Clay Madsen," Maggie said, winking.

A waiter wearing a white waistcoat with a red rag sticking out of the front pocket of his black trousers came through the door nearest Trap and started for the O'Shannons' table. He was a young man with a wispy blond mustache and a matching attempt at side-whiskers.

The frowning woman cleared her throat and glared. "I believe I was here first," she hissed.

The young man shot a caged glance at the woman, then looked sheepishly at the O'Shannons. "I'll be right with you folks," he said, smiling. "Won't be a moment, I'm . . ."

"Did I mention I was seated before that little man and his squaw?"

Trap flinched at the cutting tone in the woman's voice. Calling his sweet wife a squaw would have earned another man a sound thrashing. Maggie released a quiet sigh, but held him in his seat with her eyes.

He wouldn't be able to put up with this sort of behavior all the way to Arizona.

"Can I help you then, ma'am?" The waiter stood back from the table a few feet as if the woman might strike if he got too close. "Would you like some coffee—or maybe some spice cake? Gerta, that's our cook—she makes excellent spice cake."

The woman shook her head. "I don't want any spice cake. My name is Birdie Baker. My husband is Leo Baker, the postmaster of Dillon, Montana." She waited as if the waiter might bow or otherwise yield to the influential status of her name.

"What can I do for you then, Mrs. Baker?"

Birdie lowered her husky voice, but kept it loud enough that the O'Shannons could hear every word. "Tell me your name, young man."

"Sidney, Mrs. B-Baker." He began to stammer. "If you'd like to order, then I'd be g-glad to . . ."

"Well, Sidney," she said, cutting him off and folding her hands as if she were passing sentence. "Here's what you may do for me. You may make certain that I have a decent place in which to eat my breakfast."

Sidney looked up and down the dining car and then at the table where Birdie sat. "I swear, ma'am, this is the most decent dining car we have on the train."

"The car is just fine, young man," she said with an acid tone. "I'm speaking of the company." Birdie jerked her big head toward the O'Shannons. "You run along and fetch the conductor for me. There are laws of common decency, you know. Honestly, does the railroad expect me to have an appetite while practically sitting at the same table with this Indian slut?"

Trap crashed his hand flat against the table. The slap was loud enough to make poor Sidney jerk. The boy swayed on his feet in fright.

Maggie might be tough, but that wasn't the point. Trap was her husband, and though she was capable enough on her own, *no one* was going to get by with this sort of behavior—not even the postmaster's wife from Dillon, Montana.

CHAPTER 3

"What do you mean, pox?" Blake eyed the doctor. "Tell me exactly what happened."

Holier sighed, stroking his gray beard. "I apologize, young man. I suppose I am rambling. Can't remember the last time I slept."

Blake kicked a drift of snow off the peeling wood on the platform and rested his foot there. It took some strain off his aching thigh. "You say someone with smallpox ended up on this train?" He pointed down the empty tracks.

"It does appear that way." Holier shrugged. "His three friends have already broken out into sores. That's why you have to stop the train. Smallpox carries a hell of a lot of pain with it once the sores come. Double you over like an ax in the belly. Usually puts a body in bed straightaway. But if this fellow's able to move around by train, he could infect countless people who get on and off before anyone figures out what's going on. This could be the beginning of an epidemic."

The gravity of the situation hit Blake like a cold slap. As far as he knew, neither his mother or father had ever been exposed to full-blown smallpox. Many people in the West had had it in one form or another, but there were just as many who hadn't. One thing he knew for sure—when an Indian was exposed, the outcome was usually a horrific death.

"And the lines are down?" Blake looked up at the gray sky. It still sifted a steady powder of snow.

"Completely cut off, that's what we are," Holier said.

Blake climbed back into the saddle and tugged his hat down against the wind. "If anyone is able to get the lines repaired, get word to Coeur d'Alene to stop them. Use the Army out of Spokane if they have to, but keep everyone on board that train. I'll ride until I can either catch them or find a place to send the same message."

Blake tipped his head to the grim-faced doctor and spurred his Appaloosa into the snow. The news he carried for his father still weighed heavy on his mind.

CHAPTER 4

Raucous laughter erupted from outside and the door behind Trap swung open with a gust of cold air. Clay Madsen had his silver-belly hat thrown back in his normally rakish manner. He gestured high over his head with both hands and lowered his voice to finish his bawdy story as he came into the dining car behind the conductor.

Cold and laughter pinked both men's cheeks. Madsen smoothed the corners of his thick, chocolate mustache and wiped his eyes. Tears rolled down the conductor's round face.

"No need to stand on my account." Madsen nodded at Trap when he came up alongside the table. The big man's presence calmed O'Shannon, but not much.

Birdie Baker piped up like a pestered wren when she spied the conductor. His smiling face fell at once.

"I am so glad you arrived when you did," she keened.

"How can I help you, Mrs. Baker?" The conductor

motioned an addled Sidney back to the cook car with a flick of his thick fingers.

"I assume there are two dining cars on board this train."

The conductor nodded. "That's right, one to the fore of the cook car and one behind it."

"Would not the Jim Crow dining car be up front?" Baker folded her arms across her chest, barely containing her huff.

It was the custom of the railroad to put higher-class patrons in the cars further away from the ash and smoke of the engine. The dining car behind the cook car was usually considered preferable and reserved for the upper crust. Negroes, Indians, and other "undesirables" were supposed to use the forward car.

"I reckon it would, ma'am," the conductor said. "But the windows are busted out on the forward cars on account of an avalanche last week. There's no one riding up there on this trip."

"The railroad's broken windows are none of my concern. I have the right to take my breakfast without the presence of a filthy red savage nearby."

O'Shannon fought back the urge to stomp across the car and keep stomping. He seethed inside, but beating on women, even rude ones, gave him pause.

Clay let out a deep breath and shot a sideways wink at Trap. The big cowboy took off his hat and moved up next to the conductor.

"I see your predicament, dear lady," he said, giving a slight bow. "To tell you the truth, I was a mite surprised to see these folks here as well."

The conductor's mouth fell open.

"At last, a man who understands the laws of common decency," Birdie sighed.

"Perhaps I can be of service to you somehow in this"—Madsen shot a glance over his shoulder at Trap, who remained standing with clenched fists—"delicate matter."

"I'd be grateful for any assistance you could offer, sir," Birdie said, turning her hooked beak up at the conductor. "The railroad appears to have its priorities askew."

Clay nodded. His deep voice was soft and honey-sweet. "Here's what I propose. If the company in this particular dining car upsets your tender digestion, may I suggest you take your fat caboose back to your own compartment and have your meals delivered—or better yet, skip a meal or two entirely? Looks like it might do you some good."

He smiled to let the words sink in and twirled the handlebars of his dark mustache. "If you continue to speak rudely to my friends, I'll be compelled to pitch your broad ass off this train." He turned again and tipped his hat toward the O'Shannons. "Forgive the language, Maggie darlin', but I fear this woman will only respond to the harshest words."

Birdie blustered and looked to the conductor for help. He offered none.

"Well," she harrumphed. "Never in my life have I been subjected to this sort of . . ."

Clay cut her off. "Ma'am." He shook his head. "I believe we're done. I'm about to buy my friends breakfast. If you aim to perch here any longer, you best keep your pie hole shut."

"I must advise you that my husband is the postmaster of Dillon, Montana, and you, sir, shall hear from him on this matter." Birdie pushed her chair back and strode for the doorway.

"The postmaster, huh?" Clay shrugged. "Well, that's damned lucky. If he talks like you, I'll give him the whippin' he deserves, put a stamp on his ass, and mail him straight back to Dillon, Montana. I find it's a hell of a lot easier to deal with rude menfolk."

Clay sat down next to Maggie and tipped back his hat to reveal a forelock of dark hair.

A blond woman in a red shawl and with a matching smile on full lips came in as a fuming Birdie Baker left the swaying dining car. Her tea-green eyes fell straight on Clay and the smile became more animated. She was tall and lean with a strong jaw. Flaxen hair hung in loose curls at her broad shoulders, and a healthy crop of freckles splashed across the bridge of a button nose.

"I'd have been here sooner but there's a man in the next car looks like he's about to throw up on somebody. I was afraid to pass him until he sat down." She was in her early forties—just a few years younger than Clay and vibrant enough to make the air around her buzz. Clay and Trap both stood.

"This man, what did he look like?" The conductor shot a worried glance at the door. "I've had two reports about him already."

The woman shrugged. "I don't know. My age, maybe—a little taller than me, stoop-shouldered. Hard to get a good look at his face because he was so downcast. Look for the man who's green around the gills. That's him."

"Likely the postmaster of Dillon, Montana, drink-

ing away his troubles at being married to such a"—
Clay looked at both the ladies and changed his tack—
"awful woman."

The conductor tipped his pillbox cap and strode
off in search of his troublesome passenger.

"Have I missed something?" asked the blond
woman. "The tension is thick enough in here to cut.
Clay dear, did you just tell one of your rough-hewn
stories?"

Clay took off his hat and gave the grinning woman
a kiss on the cheek. "Nothing that exciting. That gal
with her snoot up in the air is just going to get her
husband to come back and have a go at kicking my
tail." He turned to the O'Shannons. "Maggie, Trap,
I'd like to introduce you to Hanna Cobb, a schoolteacher who finds herself in between appointments.
She has a grown daughter in Phoenix, so I convinced
her to accompany us on our little journey with the
captain."

Trap took off his hat and smiled. It seemed that
Clay Madsen could convince just about any woman
of just about anything. Maggie reached across the
table and offered her hand. "Won't you join us?"

Hanna took the seat next to Trap. "Sounds like you
were all having another one of your adventures before
I came in."

Clay scoffed. "I wouldn't call it much of an adventure. More like a case of prickly heat."

"Mr. Madsen has told me so much about the two of
you," Hanna went on. "In fact, that's one of the reasons I looked forward to coming on this trip, to get to
know the both of you better. He said the three of you,
along with your poor departed Captain Roman, have

quite a history together. Besides . . ." She looked at Maggie with a hint of mischief budding on her full lips. "Mr. Madsen informs me he is a widower many times over. I understand he has the reputation of being quite a scamp between marriages. Perhaps you could speak with me, woman to woman, a little later on that particular matter."

Clay raised a beefy hand. "You may ask Maggie anything you want about me, my dear Mrs. Cobb. I admit that I have been a rounder in my time, and may very well continue to be one. But I am honest about it. And if I may say one thing in my own defense, I never once jumped the fence while I was married."

Hanna grinned. "Ah, you never jumped the fence, but from what I hear, you were a bull that was all too happy to play with every heifer in the herd when the Good Lord opened the gate between engagements."

Trap had to hand it to this Mrs. Cobb. It looked like Madsen had finally met his match.

Clay took her hand across the table and gazed at her as if she was the only woman in the world, his hat thrown back on his head like a lovesick puppy. "What you say is a fact, my dear. But I do believe I feel that gate swinging shut again."

The Widow Cobb narrowed her eyes. "Oh you do, do you?" She withdrew her hand and turned to a smiling Maggie, who sat enjoying the show. "I hear you all met when you were quite young."

"I was fourteen."

"And you've been married how long?"

"Thirty-two years," Maggie whispered.

"Thirty-two years with this little wart?" Clay shot a grin at Trap. "I reckon I've known you for all of that but a day or two. I was just tellin' Hanna how we got started, the three of us. It makes a mighty good story when you think of it. The country was still so fresh back then. . . ."

Hanna rested both elbows on the table in front of her and leaned her chin on her clasped hands. Her green eyes twinkled and she suddenly looked more like a schoolgirl than a teacher. "I don't mean to pry, but we have a long trip ahead of us while we wait for that huffy woman's husband to come challenge Mr. Madsen."

Trap chuckled in spite of himself. "The way Clay spins yarns, it would likely be a heck of a lot more interesting than it really was. . . ."

He stared out frosted window, watched the snowy landscape lumber by—and remembered.

CHAPTER 5

April 1878
Near Lebanon, Missouri

Patrick "Trap" O'Shannon was about to leave the only woman he'd ever love, except for his mother, before he even met her.

He slumped in a high-backed wooden chair and stared at the buds on huge white oaks outside the rippled glass of the second-story window. His father, the Right Reverend James B. O'Shannon was a head taller than him, lean and wiry of build with the keen eyes of a boxer. He had a ruddy complexion with thick, sandy hair. More often than not, he showed at least a day's growth of dark red beard when he became too engrossed in his studies to remember to shave.

Though in coloring and complexion they were complete opposites, both father and son shared a short button nose and the propensity to grow a heavy beard if left unattended by a razor. They also shared the same intensity, albeit about different things. When he wasn't doting on his wife, the Reverend O'Shannon spent his days at study of the Scripture and other zealous pursuits in better understanding the ways of God. Trap had inherited a love for the outdoors from his mother, and preferred the woods and what they had to teach to any book or chapel.

The reverend broke the news in his customary way. A Scots-Irish Presbyterian, he believed a sharp knife cut quickest and always went directly to the meat of the matter. His Apache wife, Hummingbird, was spirited but tenderhearted, so he always followed his direct pronouncements with quiet explanations, allowing room for understanding if not debate.

The elder O'Shannon sat across from his son in an equally uncomfortable chair, his hands folded across his lap. Trap's mother once confided that when his father folded his hands in his lap, his mind was made up for good. In all his sixteen years, Trap had never known his father to change his mind once he'd voiced an opinion, so he doubted any hand-folding made much of a difference.

"It will do your mother good to be nearer her family," the reverend said. His voice was soft and sure as if he was trying to calm a frightened horse, but his green eyes held the same passionate sparkle they had when he preached. "God wants us in Arizona."

Trap had been to Arizona once before when he was very young. He still remembered the oppressive heat and bleak desert. If God sent a person to a desolate piece of ground like that, they must have done something particularly bad to displease Him.

Trap stood and stepped across the polished hardwood to the window, looking out but seeing nothing.

"Is she unhappy here?" He could force no spirit into his words. The thought of leaving behind the rivers and oak forests of Missouri caught hard in the boy's throat. His mother often walked with him and taught him the ways of her forebears—how to hunt and track and make his way in the woods. He'd always believed she liked it here. It didn't matter. His father hadn't called him to the office to ask for his opinion. To James O'Shannon things were as they were, and that was that.

"No, she is not unhappy," the reverend said. He moved to the window beside his son. Coach wheels chattered across the stone drive below. "But she could be happier. My duty as a husband is to see to her complete happiness. You're what now, sixteen? Nearly a man. One day you'll meet someone—and nothing else in the world will matter. Everything you do, down to the very breath you draw, will be meaningless unless that person is content. . . ."

Trap's head felt numb. His father's words hit his ears but went no further. Arizona was a world away from White Oak Indian Academy and the place where he'd grown up—the place where he thought he would live forever.

He watched as the door on the newly arrived coach—a refit Army ambulance—opened slowly. Three Indian girls in their early teens stepped timidly onto the drive, a toe at a time, as a doe might enter a clearing from the safety of the dark wood line.

Four horses of mixed size and heritage pranced in the morning mist, tugging at the harness. The heavyset driver hauled himself out of the seat and climbed down to grab the lead horse, a thick roan, by the head-stall. His presence only seemed to irritate the animal, and the entire team began to rock the coach back and forth in an effort to move forward.

A flicker of movement inside the dark ambulance caught Trap's eye. A moment later, a fourth girl appeared at the door. She was young, no more than fifteen, but had the sure movements of a woman who'd seen a great deal of life. A loose, fawn-colored skirt covered her feet and made her appear to float in the air.

All the new arrivals, including the fidgety driver, wore various designs of frock or coat, but not the floating girl. A loose white blouse fell unbuttoned at the neck and hung open enough; Trap could see the bronze lines of her collarbone and the smooth beginnings of young breasts. Despite the morning chill, she'd pushed her long sleeves high on her arms. The garment was an afterthought, something she'd be more comfortable without.

The horses kept up their jigging fit while the driver continued to make things worse by facing them and shouting. The new girl hopped from the rocking coach and floated up next to him. There was a liquid grace in the way she moved that reminded Trap of a panther. For a moment he wasn't sure if she intended to melt into the shadowed oaks or pounce on the horses and kill them all.

The animals knew, and calmed immediately at her presence.

The big driver cocked his head to one side, scratched his belly under a baggy wool cloak, then walked back to check the brake.

Vapor blew from the horses' noses. Steam rose

from their backs. The floating girl rubbed the big roan's forehead. Then, without warning, she turned and looked directly at the window—and Trap.

Trap felt a sudden knot in his gut. His face flushed and he glanced up to see if his father had noticed.

The reverend spoke on, his hands clasped behind the small of his back; touching on the varied reasons the move to Arizona was inevitable, sprinkling his discourse as always with liberal points from the Scriptures.

Trap turned his attention back to the girl. He was at once relieved and disappointed that she was no longer looking at him. She'd calmed the spirited horses, but even from the second-story window, Trap could see there was nothing calm about her. Where the other girls looked small and frightened in their new surroundings, this one looked around the brick and stone buildings of the Indian school as if sizing up an opponent—an enemy she had no doubt that she could beat.

Thick, black hair flowed past full hips in stark contrast to the bright material of her blouse. Trap felt his mouth go dry. He'd never seen such long hair; so black in the morning light it was almost blue.

Mrs. Tally, the mistress of girls, waddled out like a redheaded hen to welcome her new charges. She spoke briefly to the driver, then turned her attention to the newcomers, three of whom huddled around the floating girl with the long, blue-black hair.

Mrs. Tally's shrill voice made the second-story windows buzz. She never could get it through her head that English spoken succinctly and at a great volume did not automatically translate into every other language in the world. He could see the girls flinch at the well-intentioned but earsplitting words the heavy woman hurled at them as she pointed toward the double doors that led into the main lobby.

The wild girl appeared to ignore the barrage, and let her eyes crawl back up the red brick face of the building until again they settled on Trap. She cocked her face to one side and ran a hand over the top of her head, sliding her fingers through the black mane. Her eyes caught his this time, and held them while she gently fingered a small leather bag that hung from a thong at her breast. The tiniest hint of a smile twitched at the corners of her mouth, and then vanished as quickly as it had appeared.

Mrs. Tally interrupted the moment and shooed her new charges in the front door and out of sight.

Trap blinked to clear his head. He felt an overpowering need to flee his father's study and rush headlong down the stairs to see the beautiful apparition again. As far as he knew, no girl had ever singled him out for a smile.

". . . and you should remember, the Chiricahua Apache are your people as well," his father was saying. Reverend O'Shannon stared at the window at his own reflection. His hands were still clasped behind his back. "Someday, you'll meet someone. When that day comes, you will see what I mean. Nothing else will matter but her."

Trap looked at his father. His mind filled with the vision of the floating girl with blue-black hair. Now, more than ever, he understood what his father meant—and they were moving to Arizona in five days.

CHAPTER 6

"Carpe diem," Trap's father would often say. "Seize the day and worry not for the morrow; the Lord has your future well in hand."

Mrs. Tally had the new arrivals shuffled off to the girls' dormitory behind the main building by the time Trap was able to escape his father's study and make it downstairs. She would keep them busy settling in and getting them fitted for uniforms until lunch, so Trap resigned himself to a dry morning of lessons and pretended study.

Trap had never been the kind of boy to make long-range plans. He walked for hours in the woods with his mother, enjoyed yearly hunting trips with his father in the fall, but the future and the world of adulthood rarely came up. Each day provided a new sort of adventure, and he was happy to tend to each one as it presented itself. *Carpe diem* indeed.

The arrival of this mysterious girl who floated across the ground sent a sudden whirlwind of thoughts spinning through the boy's head. For the first time in his life, Trap thought about the eventuality of providing for someone else, and came to the sad realization that he didn't have many marketable skills. This thought alone put him into a quiet stupor, and he spent the morning brooding into his arithmetic primer, seeing nothing but a blur.

At sixteen, Trap was among the oldest of the twenty-five students at White Oak. Girls of any age outnumbered boys six to one. The only other boy close to his age was Frank Tall Horse, a gangly Ogallala Sioux. None of the other male students was older than twelve.

When he was ten, Trap had asked his mother why there were few other boys his age to play with.

"Indian boys of all ages are fighters," she'd told him. "Most are killed in battle. A few more of the girls survive. If they aren't taken as slaves by other tribes, well-meaning soldiers sometimes bring them here." Hummingbird was a quiet woman, but she wasn't one to beat around the bush.

Morning classes ground by with a glacial lack of speed. When it came time for midday break, Trap felt as if he might jump out of his skin if he didn't get another look at the floating girl.

A bright sun filtered through the new foliage on the tall oaks and cast dimpled shadows around the spring grass in the exercise yard below.

Mrs. Tally was in the habit of having what she called an early lunch, which everyone knew was a nap. Trap was certain she would let the new girls out for some fresh air while she retired to her quarters for an hour or so.

Knowing the new girl would likely come out the

large double doors off the front hallway, Trap resolved to station himself in the grassy area nearby.

Frank Tall Horse was a quiet boy, a head taller than Trap. He'd been orphaned at three—too young to be a warrior when he was brought to White Oak. Prone to spending hours with his nose stuck in fanciful tales by someone named Jules Verne, he knew little of his native ways except for what Trap's mother had taught him. He liked to joke that he'd been raised in captivity.

Trap stared at the door and bounced with nervous energy.

"How about a leg-wrestling match?" Tall Horse suggested. He had a new book, but sensed his friend's anxiety and genuinely wanted to help.

Trap watched the door while he spoke. He'd wrestled the long-legged Sioux at least two dozen times over the years, and bested him every time though he was over a head shorter. Suddenly, the thought of this new girl seeing him doing nothing but standing around waiting seemed foolish. It would be better if he were engaged in some sort of contest. Especially a contest he was likely to win.

"Sure," Trap said, trying to sound disinterested. "A game might be good."

The two boys lay down on the grass elbow-to-elbow, Trap's feet toward the building and Tall Horse's toward the trees. In unison they counted to three, then raised their legs to hook each other at the knee. Locked together, each struggled to roll his opponent backward over his own head.

Trap beat the taller boy soundly on the first round.

"Two out of three?" Frank picked bits of grass and twigs out of his close-cropped hair.

Trap shrugged. "All right by me," he said resuming his position.

"I've learned your trick, Apache," Tall Horse said as he raised his leg the first time. "This time the mighty Sioux will be victorious."

On the count of two, the front doors of the school opened. Trap felt the strength leave his legs when the new girl floated out in her crisp blue uniform dress. The sight of her hit Trap like a bucket of springwater. The ability for all concentration drained from his body. She looked directly at him. A smile crossed her oval face.

Tall Horse took advantage of the momentary lapse and sent the befuddled Trap flying backward into the grass. When he rolled to his feet, the girl was gone.

The Sioux boy ducked his head and gave an embarrassed grimace at having won the contest. He never won at anything physical, and seemed uncomfortable with the thought of it.

"Want another go at it?" Tall Horse grunted.

Trap popped his neck from side to side and grinned. "No. It was fair."

He left a beaming Tall Horse to his book and moved immediately toward the place where he'd last seen the floating girl.

The other new arrivals milled around at the edge of the yard, bunched in the same nervous group. Two of them looked as though they might be sisters; all were surely from the same tribe.

It was easy to find the girl's track. The stiff leather soles of her newly issued shoes couldn't hide the soft, toe-first way her feet struck the ground with each step. His mother walked the same way, and Trap had grown up mimicking it.

The tracks led around the corner, toward the delivery entrance to the kitchen and the root cellar he'd help enlarge the previous fall. The constricting pair of new shoes lay abandoned beside the worn path.

Trap knelt to study the small print of the girl's bare foot. His open hand almost covered it. Trap's mother often told him to feel the track—*talk to it,* she said. He touched each tiny indentation where toes had dug in lightly to the dark earth, closed his eyes to see what these tracks might tell him.

He heard a sharp yowl, like a bobcat caught in a snare.

Trap's eyes snapped open and he sprinted around the building.

The Van Zandt's Creamery wagon was parked beside the kitchen entrance. Another yowl came from the open door of the root cellar. Moments later a fuming Harry Van Zandt scampered out of the dark opening, the remains of a jar of currant jelly dripping off the top of his head. At seventeen, Harry was nearly six feet tall with menacing features and a permanent scowl on his long face. His younger brother Roth was nowhere to be seen.

Harry cast his eyes back and forth on the ground while he wiped the sticky red goop off his face.

"Watch her, Roth," he yelled into the cellar as he

found an oak branch the size of his arm. "She's a scrapper. Them jars hurt, I'm tellin' ya." He tested the club on his open palm and started for the door again.

There was a commotion of breaking bottles and more cries from the cellar.

"Where you aim to go with that?" Trap nodded toward the piece of oak in Harry's hand.

"None of your damned business, runt," the other boy said. "I'm gonna teach that little red whore some manners. She's a looker, but that don't give her no right. . . ."

The stone caught Harry high in the side of the head, glancing off a glob of current jelly. Dark eyes rolled back in his head, lids fluttering life a leaf on the wind. He swayed on his feet, teetered for a moment, then collapsed into the dirt by the back wheel of his delivery wagon.

He was still breathing, but a nasty knot was already rising over his left temple. That was *his* problem.

Trap bent to scoop up the oak club and trotted the two steps to the open root cellar. A jar of tomatoes shattered against the timber door frame.

Once his eyes adjusted to the dim light, he could see Roth Van Zandt holding a wooden barrel lid like a shield as he advanced on the new girl at the far end of the narrow earthen room.

Tomatoes had been a bumper crop the previous summer, and there was an almost endless supply of jars she could use to defend herself.

"Almost there, darlin'," Roth giggled as another jar of tomatoes exploded off the wooden lid. He didn't look up as Trap moved up behind him. "Me and Harry here gonna show you some fun, that's all. . . . We ain't gonna hurt you, are we, Harry?"

Trap moved up so he was within striking distance with the oak club. "No," he said. "We're not."

Roth lowered the barrel lid in time to catch a quart jar on the point of his chin. Glass shattered and Trap stepped back to avoid getting splattered.

"Your brother's outside with a bad headache," Trap said, gesturing with the wood. "Take him on back to town before this girl knocks your head off."

Van Zandt wiped the red juice off his face and chest. His tongue flicked across his lips in disgust.

"Havin' a white pa didn't help you much when it came to brains, O'Shannon." Roth spit. "Just goes to prove it only takes a drop of the heathen blood to ruin a body."

Trap raised the club. "Go ahead and say another word about my mother," he whispered. "I'll finish what the girl started."

Roth talked big, but he had no intention of facing Trap alone. He backed outside with the barrel lid in hand before helping his half-conscious brother back to the wagon.

"You ain't heard the last of us, O'Shannon." Roth gathered up the reins and clucked to the Cleveland Bay mare to get her moving. "Or you either, Miss Tomato Chucker. You're bound to see us again, that's for damned sure."

Trap threw the oak club at Van Zandt to hurry him along. When the wagon was safely down the gravel drive, he turned to face the new girl. She was even more beautiful up close than from his father's window. He could think of nothing to say, so he just stood and looked.

"You are Indian?" she said at length. His staring didn't seem to bother her.

Trap swallowed hard. "Yes. I mean, sort of. My mother is Chiricahua Apache." He felt as if he was tripping over every word.

"My name is Maggie Sundown of the Nimi'ipuu—the whites call us Wallowa Nez Percé." Her chest still heaved. Her eyes, the color of black coffee, glistened as she calmed herself from her run-in with the Van Zandts.

"I'm Patrick O'Shannon, but everyone calls me Trap."

"Reverend O'Shannon is your father?"

Trap nodded.

Maggie smiled. "So you live here, like I do."

All Trap ever wanted to do again was stand there and watch this girl smile. Then he thought about what she'd just said and the happiness drained out of him.

"Only a few more days." The words tasted bitter as he said them. "We're moving to Arizona."

Maggie brushed a lock of hair away from her full cheek. The smile was gone.

"That is a very sad thing to hear, Patrick Trap O'Shannon of the Chiricahua Apache."

The promise of an interesting week hung heavy on her sigh.

CHAPTER 7

Trap decided early on that whatever he decided to do with his life, it would not involve wearing a necktie. Even if he had shared his father's zeal for the ministry, the way he'd have to dress alone was enough to keep him from following in the man's steps. He considered the infernal things instruments of unbearable torture, and avoided them as he would any other form of slow, strangling death.

Unfortunately, the reverend saw things differently and required a tie for church and all important social events—like dinner with the new superintendent.

The Reverend Tobias Drum had arrived that morning by wagon with a pile of worn carpetbags and a fine Thoroughbred gelding, the color of a roasted chestnut. His coming was like a dark cloud over the school. The students had lined up at the windows in stunned sadness to witness the proof that the O'Shannons were leaving very soon.

Trap tried to keep an open mind, but Drum seemed to him a particularly oily man, both in body and demeanor. He was stout, a half a head taller than Trap's father, who stood nearly six feet. Where the Reverend O'Shannon possessed the gaunt appearance of a hungry boxer, Drum was a blocky brute with the well-fed look and sullen eyes of one more accustomed to barroom brawls. Bushy sideburns covered pink jowls, and a greasy ponytail dusted the collar of his black frock coat with a steady sifting of dandruff.

From the time the man had arrived, Trap's father had become almost subservient to him, yielding the school as if he'd turned over the reins already. What was worse is that Drum appeared to expect such treatment.

The men's voices hummed through the panel door off the dining room while Trap helped his mother fill crystal water glasses and finish setting the table. He tugged at the knot in his silk tie.

A sumptuous meal of roast pork, turnips, string beans, and hot bread spread across the expansive oak table—the table his mother would have to leave behind in two days time when they left for Arizona.

"Why don't you take this fine table and leave me behind?" Trap said before he thought much about it. He would never have spoken so directly to his father.

Hummingbird smiled softly as she always did, reacting to what he meant, not what he said. "The table is only planks and sticks." She smoothed the front of her white apron with a copper hand. Her hair was long, but she kept it coiled and pinned up so Trap hardly ever saw it down. "I'm sure there will be tables in Arizona." She put a hand on Trap's shoulder. "But I do worry for you, my son. There is more to this than you can understand. I have asked your father to tell you, and maybe he will in his time. You are almost grown. . . ."

The Reverend O'Shannon's face was locked in a wooden half frown when he came through the door ahead of Drum.

"We have a job to do," Drum was saying. "It's not always pleasant, but it is, nonetheless, our duty."

Trap's jaw dropped when the new superintendent took the chair at the head of the long table—his father's spot—and flopped down in it before his mother was seated.

Reverend O'Shannon said grace and carved the roast while he listened in stony silence as Drum droned on with his philosophy about running an Indian school.

Drum began eating as soon as his plate was filled. "The United States Army has made my orders clear," he said around a fork piled high with roast pork and turnips.

"Chuparosa," O'Shannon said, calling his wife by name to get her to hold up her plate. He gave her a thick slice of end-cut. Trap knew the seasoned, outer edge of the roast was his mother's favorite, and his father always made certain she got this choice morsel, no matter who was eating with them. The reverend looked up at Drum and moved the knife to cut Trap's portion. "I was under the impression we got our orders from a higher authority than the Army," he said. His voice was tight but controlled.

Drum waved him off with the fork. "Of course we do, but the Army brings us the students. We have to learn to work hand in glove. Don't disparage the military, O'Shannon. The God of the Israelites utilized an army to work miracles."

"True enough," Trap's father said. Everyone served, he sat down to his own plate.

"I couldn't help but notice you called your wife by an Indian name. Do you believe that is wise?" Drum continued to eat as he spoke. He appeared to be numb to the fact that Mrs. O'Shannon sat directly to his right, and spoke of her more as if she were a valued hunting dog than another human being.

"Ah, yes," O'Shannon said. "Chuparosa. It's Spanish for Hummingbird. The Apache often use Spanish appellations—Geronimo, Magnus Colorado—beyond that . . ." He shrugged. "It was her name before I knew her and it continues to be so. I see no reason to call her anything else."

Drum grunted through a full mouth of meat and turnips. "This meal prepared by your lovely Hummingbird is a perfect example of what I'm talking about." Other than a backhanded gesture toward Trap's mother, he ignored her completely. "She has learned to cook as good as any white woman."

The man's flippant tone made Trap grip his knife tighter and chased away any thought of an appetite.

"See what the savage Indian is capable of when properly schooled and trained." Drum pushed ahead, unwavering in his rude behavior. "Left to her own devices—her natural and carnal state, if you will—who knows what kind of grubs we'd be eating. Likely a feast of stolen horse and potent corn *tiswin.*"

Reverend O'Shannon put his fork and knife on the table and took a deep breath. His fists clenched white beside his plate. Trap had seen his father box many times, and wondered if Drum knew he was about to get a sound whipping.

"You've overstepped your bounds, sir, in speaking this way of my wife."

Drum dabbed at the corner of his mouth with a linen napkin and flicked a thick hand. "I meant no offense, Reverend." It was a halfhearted apology at best, and Trap felt compelled to bash the man's stodgy face against the fine oak table. A look from his mother held him back.

"I did not intend to insult your family. On the contrary. I only mean to point out that you have done exactly that of which I speak. 'Kill everything in them that is Indian,' the Army says. 'Civilize them and teach them solid Christian doctrine.' That's what we are to do with our charges here at White Oak." Drum looked suddenly at Trap from under a bushy brow and pointed at him with a fork.

"How about you, boy? From what I've heard, you've grown up here. Are you a Christian or an Indian?"

"Can't I be both?" Trap said, though his thoughts at the moment were anything but Christian.

"I don't believe you can," Drum said, banging his fist on the table. The dishes rattled and water sloshed out of the glass at his side. "And neither does the Army. This was a tasty meal, Reverend. And now, if you'll excuse me, I've had a long trip and wish to retire early. I'll have a look around the school tomorrow on my own. You'll be on your way the day after?"

"We will," Trap's father said. He pushed back his chair and rose. Trap could not remember him ever looking sadder. "I'll show you to your room."

When the men had gone, Trap noticed his mother hadn't eaten a bite. "Are you all right?" he asked, knowing the answer before it came.

"I am afraid for you," Hummingbird said. "You will find that some people are like one-eyed mules. No matter how you turn them, they can only see a single point of view." She pushed her plate away and put a hand on top of Trap's. "Hard things await you, my son. I only hope we have prepared you well enough."

CHAPTER 8

Reverend Drum's presence hung over the school like a putrid illness. He lurked around every corner and at the end of every path, always with a sour look of disapproval on his pink face. For the most part, he held his tongue until the O'Shannons left. He didn't have to wait long for that.

The students threw a quiet going-away party at supper on their last night, and took turns giving the O'Shannons small, handmade tokens to remember them by. Trap's normally stoic father was moved to the point of tears by the time the meal was complete. His mother wept openly throughout the entire affair. Drum stood in the corner with his hands behind him, the tiniest hint of a sneer on his carplike lips.

As the party began to wind down, Trap felt a gnawing urgency to spend a few moments alone with Maggie.

It was Maggie who suggested they go for a walk—not with words but with a casual glance toward the door. Trap looked up at his mother, who also spoke much without speaking at all.

Hummingbird nodded gently, then turned to occupy her husband's attention while Trap and Maggie slipped out together. Drum gave the young couple a sidelong eye, but Mrs. Tally swooped in to intercept him like a fluttering mother dove when a fox is too near her nest, as if she were working in concert with Trap's mother to allow the two youngsters a few moments alone together.

Trap had never been much of a talker, finding himself more at home alone in the woods than with any other human being—until Maggie Sundown came along. He talked to her more than he'd talked to anyone, and still much of their time together was spent sitting quietly.

"The Apache value silence," his mother had always told him. From what he could see, the Nez Percé thought a lot of it too. Maggie appeared to enjoy his company, but she was just as content to sit and study the earth as he was. To Trap's way of thinking, more got said between him and Maggie in an hour of near silence than most people accomplished in a whole day of wordy conversation.

The evening was crisp, with a waning half-moon that cast dark shadows along the gravel path beyond the root cellar. Once in a while, Trap could hear the patient, baritone voice of his father drifting out amid the more tentative students' voices through the kitchen door.

Maggie found a spot on the stone wall along the path and sat down among the shadows. She said nothing.

Trap sat beside her, a few inches away, and folded his hands in his lap. A million bees buzzed inside his chest.

After a time, Maggie broke the silence.

"My people, the Nimi'ipuu, are a people of the horse." Her voice was soft and throaty—almost a whisper. She turned to look at him in the scant moonlight. "I haven't seen too many horses around here."

Trap stared down at his feet, afraid he might say something foolish if he met her eye. "I used to have a nice little bay, but we had to sell them all for this move. The school owns the ones that are left—mostly cart horses."

"I miss watching the herds running together. . . ."

"That would be a beautiful sight," Trap whispered. He could only think of leaving the next day. He wanted to say more, but didn't know how. When he looked up, Maggie held a small bracelet in her hand.

"I made this from the hair of my father's finest horses. I braided in some of my own hair as well." She held it out to him. "I wish you to have it . . . to remember me when you are in Arizona." Her voice was barren of emotion, but her eyes shone bright and clear in the moonlight. "Perhaps you will find a beautiful Apache girl and have many children with her. If you do, you should throw the bracelet away so it doesn't haunt your marriage."

He took the gift and slid it over his hand, pulling it snug with the intricately braided button of hair. "Thank you," he said, his voice catching in his throat. "I would never throw anything away I received from you."

Surely this was what his father had meant when he

spoke of meeting the person who would mean more to him than anything else. He'd thought about giving something to her as well, but never would have had the courage to be the first to mention it.

He fished in his trouser pocket for a moment.

"It's not much." He held a silver coin out on the palm of his hand.

Maggie took it and held it up in the moonlight to get a good look.

"It's the O'Shannon crest. Three stars over two hunting dogs."

"What does it say around the edge?" Maggie traced the face of the coin gently with her finger.

"It's the family motto in Latin—*Under the Guidance of Valor.*"

Maggie held it up next to Trap's face. Her fingers brushed his cheek. He squirmed.

She smiled—it at once calmed him and sent his mind spinning out of control. "I will put this in my medicine bag where I keep things most important to me," she said.

Arizona seemed like an ax ready to chop off his head. Trap had little experience with such things, but felt pretty certain that girls like Maggie Sundown didn't come along more than once in a person's life. He felt like he should give her more than a silver medallion before he left. The idea that he might never see her again was unthinkable.

"Maggie . . ." he whispered.

She took the small leather bag from around her neck and slipped the coin inside. She must have moved closer to him when they exchanged gifts, because he could feel her body move with each breath.

Her thigh was warm against him through their clothes. He found it almost impossible to think, let alone speak a coherent thought.

"Maggie, I . . ." he tried again.

Drum's acid voice cut the night like a knife.

"When the lust hath conceived, it bringeth forth sin: and sin, when it is finished, bringeth forth death." Drum stepped out of the shadows beside the low roof of the root cellar.

Trap shot to his feet. Maggie stayed where she was.

"What's going on here, young Master O'Shannon?" Drum was on them in a stride.

"Nothing, sir," Trap said, upset at his own nervousness. He took a deep breath to calm himself. "I was . . . am saying good-bye to Miss Sundown."

"I'm certain you were," Drum said, raising his brow. The way his eyes slid slowly up and down over Maggie's body made Trap want to bury the man then and there. "It's a blessing I happened to need some fresh air when I did. Saved you from your own sinful nature, I believe. You had best get back inside with the party, young man. I believe it would break your father's heart if he found his son out here in near fornication with one of his students."

"Near fornication? You know that's a lie." Trap gritted his teeth and took a half step closer to the much larger man.

"Don't begin something you aren't prepared to finish, little hero." Drum smiled through a crooked sneer as if he'd won a fight already.

"I should say my good-byes to your mother." Maggie's voice came soft and steady from the shadows. "Come with me, Trap. We have nothing to be ashamed of. The

Reverend Drum came out here for some air. Let's give it to him."

"Go with her, boy. Say your good-byes," Drum spit.

"Mr. Drum." Trap refused to call him Reverend anymore. "My family and I are leaving tomorrow. I'm only sixteen, but you should remember this: My mother is Apache, which makes me half Apache."

"O'Shannon," Drum sneered. "You and your kind are no more than a boil on my rump. A trivial inconvenience, but tomorrow I'll be shed of you. Your sweet little Miss Sundown will pine away for you to be sure." He winked and shook his head back and forth behind a wry grin. "But don't you worry, son. I'll see that she is well taken care of."

Trap found himself so mad his head throbbed. Fists clenched at his sides, he stood on the balls of his feet. His voice was quiet and sharp, as merciless as a steel blade. Like his father, Trap became stone cold when he was truly angry. He didn't so much lose his temper as focus it in a single beam of white-hot fury.

"Drum," Trap hissed. He doubted Maggie could even hear him, and she was only a few feet away. "I may not be very old, but you have my word on this: If you act anything other than the complete gentleman to Maggie, I'll cut that black heart out of your worthless body and send you straight to Hell where you belong."

"Listen here, boy . . ." Drum tried to interrupt.

Trap held up his hand. His voice remained calm, but it pierced as surely as any arrow. "No, you listen to me. I'm not fooling. I leave tomorrow. If you say another word to me or Maggie, I'll kill you now, if I have to do it with my teeth."

Trap's shoulders heaved. He almost wished the big man would try something.

Instead, Drum shrugged, tossed his head like an insolent horse, and walked into the darkness.

All the anger drained from Trap's body when Maggie came up behind him and touched his arm.

Trap turned and looked at her. He wanted to tell her he would come back for her someday soon, wanted to tell her she meant more to him than anything he'd ever known. But such words didn't come easy to his lips. The notion of leaving her behind was unthinkable, but he was only a boy. What else could he do but respect his father's wishes?

"Thank you for that," Maggie whispered, moving closer to him in the chilly night air. "I don't think people often stand up to him. He looked like he believed you."

Trap let out a deep breath. The aftereffects of the run-in with Drum and the warmth of Maggie's body combined to make him feel dizzy. "I hope he believed me, because I would have killed him."

Maggie held his arm with both hands and rested her head on his shoulder.

"I know it," she whispered in his ear, her voice matter-of-fact. "And I would have helped."

CHAPTER 9

The O'Shannons' wagon was not yet past the tall oaks that skirted the gravel drive before Drum made his first sweeping edict. The students were still lined up in neat, uniformed rows from saying their good-byes. Maggie saw bad things coming in the smug grin that spread over the new superintendent's face the further the Reverend O'Shannon got from the school.

She had watched in silence as Trap climbed into the wagon behind his parents and sat facing backward on a wooden trunk. His face was stoic, but Maggie could see the pain in his eyes. Neither had spoken a word that morning. They had said their good-byes the evening before.

"Mrs. Tally," Drum barked. Fully in charge now, he set his bottom jaw after each phrase like a jowly bull-dog. Two rough men, wearing low hats and leather braces over course work shirts, stepped from the yard behind the kitchen. The taller of the two wore a set of worn Army trousers. The shorter was as stout and wide as he was tall. A thick wad of gray hair sprouted up from the collar of his threadbare woolen shirt.

"These are my associates Pugh and Foster." Drum nodded at the men. "From here forward they will act as orderlies to assure discipline and structure at all times."

"We've never had a problem with order and discipline before, Reverend." Mrs. Tally cocked her head to one side and gave the two new arrivals a quick perusal. "Are you certain the elders would approve such an expense?"

"Don't concern yourself with the elders, Mrs. Tally. That will be my job. Concern yourself with the new rules and see that the students obey them."

"New rules?"

"First," Drum said, clasping his hands behind the small of his back and stalking up and down the line of wide-eyed students. "As of this moment, any utterance of a heathen tongue will not be tolerated. God's own English is the language of learning and that is what I expect to hear."

Frank Tall Horse stood at the end of the line next to Maggie. He smiled softly and nodded his head. He often commented that the constant jabbering of the other students in their assorted languages gave him a headache.

"*Washite,*" he said under his breath. It was one of the few Sioux words he knew. "Fine by me."

Drum spun when he heard the boy speak. "What did you say, young man?" Small stones crunched under his boots as he strode across the yard.

The smile fell from Tall Horse's lips. His brown eyes went wide and he cowered under the scrutiny of the new superintendent. "I said English is fine by me, sir."

"Before that. You said something else before that." Drum's heavy face was inches away from the boy.

"I said *washite.* It means *good.*"

"Did I not just explain the rule to you regarding use of heathen tongues?"

"Yes, sir," Tall Horse whispered. His face was ashen white. "It was. . . . I mean I was. . . ."

"Do you intend to mock me?"

"No, sir." All the joy appeared to flow out of Tall Horse's normally bright face.

"He doesn't even speak Sioux," Maggie said. She could see where this was leading and it made her sick to her stomach.

"Be still," Drum snapped. "He knows well enough not to disregard my mandate only moments after I made it." He nodded to Pugh and Foster, who shuffled up on either side of Tall Horse.

"I am a fair man," Drum said, puffing himself up like the self-important adder that he was. "But I must abide by my own rules or there can be no order." He nodded again at the two men.

They each took one of the boy's arms. He did not struggle.

"This is your first offense, so I will limit your punishment to five stripes."

Maggie stepped forward. "I told you, sir. He doesn't even speak Sioux. He is happy to speak English. You don't have to do this." She knew if she spoke what was truly in her heart, Drum would only take it out on Frank.

"I said be still, young lady." Drum turned to a quivering Mrs. Tally. "Fetch me a strong switch from that willow tree yonder."

"Sir?" Mrs. Tally's mouth fell open. "You don't truly intend to . . . ?"

"Dear Lord, forgive me my thoughts about these imbeciles with whom I am forced to work," Drum muttered. "I'll get the blasted switch myself."

Foster and Pugh made Tall Horse take off his shirt, and then took him again by each arm. There was no need; he endured his whipping without a word. When Maggie took a step forward, he only gritted his teeth and shook his head to keep her back. The younger students looked on with blank eyes. This was not the first time many of them had seen cruelty, only the first time they'd seen it at the school.

Drum could barely contain his smile as he administered the cruel lashes. When he finished, Drum dismissed the group to return to morning classes. He pitched the offending switch unceremoniously on the ground at his feet and turned a snide face to Maggie while he straightened his frock coat and tie.

"I'll see you in my office at three P.M. sharp," he said. The fire in his eyes from the enjoyment of meting out Tall Horse's punishment had turned to a lecherous glow. "I admire your spirit, young lady. I won't put up with it, but I admire it nonetheless."

Maggie knew her own limits. It would take more than Drum's pitiful orderlies to hold her. There were certain things she would never stand for. But Drum had his limits as well—he'd shown that.

She helped a tight-lipped Frank Tall Horse back inside the school, and wondered if she would be alive by nightfall.

CHAPTER 10

A thin gash of yellow light cut the dark hallway from the door to Reverend Drum's office. Maggie stood outside until she heard the downstairs clock chime three. She steeled herself for what was sure to await her and put her hand on the knob. She was not afraid to die. A month ago, she would have welcomed the thought, but since she'd met Trap O'Shannon and seen there was still something right with the world, she was not ready to rush into death either.

The door creaked when she pushed it open and stepped inside. Drum sat at his desk, a pair of black-rimmed glasses on the end of his nose. He glanced up when he heard her and gave a cursory nod to one of the high-backed chairs in front of him before going back to his reading.

He ignored her for some time. The shuffling of papers and the sound of his heavy, nasal breathing were the only sounds in the room.

When he finished, Drum closed the folder of papers in front of him. An artificial smile flashed across his face. He came around to sit on the edge of the desk, peeling off his wire glasses with thick fingers. His knees hovered only inches away from her.

"I've been reading your file," he said as if to gloat.

Maggie sat motionless, staring at the floor.

"You know that it can only help you to cooperate with me." He licked his lips.

This Maggie understood, but she pretended like she didn't. "I *am* cooperating with you, Reverend. All the students have always cooperated here at the school."

Drum rubbed his face and changed tacks. "Miss Sundown, you haven't been here for two weeks and have been branded as a troublemaker already." He nodded toward the papers on the desk at his side. "Your file has a complete report and affidavit drawn up by the delivery boys from Van Zandt's Creamery."

Maggie didn't know what an affidavit was, but if the wicked boys from Van Zandt's Creamery wrote it, it couldn't be any good.

He continued. "I am not sure what Reverend O'Shannon intended to do about it, but my course appears to be clear. You assaulted local townsfolk. We can't stand for that, can we?"

"They chased me into the cellar," Maggie said, knowing it wouldn't make any difference.

Drum shook his head. "I have to go by the facts, young lady, not your fanciful stories." He inched to the edge of the desk. He was close enough now that she could smell the foul smell of the sausages he'd eaten for lunch on his breath. "I should tell you, the Van Zandts would see you hang."

He studied her face for a reaction. She gave him none so he plowed ahead. "I could help you," he said. "I believe you would find me as powerful as I find you alluring."

"I do not understand what that word means," Maggie lied. She'd never heard *alluring* before, but she understood all too well.

He chuckled, obviously thinking she was falling under his spell. His voice was low and throaty. "It means I am attracted to you. I find you pleasant to look at."

He reached to touch her hair. Maggie's stomach churned, but she sat completely still while his clumsy fingers slid slowly, lecherously down her cheek. When they were near enough to her mouth that she knew she couldn't miss, she turned and sank her teeth deep into the flesh at the base of the reverend's thumb and hung on.

Drum tried to jerk the hand back, erupting in a fearsome growl. He clubbed Maggie brutally in the temple with his free fist, hitting her at least three times before the skin on his thumb gave way.

Stunned, Maggie slumped to the floor. Her head reeled and the room spun around her. She tasted blood and flesh in her mouth. It took her a moment to realize it was Drum's. She spat out the chunk of meat in disgust and crawled backward across the floor. If she could only make it to the door . . .

The reverend advanced on her. His hungry look had turned to a blaze of pure hatred. Grabbing her by both shoulders with powerful hands, he hauled her up to face him.

"I'll see you do worse than hang, you deceitful little bitch. . . ."

Maggie spit more blood—his blood—in his face and drove a knee hard into his groin.

He groaned, but his grip held firm and he pulled her to him, pinning her arms by her side. He kissed her brutally on the mouth, stifling the scream that hung there with the press of his cold lips.

Mrs. Tally opened the door and stepped inside.

"Reverend, I . . ." Her mouth hung open as she took in the scene in front of her.

Drum released his hold and Maggie fell to the floor, panting. He wiped the blood from his face with his good hand and made a feeble attempt to straighten his clothes.

"I . . . What happened, child? Reverend Drum, you're bleeding. What's the matter with your hand?" Mrs. Tally's face was ashen white.

Maggie took the opportunity to scramble to her feet and stand behind the head matron.

"Mrs. Tally, take this young trollop out of my sight. She still has a long way to go before she is anywhere near civilized," Drum fumed. "We must yet kill everything in her that is Indian. We'll begin with that long mop of unruly hair. See that it's cut to a respectable length at once." He took a length of white cloth from his desk drawer and began to wrap his hand. "Bring them around to God and away from their heathen ways of savagery."

Mrs. Tally bit her lip and turned to go. Maggie could feel the woman's heavy shoulders trembling next to her.

"I'll personally inspect the haircut tomorrow morning," he said through clenched teeth. "And Mrs. Tally . . ."

"Reverend?" She stopped in her tracks but didn't turn around. She swallowed hard.

His voice was acid and venomous. "If you ever enter my office without knocking again, I'll have Pugh and Foster escort you off the grounds so fast your head will spin."

CHAPTER 11

The train out of Lebanon didn't leave until after ten in the morning. It was a great, leaking beast that blew off more steam than it used to turn its massive wheels and lumbered along at a mind-numbing pace that tore a hole in Trap's nerves.

The hole in the boy's gut grew deeper with every slow, excruciating mile the rattling train took him from Maggie Sundown.

By the time they reached Carthage, the engine had about boiled dry and had to stop and take on water. It was early evening and the sun hung low on the western horizon.

A cloud of mosquitoes and biting gnats pestered a gray Brahma bull across the split-oak fence. Trap squatted next to the bottom rail looking alternately at the dusty ground and the long line of trees to the north—back toward the school. He shooed a gnat out of his face. Behind him, the train vented a gasp of steam and covered the crunch of his mother's footsteps until she was almost on top of him.

"I can see you are badly troubled, Denihii." She called him by the Apache nickname she'd given him when he was a small boy. It meant Tracker.

"I am fine, Mother." He knew she didn't believe him.

Hummingbird sighed and knelt on the ground next to her son. Trap would always remember that though his mother was the wife of a reputable Presbyterian minister and wore decent, respectable dresses, she never hesitated to sit on the ground.

"It is a good thing to respect your father," she began, studying a blade of broad grass. "But when your heart tells you something is good, there are times you must follow what it says."

Trap looked up at her. "I understand you want to be with your people."

Hummingbird smiled. "Trap, I left the Chiricahua when I was yet a girl. You and your father are my people. I go to Arizona for the same reason you do—to honor your father."

"But he said you . . ."

She put up her hand. "It will be good to see my relatives. But I was not the one that asked him to go. The church was. He will not admit it, but there are some on the board of directors—as well as in the Army—who do not approve of the way your father ran White Oak. I've heard them say he used too soft a hand." She cast her eyes down at the grass again. "Likely because of you and me."

It had always been her custom to speak frankly with her son, but she'd never spoken so openly to him about his father. "The church asked him to go to Arizona to get him out of the way."

"I didn't know." Trap found it a difficult thing to grow up—to learn that his father had a bit of an ego.

The conductor called for all to board, and the engine vented more steam in preparation to move.

Trap shook his head as if he could shake off his thoughts. "I didn't know," he repeated himself.

"He wouldn't want you to." Hummingbird let Trap help her to her feet. She took his hand and pressed a wad of money into it.

"What is this?" He stood with her beside him.

"In the world of the whites a man should always have at least a small amount of money. You are all grown up now. So much like your father—and yet your own man . . ."

The conductor called again, giving them an impatient glare.

"Walk with me to the train," she said, still holding his hand. "I have a little more to say. People will tell you that you must choose between your Apache and your white blood. Do not listen to them. Choose only the good from each. My forebears were tenacious and often ferocious people. Though it is not always evident, your father is much the same if he has to be. . . . As you will soon learn, both Indians and whites can be cruel beyond belief."

By the time they reached the train Trap was speechless. He'd never had a need for money, and couldn't understand why he would need any now. He stared down at the wad of bills in his hand.

"It is not much," Hummingbird said. "But if you are careful, you will have enough to buy a good horse and a few other things you may need."

She took a small bundle of red cloth from under the smock she wore to protect her dress and placed it in Trap's hand on top of the money.

"This belonged to my father." She stepped up onto the train so she was looking down at him. A shrill whistle split the air as the huge arms on the steam engine sprang to life and jerked at the metal wheels.

Trap unrolled the cloth to find a gleaming, bone-handled hunting knife.

"It is a hard world, my son. I wish I could give you more, but it has always been my experience that wits are your best weapons—and you have plenty of those."

She stayed in the doorway, blocking Trap's path while the train began to pick up speed. She was kicking him out of the nest. A warm breeze tugged at a stray lock of hair over her high forehead. She smiled softly while she looked at him.

Trap moved along at a fast walk, shaking his head.

The train picked up speed in earnest now. Hummingbird reached out with a slender hand and touched Trap's outstretched fingers. "I'll talk to your father," she said. She had to shout as the train began to move faster than Trap could walk. "I was foolish to let you come this far. Go back and get that girl, Denihii. In the future, when you see that something is right, do not wait this long to do it."

CHAPTER 12

"It's nothing short of dreadful," Mrs. Tally sniffed. "The plight of womanhood in general, I mean to say." She stood behind a stoic Maggie, a pair of shears poised over the girl's head. "Understand, dear, that I am loath to speak out against the superintendent, but I see no reason to cut this beautiful hair except his spite for your rebuff."

Maggie sat quietly, her hands folded in her lap, her eyes shut. She could hear the metal blades whisper as they came together. She felt the gossamer softness of each lock of hair as it fell down her shoulders and gently brushed her arms on the way to the floor.

Mrs. Tally spoke through her tears as she cut. "I mean to say, I know it's the way the Good Lord made us. We are after all the weaker sex—born to a life of servitude, the bearing of babies, and the pleasures of wicked men." She stomped her foot. Maggie could hear her gritting her teeth. "But sometimes, when I meet a man like Drum, I wish I could take these snips and do some quick surgery."

She stepped back and wiped her nose with the back of her sleeve, a sure sign the normally fastidious woman was nearing a complete breakdown. "Still," she sighed. "We have to be reasonable as women and know our own limitations. Sometimes it's better to give in a little rather than suffer. What I mean to say is, if something is inevitable, perhaps one should make the best of it to survive the situation." The poor woman's face was drawn, and looked ten years older than it had the day before.

Maggie said nothing.

Mrs. Tally handed her a small mirror. "There now, I left it over your ears. You are still as lovely as ever. Perhaps he will leave you alone—now he knows I'm on to his game."

"You know that will never happen," Maggie said. "I've made him angry. Cutting my hair is but a small thing compared to what he plans to do with me. This no longer has anything to do with his pleasure; it is about resentment."

Mrs. Tally flashed a sorrowful smile. "It most usually is, my dear. It most usually is."

"I will kill him when he tries to touch me again."

"Oh, I don't doubt it, child. But I am just as certain the people in town will hang you for your trouble. The sad truth is. . . ." Mrs. Tally wrung her hands and stared at the floor, biting on her bottom lip. "What I mean to say is, if you were to let him . . . have his way, he might hurt you some in the process—but if you fight him, he'll kill you for sure." She suddenly looked up, new tears welling in her weary eyes. "I fear your options are but few and far between."

Maggie picked up the small mirror and looked at

her new hair. It made her face look bigger, maybe a little older—but not as old as she felt. Fourteen was not so young in the great scheme of things. Back in the Wallowa she would likely have been married very soon.

"Options," she whispered to herself. The sound was so soft it must have sounded like a sigh to Mrs. Tally.

There was another option. She could run.

CHAPTER 13

Maggie Sundown began to plan her escape the day she'd first set foot on the grounds of the White Oak Indian Academy. She'd stashed a water jug and a small carving knife she'd stolen from the kitchen under her bed. Her geography textbooks contained decent maps, and she had spent several evenings gazing at the angled lines that represented the mountains and rivers of her beloved Wallowa Valley. One map in particular showed hash marks representing railroads and a detailed rendition of the entire United States over a two-page spread. She'd torn out both pages, folded them carefully, and put them in the small poke with her food—some dried beef and two small jars of strawberry jam sealed with wax. The jam was sweet, and she reckoned a spoonful would keep her going for some time on the trail.

She decided to leave during the evening meal, fearing that if she waited until after dark, Drum might call her to his study again before she could get away.

The older girls took turns helping in the kitchen. It wasn't Maggie's turn, but she volunteered to trade with a timid Cheyenne girl to give her a little extra time out from under the headmaster's nose.

Drum's eyes burned at her constantly throughout the entire meal. Her stomach knotted at the thought of food, but she knew she would soon need all her strength. When she'd cleaned every last morsel of chicken from her plate, she carried it to the kitchen, retrieved her meager supplies, and walked straight out the back door.

Gray dusk had settled over the grounds by the time she made it down the little path that led to the stables. Cool air pinked Maggie's cheeks. Gut-wrenching tension sent a trickle of sweat down the small of her back, and she looked behind her in spite of herself. The headmaster was nowhere to be seen. Mrs. Tally was in the dining hall with the other students. If she noticed Maggie's absence, she wouldn't be likely to say anything.

Pugh and Foster had disappeared into the root cellar before supper. There was a supply of medicinal liquor in there that would keep them busy for some time.

Maggie knew she'd be easier to track on horseback, but she needed to get as far away from the school as she could in a night's time. Most of the animals in the barn were heavy draft types, meant for pulling one of the school wagons or plows. The choice of which one to take was easy.

Drum's brown Thoroughbred nickered softly when she stepped into the stall. It was a leggy horse with a flowing mane and long head. Built for speed, but unlikely to have the endurance for long days on the trail like the spotted ponies of the Nimi'ipuu, the gelding had the lean look of a racehorse. For the time being at least, a racehorse was just what she wanted.

She decided to saddle in the cramped stall, in case anyone happened to come in. Drum rode a light plantation saddle with no horn, a padded leather seat, and metal stirrups. It was not meant for strenuous cross-country riding, but it looked comfortable enough. Small brass D rings behind the low cantle enabled her to tie on an extra saddle blanket rolled to contain her poke of gear. The Thoroughbred turned its head and sniffed Maggie's arm as she finished tightening the girth strap. She hummed softly, and the big animal released a rumbling sigh.

Once she'd saddled the horse, Maggie slipped out of the blue-gray uniform skirt and picked up the fawn-colored skirt she'd had on the day she'd come to the school. It was lighter, but made with a fuller cut so she could straddle a horse without exposing most of her legs as she rode. She kept the gray kersey uniform blouse, but left the tail out and unbuttoned the top two buttons so it hung open at the collar. She fastened a wide leather belt around her waist and tucked the hunting knife in next to her side. Untucked, the blouse was just long enough to cover the wooden handle.

The thrum of deep voices at the outer door sent Maggie's hand to the handle of her knife. She ducked her head behind the horse and held her breath. Slowly, the voices faded as the speakers moved away.

Maggie swallowed hard. She couldn't stay in the stall much longer without being seen. She reached over the door and moved the metal latch. Her hand trembled and she took a deep breath to calm herself. If she could only make it out to the trees, she knew she could disappear in an instant.

Poking her head around the stall door, she chanced a look up and down the dim alleyway of the barn. She led the gelding out, turned her back to the door, and put a small foot in the stirrup to climb into the saddle.

A heavy crunch of gravel behind her sent a cold chill up Maggie's spine. Her throat tightened. Reins in one hand and the stirrup leather in the other, she made ready to spring aboard the horse and run for it.

"*Washite,*" a soft voice said from the doorway. It was Frank Tall Horse. "I'm glad you're getting away from here."

Maggie gave a sigh of relief and turned to face him, the reins still in her left hand. The gelding seemed to feel her mood change, and hung its head to sniff the ground. Lips gave off loud pops as the horse nibbled at the bits of hay that littered the stable floor.

"You could go too," she said. "You are old enough to make it away from this place." It was a difficult thing, leaving the tenderhearted boy behind.

Frank toed the dirt. "No. I got nowhere else to go. I been at this school nearly my whole life. I'd probably get lost and wander into all kinds of trouble."

Tall Horse stepped closer and rubbed the gelding's long neck. "Thank you for trying to help me this morning."

"You would have done the same for me."

"I'd like to think so," he said. "But I don't know. I believe you are braver than me." He smiled at her with deep brown eyes. "Watch yourself, Maggie Sundown. There are people out there just as bad as the reverend—maybe worse."

Maggie gave a solemn nod. "I know." She took the map from her breast pocket and unfolded it. There was just enough light to make out the lines. "Am I right that we are here?"

The boy studied the map for a moment, then nodded. "This is Lebanon and this is us. It doesn't show you much of what else is out there—only the big rivers and some of the mountains." He pointed to the area south and a little west of them, just north of Texas. "They call this Indian Territory, but from what I hear, it's mostly outlaws and cutthroats. I'd steer well clear of it if it was me."

Maggie shrugged that off. She tapped the map with the tip of her finger. "I am told the Nimi'ipuu, my people, are imprisoned somewhere in Kansas. That is this place?"

Tall Horse smiled. "That's what I have heard. But you can't fool me." He tapped the map on the outline of Arizona. "You are going here."

He clasped both hands and held them at waist level in front of him to give her a step up into the saddle.

"Good-bye, Frank Tall Horse of the Ogallala Sioux. You are a good Indian, do not forget that. Perhaps we will meet again," Maggie whispered, knowing the chances were unlikely.

"Good-bye." Tall Horse patted the horse on the

shoulder and handed Maggie the reins. "You are a good human being. Do not forget *that.* Say hello to my friend for me when you see him. I hope I can meet your children someday."

The road away from the Indian school led directly south, and Maggie kept to it for the first hour. Though the moon waned to less than half, the road was bumpy and rife with low branches and sinkholes. She held the powerful horse to a gentle lope for several minutes, fighting the urge to gallop until it was worn completely out or worse.

She calculated she had about nine hours until the sun rose, and she intended to use every minute of it.

Lamplights from small farmhouses flickered every few miles in the trees along the roadway and kept her moving forward. Dogs barked here and there, but none came after her. As long as she was around people, she would be in danger. The further south she got, the less of a problem that would be. According to her map, the city of Springfield lay somewhere to the southwest, but she intended to stay well away from there.

The big gelding proved to be tireless as long as she kept him pulled back in the easy, ground-eating lope. She pointed south until the lamplights were spaced further apart and she felt she was well past town. When she found a stream she took to it, hoping to throw off any would-be pursuers until she could make more distance. Twice, she wasted precious minutes to double back on her own trail, working her way through a fetid swamp, full of dark shadows and hanging vines as big around as her wrist. The terrain was anything but flat, and she made much slower progress than she'd hoped. She could only hope the thick hardwood forests and rocky creeks slowed Drum as well.

Two hours before daylight, Maggie began to look for a place to hide. She hadn't seen a house for some time, but wanted to be well entrenched before daybreak and out of the eyes of any wandering travelers who might be able to help Drum when he did come looking.

Thoughts of the wicked man sent her hand to the knife at her side. She wished for a gun, but consoled herself that it was better to play the rabbit than the wolf for the time being. If she could hide long enough, perhaps Drum would give up and she could make it to this place called Arizona.

CHAPTER 14

Trap figured the train had gone a little over a hundred miles to reach the water stop outside of Carthage. The tracks did a fair amount of snaking back and forth through the hills, so he could cut off a third of that distance if he took a more direct route. A night and a day of hard riding could get him back.

As usual, Trap spent little time planning for the future. He had no idea what he would say when he reached White Oak, but figured his father would be proud of him for letting the Good Lord take care of the morrow. He'd decide what to do when he got there.

To get there at all, he had to buy a horse. Though he was almost seventeen and comfortable enough in the saddle, he'd never had occasion to buy much of anything, let alone something as important as a horse. He knew a good one when he saw it, and hoped the money his mother had given him would be enough.

The livery stable was located about a block from the water tower across the tracks from Carthage proper. It was a low structure, cobbled together of rough-hewn lumber and rusty tin. A low sun shone through a multitude of old nail holes on the large open door, proving that the forlorn building was little more than a pile of previously used scrap.

Trap stopped halfway there and divided his bankroll into three small stacks. He put one in his vest pocket, a second in his front trouser pocket with his jackknife, and the rest he slipped inside the belly of his shirt. He knew enough to be sure there would be some bargaining involved in any horse trade, and didn't want to be in a position where he played his entire hand at once.

When he started walking again, he saw a boy about his age come out the double doors and dip two wooden buckets in the long water trough out front under the eaves. Trap waved at him. The boy looked up while he pushed the buckets down in the water and let them fill. He spit and turned his head to wipe his mouth on his shoulder. A grimy spot on his pale yellow shirt showed this was a regular habit.

"Help you?" the boy said, hoisting the brimming buckets. He was hatless, blond, and several inches taller than Trap.

"I was hopin' to buy a horse," Trap said. He came up beside the trough. "Want a hand with one of those?"

The boy shook his head. "Nope. I'd lose my balance and keel over if you took one." He stuck out his chin to point toward the doors. "My uncle's inside pouring oats while I do the waterin'. He's the man you'd wanta talk to about a horse."

Inside, the livery was as spotless as a horse barn

could be. The wide alleyway was clean and uncluttered. The warm, comfortable smell of fresh hay and saddle soap hung in the cool shadows. Well-groomed animals stuck contented noses out of nearly every stall. The interior was in all ways the opposite of what the outside of the place looked to be.

A row of polished saddles on pegs along the far wall reminded Trap that he'd not only have to buy a horse, but tack as well. He chewed the inside of his jaw and tried to look like he knew what he was doing. The boy went to fetch his uncle from a back stall.

"What can I do for you, lad?" A smiling man strode forward on a wooden leg. He wiped his hands on a towel he had stuck in his belt and reached to shake Trap's hand. "Nathan Bowdecker. I'm the proprietor hereabouts."

"Trap O'Shannon." He shook the offered hand. It seemed honest enough—if a person could tell that sort of thing from a handshake. "I need to buy a horse." He tried to keep his voice from sounding urgent.

Bowdecker rubbed his chin in thought. He looked Trap over with deep-set eyes. "It's awful late," he finally said. "How'd you get here?"

"Train," Trap said simply.

"You James O'Shannon's boy?"

Trap nodded. He wasn't surprised. His father often traveled to do a little preaching. It helped tone down his otherwise restless nature. "Yessir."

"He's a fine man, your pa," Bowdecker said. "I've heard him go to expoundin' a time or two. I'm a Lutheran myself, but I do enjoy hearing the good word of God from you Presbyterians once in a great while." His gaze narrowed. "It don't add up, James O'Shannon's boy running around Missouri this time of an evenin' looking to purchase hisself a horse. You're either running from somethin' or to somethin'. . . ."

Nathan Bowdecker had the forthright look of a man who would see straight through a lie, so Trap told him the whole story, including his observations of Drum.

"Sounds like you're on a mission," Bowdecker said when Trap finished. "I reckon a man oughta follow his gut." He rubbed his face in thought, then tapped his wooden leg. "My gut told me to go to sea on a whalin' ship when I was still a lad. Lost my leg, but I saw things I'd never seen otherwise. I reckon it was worth the price. . . . Let's get our business done then so you can be on your way. I got just the mount for you."

Mr. Bowdecker said he felt duty-bound to supply Trap with a sound animal, capable of making it all the way to Arizona.

"I ain't runnin' any charity ward here." Bowdecker smiled as he led out the short-coupled black. The gelding had a round spot at the point of its croup and a shock of white hair tucked into the thick black tail. "Skunk here will do you a good service, but he won't come cheap."

When he heard the price, Trap sucked in air through the corner of his mouth like he'd seen his father do when negotiating the price of mutton.

"I don't feel right about sellin' you anything less," Bowdecker said. "The Comanche are still hittin' it pretty good down Texas way and the trail between

here and Arizona is chockablock full of outlaws and
bandits. A man's horse is sometimes the onliest way out
of a pickle—particularly a half-Apache Presbyterian
who doesn't even appear to pack a pistol."

"Is that your bottom dollar?" Trap's heart sank as
he figured out how little money he'd have left over.
He'd have to live off the land most of the way to
Arizona—and without a rifle, that would be a pretty
tall order.

Bowdecker nodded. "Son, take a lesson from the
Greeks; never trust a man who is willin' to let you
have a horse for less than market value. It's a good
bet such a beast has a bowed tendon or some other
such malady—or at the very least is ornery as all get-
out." He leaned in close to Trap. "Tell you what I'll
do. You take ol' Skunk off my hands and I'll throw in
all the tack as a gift for the service your pa did for
this little part of God's vineyard. Those Greeks never
said a word about a gift saddle."

"He handles good?" Trap already had his mind
made up to take the deal.

Bowdecker gave him the lead. "Clamber on up
and give him a try. You'll find none better in all of
Missouri for what you have in mind."

It was nearly dark by the time Trap paid the liveryman his price and finished tacking up. He had nothing in the way of supplies, so it didn't take him long
to pack. The kind-hearted liveryman gave him a
small coffee sack with some biscuits and a battered
canteen full of water. Along with the money, Trap
gave Bowdecker his heartfelt thanks.

Skunk had a remarkably smooth gait for such short legs. He seemed to sense the urgency Trap felt to get back to Maggie, and covered the ground with a vengeance. Five minutes away from the livery, the stout little horse settled into a five-beat trot so smooth, Trap took a drink from the canteen and didn't spill a drop.

He was dog-tired, but that didn't matter. Maggie was ahead—at White Oak. He couldn't wait to see her, to see the look on her beautiful face when he rode up and finally told her how he felt.

Chapter 15

The Right Reverend Tobias Drum drew back and slapped Mrs. Tally across her round face. He wanted to punch her, but there were too many witnesses. A slap would be easier to explain away. The heavy woman staggered, swayed, and then fell back on her broad rump with a loud *whoompf*. Her face reddened, but it was not as red as Drum's.

"You were fully aware she was going, weren't you?" the headmaster raged. He towered over the pitiful woman, contemplating how good it would feel to give her a swift boot to her heaving belly. "You let her slip away to make me look foolish."

Mrs. Tally gulped for air trying to catch her wind. A river of tears poured down her cheeks. She could only shake her head.

Drum waved her off in disgust. She was too stupid to draw breath. A useless breather, that's what she was, a pure waste of good air. She contributed little to society but snivels and weakness.

He turned his attention to the red-eyed duo of Foster and Pugh. Both reeked like a whiskey keg.

"And look at you two," Drum spit. His voice shook. Dark eyes looked as though they could melt stone. "The one and only reason I hired you two idiots is to keep this sort of thing from happening."

Pugh opened his mouth to speak, but Drum raised his fist and gave it a vehement shake. "Do yourself a favor and keep quiet while you leave the grounds. I'll not have buffoons in my employ."

The useless breathers taken care of, Drum turned his attention to the problem at hand. He couldn't let the girl escape unpunished. She'd taken his horse, but worse than that, she'd usurped his authority. The Army and the church would surely look down on a man who couldn't even keep fourteen-year-old Indian children in custody.

Drum knew he'd have to follow her, catch her, and teach her a lesson she'd not soon forget—a lesson he'd enjoy teaching very much.

Van Zandt's Creamery wagon clattered up the drive, a sullen Cleveland bay mare in the traces. The boy driving it had an equally sullen look. A yellow bruise healed slowly in front of his left ear. A brindle hound slouched on the wooden seat beside him, lips pulled back in a smiling half snarl.

Drum nodded to himself. This was perfect.

"Does that dog know how to track?" Drum asked when the wagon came closer.

"It do at that," the boy said. "Toot can trail anything livin'."

"How about Indian girls?"

"Injun gals got enough stink to 'em, I reckon just about any old dog could trail one," the boy said with a grin. He knew most of the children surrounding Mrs. Tally could understand everything he said. "Why, you got one that's escaped on you?"

Drum nodded. "I do. What's your name?"

"Harry Van Zandt."

"That's what I thought," Drum said. He walked up to the wagon, ignoring the growling hound. "The girl who's gone missing is the same one who's responsible for the bruise on your face."

Harry rubbed his ear and took a deep breath. His face grew dark and began to resemble his snarling dog. "The O'Shannon runt done this to me, then slipped outta here before I could get even with him."

Drum raised an eyebrow. "O'Shannon may have done it, but he did it for the girl. And now she's run off with my horse. I'll be putting up a hundred-dollar bounty to those who ride with me. . . ."

"And help bring her back?" Van Zandt finished the sentence. His eyes sparkled at the mention of such a large sum of money.

Drum shrugged. "Let's just see how it turns out. She's a fighter—and she has stolen a horse. I'm not sure she'll let us bring her back. Some around here might say hanging's too good for the likes of her."

Harry's scowl blossomed into a full-face grin. Even the dog appeared to glow with added enthusiasm.

"I'll go get my pa. He's the best hunter you ever laid your eyes across. Toot can track with the best of 'em, but Pa's dog, Zip, he's got a mean streak, I'm here to tell you. Pa won't let us bring ol' Zip on our rounds on account of he hates redskins with a purple passion. He'd chew these young nits to pieces in no time." The Van Zandt boy giggled. "When ol' Zip catches the little tart, he'll rip her to bloody red shreds."

Drum heard Mrs. Tally gasp behind him, but she said nothing. The pathetic woman was too weak to make any sort of stand against him. At least the Nez Percé girl was a fighter.

"Very well," he said to Harry Van Zandt. "You go get your father and his mean dog, Zip. We'll leave in two hours time. She's a wily one, this Sundown girl. Be prepared to spend a night on the trail."

A string of drool dripped from the brindle dog's mouth. She growled and licked her lips in anticipation.

CHAPTER 16

Trap had covered more than half the ground he needed to by the time the sun crested the line of green-topped hickory and smaller ash trees on a tumbled line of low hills to the east. Bolstered by the warmth of the rising sun, fatigue settled around him shortly after dawn. Every few steps Skunk's smooth gait rocked Trap to sleep. Dreams of Maggie jerked him awake. Each time, the little gelding pushed on in the direction it was pointed.

Trap followed the train tracks some, cut through a newly planted field of black soil, then moved to a brushy trail along a river he didn't know the name of by the time the sun was full up.

Shaking off the weariness, he thought of Maggie trapped at the school with Reverend Drum. Dread and worry chased away the thought of sleep. He took a biscuit from the coffee sack tied to his saddle horn, eating while he rode to make better time.

Half an hour later, the heat of the day and the

food in his belly sent another wave of sleep rolling over him.

It was too powerful to fight and he lolled, relaxed in the saddle, falling forward when the gelding stopped dead in the trail. He grabbed a handful of mane to keep from tumbling into a locust bush. His eyes snapped open and when his vision cleared, he saw a muscular blue roan facing him, sniffing noses with Skunk.

A sleeping boy about Trap's age sat astraddle the new horse, his wide-brimmed hat thrown against a leather stampede string behind broad shoulders. He wore an ivory-handled revolver on his hip. His fancy white shirt was covered with dust. Sweat rendered it almost transparent.

Trap cleared his throat and the boy clutched at the saddle horn, jerking awake.

"Jeez-o'-Pete!" he said, rubbing his eyes. "How long you been sittin' there starin' at me? It ain't po-lite."

Trap grinned. "Wouldn't know," he said. "I only just woke up myself."

The boy chuckled and settled the hat back on his head. He urged his roan up next to Skunk and reached a big hand across the pommel of his saddle. "In that case, I'm Clay Madsen hailin' from Bastrop, Texas. Glad to meet you."

Trap shook the offered hand. "Trap O'Shannon."

Madsen threw a quick glance over his shoulder before he turned his attention back to Trap. "You don't look Irish."

"O'Shannon is Scots-Irish."

"You don't look Scots either," Madsen said, looking behind him again.

Trap saw no reason to start explaining his heritage to everyone he met on the trail. He didn't have time to sit and jabber the morning away, so he picked up the reins to take his leave.

"Well," he said. "It looks like you're waiting for somebody. Guess I'll just push on."

The other boy shrugged and cocked back his hat with a knuckle. "I ain't waitin' for no one," he said, casting another glance over a muscular shoulder. He brought the blue roan up beside Trap so they faced the same direction. "Mind if I ride along with you for a little spell? I could use a speck of friendly conversation."

"I reckon I'm friendly enough," Trap said. "But I'm not much of a talker."

"Perfect." Madsen gave him a wide grin. "You're just the sort of feller I like to converse with."

Trap picked up the pace and Clay Madsen matched it with ease. With the sun higher in the sky, the day grew warm and sticky. Moisture hung heavy in the hot air, and felt thick enough to drown anyone who took in a full breath.

The talkative Texan had the relaxed yet supremely confident air of a man three times his age. He spoke the miles away as the two picked their way through hardwood forests and loped through knee-high grass along lush floodplains. Even the blue roan, who must surely have heard them all before, cocked an inquisitive ear back to listen to Madsen's stories.

The Texan recounted that he'd left his father's ranch in south central Texas three months earlier to strike out for adventure and fortune on his own. In gritty detail, he described how he'd wiled away the last few weeks with a pretty young whore in St. Joe, who'd befriended him without charging a cent for her time.

Trap never considered himself a prude, but all Clay's talk of drinking, gambling, and half-naked women needled at his conscience. His father would have had him reciting Scripture until his tongue fell off.

The most bothersome fact was that he found Madsen's stories interesting. The way the boy told them made Trap feel as if he was being trusted with a family confidence.

"Her name was Vera," Clay said as their horses lugged up the crest of a red clay embankment. The going was steep, but he spoke on without any concern. He was a superb horseman and rode as an extension of the handsome blue roan. "Course, that was her given name. I called her Popper."

Trap shook his head. He didn't really think he should hear why anyone would give a nickname like Popper to a whore.

Clay gave him no notice and pushed ahead, twirling the end of his reins absentmindedly as he spoke. "Called her that on account of the way she was always a-poppin' her knuckles and what not."

Trap relaxed a notch. That wasn't so bad.

"Sometimes she'd have me give her a big squeeze around the middle, like a bear hug. Her spine would pop like a row of dominoes clinkin' over." Madsen leaned over in the saddle across the gap between the two riders. He raised dark eyebrows under the brim of his hat and spoke in a hushed tone. "Once in a while, she even had me tug on her little ol' toes and give each of them a pop." He grinned at Trap. "You ever hear of such a thing?" He sighed, looking away. "She had danged fine toes too, like peas in a pod. . . ." His voice trailed off.

"Why didn't you stay with her?" Trap heard himself ask. His mouth felt dry and he found himself pondering on Maggie's toes. He could still picture the tiny impressions they made from the first time he'd tracked her to the root cellar. As a student of tracking, if there was one thing Trap noticed, it was feet. Now that he thought of it, Maggie Sundown had some danged pretty toes herself.

Madsen interrupted his thoughts.

"A no-account son-of-a-bitch gambler named Haywood."

"What?" Trap snapped out of his reverie over the details of Maggie's body.

"You asked why I didn't stay with Popper. It was that sorry pimp gambler of hers named Haywood. He reckoned I owed him money even if she decided not to charge a handsome young feller like myself. I may be long on charm when it comes to the womenfolk." Clay winked. "But I don't have two shinplasters to rub together. I coulda taken the bucktoothed bastard in a fair fight, but I knew he'd force my hand. Be a hell of a poor start if I had to go and kill somebody before I was gone from the home place three months."

"That's good thinking," Trap agreed, but his mind was elsewhere.

They topped a hill overlooking a valley choked with

tall grass. A swift creek wound its way through groves of pecans and other hardwoods. They were still a good thirty miles away from the school.

A glint of steel and movement a scant half mile to the north caught his eye. It was late afternoon and the sun was behind them, casting long shadows to the fore. Trap figured he and Madsen were all but invisible to the four approaching riders with the sun in their eyes.

Something about the lead rider—something he couldn't put his finger on—made Trap pause.

"I need to get closer," he muttered under his breath. Thoughts of Maggie's toes still lingered, giving the boy a warm knot, low in his belly.

"It ain't Haywood," Madsen said. "Not unless he's lost, comin' from that direction." He took a brass spyglass out of his saddlebag and held it up to his eye. "I don't recognize any of them. But them dogs sure look mean. We best give them a wide berth." He passed the telescope to Trap.

O'Shannon caught his breath when he moved the metal tubes into focus. The only reason Tobias Drum would ride this far south with a group of hard cases like the Van Zandts and their vicious dogs was to hunt someone who'd left without permission. The only person he knew with enough guts to run away from the school was Maggie Sundown.

The two boys backed down the hill and watched Drum and his men move methodically through the groves of nut trees. One of the striped dogs kept his nose to the ground and tracked, the other, the bigger one, sniffed the air. Even from a distance, Trap could see the animal was a mean one, capable of tearing an unarmed man to shreds.

It took an hour for Drum and his group to move far enough away that Trap considered it safe to approach the trail below.

Trap dismounted and looped Skunk's reins around a low limb of scrub oak. Clay remained in the saddle, keeping watch.

"This Indian girl you're looking for," Madsen said. "If she knew you were comin' back for her, why'd she take to the woods like this?"

Trap knelt and touched the ground, studying the tracks left by the Drum and the others. A fifth set of tracks caught his attention. Most of the hoofprints had been walked over by the others, but a few were still visible.

"Drum must have forced her hand after I left." Trap didn't think he'd ever be able to talk about Maggie with the same easy detail Clay used to speak about women. He tapped the loose soil with his fingers. "I'm betting this is her horse. It's dragging its toes like it's getting tired. She'd likely ran it a good ways before she got here. The way it's movin', I'd say it's picked up a stone in the forefoot."

Trap stood and led Skunk toward the shallow stream. "She would have dismounted and gotten the stone out."

"This Maggie girl must know her horses," Madsen said. He threw back his hat and slid a hand over his thick, chocolate hair. "I believe I'd like to meet her someday."

Trap looked up and shielded his eyes from the low sun with the flat of his hand. "Sounds like you got women a-plenty from all the stories you tell. I only got the one. I'd be much obliged if you didn't try to steal her."

Madsen gave him a good-natured grin. "I may not have to try. She's likely to fall into my arms all on her own."

Trap stood and studied the tracks at his feet beside a leaning cottonwood. Two moccasin prints straddled a damp spot in the earth where Maggie had made water. He didn't tell Clay; it seemed too private a thing to talk about out loud.

The thought of Drum and the others chasing her gnawed hard at Trap's gut, but another, more sobering thought filled him with a feeling he'd never quite experienced. It was the same feeling he'd had as he contemplated Maggie's toes earlier, only multiplied until he felt his insides might burst.

She was not only running away from the school. Maggie Sundown was running *to* him.

CHAPTER 17

Maggie used a rock to kill a fat grouse just before sunset. Fearful of being seen if she started a fire, she hung the bird on her saddle string and rode on. She wanted to keep riding throughout the night, but her horse stumbled more often now and groaned for a rest at every step. He was a lanky beast not cut out for this type of labor, and Maggie knew he would lose flesh rapidly if she didn't give him plenty of time to graze.

The trees began to thin out not long after sunset. Here and there a lamp flickered in the window of some farmhouse, but Maggie was careful to steer clear of those. She turned more south to keep to thicker country, and was relieved when the forests began to come back. Guided by the stars and little more than the feeling inside her, she worked her way southwest until midnight. A crescent moon cast black pools of shadow among the trees and bushes.

The weary gelding jerked to a twitchy stop as something crashed through the bushes in the thicket

to the right ahead of them and splashed in the water
on the other side. Maggie leaned forward in the saddle and patted the horse's neck. A warm wind blew
across her face.

The darkness and unseen noises might have frightened a lesser girl, but Maggie had been chased by the
Army, shot at, clubbed on the head with a pistol, and
assaulted by Reverend Drum. Worse, she'd had to
watch while her once-proud people were conquered.
Few things in the night were as frightening as that.

Maggie dismounted under the protection of a
large cottonwood, loosened the girth, and let the
saddle slide to the ground. Her bones ached from
the constant pounding of riding over rough terrain.
The brown gelding nosed her hand and gave a rattling groan. She blew softly into its nose and hummed
a soothing tune her mother used to sing when she
worked around horses.

Maggie used her knife to cut a strip off the saddle
blanket about three inches wide. She knotted one
end, and after cutting a slit like a button hole in the
middle and the opposite end, wove the cloth back and
forth through itself to make a set of figure-eight hob-
bles. The horse was sweat-stained and exhausted
enough, it would likely stay near her little camp while
it grazed, but she had to be sure.

Once the animal was watered, she turned it out,
hobbled, and sank down at the base of a tree against
the soft fleece pad on her saddle. She still didn't want
to risk a fire, but the weather was cool and the grouse
would keep a while longer.

A breeze blew across her neck, and she reached up to smooth her hair. She'd forgotten Reverend Drum had ordered it cut. She hated the greasy man as much as she'd ever hated anyone. Her heart told her she'd have the chance to kill him someday. Not for cutting her hair or even what he did in his office—no, when next they met, Drum would surely give her a reason much more vile.

Leaning her head back against the rough bark on the tree, she gazed up at the myriad of stars that speckled white on the night sky, like the blanket on an Appaloosa horse.

She wondered if Trap O'Shannon would be surprised to see her—if she made it to Arizona. She wondered if he might be thinking of her at all since he left.

Drum would follow her, there was no doubt about that. She'd made good time, but he was close; she could feel it. The Thoroughbred needed rest; that was something she couldn't get around. Without the big gelding she'd move so slowly, she was sure to be caught. But the horse also left an easy trail to follow. She had to do something to discourage her pursuers—to slow them down.

Her breathing came deep and steady as drowsiness tugged at her body. Asleep only a few seconds, she was startled awake by a familiar whistling grunt in the bushes beside her. When she figured out what it was she smiled, a plan already forming in her mind.

CHAPTER 18

"I'm not too keen on them dogs hearing us," Clay whispered. Drops of dew covered the grass in front of their faces. A black and yellow spider the size of a twenty-dollar gold piece scuttled up and down the damp stems to repair a glistening web only inches from the Texan's nose. He paid it no mind, concentrating instead on the brindle dogs below. "I got bit by a dog once when I was a boy and I gotta tell you, I'd rather be in a gunfight without a gun than go through that again."

"Wind's wrong," Trap grunted beside him. "We've stayed well away so they won't even cross our trail."

The two boys watched from a thick stand of tall grass and berry brush on a chalk bluff above the river bottom. The sun had been up less than an hour when they saw Drum pick his way though a thin layer of fog that hugged the waterline. The Van Zandts followed, rifles at the ready, as if they were hunting escaped convicts instead of a fourteen-year-old Indian girl. The brindle dogs ranged in front of the group, padding up to this tree or that, pausing to sniff out every possible trail.

The small one took the lead, while the meaner one hung back a little.

"Looks like the monster's waitin' for his little buddy to flush out something for him to rip to pieces," Clay whispered.

Trap nodded slowly. The morning felt so quiet, he didn't dare speak.

Without warning the smaller dog, who sniffed at the base of a large cottonwood, let out a mournful howl and ran yelping back to Harry Van Zandt. The bigger dog broke into a ferocious snarling fit. It faced another tree, not ten feet away from the first along the water's edge.

Trap's heart jumped in his chest. He shot a glance at Clay. "I'm afraid she might be in those bushes. Wish we had a rifle."

"We don't need no rifle to shoot that little piece," Clay scoffed. "I could part their hair with this peashooter at this distance if they try and do the girl any harm."

The big dog suddenly tore up to the tree and pawed at the ground around it. Seconds later, it flipped over backward with a yowling cry, more wildcat than hunting dog. Regaining its feet, the yelping animal retreated to a dismayed master, tail between its legs.

Clay took up the telescope and studied the scene in more detail. He chuckled and passed it to Trap.

"She's a smart one, this girl of yours," Madsen whispered. "She must have got herself a porcupine last night and set some snares with the quills. Both dogs got a snootful. That little one looks to have three or four up around the eyes. Wouldn't be surprised if it's blinded. The kid holding it looks mad as a hornet."

Unable to move without being seen, Trap and Clay lay still in the grass and watched the scene below them. The Van Zandt boys were furious at the injuries to their pets. Their vehement curses and oaths carried on the stiff breeze, but it was impossible to make out more than a few words.

It took an hour to get all the quills out of both dogs. The monster bit Roth in the hand during the process, and they had to use a belt to muzzle the snarling thing. It took more time to doctor the wound.

In the end, the two brothers left with their injured little dog, while Mr. Van Zandt and Drum followed the monster up the trail that ran along the water.

Ten minutes later, Trap and Clay moved down to take a look at the sign. Five minutes of study and Trap began to chuckle. He swung back on his horse, shaking his head.

"They're following the wrong trail," he said. "You're right, she is a smart girl."

Madsen stood dumbfounded, holding the roan's lead in his hand. "How do you know it's the wrong trail?"

Trap smiled. "You ever have a dog mix it up with a porcupine?"

Madsen nodded.

"Could you ever break him of it?"

"I guess not," the Texan admitted. "Seems like they get more quills each time they tangle with one. It's like they hold a grudge or something."

"Exactly. They get all caught up in a blind rage and can't think of anything but revenge," Trap said. "Drum's relying too much on the dog." He nodded back to the northeast. "There are rocks turned over in the water heading upriver. I reckon Maggie will go that way a spell before she turns back south."

"If she headed back upriver, who's the evil reverend followin'?"

"He's following the dog." Trap waited for Clay to make the connection.

A smile slowly spread across Clay's face. "And the dog's followin' the porcupine where Maggie got the quills. . . ."

CHAPTER 19

1910
Montana

"You were some woman then and you're some woman now, Maggie darlin'," Clay said, bouncing his fist on top of the table. "I still don't see why you didn't take up with me all those years ago. . . ."

"Mr. O'Shannon, I'm amazed you didn't shoot this scoundrel two days after you met," Hanna said.

"He never had the need to." Clay shrugged. "I can't figure it out, but she picked him over big, strappin' me."

Hanna leaned forward on the table. "Clay was telling me you all rode from St. Louis to Arizona, dodging Comanche troubles, whiskey peddlers, and outlaws all the way. I suppose there were still buffalo back then."

Trap nodded. "Some. Hide hunters had already made a good mark against them, but we ran across several sizable herds." It was funny, but looking back, he'd been so focused on finding Maggie, he'd likely let half the country slip by him without really taking the time to notice it.

A blast of cold air tore through the narrow dining car when the conductor poked his head inside. His face was flushed, his hat dusted with snow.

"Sorry to bother you folks," he panted as if he'd just run the length of the train. "But Mrs. Cobb, have you by chance seen that man you said looked ill earlier?"

Hanna shook her head. "It's just us," she said. "I'm hearing an awfully good story, though. You should take a rest and join us."

"Wish I could," the conductor said, setting his jaw. "But I need to find that fellow. I've had a bucketful of complaints on him, but he keeps giving me the slip." The door shut as he withdrew his head to continue his search.

"Brrrr." Hanna leaned across the table to take Clay's hands. "It's freezing in here. Come now, I still don't know how you three got together and came to know your good Captain Roman. Finish telling me about how you got to Arizona. I wish I could have been there."

"So does Clay." Maggie grinned.

CHAPTER 20

1878
Arizona

"You ever notice how that gal of yours has a knack for pickin' the routes with the best grass for her horse?" Clay let his boot swing free of the stirrups as if there weren't a dozen rattlesnakes per square yard that might spook his horse and dump him on his hind parts. "You sure she hadn't been this way before?"

Trap grunted. Over the past few weeks he'd grown accustomed to having Clay Madsen along, even come to count on him when they spotted signs of a Comanche raiding party or any of the dozen other dangers they faced on the trail. For the most part, the brash Texan was an easy keeper, content to yammer on about whatever might be running though his mind at the moment, happy to hear himself talk as long as Trap gave him an occasional grunt or nod to show he hadn't gone to sleep.

Maggie had stayed south when she left Missouri,

just nicking the northwest corner of Arkansas before she turned due west into Indian Territory.

Trap felt certain they would be able to catch her in the wide-open country of the Texas Panhandle, but she always stayed a step or two ahead. By the time they crossed into the high country in northern Arizona, Trap felt like they were getting close.

For weeks, there had been no sign of Drum or the remaining Van Zandt and his dog.

"You certain we're still on her trail?" Clay asked the same question about every three days. Trap assumed it was when the boy's mind ran dry and he needed time to reload new ammo for his dissertations. On these occasions Madsen required more than a grunt.

"Pretty certain," Trap said. "She's a sly one. I'm able to follow her, but I have to go slow. She's an expert at blending in with game trails or old Indian roads." He was on the ground now, looking at a spot where a set of new tracks joined Maggie's in the red earth.

"Looks like a wagon," Madsen said, nodding down from the back of his horse.

Trap nodded. "Stagecoach maybe. Whoever it is, there are three riders following it." He ran his hand over the parallel lines in the ground.

"Maybe outriders," Clay shrugged. "Guarding a payroll or something."

"Maybe," Trap said. He took off his hat and squinted at the blazing sun overhead. It beat down like an unrelenting forge. "Stage throws up a lot of dust. Look how it's settled here in the wheel tracks and all of these hoofprints." He toed another set of tracks off to the side. "Not as much dust in these. I'm thinking they came along sometime later. . . ."

A low whine echoed across the barren earth, barely audible behind a long jumble of red sandstone and cactus ahead on the trail. Clay and Trap looked at each other.

"What was that?" Trap said. He shaded his eyes with his hand and stared toward the rocks.

Clay gathered up the reins and speared both boots into the stirrups. "I ain't certain," he said. "But I think it was a gunshot." His hand drifted toward the pistol at his belt.

So far, the boys had eluded contact with much of anyone but a stray cowboy or two. Following the gunshot was sure to change that.

Trap climbed back into the saddle. "Whatever it was, it came from the direction Maggie's headed. Might as well check it out, we're going that way anyway."

The boys nearly stumbled onto the robbery before they knew what was going on. Trap drew his gelding to a skittering stop. Clay's blue roan plowed into him from behind.

". . . when we find an innocent girl out here all by her lonesome like this, we got to do somethin' about it." A raspy voice came from around the red rock outcrop in front of them.

"Yeah, yeah, that's it, our hands are tied," another, higher voice cackled. "We got to do somethin' about it. It's almost a law out here."

"I am Pilar de la Cruz," a fiery female voice spit.

"My father is Colonel Hernan de la Cruz of the Mexican cavalry. He will surely hunt you all down for this outrage. Poor Gerardo did nothing to deserve being shot."

"Pilar de la-la-ti-da Cruz," the cackling voice said again. "Ain't that somethin'? We done captured the daughter of a real live Mexican cavalry colonel."

"You boys shut up and drag her outta the coach," another voice said. This one was calm and in complete control.

Trap looked at Clay and held up three fingers.

The Texan already had his pistol out. "It was four months last week since I left home. I guess I been good as long as can be expected. I'm sure wishin' you had a gun about now," he whispered.

Trap drew the bone-handled knife and took a better grip on the reins. "Me too," he said. "What do you think? Can you shoot all three without hitting the girl?"

Clay shrugged. "I won't know until we ride around the rock and take a look. For all we know, there could be another ten of them who haven't said anything."

"Stop it!" Pilar de la Cruz screamed. "Take your filty hands off me."

"Careful, Buster, she'll cut you," the raspy voice snapped. There was a yowl from Buster and a laugh from the other men.

Trap set his teeth. Attacking at least three bandits with nothing but a knife in his hand was a foolish endeavor and he knew it, but he couldn't very well let Clay do all the work by himself.

"That's enough," the calm voice said. "You listen to me, your little highness; I don't give a mule's dirty ass if your daddy's the potentate of your stinkin' greaser country, you got no choice in the matter. My compadres are in need of a little company." The voice grew in volume and timbre as he spoke. "Now get out of the damned coach or I'll shoot you in the gut. It won't bother the boys a speck if you got a little hole in your belly."

Clay settled his hat firmly. "I do believe I'll shoot that one first," he whispered.

As the two boys gathered their reins to charge, a bloodcurdling scream rent the air high in the sandstone above them. Trap shivered in spite of himself. The cry came again, echoing like a banshee scream from one of his father's stories, through the cactus and sheer cliffs above them. Trap fully expected to see either the devil himself or a whole party of Apache warriors swoop down at any moment.

The black gelding bolted around the rock in the excitement and Madsen's roan followed.

Three men stood by the coach. One of them went for the pistol at his belt and Madsen sent a bullet through his chest. The pistol slipped out of his hand and he tumbled out of the saddle as his wild-eyed horse squirted out from under him. Trap grabbed the animal's reins as it went past.

The remaining two men stood with their hands above their heads, frozen in time on the ground beside the coach and their intended victim. Dressed like gamblers, they looked out of place in clothes too fancy for desert travel. Closer inspection showed their dirty faces and hands didn't quite match up with the rest of the outfits they'd likely stolen from unsuspecting travelers on the trail.

When the men saw they were being faced by two boys, they both relaxed a notch. The one nearest Clay grinned.

"What do you aim to do now, kid? You think you can take both of us before one of us gets you?" He tipped his head toward Trap, then shot a nervous glance at the rock above. Beads of sweat dotted his grizzled upper lip. "Your partner there don't even have a gun. And even if you do kill us, you'll still have them Apache to deal with."

Clay kept the pistol pointed at the pair. Trap slid a Winchester out of the dead outlaw's saddle scabbard, worked the lever, and leveled it at the rough talker.

Clay sighed. "We just can't let you boys bother a poor innocent girl out here all by her lonesome like this." He mimicked the man's gravel voice. "Our hands are tied, you no-account bastards." Clay dipped his head. "Señorita de la Cruz, I apologize for my harsh choice of words there."

The Mexican girl smiled. "Think nothing of it, kind sir."

Trap heard a skittering of rocks from above and chanced a look. In the low sun, he could just make out a shadowed form working its way down a narrow trail. When the lone form dropped below the rim and into the shadows, he could see it was no Apache war party.

It was Maggie.

"Don't look now, boys," the outlaw with the cackling voice whispered. "But the Injuns are sending a squaw down to cut our cojones off. Shoot me if you have to, but I aim to kill me at least one more redskin before I die." He grabbed for the pistol at his belt.

The man's head exploded like a ripe melon and Trap levered another shell in the Winchester. The second outlaw got his gun out and ran for the safety of the coach. Both boys cut him down and he pitched headlong into the sand.

When the smoke cleared, one horse was down and bleeding in the traces while another wild-eyed beast stood blowing and shaking beside its fallen companion. Three outlaws lay dead on the ground. An ashen-faced Pilar de la Cruz trembled as badly as the surviving horse.

Clay saw to comforting the young woman while Trap spurred his gelding over the rocks and dismounted. Maggie slid down the mountain and into his arms.

The shock of finally seeing her mingled with the feeling in his gut. He'd never killed anyone before, and it made him go hollow inside at the thought of it. Then he looked at Maggie and the hollowness filled up to overflowing.

CHAPTER 21

"Your hair," Trap said. He couldn't bring himself to let go of Maggie's hand.

She gave him a self-conscious smile and ran her fingers through her short locks. "Drum decided I needed to look more like a white woman." The smile faded and she set her jaw. Her eyes narrowed. "I'll not cut it again. Not for Drum, not for anyone. I'd die first."

"Oh, Maggie darlin'," Clay said from the coach where he'd sidled up to a dazed Pilar de la Cruz. "You say that now, but poor ol' Trap would rather have you plumb baldheaded as not to have you at all."

Trap nodded toward Madsen. "He says pretty much whatever pops into his mind."

"Well, it's the damned truth and you know it." Clay pretended to sulk for a moment, but couldn't keep it up with Pilar at his arm. "Your little friend is not near as talkative as I am, but believe me, he's easy to read when it comes to you. We been trackin' you for so long now I feel like I know you already."

Maggie's dark eyes glistened. "You were tracking me?" She looked back and forth from Clay to Trap.

"Doggone right he was tracking you," Clay said. "This boy's like a danged hound when it comes to findin' you."

A party of six Mexicans in civilian dress clattered over the sandstone with rifles drawn and wary looks on their faces. They rode with the tight formality of soldiers. Pilar put her arm around Clay to show he was friendly and waved at a young man in the lead. He had a thin mustache and brooding black eyes. A wide sombrero fell back on a leather string around his shoulders. He kept his gun trained on Clay and appeared to want to shoot him on general principles.

"Norman," Pilar cried. She spoke to him in rapid Spanish.

Norman reined his bald-faced sorrel to a clattering stop. He lowered his rifle grudgingly after Pilar repeated herself.

"I told him you saved my life," she said out of the corner of her beautiful mouth. "May I present Captain Norman Francisco Garza of my father's cavalry command. They are my escorts on my trip to the United States."

Garza dipped his head slightly and spoke to Pilar in Spanish. His tone was polite, but strained.

Trap's mother spoke Spanish and he'd learned a little as a child. From what he could pick out of the conversation, Pilar had slipped away from the rest of the group to do some exploring on her own. The captain could barely contain his anger and embarrassment that his charge had gotten away from him and almost gotten herself killed.

Trap wondered if Clay could see this man harbored strong feelings for the commander's daughter. If he did, it didn't slow him down.

Madsen stuck out his hand. "Clay Madsen out of Bastrop, Texas," he said. "Pleasure to meet you, Captain Garza. I assume you will be escorting the young lady back to safety. I'd be happy to accompany you and assist if . . ."

"That will be most unnecessary, Señor." Captain Garza turned to Pilar. "Señorita de la Cruz, we must be going. Your father expects us back in three days time. I do not wish to disappoint him." He broke into clipped Spanish again and Pilar nodded her head.

"Might I see you again, Señor Madsen?" she said while Garza's men tended to the body of the fallen driver, cut the dead horse from the traces, and hitched one of the saddle horses to the coach.

"I'll be in Arizona for some time, I believe," Clay said. He took her hand in his and gently kissed the back of it. Trap marveled at the simple act and wondered how Madsen knew to do such a thing. "I would say you can count on seeing me again, ma'am. Wild horses or a whole unit of Mexican cavalry couldn't keep me away."

Pilar smiled and handed him a slip of paper. *"Perfecto."* The words clicked off her tongue. "You may find me at this address. Please consider this a formal invitation to come call on my father and me at any time you find convenient."

Garza spurred his horse up and opened the coach

door from the saddle. "Pilar," he said curtly, holding the door ajar. The stern look he gave Clay Madsen was as much a challenge as Pilar's little scrap of paper had been an invitation.

Clay fell into a blue depression as soon as Pilar and her entourage rumbled out of sight. He vowed to hunt her as hard as Trap had hunted Maggie—a feat that shouldn't prove too difficult since he had her address.

Only the sight of the dead outlaws' firearms helped bring the young cowboy out of his love-struck stupor. He stood beside a dusky, jug-headed horse and picked through the saddle kit. He whistled under his breath when he slid a rifle out of its sheepskin scabbard.

"I do believe this is the most handsome rifle I've ever set my eyes on." Madsen ran a hand over the rich wooden stock. "A .45-90 buffalo Sharps. You can shoot .45-70s out of these too." He threw the gun up to his shoulder and sighted down the thirty-two-inch barrel. "I feel like we just saved her from a life of crime." He cocked his head to one side, like he was trying to drain something out of his ear.

Trap looked at Maggie. "He does that sometimes when he's thinking on something important." Through all the talk, he'd not moved an inch from her side.

"Seems like a good man." Maggie giggled at the funny faces Clay made while he pondered. "How long has he been with you?"

"I've got it." Madsen slapped his leg and let his head bob back to a more natural angle. "I'll call her

Clarice." He held the rifle up to Trap and Maggie. "She weighs as much as a small pony, but I always did like my lady friends on the beefy side."

Clay lowered the gun slowly and stared into the pink glow in the west. The drawn look of melancholy washed over his face again. There was a catch in his voice. "You ever feel like you're riding off from your one true love?"

Trap looked at Maggie and smiled.

"I guess I have," he said.

CHAPTER 22

Van Zandt squatted next to his brindle dog and let a handful of sand sift through his fingers. "She ain't far now," he said, spitting a slurry of tobacco juice onto the ground. Remnants of the brown goo dribbled down his chin.

"That's the same song you've been singing for the past three weeks." Drum took off his hat and mopped his brow with a dirty rag from his back pocket. His oily look had taken on a wilted appearance, like a piece of fatty bacon left too long in grease not quite hot enough to cook it.

Van Zandt rubbed his dog behind the ears. "Ol' Zip knows we're close. Tracks don't stay too long in this wind and sand. If we don't get ourselves kilt by Apaches, we should have her by tomorrow night." He squinted up at Drum. "How do you aim to get her back to Missouri once we catch her?"

Drum patted the thick leather reins against his thigh and thought about his answer. Take her back after all this? That was a funny notion. He'd be lucky if the church would let him return at all after he left without giving any notice. Of course, that idiot Mrs. Tally had surely given a full report of what she'd seen, no doubt blowing everything out of proportion as if Maggie Sundown was a white girl.

The sun throbbed against Drum's head with a vengeance and threatened to boil his brain. He squinted through the endless waves of sand and stone and heat and tried to keep his eyes from crossing. He'd sweated through his clothes many times over, and his rump was chaffed raw from weeks in the saddle on a gimpy horse.

This little Indian tramp had not only run off with his favorite horse. She'd stolen his career, his comfortable life, and his reputation. No, she'd not be going back to the school. Neither of them would.

Drum had seen the fight in the girl's eyes before, when she'd bitten him. It warmed him inside to think of it. He hoped she fought again this time. It would make what he planned to do all the sweeter. And, in the end, it would make it easier to kill her.

CHAPTER 23

A day south of old Fort Defiance, Trap decided he wanted to buy Maggie a new dress. A passing stranger, likely a deserting soldier, had told them there was a town a few hours ahead. They were still a few days out of Camp Apache, but Trap didn't know how many opportunities he'd have to buy anything like that. From what he'd seen of the frontier, new clothes and shops to buy them in were seriously lacking.

Maggie insisted her faded skirt only needed time with a needle and thread to render it good as new, but Trap showed he'd inherited his father's Scots-Irish resolution and insisted right back that she was getting a new dress. If she wanted to mend the old one, then she'd have two.

Of course, he had no idea how much such a thing might cost. He had a few dollars of the money his mother had given him, and figured he could get a little more for the extra pistols he and Clay had taken from the dead outlaws.

Buying Maggie a dress seemed like a good idea,

but leaving her to do it, even for a minute, was like pulling out a perfectly good tooth. Trap held her hand from the back of his horse, looking down at her eyes.

"Jeez-o'-Pete," Clay said from atop his own gelding, stirrup-to-stirrup with Trap. "You two beat all I ever seen. She's made it by herself across half the country. I reckon she'll survive one afternoon without us."

Trap let his fingers slide away.

"We should be back before dark," he said. "You keep the Winchester with you."

"Clay is right," Maggie said. "Everything will be fine. There is a nice pool down at the river. I'll have a cool bath while you are gone."

"Well, then." Madsen winked. "That changes things. I reckon I oughta stay around and see to your safety after all."

Trap took off his hat and slapped Clay's horse on the rump. The startled roan jumped forward and broke into a fast walk toward town. "She needs protection from you. Let's get gone so we can get back."

Trap looked over his shoulder as he urged his horse into a trot. He wondered if it would always make him so sick when he rode away from this woman.

Maggie watched the boys ride into the swaying waves of desert heat. It didn't take them long to disappear among the Joshua trees and barrel cactus. She rubbed the sweat out of her eyes and sighed. Her memories of the cool mountain air of the Wallowa Valley tugged at her heart—but her future lay with

Trap O'Shannon. If he was to go to Arizona, that's where she would go as well.

A new dress seemed a silly extravagance, but she supposed it would be nice to look her best when next she met the Reverend and Mrs. O'Shannon alongside their son.

It felt strange to be alone again after days with the two boys. Trap was quiet for the most part, but Clay Madsen spoke enough for all three of them. Maggie walked toward the line of shimmering acacia trees that lined the riverbank. The catclaw thorns on just such trees were responsible for most of the rips on her shredded skirt.

She smiled to herself at the thought of the fun-loving Texan. As quiet as Trap was, it was easy to tell he possessed strong feelings for her. Clay flirted constantly, but it was obvious he loved all womankind—the one he was with at the moment just a little more than all the rest.

Black streaks lined the red sandstone cliffs that towered over the slow-moving river like a castle wall and provided a comfortable shade from the midday sun. Long strands of lime-green moss swayed like hair in the lazy current where the river widened into an emerald pool in the mountain's shadow.

Maggie took a quick look around and leaned the Winchester against a low bush of salt cedar at the water's edge so she could get to it in a hurry if she had to. She hung her medicine bag beside the rifle before slipping nimbly out of her skirt and pulling her loose blouse over her head. Her knee-high moccasins came off last, and she hung them across a low branch. It was a tactic she'd learned the hard way·to discourage scorpions and other stinging crawlers from making a home in the dark recesses of her tattered footgear.

Naked on the bank, she let the hot breeze blow across her skin while she inspected the ragged clothes. Miles in the saddle and countless nights sleeping on the ground had taken their toll. Cactus and acacia brush had ripped the threadbare garments in countless spots. Maybe the new dress wasn't such a bad idea. She carried her old clothes into the water with her. Hopefully, they would stand up to one more good washing.

The water was warm, a refreshing contrast to the blazing air, the rock bed slick with moss. Gradually, she waded deeper into the stream until she had to hop to keep her head above water. Letting her legs come up, she floated on her back and gazed at the perfect blue sky while she kicked slowly across the deep pool. She was happy to be alone with her thoughts until Trap returned—happy to make herself feel and smell clean for him.

With her ears underwater she couldn't hear the rocks skitter down the red sandstone bluff above.

Two ravens circle overhead, cawing and playing with one another like the tricksters they were. Suddenly, one of the birds dipped its wings and plummeted straight for her. Inches above the water, the raven pulled out of its dive and flew to the acacia tree beside her rifle.

Startled, Maggie sat up to tread water. She brushed a lock of wet hair out of her eyes. The bird cawed again, then turned its head sideways and blinked a shining black eye.

A hot wind rippled the water in front of her, sending a wave of goose flesh over her body. Something was wrong.

Two strong kicks took her to the shore. Dripping wet, she picked up the Winchester and scanned the shadows among the bushes and rocks before she wriggled into her wet clothes one arm at a time.

The raven flew to a nearby mesquite and began to preen while its mate soared among the cliffs above.

Water dripped from Maggie's hair and ran down her spine beneath her shirt. A familiar feeling tugged at her chest, as if she had walked through a spiderweb. She nodded her thanks to the bird for its warning and backed slowly into the trees.

Someone was out there, watching her.

CHAPTER 24

Trap had the skinny Mexican girl at the mercantile wrap the new dress in brown paper and string. He figured Maggie hadn't been able to open too many presents in her life, and thought she might enjoy it. It took a few minutes to pry Clay away from his flirting, but after a quick trip to the dry-goods store for a few supplies, the boys were on their way back to camp.

Trap was anxious to get back, and kept his horse to a trot. He would have galloped if he hadn't been afraid the heat would kill his horse.

Skunk's ears perked up a half mile away from the river. Trap felt the little gelding tighten its gait, and scanned the area ahead. If he'd learned anything in his short life away from civilization, it was to trust his mount's instincts. He shot a glance at Clay, who was neck-deep in a convoluted story about his plans to ride to Mexico and marry Pilar de la Cruz.

Madsen stopped in mid-sentence. "What's wrong, partner? Looks like you just swallowed a bug."

"Can't tell." Trap gave the gelding its head.

Both horses slid to a stop in the trees beside the remains of Maggie's small fire. The pungent smell of cedar smoke hung heavy in the still air. Trap swung a leg over the saddle horn and hopped to the ground. His voice was tight as a skin drum.

"I shouldn't have left her."

"Aw, she's likely just enjoying her little bath," Clay said from the back of his roan. He raised his dark eyebrows up and down. "I'd be happy to go check on her."

Trap squatted and studied the petite moccasin tracks that led through the dark portal of acacias along the river. "We been gone a good while. I can't see her taking a bath that . . ."

The sharp crack of a Winchester creased the hot evening air. It came from the river.

Trap was back in the saddle in a flash. Clay drew his pistol and the boys spurred their horses into the trees.

A dead man lay facedown in the water, legs bobbing in the current, his hands clawed at the bunchgrass along the rocky bank. Blood oozed from a wound underneath him and mingled with the green moss. A brindle dog lay a few feet away. A shotgun blast had torn the animal in half. Blood streaked the rock and grass where the mortally wounded animal had tried in vain to drag itself to the dead man in the water. A swarm of flies buzzed around the dog's shining entrails and the man's open eyes. Neither had been dead very long.

"Van Zandt," Trap said in a tight whisper.

Clay scanned the waterline, his eyes following his pistol. "Yeah, I recognize that mean critter layin' dead beside him. Glad I don't have to fret over him anymore. I reckon that means Drum's lurkin' around here somewhere."

Trap nodded, walking along the river's edge in search of tracks. "Van Zandt got it with a shotgun. Maggie only had the Winchester."

"Drum killed his own man?"

"Here." Trap found the cloudy boot prints in the slow-moving water where Drum had crossed. He swung back on his horse and splashed across, keeping his eyes on the water. "Clay," he said without looking up. "I'd be much obliged if you'd keep your eyes peeled and see that I don't get shot while I figure out where Maggie went."

Madsen gave a curt nod. "I'm hurt you thought I'd do anything else. Be happy to kill that son of a bitch Drum for you too."

"If he's harmed Maggie, there won't be anything of him left for you to kill."

Two hundred yards downriver, past the swimming hole, they heard voices coming through the trees. Trap dismounted and motioned silently for Clay to follow suit. The boys tied their horses and crept forward on foot.

The evening was already warm, but Trap's mind burned at the thought of any harm coming to Maggie. All he'd wanted to do over the last few months, all he'd thought about was to find and protect her. Now, he was afraid he'd failed.

Dwarf willows and salt cedar grew thick along the sandy bank. Drum's deep voice filtered through the coarse foliage.

". . . you really believed you could get away from

me, you filthy little whore? Well, let me tell you something. When a woman makes eyes at me the way you did, I know what she wants. . . ." His voice was strained and breathy.

Maggie screamed.

"Go on and yell your fool head off." Drum laughed manically. "There's nobody out here to save you."

Trap had heard enough. He crashed through the trees with Clay tight on his heels. What he saw was like a kick to his stomach.

Maggie's shirt hung from her shoulders. Drum knelt on top of her, pinning both arms up above her head with a powerful left hand. His right gripped cruelly at her face, pinching her cheeks into a pitiful grimace.

Her screams came out in a muffled groan and she arched her back, trying to throw him off. He was a big man and as feisty as she was, Maggie was no match for him in strength. Blood oozed from a jagged bite wound on her neck. The ground was plowed around them. Her bare feet bled from her kicks and struggles.

Trap felt Clay bring up the pistol on his left. He raised a hand to stop him. "Don't want you to have to live with this one," he heard himself say.

Trap's bone-handled knife hissed from the sheath and he flew at Drum with a fury he'd never known. A brutal kick to the big man's ribs sent him flying off Maggie with a *whoof* as the air left his lungs. Trap heard bones crack, but Drum lashed out with a powerful hand and swiped him off his feet. Buoyed by rage, the boy rolled quickly and was on his feet in an instant.

Maggie ripped away the remainder of her torn

blouse and moved in with him, shoulder-to-shoulder. Blood from her nose and the wound at her neck covered her heaving chest. A blade gleamed in her hand.

"Good Lord," Clay gasped.

Drum lay on his side, panting and clutching his injured ribs. His eyes grew wide when he saw the knives. He shot a glance at the shotgun ten feet away, then raised a hand to ward off the attack, trying to push himself to his knees.

It was too late.

Trap and Maggie fell on him as one, a flash of steel, blood, and teeth—a flurry of black hair, bronze skin, and righteous indignation.

It was over as fast as it had begun.

"Van Zandt wanted him to share me. Drum didn't feel like sharing." Maggie stooped to clean her knife and hands in the river. "I guess I need another bath."

Trap stood beside her. They were both covered in blood. "Are you all right?" he asked. His voice was distant in his head, as if it were coming from someone else's mouth.

Maggie used a bit of her torn shirt to dab some blood out of his eye. It didn't appear to bother her that she was naked from the waist up. "He never got to do anything but bite me." She touched the same piece of cloth to the crescent-shaped wound below her ear. "I hid in the trees as long as I could. I knew you would make it back in time." Her eyes sparkled in the low light. Her bare shoulders trembled, but she didn't cry.

Clay Madsen, who talked about naked women more than any single thing in the world, took off his own shirt and held it out to Maggie. "You need this more than I do, Maggie darlin'," he whispered gently. For all his talk, he kept his eyes pointed at the ground. He shook his head, his face a little on the pale side. "You two beat all. I seen of some strange ways of consummatin' a relationship in my short years, but I ain't never even heard of anything quite so unifyin' as two lovebirds fighting side by side to hack a common enemy to pieces."

CHAPTER 25

The train chugged over Lookout Pass a little before noon, belching thick clouds of smoke and steam, a long black snake against a white backdrop. It lumbered slowly through the deep snow, and the engineer made frequent stops to clear downed trees or heavy drifts in the narrow canyons.

The passengers were used to such stops and starts, so when gears ground and wheels squealed against wet tracks and they began to slow, hardly anyone gave it a second thought.

"We oughta be getting into Mullan anytime," Clay said. His eyes sparkled with the memories of their conversation. "I could use a little stretch. How about . . . "

The throaty boom outside the train cut him short. Trap shot a worried look at Clay, then at his wife.

"Was that what I think it was?" Hanna's green eyes went wide.

Trap stood, his hand on Maggie's shoulder. "Let's move away from the window until we figure out what's going on out there." He took a black pistol from under his coat and gave it to Maggie. "We'll be right back."

Clay gave Hanna a peck on the nose. "Stay with Maggie."

They met the red-faced conductor stepping back inside the door.

"What's the news?" Clay put a hand up to stop the blustering man. "Somebody get shot?"

"Not as of yet." The beefy conductor's face glowed red, more from a brush with death than the cold. His chin quivered a little as if he might start to sob at any moment. "There's a mob of men out there threatening to shoot anyone who gets off the train." He took his hat off and ran a hand over a sweating scalp. "This has been one hell of a day: a phantom passenger, that high-toned Baker woman, and now I almost get my head blown off. I don't get paid enough for all this."

"Did they give you a reason?" Trap needed answers, not a bunch of talk about the conductor's bad day at work.

The man scoffed. "Said they had orders to keep us on the train to protect the good citizens of Idaho." He scuttled past in the narrow hallway, eager to get the train moving again.

Clay put his hand on the door handle and shot a

grin at Trap. "I was lookin' forward to wettin' my whistle in Mullan. Shall we see what's eatin' these folks?"

"Move slow so they don't get antsy with that scattergun," Trap said. "I don't like the idea of buryin' two
friends on one trip."

"You always were the brains of this outfit," Clay
said as he pushed open the door.

A cold blast of air hit them full in the face. A bel-
lowing order followed.

"We mean business," a gruff voice shouted from
the tree line. "I'll cut down the first man who steps off
that train."

Clay held both hands out the door. "We're not
armed."

"I don't give a ding-dong damn."

Clay turned to Trap and shrugged. "Never heard
that one before." He shouted back out the door.
"You want to tell us what's got into you folks? Mullan
used to be a right hospitable place."

"We got orders from the United States marshal to
keep all of you on that train. Deputized me over the
phone, he did." The voice was pinched, as if the
speaker had a hand caught in a vise.

"The marshal?" Trap began to chew the inside of
his cheek, wondering how Blake might fit into all
this.

"That's right. So you best stay on that train just like
I tell you and nobody'll get hurt."

"You allowed to tell us why?" Clay always sounded
like he was in charge—mainly because he believed he
always was.

A buzzing silence followed while the men at the tree

line conferred with each other. Finally, the leader spoke up again. "We're supposed to keep you on this train until a deputy gets here from Montana this evenin'. Somebody on your train has the smallpox."

"Smallpox?" Clay pushed the door open and put his foot on the top step. "Do I look like I have smallpox?"

The roar of a shotgun split the cold air. A splattering of snow kicked up on the ground twenty feet away.

Clay moved back in the doorway beside Trap. "Whoa, whoa, whoa, I'm not gettin' off the train."

He slammed the door shut behind him.

"Good thing he fired another warning shot." Trap smirked and let out a tense sigh.

"I don't believe it was a warnin'." Clay winked. "I reckon that ol' boy just didn't know the shotgun would shoot so low at that distance. You think Blake is the one comin'?"

"A deputy from Montana . . . ." Trap mused. "The chances are good. I guess we'll have to wait and see. I want to get back to Maggie as quick as we can." Waiting was something Trap was never good at.

"Know what you mean," Clay whispered, digesting the news. "I should check on Hanna."

"A word with you, sir!" a low voice said from the wood-paneled aisle behind them.

"Me?" Trap said, turning. He relaxed his shoulders, ready to block a punch.

A broad man with wire glasses and a thick neck stood square in the middle of their path. The sleeves on his white shirt were rolled up to reveal thick forearms and huge hands. "No, not you. I'll deal with your issue later. I'm looking to settle with this man here." He nodded his balding head at Madsen.

"Are you Mr. Baker, the postmaster of Dillon, Montana?" Clay moved up beside Trap, shouldering in front of him slightly.

"I am."

"Well, sir, that's impressive, a real live, honest-to-goodness postmaster." Clay fawned, bringing both hands up to his face as if he was smitten with a bad case of puppy love. "Now . . ." Madsen's face grew dark. He let his hands fall to his side. "We have business elsewhere and you're in our way. I'll ask you once to step aside. I hope you heard me because I said once."

Baker's eyes flamed. He wasn't going anywhere. "You, sir, were extremely ungentlemanly toward my . . ."

Clay's right hand shot out and connected with Baker's nose. The man's glasses shattered, then swung from one ear. Blood covered his lips and chin. He swayed for a moment, blinking, then pitched across the back of a padded bench.

"Now, that's what I wanted to do to his wife." Clay smirked. He rubbed the back of his hand, grimacing when he touched his knuckle. "Damn, those postmasters sure have hard faces in Dillon, Montana."

Sidney, the waiter brought four coffees and set them on the table. Jittery about the prospect of smallpox, but resigned to a long wait, the passengers were circumspect. Every seat in the dining car was full, but conversations were hushed and tense. Birdie was nowhere to be seen.

"Don't you think Mr. Baker will come for you again?" Hanna said. She was sitting beside Clay now and Trap was next to Maggie.

"I hope so." Clay grinned. "Hate to leave anything unfinished. Trap and I were in a hurry to get back to you beautiful womenfolk so I didn't have time to do things proper."

Trap lifted his coffee, eager to change the subject. "Here's to Hezekiah Roman, the best captain a man could have."

Clay clinked his cup against Trap's. "You got that right, partner."

"So you joined the Army and got assigned to Roman's Scout Trackers after you made it to Arizona?"

"Not exactly." Clay shot a knowing glance at Trap. "We didn't meet up with him for some time—and the Scout Trackers didn't even exist before us. We were the first."

Hanna peered across her cup at Maggie as she took a sip. "But you and Trap got married as soon as you got to Fort Apache?"

"Not for a while," Maggie said. "And Camp Apache wasn't even a fort yet. It was still just a pile of buildings and squad huts."

"This is all so fascinating. Here you are taking your captain—your dear friend—back to his wife in Arizona to be buried—that's an extraordinary friendship."

"Ky Roman was an extraordinary man," Maggie sighed. "When Trap went out under his command, I knew things would be all right."

"I should write down all those stories you told me." Hanna leaned her head against Clay's shoulder and sighed. "A half-Apache tracker, his beautiful Nez Percé wife, a stalwart Mormon captain, and a handsome Texan who flirts with everything in petticoats . . ."

Clay let the comment about his past indiscretions slide. "It was a moment in time, Hanna, darlin'. When the Scout Trackers were up and runnin', we were a force to be reckoned with . . . and the force behind us was Captain Hezekiah Roman."

"Tell me more," Hanna said.

Trap shrugged. "I'll leave the storytellin' to Clay. He's got a way of making tales considerably more interesting than they really were."

Hanna snuggled down in her shawl, like a child getting tucked in for her nightly bedtime story. "I've read my last good book," she said. "What else is there to do on such a chilly afternoon?"

Clay grinned down at her through narrow, wolfish eyes. "I can think of a thing or two."

"You hush," she said. "Now, go ahead and start telling. I'm waiting. . . ."

PART TWO

PART TWO

CHAPTER 26

October 1878
Camp Apache, Arizona

When they reached the camp, the three adventurers decided it would be better to leave out any mention of Tobias Drum. They spoke only vaguely about Pilar de la Cruz and the bandits, but Trap could tell his mother viewed him differently. She seemed to know he'd moved to another level in his life, to sense that he'd spilled blood.

The fact that he'd survived months on the trail, tracking Maggie all the way to Arizona, wasn't quite enough to prove to the O'Shannons that their only son was old enough to get married. Though it was not uncommon for girls Maggie's age to tie the knot, the reverend insisted the two lovebirds wait a year at the very least.

Unwilling to throw Maggie to the mercy of the Army, the reverend and Hummingbird informally adopted the girl and let her live in the other half of their dog-run cabin beside the crude log school. He'd clasped his hands behind his back as he made the pronouncement.

Trap and Clay were able to secure jobs working as packers and mule handlers for the Army's campaign against renegade Apache. Clay was a talker, but he was a hard worker as well. The two were well liked by their superiors, and life around the Camp Apache, though full of sweat and long hours, was better than bearable.

"I've got to draw a new pair of gloves," Madsen allowed one evening on the way to check on a string of new shavetail mules. "These old ones are about rotted through with sweat." As junior teamsters on the mule crew, Clay and Trap invariably drew the short straw when it came to work details. Breaking a rank mule was smack at the bottom of everybody's list of enjoyable things to do.

In keeping with post orders, both boys led their horses rather than riding them through the dusty parade ground. It was a sore spot with Clay, who considered it demeaning to have to walk anywhere he could ride. He squinted at the low orange sun and used a sweaty bandanna to wipe the grime and dust off the back of his neck. "King James is likely still puttering around in his shack. I bet he'd let me have a new pair of gloves if I took him some whiskey. We have to go by there anyway to get to the mules."

Sergeant Riley James, King James to those who dealt with him, was the quartermaster in Camp Apache. A grizzled and bent man in his early fifties, he appeared as old as dirt to the sixteen-year-old boys. In charge of uniform and equipment issue, King James held the ultimate power of comfort over men in employ of the Army. Uniforms only came in three sizes: small, medium, and large—and the large sizes went quickly. Though cavalry soldiers were normally chosen for their small build, there were plenty of hefty troopers. If offered a tot of whiskey, the king could usually be counted on to turn up at least one pair of large trousers. For a little more, he'd search until he found a large tunic hiding among his stores.

His power alone was enough for the men to dub him King, but the real reason everyone, including his old friend General Crook, called him King James was because of the way he spoke. A whack on the noggin from an Apache war club had addled his brain, and though he still had a head for numbers, everything he said came out of his whiskered mouth like a verse from the Good Book. He did his job, but everyone knew Crook had asked his subsequent replacements in Arizona to look after him as an act of kindness for his previous loyalty in battle.

A huge padlock hung open on the hasp at the front door to King James's adobe storehouse. Both boys removed their hats—a covered head could bring forth an entire barn-load of damnation and wrath—and stepped into the dim interior. The smell of oiled paper and mothballs hung heavy in the musty air. A wooden counter ran the length of the place, separating the bulk of the stores from the narrow lobby area out front. On busy days the king opened both front doors so troopers could come in one entry for issue and go out the other. Today, only one door stood open.

Trap waited just inside while Clay stood at the

counter and cleared his throat. Wax-paper bundles, piled almost to the rafters, lined the back walls. Wooden crates of varying sizes marked "U.S." in bold black lettering were stacked to the ceiling. For a soldier, it was like a candy store. Many of the items would bring a tidy sum if sold on the civilian market, and thus were kept under lock and key. The quartermaster was nowhere to be found.

"Odd he left and didn't lock up," Clay muttered. "Sergeant James is particular about his kingdom."

There was a bundle of leather gloves tied with twine at the far end of the counter, but it didn't occur to either boy to take anything without the king there to issue it. The wrath of King James would only bring the wrath of the iron-fisted Colonel Branchflower— and no man in his right mind wanted to risk that.

"Maybe somebody already brought him some whiskey and he went to enjoy it while he watched the sunset."

It was common knowledge that James often drank a little on the job, but he waited until sundown to get really drunk. Trap suspected the man lived with a powerful headache from his injuries and used the whiskey to dull the pain.

"I reckon my poor old paws can get by another day with the rags I got now," Clay muttered. "Expect we better lock up as we go, in case he don't come back tonight."

Trap gave a grunting nod.

Two of the new shavetail mules were branded as incorrigible the day after they jogged grudgingly into Camp Apache. The big red animals had nearly kicked a young private's head off when he got too close during Call to Feed. Had the mules been of lesser quality, the chief packer, Jose Morales, said he would have run the lot of them over the rim of the canyon to drown in the White River. As it was, the two culprits, along with three other white-eyed beasts, had been quarantined from the gentler stock and placed in a stout cedar corral out behind the quartermaster's shack for Clay to work in the cool of the evening.

Trap could tell the animals were gone as soon as he rounded the corner of the long adobe building. There's a forlorn and lonely look about an empty corral, even from a hundred yards away. No guards were in sight and the double corral gates yawned open toward the far-off hills.

A brooding line of gray-black thunderheads boiled on the horizon. The warm, earthy aroma of a distant rain mixed with the ever-present odor of cavalry horses and hung on the stiffening breeze.

A jumble of tracks scratched the dust around the corral. Trap counted two distinct pair of flat-toed moccasin prints and an equal number of horses. He was easily able to pick out the slimmer, more U-shaped tracks of the Army mules, all of which were yet unshod because of their foul tempers and snakelike speed when it came to dealing with shoers.

"Renegades," Clay hissed under his breath. The young Texan's attempt at a mustache finally had a good crop of brown whiskers cultivated on his upper lip. He'd taken to toying with the end of his new accessory when he was deep in thought. "They must have snuck in here while the sentry was off on some kind of frolic. There'll be hell to pay when Colonel Branchflower finds out about this. Makes me glad I'm just a lowly civilian."

"The Army hangs civilians too," Trap said under his breath.

Clay shuddered. "You always do come up with words to comfort me."

Trap studied the rocky line of tree-topped mesas in the direction of the tracks. Dark clouds loomed closer by the moment. In a short time, all sign would be as gone as the mules, washed away in the rain.

A voice from behind the loafing shed snapped him out of his thoughts and sent Madsen's hand to his pistol.

"Verily," the wobbly voice proclaimed. "The wrath of the Lord will surely come upon one Private Penny for abandoning his post to chase strong drink and all manner of abominations."

Clay let his gun hand relax and grinned. "I can't believe they didn't finish off the old fool."

"I hear your words, my sons," King James called from around the shed. "Come hither while I bear witness of what terrible deeds have come to pass."

Trap sighed. "Most Indians look at crazy folks like they got a little better chance at communing with the spirits."

"Lucky for Sergeant James he's as numb in the head as they get."

King James leaned against the stack-pole wall of the loafing shed. He was bound hand and foot with frayed bits of hay twine. Flecks of straw mingled with his gray beard. Dirt covered his normally impeccable uniform. In ornate Biblical detail he explained that he'd heard a commotion coming from the mule pen. Worrying that Private Penny, the sentry on duty, had gotten too close to one of the rank mules, he'd gone to check on him and received a club to the head for his troubles.

"Lo, they have fled with the wretched beasts, fled I say." His voice rose in pitch and timbre. "Sound the trump and shout from the rooftops, heathens are among the tents."

Trap unfolded his jackknife and bent to cut the old man free. "Sergeant," he said. "Begging your pardon, but can you walk?"

"Yea, I say, verily I say, it would be easier for a camel to pass through the eye of a needle than for any damned Apache to rob me of my power to ambulate."

Trap shot an entertained looked at Clay, then turned back to Sergeant James. "Would you be so kind as to go back and sound the general alarm? That storm is coming in fast. If we don't take up the trail now, we'll lose the stock for certain. Clay and me will get right on it. You send reinforcements out as soon as you can."

"Yea, ask and ye shall receive, knock and the very same shall come to pass," King James decreed with a wobbly head.

"Does that mean you'll get us some help?" Clay raised a wary eyebrow. He was losing patience fast.

"Yea." The man groaned up on bent knees. He grabbed Trap's hand with gnarled fingers and pulled himself the rest of the way to his feet. "It doth."

* * *

At first, the tracks were easy to follow—down the brushy slope, along the White River, and then back south down a narrow canyon. The spot where the renegades forded was plainly visible, and Trap was able to keep the speed up for almost two hours while Clay kept his eyes on the surrounding trees and rocks, watching for signs of the mule thieves with weapons.

The air crackled with the excitement of hot pursuit. Long hours on the trail together had taught them to anticipate each other's movements. Both had learned enough of life to know that what they were doing was extremely dangerous. But neither considered turning back. The trail was before them, so they took it.

The advancing storm pushed columns of wind before it, sending twirling dust devils through the piñons and scrub juniper.

Evergreen trees gave way to sandstone and cactus about the time the first large drops of rain plopped against the brim of Trap's hat.

"Ashamed we don't have a bugle with us so we could blow Call to Feed. I bet them mules would come runnin' back to their oats no matter how mean they are." Clay slumped in the saddle, both hands resting across the horn,

"I don't know how to play the bugle," Trap said. He studied a pinched draw almost choked closed by a tumbled pile of gray rock. "And unless you been practicin' while I wasn't looking, you don't know how either."

Clay smiled. "That's the trouble with you, O'Shannon. You're too damned practical." He followed Trap's gaze to a tower of sandstone, sculpted over time by wind and water. "You think they went up there?"

"I do," Trap said over a rising wind. He had to squint against the blowing dust and ducked his head to keep his hat from blowing off. "Those mules are mean as snakes, right?"

Clay nodded. "I guess I seen meaner down home."

To Clay's way of thinking everything was meaner, prettier, or hotter in Texas. "Well, if they gave us trouble, they're sure to do likewise to these Apaches. I only count two sets of tracks. Five vicious mules can make a handful of trouble for two of anybody—even renegade Indians. The tracks go every which way here, like the mules pitched a huge fit. I'm betting the thieves won't go much further before they hide the stock and go for help—particularly with this storm coming in."

It was a long speech for Trap.

"Well, sir." Clay nodded at the rocks while he held his hat on against a howling wind. "If I was going to hide a passel of sorry mules, I guess that's as good a place as any." The Texan snugged his hat down over his head and pulled the Sharps out of its scabbard. "We best keep a sharp eye peeled. If the mules didn't kill 'em, them boogers are likely to be holed up in there. Best I let Clarice out to play."

Trap grinned. "That's why I brought you along."

CHAPTER 27

Madsen hung his head in mock disappointment when they found the mules bunched in a piled-brush corral and no Apaches around to fight. He returned Clarice to her rifle boot and untied his lariat to build a catch loop for the brawny red boss mule.

Rain pelted the rock with a fury now, splattering off every surface. It seemed to come just as hard from the ground as it did from above. Lightning periodically forked across the gray sky. Thunder cracked, echoing through the sandstone hills, dark red now from the sudden rain.

The mules, still tied together with short lengths of rope between halter and tail, milled and bunched against the rock face at the far end of the thorny enclosure. Steam rose from their wet backs and disappeared in the chilling rain. The whites of their eyes rolled back and they stomped their feet nervously at each clap of thunder. Trap had watched one of these mules nearly bite the head off a stable hand. He'd narrowly missed getting his own skull kicked in on more than one occasion. It was a marvel that anyone, even an Apache warrior, had been able to even get near them, much less tie anything to their tails.

Clay's lariat settled over the neck of a snorting beast as Al Seiber, chief of scouts, splashed up the little canyon on a copper sorrel. A squad of mounted troopers from C company followed a hundred yards to the rear, flankers out as far as they could get in the narrow confines of the canyon.

Clay took a dally around his saddle horn and came as close to attention as Trap ever saw him. The strong-jawed chief of scouts was one of the few people who caused Madsen to go quiet. Trap didn't ever mention it, but he was pretty certain Clay hadn't even considered growing a mustache until his met his new mentor.

Seiber was an affable man, with a direct manner that made him either feared or admired. His Apache scouts followed him faithfully and trusted him as they did one another. "I always tell 'em the truth," he would often say. "When I tell an Apache, 'If you do thus and such, I'll kill you,' and he does it, well, then, he knows I'll keep my word, because he's seen me do it before. If I promise one I'll help him, he knows he can count on that too, just as sure as the other."

The capable frontiersman lived an honest life out in the open and his motives lived out there too for everyone to see. Seiber reined his Roman-nosed gelding to a sliding stop and pulled his oilskin tighter around his neck to ward off the pelting rain.

"Good work, boys," he shouted above the squall. He eyed the brooding herd of mules with a jaundiced gaze. "Don't know whether you saved the Army some money by recovering stolen stock or cost it in the way of medical bills for the damage these cursed animals are bound to inflict." The rain began to ease as quickly as it started. Seiber took a kerchief from the crown of his wide-brimmed hat and wiped rain-water off his face and high forehead. He took great care to smooth his thick mustache before he replaced the hat.

"Still," he continued. "We can't have the hostiles stealin' our animals, no matter how wicked the beasts are. Did you boys catch sight of the renegades? It took some cojones for sure—you almost have to admire 'em."

"No, sir," Trap said.

Seiber rubbed a strong jaw in thought. "I got me a little problem, boys."

Trap watched as the ramrod-straight lieutenant in charge of C Company broke away from his men and picked his way through the rocks toward them.

"My problem is thus," the chief of scouts continued. "Victorio and that spooky sister of his are causin' quite a stir since they slipped away. I'm to guide a company of troops east to join forces with men from Grant and see if we can't catch the wily son of a bitch."

The tall lieutenant dismounted and checked his cinch while Seiber continued with his explanation. The rain had stopped, but a bitter wind blew down the mountain like an omen of things to come.

"To be honest," Seiber said, "I didn't have a lot of faith that you boys would be able to hold the trail with the rain and all. I should have brought a couple of the White Mountain scouts with me."

The lieutenant removed a gauntlet and stepped forward to shake Trap's hand and then Clay's hand in turn. Gray eyes peered over a slightly hooked nose. There was a hint of honest weariness about his angular face, as if he carried the burden of the world on his shoulders.

"Hezekiah Roman," he said, leaving off his rank since he was speaking to civilians. It didn't matter. Though he was no more than five or six years older than Trap, Roman had a dignified air about him that left no doubt about who was in charge. Even Seiber took note of the young officer's quiet, yet piercing voice.

"I wonder if you men would feel comfortable tracking for my column while we go after these renegades." He scanned the surrounding mesas with a gaze so flinthard, it looked as though he might set fire to every tree. "It was a bold move to come right onto the compound like that—a move that can't go unpunished."

Trap shot a glance at Clay, who looked at him and shrugged.

Seiber cleared his throat. "They're young, sir—young but capable. I've been watching them and I've not seen many of my Apache scouts that can track as good as young O'Shannon here. Both know their way around a horse. And if you can get past his constant jabbering, Madsen is as stalwart a hand on the trail as any man in the Army. He's got an eye like a hawk and can use that fancy long gun of his to shoot the heads off turkeys for the camp pot at two hundred paces."

Trap hated to admit it, but the prospect of tracking the mule thieves appealed to him. He could see by the glint in Clay's eyes he felt the same way. The adventure would be a welcome change to the drudgery of garrison life even if it did mean time away from Maggie. Under the watchful eye of the Reverend O'Shannon, the two hardly got to spend any time alone together anyway.

"We'll do our best for you, Lieutenant Roman." Trap held out his hand to shake again. It seemed to be the proper thing to do since an agreement had been reached.

"Excellent," Roman said. He remounted immediately and nodded up the canyon. It was apparent that he was not the sort to sit around and contemplate things once a decision was made. He turned and spoke over his shoulder to a gaunt sergeant who'd ridden up behind him. "Sergeant Martini, have a detail of two men fall out and take that string of mules from Mr. Madsen and see them back to the camp. The rest of us will take up the trail."

"Aye, sir," the sallow sergeant said in a clipped Italian accent. "Fitzsimmons, Wallace, fall out for detail!" His barked orders belied his slender build.

"You'll need supplies, men," Roman said, turning matter-of-factly back to Trap and Clay. "I took the liberty of packing you each a kit when Sergeant James came in with the news. Mr. Webber." Roman didn't so much raise his voice as he put more energy into it. A redheaded trooper riding a massive bay gelding trotted up from the ranks.

The lieutenant dipped his head at the trooper. "Private Webber will see that you have your gear. From this point on, I'd suggest neither of you leave the camp without at least enough supplies to spend the night. It's been my experience that things seldom go as planned."

Trap O'Shannon knew how to track, but the idea of having a column of twenty armed soldiers behind him was a big responsibility and it put him a little on edge.

The steady rain had washed away almost all sign of the renegades. For the first two hours, Trap went on little more than instinct and the fact that there were very few directions meant anyone could take a horse in the jagged confines of the red rock canyon. As the sandstone walls began to fan out, the options for travel increased and the tension mounted inside the young tracker.

He moved slowly, leading his little black gelding, stooping now and then to study a bit of compressed gravel or crushed vegetation. Often, he had little more to go on than a flake of earth that looked out of place for its surroundings or the telltale scuff a hoof might leave behind on wet rock. Always, he was aware of the soldiers behind him, pressing him. The rattle of bits and groan of horses added to his stress.

Luckily, the rain had not come as hard on the far side of the mountains. Trap was relieved to find the faint tracks of unshod horses weaving in and out between the pungent creosote bushes and chaparral. The ground softened and the trail became easier to follow just before sundown.

"We'll stop up there by that little creek and rest

the horses," Roman said, pointing with his gauntlet at a line of scrubby salt cedars.

"Beggin' your pardon, Lieutenant," Clay said, drawing rein beside the officer. "But these animals look mighty near worn out and we haven't been gone more than a few hours."

Trap had been so focused on the trail he hadn't noticed how poor and stumble-footed most of the Army mounts were. Roman's was in good flesh, as was Private Webber's bay and a handful of others, but by and large the horses were winded and holloweyed.

Lieutenant Roman rested both hands on the smooth pommel of his McClellan saddle. "Yes, Mr. Madsen, I'm afraid they are. All the best stock went out after Victorio, along with Mr. Seiber and Captain Rollins' company. I'm afraid bringing in a couple of renegade mule thieves didn't rate high on the colonel's priorities when it came to doling out supplies and horseflesh."

Fifty yards from the creek, Trap pulled up short and scanned the darkening horizon. He slid off his horse and studied the mass of tracks before him in the dust. At least ten new riders had joined the two renegades, maybe as many as fifteen.

It was getting too dark to see well, but Trap could tell the new horses were shod, so if they were Indians they were riding stolen ponies.

Still, something nagged at Trap as he studied the tracks in the long shadows of waning light. He nodded his head slowly when he'd figured it out.

Trap looked up at Roman as the young officer rode up alongside him.

"Sir." Trap gazed into the gathering darkness and

shivered in spite of himself. "Someone else is chasing the Apaches. Somebody besides us."

"Chasing, you say?" Roman raised an eyebrow.

"Yes, sir. The two that took our mules have picked up their pace some. They spin every now and again to catch a look behind them. The new tracks never look back, and they're moving at a pretty good clip."

"Another cavalry unit?" Clay smoothed his fledgling mustache.

"Could be," Roman said.

Trap put a hand flat on the ground, feeling the tracks. "I don't think so, sir. No rank and file to this group. Whoever it is, they ride as a bunch, not a disciplined column."

A drawn look spread over Roman's weary face. "That's what I was afraid of," he whispered. His breath clouded in front of him in the cold night air. "This is troublesome," he said, as much to himself as anyone else. "Extremely troublesome."

He didn't say why.

Lieutenant Roman chose the only seven men with fit horses to ride before dawn, Private Webber and Sergeant Martini among them. "We need to make good speed, men," he said as the group mounted up in the gray darkness. He was not a man to explain himself any more than that.

The remaining horses appeared unable to follow at any speed, and though he was loath to split his forces, Roman left thirteen men behind to pick their way back to Camp Apache as their mounts were able.

The trail was a bold one, with at least a dozen shod

horses producing a considerable amount of sign. Trap had no trouble following it even in the scant light of false dawn.

When the sun was still a faint orange wafer on the knife edge of the eastern horizon, Trap reined in his horse and motioned for the others to stop. Crows circled above a distant pueblo, whirling black dots against a gunmetal sky. Their grating caws added to the chill of the morning air and sent a shiver up the young tracker's spine.

"Can you smell it, Lieutenant?" Private Webber stood in the stirrups and inclined his red head toward the handful of drab adobe buildings and rough goat pens.

"Keep to your column, Mr. Webber," Roman said without looking back.

"Yessir." The private lifted his reins and moved his gelding back two steps into the ranks.

"Smell what?" Clay turned in the saddle from his spot beside Trap. "I don't smell anything but dirt and wind."

Roman rode forward and motioned for the column to follow with a flick of his hand. "Death, Mr. Madsen," he said over his shoulder. "That smell on the wind is the smell of death."

CHAPTER 28

Huge flies crowded around the exposed white skull of a butchered Mexican goatherd at the outskirts of the little town. A shotgun blast to the chest had torn half of his slight body away.

The tracks showed how a group of mounted men had swept through the village like a bad storm. A dozen other bodies littered the street, each mutilated and scalped like the goatherd. Three women lay clumped together in the threshold of a tiny pink church. Bullet holes riddled the adobe walls like pockmarks where the women had been cut down, seeking refuge in the only sanctuary they knew.

The troopers dismounted and led their skittish mounts through the grizzly scene, checking for survivors. Trap knew there wouldn't be any.

"Those two Apaches we're after didn't do all this," Trap said in a husky voice, full of disgust.

Lieutenant Roman took a deep breath and looked south toward the Black River. "No, Mr. O'Shannon," he whispered. "This is the work of scalp hunters. The

Apache kills his share of Mexicans, mind you—and in some awful ways. . . ." Roman closed his gray eyes, remembering. When he opened them again, he moved off to survey the rest of the scene.

"The Mexican government still pays quite a few pesos for Apache scalps," Johannes Webber said. His voice was quiet but stoic, as if he was reading all this from a book and not living in the middle of it. He flipped his gelding's reins around a broken fence rail. "It was big business back in the forties and fifties. Lots of folks came down to collect a quick fortune. Now, only Mexican citizens can collect the bounty, but that doesn't stop the determined ones. Hard to tell the difference between an Apache scalp and a peon goat-herd's."

The red-haired trooper toed at the body of an elderly woman. "They took both her ears. That's the only way the Mexican government can be sure the scalp hunters aren't cheating them—you know, trying to get two for one."

"Oh, no, no, no . . ." Clay Madsen's voice drifted soft and piteous from a slumped adobe shack on the sad little street. He appeared a moment later, framed in the black backdrop of an open doorway. The lifeless body of a girl in her teens was draped across his arms. Slender arms and legs hung in the air. Her face and bare chest were covered with blood. A modest peasant dress was ripped to tattered rags. Her scalp, along with both of her ears, had been peeled away.

Flecks of vomit dripped from Madsen's chin. He shook his head solemnly and held the dead girl up to Roman. "Who would do such a thing, Lieutenant? She ain't no older than I am."

Fire burned in the back of Trap's throat and he thought of Maggie. Whenever he worried, his thoughts always turned to her.

"Sergeant Martini," Roman said. His voice was clipped and quiet.

"Aye, sir." Martini stepped forward leading his mount.

"Get the men to move these bodies into the pueblos where the birds and coyotes can't get them."

"Yes, Lieutenant." Martini turned to carry out his orders.

"Sergeant," Roman said, removing his hat. "One more thing; you're Catholic, I believe."

Martini turned back on his heels. "I am at that, sir."

"Very good." Roman's voice was little more than a whisper. "I imagine most of these people were as well. Please see to whatever it is good Catholics need at times like this. We'll come back and bury them after we tend to our more pressing matters." He returned the hat to his head and stepped forward to put a hand on Madsen's shoulder.

Tears streamed down the boy's cheeks. "I'm sorry to be such a bawl-baby, Lieutenant Roman." Clay set the dead girl gently at his feet. He sniffed and wiped his face with the back of his sleeve. "I won't let it happen again."

"You're a strong one, Mr. Madsen, chock-full of wit and humor. I know, I've watched you." Roman looked wistfully at the ground. "This world is full of wicked men—and what these wicked men chiefly lack is heart. I've seen a bundle of evil men who were chock-full of bravery, but I've never seen one of them cry for anyone but himself. In my book, a man who'll weep for the soul of another is a man indeed."

Roman turned and started for the edge of town. "You two come with me," he said over his shoulder. "Mr. O'Shannon, can you find us the trail?"

Trap took off his hat and rubbed a hand through his hair. "The scalp hunters are all riding shod horses. There's fourteen or fifteen of them. Should be a simple trail to follow."

"Good," Roman said. "Our Apaches are most certainly heading back to their own people. The time to punish them for their thievery will have to wait. Our primary mission now is to save their lives."

CHAPTER 29

No matter how the O'Shannons saw it, Maggie already thought of Hummingbird as her mother-in-law and gave her all the respect and deference a daughter should. For the first time in two years, she found herself truly happy—even with Trap gone on frequent little forays with the Army. Just knowing he shared her feelings was enough to make her glow.

Though not as beautiful as the Wallowa, the mountains around Camp Apache held their own quiet splendor and enjoyed a pleasantly cool fall. A nice breeze blew through the canyon along the White River, and the hot-natured girl would often go sit on a rock below a twisted pine to think and feel the wind. While others layered on cloaks and woolen wraps of assorted sizes, Maggie stalked about the camp with nothing more than a light shawl and her feelings for Trap to keep her warm.

Maggie drew plenty of looks and smiles from the enlisted men when they were in garrison. Not so much because she was an Indian. Most of the Apache had been moved to San Carlos, but there were plenty around camp. Some worked as domestic help for the married soldiers. Most of the others were little more than beggars, dressed in rags and begging for their rations. Some of the Apache women were pretty, or would have been if given their freedom, but reservation life had taken its toll.

Star, a young woman only a few years Maggie's senior, worked as a housekeeper for the colonel's wife. She seemed happy enough, and often joked with Maggie when they bumped into one another around camp. Star stood out as one of the true beauties among her people, until her husband, a sullen, filthy man, accused her of infidelity and cut off the fleshy part of her nose. She disappeared from the camp shortly afterward and forced the colonel's wife to find a new maid.

After that, Maggie resolved to keep to herself and save her friendships for Trap.

Maggie's hair had always grown fast, and by October hung well below her shoulders. Sometimes, the way the soldiers looked at her made her smile. Other times, it put her on edge and she longed for Trap's quick return.

Apart from working around the modest school, Maggie had little to do but help Mrs. O'Shannon when she could. Trap's mother was a quiet woman, pensive and slow to speak, when she said anything at all, but she had a kind look in her deep brown eyes. There was no judgment in her words, as one might expect from a mother-in-law, and Maggie enjoyed their time together.

She especially liked shopping. Even the modest

sutler's store at a remote post like Camp Apache had so many things to choose from, a girl like Maggie, who was used to a frugal life, could spend hours browsing at the buttons and fabric and letting her imagination run wild. The only trouble was, the Reverend O'Shannon enjoyed shopping with his wife as well, and Maggie couldn't quite tell how he felt about her.

Rather than acceptance from the man she considered her father-in-law, she felt a sort of quiet resignation to the fact that Trap had chosen to spend the rest of his life with her. He was always kind, but distant in all his communications. Hummingbird smiled and looked at her whenever he spoke, but never made any apology for his cool behavior. The poor man appeared to be exhausted by the mere act of living since he'd had to leave White Oak.

"I must speak to Mr. Sorenson about some socks," the reverend said as they entered the long adobe-and-log store, one end of which sold spirits to the troops. His wife and Maggie both knew the talk about socks would be preceded and followed by a whiskey toddy to warm his bones. The store was not so large as to hide the fact that he was drinking, and he did not try. He just saw no reason to mention it out loud.

Hummingbird gave her husband a soft look and motioned Maggie toward the bolts of cloth. They'd spoken of making some new winter dresses. "I'll fill my list while you talk to him," Hummingbird said to the reverend, touching him on the hand as she always did when they parted ways. "Tell me if you think of anything else you need me to buy."

A copper cowbell clanked on the door behind

them and a familiar voice cut the close air inside the building. Maggie had her back to the entrance and couldn't place it for a moment. When she did, her blood ran cold.

"Peter Grant!" James O'Shannon's face brightened and he took the new arrival by both shoulders. "What brings you to Arizona?"

The baby-faced lieutenant removed his hat and nodded politely to Mrs. O'Shannon. He smiled at Maggie and blushed. His entire face fluttered with nervous energy.

She tried to keep her eyes from darting back and forth, looking for a way to escape. His countenance held the same missionary zeal as when she'd seen him last. Except for the fact that his hands were not blackened with gunpowder from shooting her people, he looked exactly as he had the day they'd met almost a year before south of the Canadian border.

"How is your uncle these days?" Reverend O'Shannon clapped his hands together, genuinely pleased to see a familiar face in such a lonely place as Camp Apache, Arizona.

"He's well, thank you," Grant said. "He sends his regards and hopes you don't think ill of the council for sending you to this duty." The boy's words were guarded, as if he knew more than he said.

"We were pleased for the opportunity to come and minister among my people," Hummingbird said, her interjection a little out of character.

James O'Shannon nodded in hearty agreement as

if he was still attempting to convince himself. "That's right, that's right," he said. "This is a wonderful opportunity for Chuparosa and me both. And the Lord knows her people need help."

Lieutenant Grant had stopped listening to either O'Shannon and stared intently at Maggie. "The truth is, I went to White Oak a few weeks ago, hoping to look in on Miss Sundown."

Maggie swallowed and bit her bottom lip, trying to keep her face passive. Her head spun, her breath came in shallow gasps.

Cocking his head to one side like a disapproving father, Grant raised his eyebrows. "I found things in a shambles. A young Sioux boy named Big Horse or something or another was virtually running the school. Tall Horse, that's it. He was doing a fair job of it too.

"Mrs. Tally has undergone a complete nervous collapse. She can do little but cry, the poor old girl. She told me between sobs that you and Reverend Drum had both disappeared." He studied Maggie's reaction. "I'm relieved to find you safe, but left wondering what brought you all the way to Arizona. Have you got any notion of what happened to Reverend Drum?"

Maggie shot a glance at Mrs. O'Shannon in spite of herself. Her jaw felt loose, as it did before she got sick to her stomach. "I do not know what became of him," she whispered. She assumed what was left of his butchered body had been torn apart and devoured by coyotes, but she kept that thought to herself.

"Peter." James O'Shannon stepped in. "With all its

other endeavors, surely the Army isn't going to concern itself about which Indian school Maggie attends. I can assure you, she won't run away from here."

Grant clenched his freckled jaw, unconvinced. "Reverend, I can assure *you,* the Army takes escape very seriously. The last thing I want to see is for Maggie to be sent to a reservation or, worse yet, a prison."

"Prison?" Hummingbird scoffed and touched Grant lightly on the shoulder, as if he'd just told a joke. "That is funny. She's under the nose of the Army all day long here at Camp Apache. She's done nothing wrong but run away from a tyrant who, from the sound of things, has disappeared himself." Mrs. O'Shannon could be as protective as a mother bear when provoked. Her eyes suddenly blazed. She pulled Maggie closer with both hands.

Maggie knew no one at Camp Apache, not even Trap's parents, could really protect her if the Army— or more particularly Lieutenant Grant—decided she needed to be somewhere else. She was truly a prisoner of war. Her heart began to flutter in her chest. Her breath came in short gasps and she struggled to remain in control. She would have to run again.

"I've seen it before." The young lieutenant looked defiant. "There's a women's prison in New York with girls in it every bit as young as her. As long as she is a single girl with no one to claim her, she's too vulnerable to be wandering around the frontier."

"We've as good as adopted her," Hummingbird said. "I think of her as a daughter."

Grant stood resolute. It was apparent that he'd given this a lot of thought.

"If you wish to adopt an Indian child, you need to go through proper channels, Mrs. O'Shannon. I'm afraid I have no choice but to take her back."

Maggie moved back a step. She looked for a window, a door—a weapon to defend herself. If she couldn't find a weapon she'd use her teeth and nails.

"Peter." James O'Shannon took Grant by the arm and led him aside. "I can see that you harbor strong feelings for our sweet Maggie. She is a beautiful young woman and I admire your judgment. But now, I must tell you some things that will only break your tender heart. . . ." The two men stepped down the aisle beside a stack of wooden buckets until they were out of earshot.

Maggie steeled herself and made ready to flee out the front door. Hummingbird's calm, summer-breeze voice stopped her.

"He must truly love you, my child," she said.

Maggie gave a frustrated sigh. "I am not sure if what he feels could be called love."

Hummingbird chuckled and shook her head. "No, no, not Peter. I speak of Trap's father. James loves you more than he lets on—to do what he is doing now."

Maggie stopped in her tracks. "What do you mean? What is he doing?"

"Something I have only known him to do twice in all the years I've been with him." A proud smile crossed Hummingbird's face. "He is going to lie."

CHAPTER 30

"Their position is defensible, but they'll run out of water sooner or later," Lieutenant Roman said grimly, and passed a pair of binoculars to Trap.

Roman and his men lay on their bellies surveying the scene before them. A red sandstone monolith rose up from the desert floor. Boulders lined a lip a third of the way down from the top, and a few gnarled trees found purchase in the meager soil among the cliffs. The cutback area in the rock was well fortified and looked big enough to hide a sizable band of Apache if they had enough supplies.

From what Trap could tell, the scalp hunters had surprised the little band, mainly women and children, judging from the tracks, and sent them fleeing for the nearest refuge. Two boys in their teens, who'd stayed behind to give their little group time to escape, had been cut down like summer hay, scalped, and left to rot in the sun. Cedar campfires still smoldered in the sand, and much of their meager equipment lay strewn along the trail.

They couldn't have taken much with them. Trap doubted the whole group had more than a few gourds of water. Some barrel cactus grew up in the cracked rocks. They'd be able to squeeze some moisture out of them, but it wouldn't be much.

The scalp hunters had tied their horses out of rifle range and taken up positions in a sickle-shaped crescent at the lip of a shallow arroyo a hundred yards from the base of the mountain stronghold. Others ghosted in and out of the trees along a narrow creek. A scattering of boulders gave them plenty of cover.

One of the hunters must have gotten bold and underestimated the Apache marksmen. His body pitched forward in the sand. Through the binoculars, Trap could see blood running from a wound in his contorted face. After seeing what he'd seen at the little pueblo, Trap found it impossible to feel anything close to sorrow for the filthy man.

Potshots rang out intermittently from below. Their echoes whined across the desert on the cool evening breeze. In the rocks above, the Apache conserved their ammunition, waiting for someone else to get careless.

Another storm boiled gray-green to the north and threatened to bring snow or hail. If it rained, the Indians could gather water and hold out a day or two more, but as long as the scalp hunters held their positions, it was only a matter of time.

A curving line of trees at the western edge of the mountain base signified the presence of a small spring. The Apache might make a try for it in the dark of night, but Trap was certain it was guarded.

"Beggin' your pardon, Lieutenant." Private Webber

took a turn with the glasses. His voice was muffled against his own fists. "But neither one of those little groups has any love lost for the United States Cavalry. We're liable to charge in there and get ourselves killed saving the day."

Trap shot a glance at Clay. He'd spent enough time around the military to know low-ranking enlisted men did not often speak so freely with an officer—even a young lieutenant. There was talk that Roman put up with it because Webber was a genius and could speak six or seven languages, including Apache and Spanish, as well as his native tongue.

Roman demanded respect from the ranks, but he seemed to give Webber a little more leeway than normal. Martini said it was because the lieutenant knew about the man's rough upbringing and wanted to give him an extra chance to make something of himself. Whatever the reason, Roman treated the young redhead like a wayward son who showed promise, if not forethought, in his actions.

"Surely you have heard the old adage," Roman patiently explained so everyone on the line could hear. "The enemy of my enemy must be my friend."

The troopers nodded in agreement up and down the line. Webber grinned and gave a little shrug before handing the binoculars back to his commanding officer.

Roman scooted back a few feet behind the cover of Joshua trees before pushing himself to a kneeling position. He used a dried stick to scratch a rough map of his plan in the alkali dirt. "Mr. Martini, we'll loop around from the west there and hit the main body of the scalp hunters from the arroyo in which they sit.

Mr. Madsen, see that lone rock there above the scalp hunters and behind them?"

Clay nodded. "Yes, sir."

"Think you can take your fancy rifle up there and pick off the ones hiding in the trees, give us a little more of an edge until the Apaches join the fight?"

"Nothing would be easier," Madsen said with a grim stare at the ruthless outlaws in the distance. Trap could see in the flash of his eyes he was remembering the mutilated girl back at the pueblo. "Or more of a pleasure."

"Very well," Roman said. There was a fire in his eyes. He was pleased to enter into battle against such evil men. "Mr. O'Shannon, you go with Madsen and watch his back. When we take the butchers at their flank, the Apache will see we've given them an advantage and join the attack. That's Juan Caesar's band up there—not a coward in the group, I assure you." The lieutenant looked over his small command. "We're not great in number, but we have surprise and right thinking on our side. When the course is clear, gentlemen, never pause—proceed. Mr. Madsen, give the men ten minutes to get into position, then take the first shot that presents itself. Your gunfire will be our signal to attack."

"An enemy of my enemy is my friend," Clay repeated as the group made their way, bent at the waist, through the cactus and back to their horses. "That's an Apache sayin' I've never heard of."

Roman chuckled, then whispered so only Trap and Clay could hear him. "That's because it's not an Apache saying, Mr. Madsen. It's a custom of the Arabian sheiks." The lieutenant speared a dusty boot through a stirrup and pulled himself up in the saddle. "But I can only assume the Apache feel the same way in that regard. I know I would."

The two boys worked their way along a rocky incline across the arroyo toward a jutting stone tower. They were in full view of the besieged Apaches the entire time, but well out of rifle range.

"Those scalp hunters are focused on the Apache and don't know hell's about to rain down on 'em from behind," Clay panted as they took up a position behind a lump of orange sandstone the size of a large ox.

He dampened the bead on his front sight with the tip of his finger so it would catch the light better, and looked down his barrel at the dark form of one of the outlaws hunkering beneath a lip of cactus and rock, out of sight of the Apache.

"How far away you think we are?" Trap asked, taking up a position with his own rifle.

Clay picked up a bit of sand and let it stream out between his thumb and forefinger to check the wind. He sighted down the barrel of his Sharps and adjusted the ladder on his Vernier sights. "I don't know, two hundred yards, give or take—not far enough to fret over. You know what's funny about this group?" Madsen looked up at Trap. "They all still got blood on 'em."

Over the last few months, Trap had learned that Madsen's eyesight was impeccable. He squinted at the men squatting or kneeling here and there among the rocks below the mountain, then grunted. "Sure enough," he said. At two hundred yards, the Texan could see as good as most people could at fifty.

"It's like they don't even care if decent folks know they're bald-faced killers." Clay sighted down the barrel again and settled the long rifle firmly against his shoulder. "Well, sir, I'm proud to do my part to send a few of the buggers straight to Hell."

Clarice barked once. The big rifle bucked against Madsen's shoulder, but her twelve-pound heft helped dampen the recoil some. A low whine flattened out against the desert sand culminating in a faint thwack an instant after one of the killers slumped to the ground. His stone hiding place was now his tomb.

Smoke curled out of the breech as Madsen slid another round into the chamber and closed the block. He swung the Sharps to search for another target.

There was no bugle call to signal Roman's attack, only a wilting volley of gunfire as eight troopers swept down the arroyo at the gallop, engaging everything in their path.

"There's another one in the rocks over there with a gun pretty near like this one." Madsen's voice was tight and he spoke into the cheek-piece of his rifle. "If he gets above the lieutenant, it'll be a cinch for him to cut 'em all down one by one."

"Can you take him?" Trap asked, looking down the barrel of the Winchester and wondering if he should even try a shot at such a distance.

"It's better than three hundred yards," Clay whispered. "Almost four. That's a hell of a long shot, even for me. I think I got. . . ."

Instead of shooting, Clay yelped and rolled to his

left. "Damned scorpion!" he hissed, clutching at his right leg.

When the boys looked between them, they saw not a scorpion, but the feather fletching of an arrow sticking up from the sand next to Clay's leg. They made it behind the safety of a boulder, just as another arrow whistled in, zinged off a stone and careened into the canyon below.

"Well, this mucks things up considerably," Clay snorted. He checked the wound at his leg and found the arrow had only nicked him. "They likely dipped the damned thing in dog crap or some other such nasty thing. You think it's Apache?"

"Could be." Trap lay on his back, staring up at the sky. He clutched the Winchester to his chest. The weapon felt useless against an opponent he couldn't even see. "Webber told me there's a big Comanche who rides with the scalp hunters. He's called Slow Killer because he likes to scalp his victims before they're dead. I caught a glimpse of a big boy. I think it's him out there."

"Well, that's dandy." Madsen gritted his teeth. "I need to take care of that other shooter across the canyon before he starts takin' out troopers, and here we are penned in by a big Comanche who wants to torture us a little before he kills us."

Trap glanced across the arroyo. He could just make out a lone figure picking its way through the high rocks. Gunfire in the valley said the fighting there was intense. "I see him," Trap said. "Can you make the shot from here?"

"I think so," Clay muttered. "If you'll keep Slow Killer from raisin' my hair while I work."

"Do my best." Trap gave his friend a pat on the shoulder. "You do yours."

When Trap chanced a look around the boulder, Slow Killer jumped him. Webber had been right; this Comanche was one huge Indian. He hit Trap full force, swinging an ironwood war club that missed the boy's skull by mere inches. Trap felt the wind of it on his cheek. He brought the Winchester up to ward off a second blow just in time, and felt the gun give way in his hands like splintering stove wood.

On his back again, he rolled to one side as the heavy club pounded the ground where his head had been. He lashed out with the rifle barrel and connected with the Comanche's leg, but the force of the blow tore the weapon from Trap's grasp.

Slow Killer grinned, pulling up his long nose like a snarling wolf, and fell on top of him. The Comanche screamed like a wild man and drove a knee into the boy's belly. Trap brought a leg up to defend himself, but felt all the wind gush from his lungs. His head reeled and he struggled to stay conscious. If he passed out for even a moment, he knew he would die.

The Comanche wore leather leggings but no shirt. He was smeared with some kind of rancid grease, and though Trap clawed and grabbed with all his might, he found it difficult to find anything to hang on to.

The two combatants rolled in the dirt, locked in mortal combat only feet from Clay Madsen.

"He's settin' up to shoot," Clay shouted above the fray. "Hold on one more second, Trapper, and I'll be over there to help you. I might not get another chance at this."

Trap knew he didn't have much more than a second left. Slow Killer was a powerful man and though Trap was holding his own, none of his blows or kicks appeared to have any effect on the huge Comanche.

Summoning all his strength, Trap pushed off with both legs and rolled toward a low rock ledge. It was just high enough off the ground that both men wedged underneath it, scraping their shoulders on the top. They'd likely be sharing it with a snake or two, but that was the least of Trap's worries. He tried to pull away and go for his knife, but the Comanche caught him in a bear hug and pulled him back, baring his teeth.

"You stay with me, little man," Slow Killer grunted, bashing his forehead into Trap's nose. "You're Apache, I can smell it."

Trap tried to push away, but found his strength was failing. The big Indian had him in a death grip now, pulling and threatening to break him in two. Trap struck out with his free hand, bloodying his fists as he hit sandstone as often as he connected with Slow Killer's greased face.

Then, Trap's thumb slid across the Comanche's eye. The Indian tried to jerk away, but the back of his head was tight against the rock overhang. Trap pushed hard, gouging as deeply as he could, aiming for the back of the Indian's skull. He felt muscles separate, then tear as Slow Killer yowled and flailed wildly under the rock. There was nowhere for him to go. The Comanche vomited when his eye tore free and hung on its stem, mingling with the blood and grease on the side of his cheek.

The crushing grip around Trap's ribs relaxed. He gulped in air, the sound of his own wheezing loud in his ears. As soon as he could work his hands again, he drew his knife and finished the big Comanche quickly.

Slow Killer ceased his struggles just as Clay made his shot and drew his pistol to help.

"Damn, boy." Clay blinked and stared, mouth agape at the gruesome scene in front of him. All the color had drained from his normally robust face. "Can't you get in a fight without gettin' covered in blood and guts and who knows what else?"

Trap tried to straighten his stiff neck. His nose was completely plugged with blood from the head butt Slow Killer had given him. He panted through an open mouth.

"Did you get him?" His vision was too cloudy to see the rocks across the valley.

Clay grinned. "I got him. You sit down so you don't fall down while me and Clarice give the lieutenant a little more help." Clay picked up the Sharps again and spoke out of the corner of his mouth. "If I ever decide to fight you, remind me to shoot you from a distance. You're too damn mean to go toe-to-toe with."

True to the lieutenant's presumption, Juan Caesar and his band poured from their hiding places among the rocks to join the battle. There were no more than a half-dozen fighting men among the Apache, but their addition demoralized the surviving scalp hunters.

Five of the bloodstained killers attempted surren-

der. The Apache shot at them in any case and Private
Webber, at full gallop with his saber drawn, took the
head and one hand off one of the outlaws just as he was
raising his arms. Only two were left alive by the time
Roman called for a cease-fire and gained control of
the Apaches.

Trap and Clay stood when they saw things were well
in hand below them, and half-slid, half-ran down the
arroyo. By the time they arrived, Martini had the two
prisoners bound with their hands behind their backs.
Webber was acting as translator between Roman and a
dark, pockmarked man. He was taller than the others,
with a round chest that was set on somewhat gangly
legs. A feather and grass hat haloed deep-set eyes that
looked as though they had the capacity to melt stone.
A splash of blood dripped from his right arm and the
side of his ragged face where he'd killed one of the
scalp hunters at close range.

The Apache demanded control of the prisoners.
Roman said the men were the Army's problem and
they would be dealt with fairly and justly for what they
had done. Webber spoke excellent Apache. Better
than Trap, and his rapid-fire words shot back and
forth between the two leaders.

At length, Juan Caesar tired of using a go-between
and fell into halting English.

"Will the Army use the same fairness the lying Indian
Agent Brandywine uses to weigh our beef? Will it give
them the same justice it gives the white settlers that fool
with our women?" Juan Caesar spit vehemently on the
ground, then looked directly into Roman's face. Trap
wondered how he'd fare if this man ever looked at
him so directly. "I believe the words, Lieutenant-with-

the-crooked-nose, but I know enough to know you cannot speak for all white eyes. You are not all places at once. Bad things happen, no matter what you say."

"Juan Caesar," Roman said. "You know I am a man of my word. These men will stand trial in a military court and I myself will bear witness of the evil they have done. I will look into Mr. Brandywine and make certain he treats you with fairness. But you and your people must return with me to Camp Apache."

The two leaders looked at each other for a time, their eyes locked in a silent battle of wills. A dozen men, Apache and soldier alike, stood tense and ready to fight again. It was quiet enough to hear flies buzzing around the freshly fallen bodies. No one breathed.

Juan Caesar let out a great sigh as his eyes darted from a ragged group of Apache women and children to the approaching storm clouds. His proud shoulders slumped and he appeared to deflate to half his former size.

"We will go with you, Lieutenant Roman." The Apache stared, blank-faced and focused on nothing. "What other choice do I have but to fight and die? Someday it will come to that, I think—but not this day."

A baby whimpered until a short woman with a scarred face hushed it with a rough hand over its mouth. Trap shuddered to think of what the ruthless scalp hunters would have done to the child.

The Indians traveled light and were ready to go from the moment the battle was over. Trap could tell Lieutenant Roman wanted to get back to garrison with all due speed while the Apache were being agreeable. But the coordinated movement of troops was an easy thing compared to keeping fourteen tired, hungry Indians on the trail, no matter how stoic they were.

Roman studied the storm clouds for a moment, then turned to Sergeant Martini and spoke so Juan Caesar could hear. "We'll ride back north for a few hours and get to the cliffs by Black Mesa. That will give us some shelter in case this weather doesn't pass us by. Bring that sorrel gelding we saw tied in the thicket back there. We'll butcher him when we get to camp. It looks as though these poor people haven't had a good meal in some time."

The soldiers had all eaten their share of horse during hard campaigns, but none of them relished the idea of killing a perfectly good animal to feed Apache renegades. The Indians, on the other hand, lengthened their stride at the thought of fresh meat, and the party began to make good time. Two of the younger children climbed into the saddle with Clay. The Texan's genuine smile was enough to calm the fears of the Apache mothers.

Trap kept to the rear of the column now that his services as a tracker were not needed. He wanted to listen to the Apaches as much as he could, study the way they walked, and bone up on the language. The women and children grew more animated at the thought of food, and chattered enough for Trap to pick up a word or two.

Juan Caesar, who had secured a piebald buckskin from the scalp hunters' horses, trotted up next to him.

"You are Denehii—the tracker," the Indian grunted. He rode with his legs out of the stirrups.

"That's the name my mother calls me," Trap answered.

"Your mother, she is Chuparosa, an Apache?" There was a wildness about this man that set Trap's nerves on edge, as if he was always on the brink of losing his temper and lashing out with bullet or blade.

"She is Chiricahua."

Juan Caesar rode for a while before speaking again. "The holy men have spoken of you and your woman."

"My mother?"

The Apache scoffed. "Your woman—the Nez Percé."

Trap smiled at the thought of Maggie being identified as his woman.

"The holy men say this girl from the north has power," the Apache continued. "They say she is like Lozan, the sister of Victorio. Some are afraid."

"Is that so," Trap said, suddenly worried about what else Apache holy men might be saying about Maggie.

Juan Caesar urged his horse faster, bolting ahead, then wheeling to block Trap's path. Skunk pulled up short, nose-to-nose with the crazy-eyed buckskin. The Apache leaned forward in the saddle and glared with his molten eyes. He jerked a thumb back toward his chest.

His voice was low, but strained, like a whispered shout. "I am not afraid. I see the truth about you and your woman."

With that, he spun the beleaguered horse again on its haunches and trotted off toward his men without looking back.

CHAPTER 31

There was a fair amount of backslapping and congratulations from the garrison soldiers as Roman's troop returned to Camp Apache.

Juan Caesar and his band were confined to the camp until a detail could be formed to take them on to San Carlos.

Ever mindful of the dangers that faced their husbands in the field, the troopers' wives lined the dusty parade ground as soon as they received word their men were returning from patrol. Officers' and enlisted men's wives mingled together at a time like this when no one knew for certain if their husbands would be part of the patrol trotting back through the gate, or slung over the back of a horse, a casualty of the mission. When Roman led his entire troop back alive, with the band of renegades, he was a hero in the eyes of the military, and more especially the military women.

A tall blond beauty, with robin's-egg eyes to match her smock and a smile powerful enough to knock a man off a horse, looked wistfully at Lieutenant Roman as he brought his horse to a stop and dismissed his troop to see to their mounts. An officer's wife to the very core, she kept her distance while Roman handed his reins to a young man wearing a tan stable smock and farrier's leather apron. He gave the man some last-minute instructions about the horse's feet. When his business was done, he removed his gloves and hat just in time to receive a proper welcome-home kiss.

Trap was thrilled to see his beautiful Maggie waiting for him at the far end of the parade ground, a few yards apart from the wives. His mother and father stood behind her. The looks they bore didn't add up.

Maggie's round face was passive, but she bounced on her feet while she waited for him to dismount, as if she was standing on a bed of hot coals. His mother carried an expression of fatigued happiness, the way he'd seen her look after an exhausting walk in the woods. A stray lock of black hair hung across her face and fluttered with the breeze.

The reverend looked as if he'd just taken a mouthful of sour milk and didn't quite know where to spit it.

Hairs stood on the back of Trap's neck. Something was very wrong.

Clay noticed it too. "Here you go, little buddy," he said, drawing his face back in a mock grimace. "I'll take Skunk for you and give him his oats and a good brush-down." He tipped his head to Maggie and the O'Shannons, but kept his voice low, speaking from the corner of his mouth. "I'd rather face a firin' squad than face whatever slow death they got lined up for you."

All instincts told Trap he should go with Clay, but the thought of being with Maggie after the long absence drew him forward. "Much obliged," he croaked through a rapidly tightening throat.

"You look as though you've taken quite a beating, son," the reverend said as Trap approached the tight-lipped group. He could tell his father had worried about him—was glad to see him home. The poor man winced slightly at every word he spoke.

Trap looked more like a raccoon than a man with his two black eyes and swollen nose, all courtesy of Slow Killer.

"I am fine, thank you," he said. "Just took a little punch in the nose." Trap shook the reverend's hand, kissed his mother on the cheek, and put an arm around Maggie's shoulders to give her a squeeze. "Is everything all right here?"

The three looked at each other. Maggie leaned into Trap, nuzzling her head against his shoulder, hiding from the rest of the world. Her whole body trembled. She appeared more vulnerable than Trap had ever seen her.

The reverend chewed on the inside of his cheek and released a tortured breath.

Hummingbird used both hands to smooth the front of her white smock before clasping them together in front of her. It was she who broke the awkward silence.

"Things have happened while you were away," she began. It reminded him of the way she'd spoken to him when he was a small child and his favorite puppy had died. "A soldier has come to call on Maggie—the very same soldier who captured her from her people and sent her to us at White Oak. It seems he has always thought to return and take her as a wife."

A shot through the heart would have pained Trap less. He pulled Maggie even closer and shook his head violently. "No! He can't. I'll fight him—we'll run; I don't care what I have to do." He turned to his father. "Whatever it takes, sir, I'll not give her up again."

"I know." Tears rolled down James O'Shannon's red cheeks.

Hummingbird put a hand on her son's shoulder. Her eyes wandered across the parade ground to a group of soldiers while she spoke. "Your father had to tell a little lie in order to keep Maggie from having to return to Missouri before you got back. The young man, Lieutenant Peter Grant is his name, wants to meet you."

The reverend suddenly took Trap by the shoulders and spun him around. His lips pursed until they were almost white and he glanced heavenward. "Forgive me, Lord," he whispered. He shook Trap's shoulders. "Now, son, listen to me carefully. Lieutenant Grant is crossing the parade ground as we speak. In bearing false witness to him, I have become something I despise. I don't wish to turn my son into a liar as well."

Trap looked to Maggie, then his mother for some clue about what was happening. Maggie sighed. Hummingbird's nose turned up and her eyelids fluttered with a hint of quiet amusement.

"What is he talking about?" Trap asked.

James O'Shannon pushed his son's hat off his head so it fell back behind him against the stampede string. He straightened the boy's hair as he'd done so many times before, when they had prepared for church on Sunday mornings. He then took a step back and gazed through moist, resigned eyes.

"Patrick 'Trap' O'Shannon, I ask you, what is the chief end of man?" he said.

Trap answered out of rote habit from years of reciting the Scripture. "The chief end of man is to glorify God and enjoy him forever. . . ."

"Will you be able to accomplish that as the husband of Mary Margaret Sundown, otherwise known as Maggie?" The reverend's face grew somber.

"Yes, I would, but . . ."

"Hush, Trap," the elder O'Shannon snapped, looking across the parade ground. "Grant is less than a stone's throw away.

"Maggie," the reverend said. He took her hand and placed it on top of Trap's, cupping them both between his own trembling fingers. "Would you be able to do the same as the wife of young Patrick?"

"Yes, I could, my father." Her voice was soft as a feather. "And I will."

Hummingbird dabbed a tear out of her eye and sniffed.

Trap looked up and saw a cavalry officer twenty steps away, approaching them at a fast walk, fists clenched at his sides, a determined look on his freckled face.

"Very well then, in the name of Jesus Christ, Our Lord . . ." James O'Shannon gave an exhausted sigh and resumed his sour-milk expression. "When Grant asks you, you may tell him honestly that you are married to Maggie Sundown O'Shannon."

Trap's head spun. He glanced down at Maggie, at his parents, then back to Maggie again. She was the most beautiful thing he'd ever seen in his life. He wanted to speak, but some unseen force worked to bind his tongue. He swallowed hard, trying to keep standing on wobbly legs that felt like they were made of fresh-cut hay instead of bone and muscle.

Grant walked up behind them and cleared his throat. Maggie must have sensed Trap's predicament because she turned and stepped forward. "Lieutenant," she said with an air of staunch formality. "I want you to meet my husband, Trap O'Shannon."

CHAPTER 32

Lieutenant Grant slinked away, hat crumpled in his hand after a few moments' polite conversation. The poor man was heartbroken at having lost all chance with the beautiful Indian girl who'd no doubt haunted his dreams for the past year.

Trap's knees still felt too weak to operate. He sank on the steps of the modest white house that served as the adjutant's office and attempted to gather his thoughts. Maggie and his parents had had a little time to chew on all this; he was forced to digest it all in one sitting.

"We've moved your things across the dog-run with Maggie," Hummingbird said. "I've been making you a new quilt."

"She stayed up half the night to finish it," Reverend O'Shannon said. Only the hint of a smile perked the corners of his stern lips.

Trap gave a weak grin. He felt like he should say something to Maggie, some words that she might remember on her wedding day, but his brain and tongue conspired against him. When he looked at her and opened his mouth, nothing came out but stutters.

Maggie sat beside him, moving close. He could feel the warmth of her thigh next to him. She sensed his tongue-tied predicament, and rescued him with kind words and the gentlest smile he'd ever seen.

"I remember the missionaries in the Wallowa reading to us from the Bible when I was a little girl. I had a favorite verse: 'Entreat me not to leave thee, or to refrain from following after thee . . . thy people shall be my people and thy God, my God. . . .'" Maggie took his hand in hers and held it on her lap. Her breath came fast and she trembled like a small bird. "I don't remember much of the Bible, but I remember that."

James O'Shannon beamed at the quotation of Scripture from his new daughter-in-law. "I suppose I have only been putting off the inevitable." He gave Trap's hand a hearty shake and patted him on the back. "Remember our talks, son. Her happiness is paramount now."

"It has been for some time, sir."

"Well, then . . . your mother and Mag . . . your wife has been hard at work preparing something of a feast once the word came you were returning today," the reverend said.

"Yes, we have." Hummingbird sighed. "Papa, I suppose you and I should go make the final arrangements while Trap and Maggie sort a few things out and he gets cleaned up."

"I suppose so." The reverend stood his ground, unwilling to leave the newlyweds alone right away. He shook Trap's hand again. Maggie stood and kissed him lightly on the cheek. In all the years he'd known his father, Trap had never seen the man blush before. "Yes, well . . . yes, I suppose we should go and . . ." He turned to his wife. "After you, Chuparosa."

Before the O'Shannons could take their leave, Clay Madsen came striding across the parade ground like a man with a mission. He took off his hat when he neared Maggie and Trap's mother and acknowledged the reverend with a polite nod. He twisted the hat in his hands as he stood.

"What's the matter, Clay?" Hummingbird asked. "You look a little out of sorts."

"I'm fine, ma'am," Clay said. His dark brow was knotted in a strained arch. "Thank you for asking." He looked at Trap and shrugged. "Sorry to drag you away from your sweetheart so soon . . ."

"My wife," Trap corrected. It felt good to say the words.

"Your wife?" Clay's jaw fell. "You hauled off and got married in the last ten minutes?"

"As a matter of fact I did." Trap filled him in about the recent events with Lieutenant Grant.

Maggie eyed Clay like she might carve off a piece of him. "What did you mean drag him away?"

Clay took a defensive step back and raised his hand. "Sorry, Maggie darlin', but the colonel wants to see me and your new husband in his office within the hour—and with the colonel, 'within the hour' means as soon as we can get our behinds over there."

"I'm sure it won't take long," Trap said. He groaned to his feet. Fatigue suddenly overwhelmed his body, and he found himself wondering if getting married was supposed to make a person feel so much older than their natural years. One thing he did know. He thought leaving Maggie had been difficult before. Now, stepping away from her, even for a minute, was nigh to unbearable.

Colonel Branchflower's aide-de-camp was a weasely little lieutenant named Ford Fargo. He had big ears and a shining forehead that reached the uppermost point of his sloping scalp. Fargo's wooden desk was known to be immaculate and polished to a sheen that competed with his gleaming head. He was fastidious in his clerical skills and bordered on maniacal in his grooming.

When Trap and Clay arrived at the office, he was sitting in a wooden chair on the porch cleaning his toenails with a jackknife. His uniform coat was folded neatly across a matching chair at his side.

"Hope you don't peel apples with that thing." Clay curled up his nose at the sight of the other man's feet. "We're here to see the colonel."

"Go right on in." Lieutenant Fargo flicked his knife toward the whitewashed door behind him. "The others are already here."

Trap and Clay exchanged glances. "The others?" Trap said what they were both thinking.

"Umm," Fargo grunted through a nod that flattened his chin to his chest while he concentrated on his ghost-pale foot. "Lieutenant Roman and Private Webber are in there waiting." Fargo wiped his jackknife on a scrap of paper and returned it to his pocket. He took his socks from the chair beside him and began to pull them back on. "Go on inside with them, but don't go past the rail until I come in and announce you."

Both boys stepped onto the small covered porch and hurried through the door. Neither liked spending any more time than necessary around the odd little man.

Thanks to Lieutenant Fargo's compulsions, the front office was spotless. His desk was situated in front of long oaken rails that separated a cramped, but tidy waiting area and telegraph station from the colonel's office proper. Even the trash in the lieutenant's wastebasket appeared to have been arranged with a particular order. A single painting of a matronly redhead in a green dress with eyes remarkably like Fargo's hung on the wall behind a padded chair.

"I bet she digs at her toenails too." Clay smirked.

Roman put a finger to his lips at the comment.

Webber wore a cat-ate-the-canary grin.

The door to Branchflower's office suddenly swung open and the colonel's voice bellowed out like a Biblical whirlwind.

"Fargo!" The shout rattled the painting on the wall.

Roman snapped to attention. "He's not out here, sir."

"I'll be go to hell," the colonel muttered. His chair clattered back from a desk. Heavy footfalls approached the doorway. Branchflower waved the men inside with a hand the size of a shovel blade, his muttonchopped jowls set in annoyance. His bright green eyes narrowed. "He's out cleaning his damned toenails again, isn't he?"

Roman nodded, shooting a wry grin at the others. "He is, sir."

Branchflower moved his massive head back and forth. It reminded Trap of a buffalo bull standing up from a wallow to shake off the dust.

"You know," Branchflower said, his nose turning up in disgust. "A soldier's feet are important, I'll give Fargo that much. But if a man keeps them clean and changes his socks on a regular basis, his damned toenails ought to take care of themselves." The colonel sank back in a huge leather chair behind an expansive desk, which was far more cluttered than Lieutenant Fargo's. He leaned forward to rest his chin on huge fists. "That peculiar little bastard spends far too much time picking his hooves if you ask me."

The other four men in the room remained on their feet, Roman and Webber at attention, their knuckles planted firmly against the stripe on their uniform britches. Trap was learning early that men in power often took their time to get to the point when they had a captive audience.

"At ease, gentlemen." Branchflower nodded curtly. "I appreciate the speed with which . . ."

Lieutenant Fargo poked his head in the door and smiled under his pencil-thin mustache. "I'm right outside at my desk if you need me, sir."

"You're dismissed for the remainder of the day, Lieutenant," the colonel said without looking at him.

Fargo's face wilted. "But sir, I don't mind staying. It's not yet two P.M."

Branchflower waved him off. "Go get a haircut, then. A visit to the tonsorial parlor will do you some good. You can catch up on the local gossip and give me a full report tomorrow."

"Aye, sir." Fargo's voice was despondent. He seemed to sense something was about to happen and hated to miss out on it. He started to shut the door, but Branchflower stopped him.

"Leave it open. I want to know if anyone is out there spying on us. If someone comes in—or doesn't leave—I'll hear it."

Once his aide was gone, the colonel closed the wooden shutters over the single window in his office. "Every commander needs at least one sycophant—but the need is just as strong to be rid of them once in a while." He lowered his voice to a conspiratorial whisper when he got to the matter at hand.

"Gentlemen, you all know that Victorio has jumped the reservation with his Membreno band of hostiles. We believe he's headed for somewhere in Mexico." The colonel slid a stack of papers to one side and un-rolled a parchment map on his desk. He used his ivory pipe and a clay ashtray to hold down the curling edges.

"Lieutenant Gatewood is in pursuit with one company along with Al Seiber and seventeen Chiricahua scouts." Captain Hotchkiss has Company F over here"—he tapped a range of mountains to the south-east—"just in case the hostiles move this way. Troops from Fort Grant are also engaged in the search. We're hoping to catch the wily bastard in a pincer."

Trap and the others studied the map. There were thousands of places the Apache could hide—too many for the cavalry to find Victorio if he didn't want to be found.

"Are we to join in this campaign then, Colonel?" Lieutenant Roman looked up from the map.

"You are not," Branchflower said, surprising them all. "All my men, including the Apache scouts, are either on patrol or needed here in garrison. That said, a delicate issue has arisen that requires our immediate action." Branchflower leaned back in his chair and folded his hands over a ponderous belly. He kept his voice low. "A prominent Mexican colonel named Hernan de la Cruz reported his daughter missing three days ago. She and one of her male escorts were taken while on their way to Phoenix."

"Pilar!" The word came softly under Clay's breath.

The colonel cocked his head to one side. "You know this girl?"

Trap stepped forward. "We do, sir. Mr. Madsen and I helped her out of a little trouble on our way to Arizona last summer."

"I see," Branchflower mused. "That makes things a touch more . . ." The colonel stopped in mid-sentence and shrugged his massive shoulders. He seemed to think better of what he was about to say. "We received a ransom demand, shortly after the girl went missing. It asked for a hundred thousand U.S. dollars."

Webber whistled under his breath, bringing a stare of disapproval from Roman.

"Sorry, sir," the private said without looking a bit sorry. "But that's a lot of money for one girl."

"Yes, it is," Branchflower muttered, almost to himself. "It's as if . . ." He stopped himself again.

He looked up at Roman without elaborating on his last utterance. "The girl's escorts were American. The one who was taken has already been killed. They left his head with the note." Branchflower pulled on his reading glasses again and glanced at some notes on his desk. "Men, the issue is forthright. Relations between Mexico and the United States are strained at best. There's still some fighting going on over on the Nueces Strip. A lot of old grudges have yet to be settled. This Apache issue isn't helping matters at all.

"To make things worse, the girl was under escort by the United States Army. It appears that a member of the military may have been involved in the kidnapping."

The colonel rested his elbows on the table and steepled his fingers, tips together, in front of his face. "General Sheridan has authorized me to assemble a special unit for missions exactly like this one—a group of unconventional fighters—somewhat like Rogers' Rangers during the French and Indian War.

"This mission is more important than you can possibly imagine. Unfortunately, I'm not at liberty to share everything with you at this moment." The colonel's gaze shifted back and forth among the men for a time before it came to rest on Clay. "Mr. Madsen," he said, rubbing his great chin. "Al Seiber tells me you're one of the best horsemen he's ever seen. He also informs me that you have a gift of gab that could ingratiate you to Geronimo himself."

The colonel left Clay to glow from the compliments and shifted his attention to Trap, letting his eyes slide up and down as if he was perusing a horse. He raised a bushy eyebrow. "And you, Mr. O'Shannon. Seiber says you track as well as any Apache he knows— maybe even better. Hell, I guess you are Apache. Is that right?"

"My mother is Chiricahua. My father is Scots-Irish." Trap stood perfectly still and endured the scrutiny. He never tried to hide the fact that he had Apache blood, but he didn't go around wearing the fact on his sleeve either.

"I'm told by many that both of you youngsters would fit the bill nicely for what I have in mind." He sighed and turned to Johannes. "And that brings me to you, Private Webber. From what I hear, you possess a remarkable gift for languages and learning. I need a man with such skills, but I have to be honest with you and say that I am left to wonder why you're not an officer."

Webber didn't answer, and Branchflower didn't pursue the issue. It was obvious any decision about Johannes had already been made or he wouldn't have been present at the meeting.

"Lieutenant Roman," Branchflower continued. "You have the integrity and perseverance I need in a commander. No offense to the good men on Victorio's trail, but if your record was not so stellar, you'd be out with them right now. As it is, I need you here.

"Hear me good, now; this special unit of Scout Trackers will answer only to me." The colonel thumbed his chest. "Me, and no one else; am I clear?"

"Understood," Roman said.

"No staff officers to get in the way and muck things up. I need fresh men, men in the Army but not yet jaded by its politics. Understood?"

Roman nodded. "Yes, Colonel."

"Begging your pardon, sir." Clay cleared his throat.

"Go ahead, Mr. Madsen," Branchflower said.

"Well, sir, it's like this. . . ." Clay stumbled a little,

unaccustomed to speaking to the commanding officer of the camp. "Trap, I mean . . . Mr. O'Shannon and me . . . I mean, we ain't exactly in the Army."

Colonel Branchflower gave a knowing smile and produced two parchment documents from the lap drawer of his desk. He'd thought all this through already.

"That is next on my list of problems to address. Lieutenant Fargo is an odd little bird, but he's a damned good penman, don't you think?"

He pushed the papers across the desk. "Sign on the line at the bottom, gentlemen, and this last issue will be solved. It's a formality really. What with one out of every three men deserting on me, the thing I truly need is your word more than any scrap of paper."

Trap scratched out his name without thinking. From the moment he'd arrived at Camp Apache he'd known, down deep, that it would come to this. He handed the pen to Clay, who paused for a moment. The quill hung over the paper while he thought, rising and falling with each breath.

"It's awful funny, the twists and turns of life," Clay whispered loud enough for all to hear. "I'm about to sign away the next five years of my life, all because I fell asleep on a horse and ran into you, O'Shannon."

"It's voluntary, Mr. Madsen," the colonel said. "No one will force your hand, but we could use your talents." His voice held the closest thing to a plea Clay—or anyone else—would ever get from the proud man.

"The truth is"—the young Texan grinned—"I don't know anything else I'd enjoy doin' more now that I got a taste of this." He gave a resigned sigh and leaned over the desk to scrawl out his name.

"Excellent." Branchflower picked up the enlistment papers and blew on the ink to dry it before slipping them back in his lap drawer.

"Now," the colonel continued. "Webber, Madsen, and O'Shannon, the assignments I have in mind for this unit, hereafter known as the Scout Trackers, will certainly be extremely dangerous and more or less secret in nature. Because of this, I'm promoting each of you to the rank of sergeant with all attendant pay and privileges. Roman, it's a little trickier to promote an officer, what with all the competitive eligibility lists and such, but I did receive permission to brevet you to the rank of captain. I imagine many of your missions will put you all in civilian dress, but if anyone has a problem with your new ranks, direct them to me."

He took a leather dispatch pouch from his desk and slid it across to Roman. "Here's the formal brief describing Señorita de la Cruz's abduction, along with descriptions of her abductors and full accounts from the sole survivor of the ambush. Review it, and then destroy it. I'm not sure who we can trust with this information."

Branchflower stood and shook each man's hand in turn. "Gentlemen, you will come to realize that five dollars a month extra is small compensation for the harsh and dangerous duties I will assign you. But rest assured, a great deal of thought went into this decision. I have all confidence that you are the right men for the job. I urge you to make all haste in this rescue."

The colonel's tone suddenly became curt and formal. "Sergeants, you are dismissed for the present. Captain Roman, if you would be so kind as to remain behind for a moment. I have another matter I need to discuss with you."

"Yes, sir." Roman fished a gold watch from his trouser pocket. "Men, it's twenty minutes to three. Go and bid your sweethearts good-bye. But don't tell them where you're heading. Meet me in front of King James' at four for gear issue."

"My noggin aches like it's been filled to the brim," Clay muttered after they walked outside.

Webber rolled his eyes and gave Madsen a good-natured slap on the back. "That's not such an accomplishment for our good colonel."

"I mean it," Clay said. "Why so much secrecy over a kidnapped girl? Even if Pilar is a colonel's daughter. Let's just ride in there and take care of it like we took care of those scalp hunters."

"If it were always that easy, we'd let the girls in town do it," Webber scoffed.

Trap touched his sore nose. He didn't remember it being all that simple.

"Whatever you say." Clay went on with his thought, unperturbed by Johannes. "He gave us a heck of a lot of information without telling us much of anything—except that our job would be dangerous."

"Welcome to the Army." Webber gave him a slap on the back.

Clay narrowed his eyes. "That Colonel Branchflower reminds me of a tight silk nightie on a curvy woman—everything gets covered, just not very well."

"I hate to leave her so soon," Trap confided to Clay a few minutes later, after Johannes excused himself to say his good-byes to a Mexican girl he'd been seeing. "An hour isn't gonna be much time for a honeymoon."

"No offense intended, partner." Madsen took off his hat. He grinned wide enough to show all his teeth. "But I seen the look in your child bride's eyes when you walked away from her a little bit ago. Maybe you didn't recognize it, but I sure enough did. I reckon an hour will be more than enough time . . ."

Trap nodded slowly, thinking about what he'd seen in Maggie's eyes. It was what had made his legs go so weak—a hungry look that bored into his very soul. "Well, then," he said. His mouth was dry. Thoughts of Maggie's toes, her face, her smells all flooded in around him like a warm and comforting breeze. "Reckon I should hurry along . . . I guess . . ."

"Go ahead and go then." Clay smirked. "Your damned feet ain't nailed to the ground. Get a move on, she's waitin' for you."

Trap snugged his hat around his ears and took off at a run.

CHAPTER 33

"Yeah, verily." King James wagged his finger at Clay. "If the United States Army sayeth thou shalt be issued a Smith & Wesson Schofield, then that is exactly what thou shalt receive."

Madsen grimaced and shot a pleading look at Roman.

"It's a free pistol," Webber whispered. "He's not saying you have to throw your Colt down the crapper. Just accept the damned thing so we can be on our way."

It took a little over half an hour for Sergeant James to finish gear issue for all four men. Although Clay accepted the Army's new sidearm, a Schofield break-top revolver chambered in .45 Smith & Wesson, he tucked it away in his saddlebag with a snide look and a few choice words. He was comfortable with his Colt Peacemaker, and made it clear that although he enjoyed fine new rifles, as far as pistols were concerned, his old friend with ivory grips and a comfortable feel would remain by his side for as long as he drew breath.

The other three men each took the new-issue sidearm as well as a Winchester 1876 chambered in the new .45-75, a necked-down but still powerful cartridge similar to the .45-70. While not as accurate as Clay's Sharps .45-90, the Winchesters were capable of throwing big chunks of lead downrange at a high rate of speed—a quality that was sure to come in handy in the sort of mission Colonel Branchflower had promised the Scout Trackers.

With no pack mule, each man had to carry all his own gear. Rations consisted of hardtack and salt beef, some of which Webber insisted was left over from the War Between the States. Each man drew two canteens and a new blanket roll.

"He's a straight shooter, that Lieutenant . . . I mean *Captain* Roman," Clay said outside the quartermaster's store. The captain was still inside taking care of a few last-minute details with King James. "I'm sure proud he let me keep Clarice. Reckon he'll do to ride with on this kind of engagement."

"He's more than capable," Webber agreed. He struck a match with his thumbnail and touched it to the end of a short cigar clenched between his teeth. "I'm thinking this will be good duty." He puffed the smoke until the end glowed orange and lit his ruddy face. "Anything is better than the drudgery of garrison duty. Give me the trail any day of the week."

Trap thought about that for a minute. As long as he had Maggie, life at Camp Apache would be a lot of things, but dull wasn't one of them.

Johannes puffed happily at his cigar and smirked at Trap. "Maggie get upset about you leaving so soon when we just got home?"

"She knows I have a job," Trap said. "She wants me to do the right thing. Honor means a lot to her."

"*I tan i epi tas,*" Webber said, nodding his head. "So, our Maggie's a warrior too."

Clay turned around from tying a canvas nose bag full of oats to his saddle and balled up his fists. He had *fight* written all over his face. "*I tan* . . . what the hell did you just call Maggie?"

Webber tapped the ash of his cigar and gave Madsen a patronizing smile. "Hold on there, righter of all wrongs to womanhood. I didn't say anything bad. It's Greek."

"It damn sure is," Clay snorted.

"It's what the Spartan mothers used to tell their sons when they left for battle: *Return with your shield or on it.* Like Maggie, those women were warriors. They believed in honor."

"I heard my father talk about the Spartans." Trap nodded. "Good fighters, lots of honor, but an awful rough life."

Webber gave Trap an approving look. His brow rose as if he was a bit surprised. "You, or at least your father, knows his Plutarch."

Clay shook his head. "We may not all be as learned as you, Mr. Webber, but even I heard of Plutarch."

"Is that so?"

"I told you I was pretty near raised by my pa's string of whores." Madsen grinned. His ire faded immediately once he found Johannes wasn't saying anything derogatory about Maggie. "Them poor old girls gotta have somethin' to do during the day. Most of 'em develop a powerful appetite for books. When I was a sprout, I just hung around and listened; some of it must have sunk in accidentally."

"Well, I am a happy man," Webber said. "I've not only been made part of an elite team of adventurers, they happen to be semi-learned adventurers as well. I thought I was going to have to do all my philosophizing to Captain Roman. He'll break into a good erudition once in a great while, but most of the time, he likes to keep quiet."

"He strikes me as being very well educated," Trap said, meaning it as a high compliment.

"I heard he's a Mormon." Clay turned to tighten the cinch on his roan. The horse was prone to take in air and snugging the girth was a chore best done in steps. "I don't reckon I ever met a real live Mormon before."

"Hell." Webber picked a bit of tobacco leaf off the tip of his tongue. "You'll meet plenty of 'em out here. They're thick as thieves in some parts of this godforsaken desert. For some reason, the Mormons flock to these desolate places." Webber lowered his voice to make certain Roman, who was still inside, didn't hear him. "I figure they identify with the ancient Children of Israel, running after the Promised Land all the time. The ones I've met are right and honest enough, if a little quirky. Some of them even marry more than one woman at a time."

The way Webber shifted his eyes put a sinking feeling in Trap's gut. He never did like talking about someone when they weren't around.

"I've seen the captain's wife." Clay grinned. "I

don't think he'd need another one. I do believe she's the only one he's got."

"She is at that, Mr. Madsen." Roman's voice poured from the dark interior of the adobe building. He followed it out into the flat evening light. The air and the conversation were just cool enough to pink his cheeks. "Her name is Irene and you may address her as such. She is the light of my life."

The captain looked around at the three members of his little group. His face was impassive, a blank page, impossible to read. "She is the only wife I have, or ever will have for that matter."

He took a deep breath, held it a moment while he pondered, then slowly exhaled. "Gentlemen, I should clear the air regarding my religion from the outset. You're welcome to speak to me about it at any time, but I won't push it on you. I attend church with my dear wife when in garrison, but I am not your preachy brand of Mormon. It is my sincere belief that the Good Lord made us each with a purpose: some to be preachers and some to be warriors—each a righteous instrument in His hands. I assume I am riding with warriors.

"Please do me the service of asking if you have a question. I don't want there to be anything unanswered from those who may have to die beside me. Here are a few things to get you acquainted with me. I don't use tobacco, I never consort with lewd women, and I won't partake of beer or hard liquor. The funny thing is, I didn't do these things before I converted, so it hasn't been much of a switch for me. Additionally, I don't happen to drink coffee or tea, though I don't look down on those who do."

The men all stood, still as glass, by their horses. Webber's cigar hung limply in his lips, Trap stared at the ground and Clay wrung his hat in his hands.

A wry smile started slowly at Roman's eyes, spread over his high cheekbones, and down to the corners of his mouth.

"And one more thing. I rarely ever curse, but take heed when I do, for then you can be sure I'm damned good and mad. Now, carry on, men. I'd like to be on the trail inside the hour."

By five o'clock other soldiers began to drift past the quartermaster's store on their way to supper or evening duties. Webber and Madsen were already in the saddle. Their horses seemed to sense their eagerness to regain the trail and pawed the ground, snorting with impatience. Clay let his roan step out a little to work off some of the tension. Webber followed, still talking on about Plutarch, the warriors of Sparta, and their hard-hearted mothers.

Trap thought about leaving Maggie while he put the finishing touches on his gear and checked his cinch one last time. In a way, he supposed, coming back for a short time, then leaving again so soon made it more difficult than if he'd just stayed away. It was like picking off a scab—no, that wasn't it, because riding away from Maggie produced a wound that didn't quite heal.

He resigned himself to the fact that he had to make a living. He hadn't chosen a life on the trail; it had chosen him—or at least Colonel Branchflower had—and Trap had to admit he enjoyed the challenge.

He'd just picked up Skunk's front foot when he caught a hint of something different on the wind. When he looked up, Maggie stood in front of him, smiling softly in her own understated way.

She wore one of his mother's dresses with blue and white checks and a matching ribbon around her loose hair.

"I got you a little something for the trail, husband." She handed him a small parcel, no bigger than a cartridge box. The dress had buttons that went up the front, all the way to the neckline, but Maggie had left the top four undone. The soft skin at her collarbone was flushed and pink. "I wanted to give you this before, but I . . ." Her voice was low and breathy. A mischievous gleam sparkled in her eye. "But my mind was on other things."

Trap blushed. He didn't dare say what he was thinking. Sometimes he wished he had Clay's quick wit so he could make Maggie laugh. He was vaguely aware of Madsen and Webber working their horses a few yards off, and of the creak of saddle leather as the captain climbed aboard his tall bay. Everyone else was mounted and Roman wasn't one to dawdle horseback. Trap knew he didn't have much time. Instead of speaking, he opened the package.

"It's a compass." Maggie lifted the small brass instrument out of the box in Trap's hands and held it up in front of him. "You are a man on the move, Trap O'Shannon. You have been leaving me since the day I met you. This will help you always find your way home."

"Where, I mean how . . . ?"

"Your father paid me a little for helping at the

school. I wanted to give you something as a wedding present."

"But I didn't. . . ."

She put a finger to his lips. "Yes, you did. You are my husband. That is all that matters."

A blond corporal leaned on gangly legs against a cedar support post in front of the quartermaster's store and smirked behind a mouth full of crooked teeth. "Well, ain't that just the most precious thing you ever heard, Costello. 'My husband'?" He elbowed a swarthy Italian trooper next to him in the ribs. "We're beddin' down with the enemy now?"

Costello gave a nervous chuckle. "Come on, Fannin. Watch what you do now."

Trap's neck burned. He knew a fight between two soldiers generally saw them both in the stockade— no matter who started it. But some things could not be tolerated. He took a deep breath. Maggie shook her head.

"Don't." She mouthed the word. "If you fight him, you will lose all you have gained today."

Corporal Fannin spit into the sand, then sucked air in through a large gap in his top teeth. "I wonder what it's like to bed a red woman."

Trap gave Maggie the reins to his horse and gave her a pat on the shoulder, moving her gently out of the way of what was sure to be an all-out brawl. He spun, both fists doubled, to face his loudmouthed adversary.

"I bet they're all hot like a fire coal," the instigator rolled on, raising his eyebrows and rolling his shoulders like he had a chill. "That's the only reason I could see to be with one of the little . . ."

Hezekiah Roman backed his muscular bay straight into the gabby corporal, pinning the surprised man against the cedar post.

Unaccustomed to having anything but a tail occupying the crack of his backside, the molested gelding flattened its ears and pitched, sending the offending man into the air and catching him with both well-shod feet on his way back down.

Corporal Fannin hit the ground with a sickening thud, clutching his groin with both hands. What little color he'd had drained from his pallid face. His Italian friend wisely stepped out of the way as if they'd never met.

"Mr. Fannin," Roman snapped, giving his snorting horse a pat on the neck. "You'd think a man such as yourself, employed in the United States Cavalry, would have the brains to stay out from behind the rear end of a mount. You will assign yourself to stable duty for the next month so you may learn proper horse-handling procedures and protocol." The captain spun his bay, and then side-passed over to the moaning soldier. He was an artist on the back of a horse. Madsen's jaw hung open in pure, unabashed hero worship.

The huge gelding stretched its neck out and nibbled at Corporal Fannin's uniform trousers.

Roman leaned down, his voice a firm stage whisper from which all around could listen and learn. "Cavalry troops of old utilized that move in battle to kill any enemy foolish enough to try and attack them from the rear. This horse could easily jump up flat-footed and kick your fool head off. All I have to do is give the command. Mister, you speak to one of my men or their women like that again, and I'll give that command. Are we clear?"

"Yes, sir," the corporal blubbered, his voice considerably higher than it had been.

As when garrison women lined up to welcome home the troops when they came in, they lined up to say good-bye when their men left. In this case, only Roman and Trap had wives there to see them off, but Clay and Webber both had pretty young things to send them off with a kiss.

"Good-bye, my son of Mars," Irene Roman shouted as the little group trotted out into the piñons outside Camp Apache. "You are my hero!" The captain blew her a kiss and tipped his hat.

Maggie's good-bye was more subtle. She stood watching as the group left, fingering the leather pouch around her soft neck. A smile Trap could feel on the back of his neck blazed like a flame in her black coffee eyes.

Trap turned back to look at her until the trees blocked her from his view.

"I only been in the Army two hours and I hate it already." Clay twirled the reins absentmindedly in his hands and looked up at the darkening sky as he spoke. "I only joined this escapade to get a chance to see that little darlin' Pilar again. Women," he sighed. "What's a man supposed to do?"

Trap kept his eyes forward, studying his horse's twitching ears. He thought about Maggie's tender good-bye to him back at their little dog-run cabin only an hour before. The last thing he wanted to do was talk to Clay about something so private and intimate. He'd surely rib him for the rest of the mission.

Afraid his face was still flushed at the thought of it, Trap kept his eyes focused on the rock-strewn terrain ahead.

"Females can sure enough cause a body a considerable amount of grief." Clay shook his head and sighed again, too caught up in his own thoughts to notice Trap's discomfort. "Ain't that right, partner?"

"I reckon they can," Trap said.

Roman reined up so all four men traveled abreast.

"Leaving is always difficult," he said. "I hate to leave my loved ones as much as the next man. When I am home, I dread the thought of a lonely expedition. I must confess that I truly despise the thought of leaving a hot bed and a hot woman for the cold and bitter trail. But . . ." He stopped his horse and looked his men each in the eye in turn. "Once I'm on the trail, I realize this is where I can be the most use to society. What good am I if I sit at home and tickle my wife? What good are any of us? I know you all want to get home, except maybe for Webber." He grinned, showing he was almost human. "Well, mark my word on this. I'll see that each of you gets back or die trying.

"Remember, though we are few in number, a small but persistent cadre of disciplined men often has an advantage over a much larger force." With that he trotted back into the lead.

Clay turned to Trap and grimaced. "I don't like them odds, partner," he whispered. "I ain't had a disciplined day in my life."

"Today is as good a day as any to begin, Sergeant

Madsen," Roman said over his shoulder, proving his hearing was truly beyond human.

"*Sanguis frigitis,*" Webber mused, under his breath.

Now Clay lowered his voice. "Hell's bells! More Greek already? You're making my head hurt."

"Not Greek, oh, wise student of learned whores. Latin. *Sanguis frigitis* literally means *cold blood*—more figuratively, it means *steady under pressure*—calm in the face of danger. Suits the captain right to the core."

Trap stood in the stirrups to stretch his back. "Can't argue there."

"Hell," Clay snorted. "After what I've seen in the last three days, I guess it suits you two as much as him. Gougin' folks' eyes out and loppin' their heads off at the gallop . . . I reckon I'm the only one that gets shook up over anything anymore."

"I don't know about that," Trap said. "You seemed mighty calm making a three-hundred-yard shot to save the captain and his men from that scalp-hunter rifleman."

"Four hundred and thirty," Clay corrected with a wink. "I stepped it off."

"Well, there you go then." Webber raised his fist high in the air, as if in a toast. "I hereby declare the motto of the Scout Trackers to be *Sanguis Frigitis.*"

"*Sanguis Frigitis,*" Trap and Clay repeated, nodding their heads.

"Has a nice ring to it," Roman said without turning around. The other men jumped when they realized he'd been listening. "*Cold Blood.* I'm afraid we'll need it."

CHAPTER 34

When she moved, she threw up, and throwing up made her move. Beads of sweat covered her forehead, pasting ringlets of black hair against pallid skin. Her body burned with fever, shivers sending bolts of pain down her shoulder and through her right arm. A normally petite hand throbbed purple and yellow at twice its normal size.

The filthy, merciless men had dragged her from her bed in the dead of night and thrown her to the ground in her nightgown. Horses squealed and stomped amid acrid smoke and the clap of gunfire. Riders cursed and shouted at each other in the darkness. She'd tried to crawl away in the confusion, but a horse had stepped on her hand.

The pain had been unbearable. She heard the bones crunch between hoof and rock. Nausea overwhelmed her before unconsciousness silenced her choking screams.

Three days in this sandstone hell had pressed every tear out of her bloodshot eyes. Grit and grime covered every inch of her body, grating and inflaming her pink skin until even a light breeze brought on dizzying waves of agony.

Red sand caked her face where it had pressed against the ground without benefit of a blanket or pillow. Her lavender gown, once a sight to behold, made in Mexico City from the finest cotton, was now reduced to filthy rags. It did little to protect her from the bone-numbing chill at night, and even less to cover her bruised nakedness.

Vile men who cared nothing for her survival squatted and knelt in tiny groups around a crackling cedar fire under the deep rock overhang. The sight of them racked her slight body with sickening panic that made her teeth ache. The things they'd said, the things they'd done to poor Charlie before they finally cut off his head—his pitiful wails still tore at her ears and haunted her fitful dreams. Their gruff voices echoed inside the rock tomb, bouncing around in her head until she thought it might explode.

The flames cast huge shadows along the back of the shallow cave, dancing and crackling with the night wind. Orange sparks rose and swirled like ghostly spirits on the air, stark against the blackness beyond the rocks.

Locked in a game of dice, the men drank and cursed and sometimes hit each other, but they seldom wasted a glance on the pitiful Mexican girl in the corner.

A half-cooked joint of antelope meat lay covered with flies on a greasy rock beside her. She'd eaten a few bites out of desperation earlier that day, but vomited them back up again a few moments later.

She knew she should eat something to keep her strength up, but her stomach churned and boiled every time she looked at the foul thing. Her lips were dry and split from lack of water and purple from slaps and rough taunts.

"Damn every last one of you, you lousy sons of bitches," the man called Jack Straw shouted as he rose from the main game of dice across the flickering chamber. He shook a bottle of liquor at the others. "I ain't gonna hunker here and get cheated by your sorry hides." His stooped shoulders heaved with anger. His craggy face appeared to twitch in the orange firelight. The big Indian slid a huge knife half out of the beaded sheath stuck in his belt. He glared through cruel eyes that shut Straw up as surely as a cold slap in the face.

The girl held her breath. They fought like this all the time, especially in the evening. She'd never seen people argue and scream at each other so violently. Someone would certainly die before long. In the beginning, she was afraid it would be her. Very soon, she knew, she would welcome the thought of it.

Straw skulked to the rear of the cave with a bottle in his hand. Back to the wall, he slid to the sandy floor, shoulders slouched in defeat. His dirty blond head hung between his knees.

When he sat up to take a drink, he caught her looking at him. She held her breath and turned away, but it was too late.

"What the hell are you gawkin' at, Miss Purebred?" Whiskey ran around the mouth of the bottle as he took a pull and dribbled down on his torn shirt. "You ain't never seen a man drunk before?"

She clenched her eyes shut. It did no good to talk to these men. She pressed her face against the sand, hoping against hope that Straw would keep drinking and leave her alone.

She smelled the fetid stench of his body and the sour odor of cheap whiskey before she opened her eyes. The coarse weave of his homespun shirt brushed against her bare shoulder. She flinched, wishing herself deeper into the sand.

"Here you go, Little Highness," Straw slurred, shaking the bottle in her face. His knee bumped her broken hand, and she bit her lip to keep from crying out. Her stomach roiled from the pain and the man's awful smell.

"Have a little drink, Honey Pot. It'll loosen you up."

Clenching her eyes shut, she shook her head and turned away. Her shoulders trembled with fright.

Straw clawed at her shoulder and gave it a brutal yank. "I said have a drink, damn you." He hauled her up by her arm. She moved with him to keep from causing any more pain to her broken hand. His face was only inches from hers. Yellow teeth gleamed dully in the shadows. She winced at his rancid breath, dumb and frozen with fear.

He grabbed her by the face and squeezed until tears poured from her eyes. He slurred through clenched teeth, "Just because them bastards cheat me don't give you the right to give me no sass." He rubbed his greasy forehead against hers as he spoke. "I don't give a damn about the money anymore. I can't spend another minute in this cave with your sweetness a-waftin' up to my old nose just a few feet away. I reckon I'll take my cut of you now."

The other men laughed at their new game of dice. Someone was losing badly, and now that Straw was gone, the group had homed in on him.

Straw was oblivious. He shoved her head tight against the rock wall, pressing her jaw with his thumb and forefinger until he forced her mouth open. She tried to scream, but could only manage a moaning gurgle.

"Come on, take a little swig." Straw leered. "You're gonna need it."

He forced the heavy whiskey bottle through dry, cracked lips. She tasted the saltiness of her own blood an instant before glass hit her teeth with a sickening thud. She gagged as the searing liquid poured against her throat and spewed down her chest.

The pain was excruciating, but she summoned enough strength to struggle, flailing against her attacker with both hands. She felt one of her front teeth snap, and retched as he jammed the bottle deeper against the back of her throat.

Suddenly, Straw stopped. The whiskey bottle fell away and splashed harmlessly to the sand. The panting girl shielded her face with her good hand and braced herself for another attack. When none came, she opened her eyes.

Straw knelt above her, his back arched in agony, his mouth open in a noiseless cry. The big Indian stood behind him, one hand on the hilt of the huge knife that was buried in Straw's spine, the other gripping a fistful of greasy hair.

Straw dropped the bottle and reached over his shoulder with both hands, clawing in vain at his back.

His shoulders twitched when the Indian jerked out the knife and stabbed him again and again.

The girl collapsed against the ground and watched in detached silence as Straw's glowing red eyes rolled back in his head. Blood poured out of him, drenching the sand. He lay at her feet, twitching and taking a long time to die.

CHAPTER 35

"Something's been eatin' at me, Webber," Clay confided as the group rode along three abreast. Roman was well in the lead. It was early afternoon on the second day out of Camp Apache. The first night had been chilly, but the sun now hung in a cloudless sky and the weather had warmed considerably.

Trap and Webber rode on without speaking. Both knew they didn't need to say anything to prod Clay into explaining what he meant.

"It's something the colonel said back there." The Texan looked at Johannes. "Webber, don't take this the wrong way, but you're one of the smartest men I ever met when it comes to book learnin'. If you don't mind my asking, how come you never did apply to be an officer?"

The three rode on in silence for quite some time with no sound but the heavy thud of hooves on rock and the lumbering groan of the horses.

"Plato," Webber said, looking ahead. "Among others."

Clay gave a swaggering laugh. "I figured you'd say something about the Greeks. Plato told you not to be an officer?"

Johannes shrugged, not upset from the question, but deadly serious. "Plato believed philosophers should be kings and all kings should be philosophers. He also said a man should do what he was born to do—stay in his own class."

"Well," Clay said. "I ain't sayin' you should be a king, but your philosophizin' ought to at least qualify you for lieutenant."

"Kings," Johannes pointed out, "and other powerful men tend to use their power to further their own selfish goals. They have a way of becoming corrupted."

Clay chewed on that for a while. Trap watched the captain riding out ahead of them. Now there was a man with philosophy and power—and he seemed virtually incorruptible.

"I think you'd make a good enough officer, even with the power it brings." Clay gave a sincere nod as if he was passing judgment.

"My friend," Johannes said, "that just proves how little you know about me."

The wind shifted and sent Clay's mind drifting another direction before he could think of a comeback. He stood in the saddle and sniffed the air. "Reminds me of a pig roast." He turned to Trap, who rode beside him, eyes on the ground looking for sign. "A pig roast and burnt rope. Do you smell what I'm smellin'?"

Trap looked up, took a moment to inhale the dry desert air, and nodded. The smell of cooked meat did hang on the faint wind. He chided himself for not noticing it before Madsen. His mother had often warned him about depending too much on one sense and forgetting the others. Humans had a way of relying only on their eyes while their ears and nose went virtually unused. The little tracker reined in his horse and drew another lungful of air. Something else mixed with the familiar smell—just a whiff. It wasn't rope—it was hair.

Roman and his men saw the buzzards ten minutes later. Some circled lazily overhead, dark specks against a blinding blue; others perched on the gnarled branches of a dead mesquite in the wavy, heated light of midday. The raucous coughing of crows grated the air shortly after. A sprawling stand of prickly pear cactus hid whatever produced the smell from view, but it was causing quite a fight among the scavenger community.

A heavy sense of doom permeated the air as the men neared the cactus. The smell grew stronger and pinched at Trap's nose. He knew what it was. They all did.

Five turkey buzzards tried to lift off from the nearest of two bodies as the riders approached on snorting horses. Two of the birds found they couldn't fly with their bellies full of rancid meat, and regurgitated it up in a splattering slurry as they winged away. Trap shot a glance at Clay, who was highly likely to throw up at the sight of such a thing. For all his braggadocio, the Texan had a tendency toward a weak stomach. Luckily, he was busy scanning the horizon for trouble and missed the buzzards' display.

"My Lord," Clay said when he finally let his eyes come to rest on the bloated bodies. His voice was shallow. "My poor eyes keep seein' things they don't want to see."

Roman dismounted and looped the bay's reins around the dead mesquite. The buzzards, crows, and a handful of magpies winged off to wait their respective turns after the interloping men moved on. There was a hierarchy among the birds, and they ate in ascending order of their looks.

"O'Shannon," the captain whispered. Trap would come to know that Roman generally spoke quietly around the dead. "Take a look around the bodies and see if you can get an idea of what happened here." He turned to Webber and Madsen, who both stood wide-eyed, entranced at the two naked bodies staked to the ground in front of them. "Men! Snap out of it and secure your horses. Get your rifles and keep a weather eye on those hills. I wouldn't put it past an Apache to use a massacre like this as bait to catch us unawares."

That bit of information was enough to jog Clay out of his stupor. He had Clarice out glinting in the sun in a matter of moments. Webber stood with his Winchester, facing the hills in the opposite direction.

Trap surveyed the grisly scene. Two men, it was impossible to tell how old they were, lay spread-eagle, feet pointing in opposite directions on the rocky ground. Stout leather cord and wooden pegs kept them there. The remains of a fire blacked the earth between what was left of their swollen heads.

Death had not come quickly for the poor souls. Trap could make out the square-toed tracks of Apache moccasins where they had fed the fire a bit at a time, keeping it just large enough to cause excruciating pain without bringing an end to the doomed men's suffering. Trap wondered how long they'd screamed while the flames singed their hair, blistered the tender skin, and finally boiled their brains.

He had to look at them like tracks to keep from getting sick. If he considered them as human beings, his stomach began to rebel. He thought of them as nothing more than sign with a story to tell, and quelled his unruly gut.

The buzzards had started with the cooked parts, and the men stared up at nothing with swollen, eyeless skulls. The sun had taken its toll on the lower half of the bodies, and though the fire had not cooked them, they were bloated and dark.

After he studied the area around the bodies, Trap worked out in ever-growing circles, checking behind every rock and shrub within a fifty-yard circle.

"They been here a while," he said when he was satisfied he had the complete story and came back to the group. "A day or two at least." He stuck his hand in the coals. There was no heat left, even a few inches down. They were as dead as the men they had killed.

"Apache?" Webber shouted from his position a few yards away.

"Looks that way." Roman nodded, slapping his leather gloves against an open hand.

"Victorio's band?" Webber scanned the hills to the east. There was no fear in his voice. He was merely thinking out loud.

Trap stood and walked toward his horse to put some distance between himself and the mutilated bodies. "There are too many hoofprints to count, Captain. Most are unshod. The whole place is covered with moccasin tracks. One set is smaller like those of a woman. It could be Victorio and his sister, Lozan. She relieved herself behind that square stone there." He pointed with an open hand.

Webber took a break from his vigil and cast a sidelong glance over his shoulder. "You can tell it was a woman by looking at where she . . ."

Trap shrugged. His mother had been blunt and open about such things as part of his tracking education. Talk of sex bothered him, but this was different; bodily functions were sign and deserved study. Trap was finding himself a teacher more and more each day.

"A female is generally wary of being discovered in such a delicate position," he pointed out calmly, as if he was instructing a class. "They will look over their shoulder, this way, then that way, back and forth several times during the process." O'Shannon mimicked the motion himself, letting his entire body sway with the movement. "Whatever they leave behind, liquid or solid, is usually in a little crescent shape instead of a circle."

Webber smirked. "Well, sir, that's about as much as I need to know about that." He resumed his guard duties, shaking his head.

Clay giggled, then nodded slowly to himself, obviously picturing the whole thing in his mind. "Victorio and Lozan it is."

"Could be," Roman mused. "But we have other business."

"Well, I'm glad to hear that." Clay gave an exasperated sigh. "I got no real desire to go up against an army of Apache who would roast what little brain I got just to get their daily entertainment."

"Let's get some dirt pushed up over the bodies," Roman said, walking to his horse for a hand shovel. They'd brought with them two of the Rice-Chillingsworth trowel-style bayonets the Army had experimented with. Roman wouldn't allow them on the end of a rifle, said it was too much temptation to stick the muzzle in the dirt, but he did find them useful as digging tools and easy to pack on such a mission where space was at a premium.

"Poor souls deserve a decent burial, whoever they are." Never one to leave the distasteful work solely to his men, Roman started for the bodies with his trowel. Trap joined him while the other two stood watch. Sweat dripped off both men by the time they had a sizable pile of dirt and rock piled over the bodies.

Trap knew it might keep the birds away for a while, but would never discourage scavengers like wolves or coyotes. He reckoned that out in the desert like this, decent folks like Captain Roman buried the dead so they could look at something neat and tidy as they rode away. If vermin and turkey buzzards dragged the bones out later, at least a man could know things were in order when he left. Burial was a luxury on the wide-open plain: peace of mind more for the living than for the uncaring dead.

A cool wind kicked up while Trap repacked the trowels. When he turned, something in the scrubby branches of a creosote bush caught his eye.

At first he thought it was a desert cottontail scurrying for shelter. Then, the wind moved the bush and he could make out straight edges, angular like something man-made.

Trap gave Skunk a reassuring pat on the rump and went to investigate. The others were already mounting up.

"What is it?" Clay asked, trotting over to see what Trap had found. It was a light brown envelope, half-burned. Scrawled in block letters, the ink smeared by an unsteady hand, was the word *URGENT!*

A single sheet of tan paper folded lengthwise down the center slid out of the envelope and into Roman's gloved hand. More than half of it crumbled into parched ashes when he tried to open it. He read what was left slowly to himself, then passed it back to Trap.

"Gentlemen, we can stop wasting our time feeling sorry for those men. It looks as though they were part of the group that kidnapped Señorita de la Cruz. I am assuming they were on their way to deliver these ransom instructions when they had the bad fortune to run into this little band of hostiles."

Trap read over the note twice to make sure he got it all, then handed it up to Clay.

"It instructs the Army to build a fire on top of Kill Devil Mesa as soon as this message is received and the money is ready." Roman rubbed his tired eyes. "Further instructions follow, but they are burned away. Whatever their plan was, it may have changed since the message never got delivered. It's dated two days ago. The signal fire should have been set by now."

Clay's mouth dropped open and he began to fid-

get with his catch rope. "You think they might spook
and kill her?"

"It's possible," Roman said. "More likely, they would
send out another note since these two never returned.
Sergeant O'Shannon. Can you pick up the dead men's
back trail?"

Trap nodded, spinning Skunk. He was already on
it. The track of two shod horses moving across the
desert was easy enough to find and follow.

"Very well," Roman said. "We'll follow the tracks
right back to the men that sent them—and hopefully
to the girl. We need to move quickly. . . ." Roman's
voice trailed off. He motioned with his hat toward a
cloud of dust billowing on the distant horizon.

Someone was coming.

Clay turned in the saddle to slide Clarice out of her
scabbard. "Apache?" he said under his breath as he
lowered the block a hair to be certain he had a fresh
round in place.

A growing red cloud boiled over the hills to the
east. Whoever it was, they were getting closer.

Roman dismounted and stood quietly. He scanned
the area around them, thinking. At length he looked
up at Clay.

"Sergeant Madsen, see that patch of rocks?" He
pointed to a long hill a hundred yards away.

Clay grunted. "Yessir."

"Take your long gun and set up a position of cover
amid those rocks. Stay out of sight until I take off my
hat. Don't rejoin us until I put my hat back on."

"How will I know if I should fire?"

Roman patted Madsen's horse on the rump. He

smiled. "Clay, if we start shooting, you go ahead and feel free to join in."

"Aye, sir." Clay put the spurs to his blue roan and loped up the steady incline to the pile of boulders. It was big enough to hide both horse and rider.

Roman stood by in silence as the dust cloud boiled ever larger on the horizon.

Trap was surprised that he felt no fear. He found himself too worried about letting Captain Roman and the others down to have any time to be afraid. He repeated Clay's earlier question. "Do you think it's Apaches? Victorio coming back, maybe?"

"They're coming in from the southeast." Roman shook his head. "It's almost sunset. That means the light is shining directly in their eyes. No self-respecting Apache would launch an attack unless the sun was to his back."

"Maybe they don't know we're here," Webber offered. His gaze too was locked on the horizon, the Winchester in his hands.

"Could be," Roman said. "But I doubt it. That cloud of dust has United States Cavalry written all over it. We horse soldiers are generally the only breed of human around these parts with enough hubris to let everyone and everything in the country know we're on our way. No, that's cavalry all right. And if it's who I think it is, I'm afraid he could pose nearly as much of a problem as Apaches."

CHAPTER 36

D Troop was under the command of Captain Fredrick Paul Lyons; Fredrick to the few friends he had, not Fred, not Freddy, or even F.P. He'd been known to correct generals if they attempted to call him anything but his proper given name.

A tall man with gray circles under matching eyes, he stood firmly on all points of formality and expected all those around him to do the same. The joke around the Army was that he required his wife to address him as Captain Lyons when he was in uniform and Your Highness when he was not.

A normal company was comprised of about a hundred men including officers, but with sickness, desertion, and other manpower shortages, D Company was lucky to have a complement of fifty. They breasted the sandstone ridge in columns of four, with Captain Lyons out front on a stodgy white horse. His aide rode next to him, followed by a mustachioed bugler. The swallow-tailed company guidon snapped on its nine-foot lance in the freshening breeze above the next trooper in line. Each man's face was set in a sort of grim, pinch-faced annoyance, as if he was being pestered by a fly but was unable to shoo it away because his hands were busy.

"The whole lot of them looks like they're marching off to Perdition," Trap muttered, moving up next to Roman.

Webber flashed a knowing smirk. "The poor bastards. You'd look that way too if you had to ride with Lyons. The man's an ass who can't . . ."

"That'll do," Roman said, his voice sharp but not unfriendly. "Explain to Mr. O'Shannon about Captain Lyons and his many idiosyncrasies another time. Just be certain you don't do it in front of me."

"Aye, sir." Webber winked at Trap, confirming he'd fill him in later.

Approaching, Lyons raised his bony arm to the square and gave the command to halt in a loud if somewhat nasal voice.

"The Lyons roar," Webber whispered, blank-faced.

Roman shot him a sideways look.

"Sorry, sir," Webber said. "Won't happen again."

Lyons urged his mount forward. "Lieutenant Roman, you're out of uniform," he barked from the back of his sullen horse. "Leave garrison for a few days and you go to hell in a handbasket, eh?"

Trap had seen the type before. Some men, officers and enlisted alike, felt like they were invincible from the back of a horse—ten feet tall and bullet-proof.

Two Apache scouts, wearing red scarves around their heads to set them apart from any hostiles, slouched on their sullen ponies and watched the two white leaders. One rolled his eyes and gave Roman a quiet, conspiratorial grin.

Roman nodded to Lyons. "I am, but not without orders. We're conducting business for Colonel Branchflower."

Lyons rubbed his receding chin and sighed. "You're filthy—covered in sweat and dirt from head to boot. A shambles, Hezekiah, that's what you are." He peeled off his glove and held out a hand. "Let's have a look at those orders of yours."

"Afraid I can't do that," Roman said. "They're classified in nature."

Lyons puffed up like a toad. "May I remind you," he harrumphed. "As long as I remain your superior officer, you are obliged to comply with my orders."

"While that's not entirely true"—Roman smiled—"it is a moot issue. Colonel Branchflower brevetted me to captain."

The bugler stifled a snicker behind his mustache.

"Is that a fact?" Lyons looked down his nose in unmasked disgust. "In any case, I am still your senior." He gave his hand a dismissive flick. "You and your men are enlisted to ride with me against Victorio. The savage and his band have been spotted raiding near this very spot."

"I know." Roman gestured over his shoulder. "We just buried two of his victims."

"Then you also know I'll need every man I can get my hand on when we find him. My scouts say he's two days away, but my gut tells me he's within a day's ride." Lyons took up the slack in his reins, preparing to move out without further discussion. His horse fought the bits, and he slapped it on the neck with a leather shoofly that hung from his wrist. "Have your men fall in at the rear. You may ride up here with me."

Trap and Johannes both looked to Roman for guidance. He stood completely still.

"Request denied," he said at length, folding his hands in front of him.

"That was not a request, Captain. That was an order."

Roman kept his voice low and calm in contrast to Lyons's high-toned quiver. "I have my orders and I intend to see them through to the end."

"I am still the senior officer here," Lyons spit though gritted teeth. "I will decide what missions are important and which ones are not while we are in the field. You *will* fall in with my command. I'll sort it out with the old man upon our return."

Every man in D Troop eased up slightly, leaning forward in the saddle to try and hear how the stand-off would play out. The air buzzed with tension. Hoarse whispers moved like a wave through the ranks. From the crooked grins on their faces, Trap decided few of these men were rooting for their commander.

Roman was calm as a summer's morning, his voice firm and matter-of-fact, as if he was speaking to a small child who didn't understand the seriousness of the situation.

"Captain Lyons, with all due respect, I suggest you continue on your mission and leave us to ours."

Lyons's eyes blazed. Feeling the tension, his horse tried to charge forward, and the captain had to yank on the reins to keep the animal under control. He shook his fist at Roman. "I've had enough of you. Sergeant Collins, put Mr. Roman in irons. If his men give you any trouble, shoot them."

Trap and Johannes both stepped forward to flank their commander. He motioned them back with a faint smile. Trap had never seen anyone so cool under pressure.

"Sergeant Collins," Roman said. There was the slightest hint of fatigue in his voice. "Delay that order."

"Collins." Lyons glared at his subordinate. "Do as I say or I'll bring you up on charges!" His head shook on stooped shoulders. His bloodshot eyes bulged in their sockets and looked like they might pop out of his skull.

Roman's voice rose at once like a clap of rolling thunder. "Captain Lyons, dismount and speak to me privately and I'll explain my orders to you."

Collins looked back and forth between the two commanders and swallowed hard. He took half a step forward, but Trap sent him a look that kept him in his place.

Lyons climbed down from his horse and handed the reins to his blank-faced aide. He stepped forward, out of earshot of his troop, and shot a dismissive look at Trap and Johannes.

"I thought you wished to speak in private. Aren't you going to have your men pull back?"

"I don't care if they hear every word I say," Roman whispered. He was smiling, so the rest of D Troop had no idea what was going on. "I asked you down here so I didn't embarrass you in front of your command."

Lyons started to turn and go.

Roman stopped him with a hiss. "My orders are more important than you could ever imagine, and I am not about to let a self-important boob who couldn't command an army of pissants dissuade me in my duty just because he thinks he has some power."

Lyons was taken aback for a moment while he struggled to regain control of the situation. A sly smile suddenly crossed his seething face. "You forget, Hezekiah. There are only three of you. If you turn this into a battle of force, I have forty-seven men at my disposal."

Roman ripped off his hat and moved nose-to-nose with the other captain. "Now you listen to me, you arrogant bastard. You may have an entire company, but the fourth man in my unit, the man you didn't even know existed until now, is up in those rocks behind you. I'm sick of your bullshit, Freddy. I don't take orders from you. I take my direction straight from Colonel Branchflower."

Roman smiled. His voice softened again. "My rifleman takes his direction from me. I'll leave it to you to figure out what that direction is."

Lyons turned his twitching face slowly to look up at the rocks. Madsen stared down the glinting barrel of his Sharps and gave him a little wave for effect. He'd moved up slightly so he could be seen once Roman removed his hat.

"He's loyal as hell to Captain Roman," Webber said. "And his skill with that rifle of his is unmatched. Wouldn't you say, Sergeant O'Shannon?"

Trap nodded. "None better, Sergeant Webber. He could part your hair at this range, that's for certain."

Lyons's face flushed a deeper shade of red. A purple vein throbbed along his temple. "I'll see you busted back to mucking stables for this, Hezekiah. I have friends in high places."

"So do I, Freddy." Roman tossed his head toward Clay and his rifle. "So do I."

Captain Fredrick Paul Lyons wasted no time in mustering his troops away after Victorio, who he no doubt would find an easier customer to deal with than Hezekiah Roman.

"I'd hate to be assigned to Company D tonight," Webber allowed as he mounted up. Clay skittered down the hill above them on his roan.

"Or ever," Trap agreed. He loped Skunk out a few paces to the east and studied the ground while the others married up and prepared to move. He shook his head and figured out another reason to hate Freddy Lyons: D Troop, with their sixty-plus horses and pack animals, had completely obliterated the outlaws' back trail.

"Can you find where they crossed?" Roman looked at the ground in disgust.

"Yessir," Trap said. "I can, but not with any speed. It'll take some time."

Roman sighed. "As fast as possible then," he said. "I'm sure the kidnappers are getting antsy since their companions have failed to return. Time is something that's in extremely short supply."

CHAPTER 37

All of the men were horrible, lewd things who melded together in the girl's fevered mind into one awful mass of putrid cruelty. Two of them took Straw's body by the heels and dragged it out of the sandstone cave to feed it to the buzzards while his blood still pooled fresh in the sand at her feet.

The big Indian had ended her torment for the moment when he stabbed Straw to death, but there was no mercy in his black eyes. To him she was nothing more than property—property he was paid to protect. If the one paying the bills gave the order, he'd stab her just as quickly as he'd killed Straw.

The short man with a cowlick and close-set eyes appeared to be the leader. In the beginning, when she was in pain, but still had some semblance of her wits about her, she'd watched the group, looked for a weakness to see if there might be a chance for escape. If the group had what could be termed a boss, this one was him. He was the one who had the plan. He seemed to be the one paying for any operating costs. The others deferred to him a tiny bit more than they did each other—and that wasn't much. Whatever hold he had on his filthy band of confederates, it was tenuous at best.

She studied him the first day, thinking him at times weak, at times just foolish. Though she was in tremendous pain, it was easy for her to feel morally superior to a little Napoleon who barely had a grip on his group of cutthroats. Then, he'd ordered poor Charlie Dolan killed.

The brutality with which the bloodthirsty group fell on her poor friend had changed her. They seemed to her like raging beasts more than men, lusting for violence the way some craved a woman. She'd been unable to turn away as Charlie, a strong, courageous man who had a wife and two daughters, screamed and thrashed in horrific pain while they cut off his head—slowly.

Now, with thirst and pain and terror eating away at her fevered brain, she could only cringe when any of the men so much as looked in her direction. She wanted to die, to be free from the pain. But she didn't want to die like Charlie.

She shuddered uncontrollably when the leader staggered to his feet and swayed over to her in the dark cave. The fire behind him cast a huge shadow against the back wall.

"I aim to turn you in for the ransom," he said, assuring her that if she cooperated she might make it home alive. "I can't have you ruined by a fool like Straw. If the Army and your papa don't pay, you'll still fetch a little money from my contacts." His small eyes narrowed when he caught her looking at the entrance to the cave. "Don't even think about trying to escape, Pilar. There's snakes and lizards out there that would kill all of us here with just one bite."

"I wish one would then," she heard herself say. Her teeth chattered when she spoke. It would serve the fool right if she died in her sleep from fever and infection.

The man chuckled. He knelt in the sand beside her and reached for her injured hand. He was gentle in an odd, uncaring sort of way, as one might carefully check an injured horse to see if it was still fit to race.

"It's been a hard-fought battle to get this far. I'll not let you run off and steal my fortune." The smirk on his pitiless face caused her to look away. "I got an awful lot riding on you, little girl. Don't you disappoint me."

She looked away, thinking she would rather brave a pit full of the deadliest of vipers as listen to one more word this man had to say.

It was as if he read her thoughts.

He grabbed her by the waist and pinched her hard in the tender belly just above her navel, hard enough to make her yelp. "Papago will cut two little slits in your skin right here; then he'll take the cord he uses to tie you up and run it through the holes." The man laughed. "Makes it hell tryin' to get away while you're rippin' your own guts out."

He gave her bare thigh a swat. "I don't want to mess you up, little girl. But I'm a businessman first and foremost. If you do anything bad for business, well, that would be an awful shame." Convinced he'd made his point, the man walked out of the cave into the darkness.

Her head drooped in despair.

A huge black fly, sticky from the rancid antelope haunch, buzzed up to investigate the crusted blood on her swollen lip. Four days ago such a thing would have sent her into a spitting frenzy to scrub her mouth with soap. Now, she couldn't bring herself to care.

Payton Brandywine hunkered against a lumpy boulder at the edge of the cave and watched his plan come unraveled right before his very eyes like a poor packknot. The rock dug into his back, but he pressed against it all the harder, letting the pain in his flesh keep him in the grim reality of his circumstances.

Since that idiot Straw had become too familiar with the merchandise and gotten himself killed, the group had begun to polarize. The Papago was still with him, not so much for the money as for revenge against the greaser girl's daddy. The sullen Indian didn't have much love for Mexicans in general, but he hated Colonel de la Cruz about as much as he hated Apaches—which was more than considerable.

Other than the Indian, he wasn't sure who was on his side. No one had killed him in his sleep yet. That was a mercy anyhow. He was pretty sure the one they called Bent Jim was with him, if only for his share of the ransom money. Bent Jim's partner was a quiet man everyone called Grunt, because that seemed to be the only way he knew how to communicate. Brandywine figured Grunt would throw in with Bent Jim, whichever way he went. That's what partners did. And out here everyone had a partner. A body had to have one to survive.

The Indian agent calculated his odds. The Papago was scorpion-quick, with the dead cruel eyes of a rattlesnake. Grunt looked to be worth any two of the others in a fight, but a bullet would kill him as quick as it would any man. Bent Jim was no slouch, but he was among the smallest of the group. Well into his fifties, he was definitely the oldest.

The two Mexicans were too mortified of Papago to go against him. Every time he stood, the two idiots nearly pissed their pants. Still, they could shoot, and he needed shooters. Hell, even he was scared of the Papago.

Haywood and Babcock, brooding whiskey peddlers Payton had known off and on for over five years, had been friends of Straw. They were none too happy to see their partner stabbed by an Indian over a Mexican girl. None of them had challenged him directly, but Brandywine knew the look when he saw it. A dispute was coming. It was just a matter of time.

A wild-eyed lion hunter named Tug leered at the girl like she was the ultimate prize instead of the money. He would choose whichever side would ultimately give him a go with her, Payton was sure of that. Tug was happy with nothing but a pile of skins to sleep on and flea-bitten hides for clothing, and the ransom meant little to him.

Tug's partner, Joe Simmons, was a filthy creature almost as old as Bent Jim. His skin and clothing were so equally stained with sweat and grime, it was difficult to tell where one ended and the other began. He would side with Tug.

A pair of cackling, towheaded twins not yet out of their teens were the wild cards. They dreamt of the money, but the thought of a few minutes with the señorita made them giggle maniacally and punch each other in the arms in turn. They were young and untested, but both were handy with their guns. Hiram, the crazier of the two, looked up to Tug the lion hunter and was apt to follow him as far as he went in any direction. Hiram's brother, Lars, would certainly go the same way, so there was a chance that whole group would band together if it came to a mutiny.

Brandywine sucked air in slowly between his teeth while he thought. "You sure got yourself a handful this time, Payton," he whispered under his breath.

If only that son of a bitch Evans would get back. He and his kid brother were supposed to deliver the ransom note two days ago and come back with supplies. The fact that they hadn't returned had tensions rubbed raw in the little group. The plan had been working perfectly until now.

If Brandywine ever had a partner it was Ponce Evans. The Army sergeant knew his way around the military. He was the one who'd heard the Mexican colonel's daughter was on her way to Phoenix under U.S. escort, the one who'd suggested how much money both governments might pay to get such a girl back. At first, the two men had thought to attempt the kidnapping with only Papago to help them, but when Evans found out the escort would consist of eight troopers, not including the coach driver, they decided to recruit more men.

To easily overpower an army, they had needed an army, so they were forced to cobble together this group of killers and misfits. If he'd known how young and inexperienced the escort was, Brandywine wouldn't have hired half the men he did. Now, they all wanted their share of the money, even if all they did was sit around and play dice and scratch themselves.

Brandywine was not a big man. For some reason, his hair had decided to thin everywhere except the cowlick at his crown. His cookie-duster mustache made him look more like a schoolteacher than a kidnapper. What he lacked in size he made up for in greed and ruthlessness. He felt confident he could hold the conspiracy together for a little while longer with the promise of money. Either the girl's father or the U.S. Army would pay. He was positive. Evans had assured him the Army considered the girl precious cargo. He'd heard enough talk from the officers about how strained relations were between the two countries. The Mexican colonel would want his precious daughter back, and the United States would pay nearly any price to avert sinking further into a squabble with their neighbor to the south.

Brandywine pushed himself to his feet. He couldn't very well stand by and watch all his planning and hard work crumble down around his shoulders. He had to do something. He needed to send out more ransom instructions before the pitiful girl died of fright or one of the men got to her in the night and killed her for the fun of it.

He didn't want to send anyone that would be on his side in a fight. In the end he decided on the Mexicans. They were too scared of Papago to go against him, and too greedy not to come back.

"Ruiz! Cardenas!" Brandywine clapped his hands together. *"Venga aqui."*

The Mexicans stood and staggered over to Brandywine. Neither was very tall, but both were strong men, with big hands and small hearts.

The remainder of the group peered up from their gambling to see what was going on. Everyone expected that the others might cheat or kill them at any moment—and in most respects, that was likely to be the gospel truth.

"We need supplies," Brandywine said, nodding his head. "I want you two to ride into Agua Caliente and see what you hear about Ponce and Sammy. I'm afraid they didn't get through. Take another letter with you and deliver it so we can get our money. If you can find that giant friend of yours, bring him back with you in case we need reinforcements." He studied the sodden, bloodshot faces of Cardenas and Ruiz.

"*Comprende?*" he said.

The men gave grunting mumbles of agreement. They brightened at the thought of a little escape from the tension of the cave.

"Very well," the Indian agent said. He turned his attention to the rest of the men. "This will all work out, boys, I assure you. In a week's time we'll all be rich."

It was Tug who proved he was the one to watch. Brandywine had been right.

The lion hunter spit a greasy brown slurry of tobacco into the sand. "You ain't got a week. If we don't see some cash inside of two days, I reckon some of us are gonna divide up our share of the spoils as best we know how." A cruel grin etched his greasy face and his hungry gaze fell on the cowering girl. He spit again. "*Comprende,* Boss Man?"

CHAPTER 38

A blind man could have followed the wide swath Lyons's troop had cut through the rough desert country. Trap kept a sharp eye out for any intersecting trails that might have been made by the dead outlaws.

His thoughts constantly wandered back to Maggie. Madsen was right about one thing. Life had a funny way of turning out a heck of a lot different than a person planned. Less than six months ago, he'd been a contented student at his father's school for Indian children. Now, he found himself married and part of a secret military unit.

As was his custom when the trail was apparent, Captain Roman ranged ahead about a hundred yards. Clay and Johannes hung back with Trap, riding on either side of him helping him try and cut sign.

"You ever think about getting older?" The words escaped Trap's mouth before he had a chance to consider the ramifications of such a question.

Clay shot a grin and a wink at Webber. "Told you he was ponderin' on the missus."

"By getting older," Johannes mused, "do you mean maturing or just getting on in years? I only ask because I don't think Madsen will ever do anything but age."

"Hell," Clay scoffed. "I'm old enough, I reckon. I expect I'll get creaky and stiff when the time comes."

Trap shrugged, sorry he'd brought it up. "I guess I meant settlin' down. You know, building a little house somewhere, raisin' some kids . . ."

Clay lifted his reins and the big roan stopped in his tracks. The other boys pulled up alongside him. "A body's got to have a roof over his head, especially if he wants to have a wife that'll stick around—and I reckon young'uns are a natural consequence of having a wife that sticks around—but I will tell you this, partner: I may be young yet, but hangin' around my papa's whores taught me a good bit about this old world. I've seen you in the scrap. You got a gift when it comes to settlin' the score—you're a damned dangerous man, Trap O'Shannon, and I can't see no dangerous man settling down too awful early in his life. Just because you up and got yourself married don't mean you have to stop fightin'."

Madsen clucked to his horse and they all three began to move again.

"Look at the captain," Webber said. "He's as married as I ever seen, and he's apt to keep doing this for as long as he lives. You've heard him. He thinks he's an instrument in God's own hands." Johannes put on a stern face and squinted into the sun as he tried his best Hezekiah Roman impression. "'When the right path is before you, gentlemen—never pause, proceed.'" Webber laughed and shook his head. "I wish I had his kind of ambition."

"Drive be damned," Clay said. "Anything else sounds plumb dull after all this." He looked across at Trap, who'd skirted a tall saguaro cactus that stood lonesome in the rocky soil. "Hell, partner, I don't see why you'd want to grow up now. We're just gettin' started with the good stuff."

Roman trotted back toward them about the time a sudden shift in the wind brought the new smell to Trap's nose: the sour scent of manure, sweat, and mescal—a town.

"Agua Caliente," Webber said, pointing ahead of them with the tail of his reins. "Been through here once on a patrol. Not much to it except for a little cantina, some goat herds, and a couple of portly women."

Clay threw his hat back and grinned. "Heavy don't necessarily mean homely. I prefer my gals to have a little hip on 'em if I have the choice."

"Well, Madsen," Webber mused. "You should be able to have your preference on this occasion. Because more-than-adequate hips are something with which every tortilla-eating beauty in this little burg are well endowed."

Madsen ran his hand through his thick head of dark hair. "I'm hoping what you just said means the girls here have nice rear ends."

The captain slowed his horse and let the others come up beside him. "If you men are finished, we'll ride in and nose around in the cantina." Roman squirmed at any talk of loose women and though he didn't come right out and stop it, he didn't encourage it either. That suited Trap just fine.

"I'd like to get a decent meal if they offer such a thing," the captain continued. "Webber, you listen to the chatter and see what you can pick up. Maybe we can get a little light shed on those roasted men back there."

The pink adobe cantina occupied the position most towns would have reserved for the courthouse. It was a long, slumping affair with exposed cedar beams, bark peeling in long feathery strips, acting as reinforcements against the periodic fall rains. A handful of rustic houses of the same material, each a sad little replica of the tavern, slouched in a loose circle around the larger establishment.

Three molting chickens, skin as pink as the sunlit adobe, pecked and scratched in the street. A black and white dog flopped in the shade with just enough energy to look hungrily at the birds and give a wide-mouth yawn.

A flimsy wooden door leaned halfheartedly across the opening to the cantina waiting for a good breeze to knock it down. Madsen and Webber wasted no time in shoving the door aside, and shouldered their way in like they owned the place.

Roman tied his horse to a split-cedar rail and stuffed his gloves in a saddlebag. Trap reined up beside him and slid to the ground. He loosened Skunk's girth a notch—not too much in case they had to leave in a rush. He wasn't in too big a hurry to go into a saloon. Growing up under the strong religious influence of his father gave him a healthy dislike for that particular kind of enterprise. He watched as Captain Roman seemed to hitch up his will to make the trip in himself.

"My poor Irene would cry her eyes out if she saw me in a place like this," Roman said under his breath.

"Beg pardon, sir." Trap wasn't certain the words were meant for him, but it didn't feel right to ignore them either.

Roman blushed a little—hardly noticeable on his already sun-pinked skin. He took on a familiar tone O'Shannon hadn't heard before—as if they were friends instead of officer and subordinate. "Nothing, Trap. I was just thinking how my dear, innocent bride would feel about me going into such a place. I think she'd like to believe we camp in the hills and fight the good fight every day we're away."

"I reckon a fight gets a little ugly sometimes," Trap said. He stepped up to the door. "Maybe we can get something to eat while we're here, sir."

It took a while for Trap's eyes to adjust to the dim interior. What little light there was filtered through the broken front door and tiny slit windows built to use as gun ports when the cantina came under attack from bandits or marauding Apaches. Two rows of upright cedar posts ran down the center of the wide building, supporting the flat adobe roof. Rough-hewn wooden tables zigzagged around the posts. Four of them had active card games and hushed conversations going. At two others, loners did their conversing with bottles of cheap mescal. All told, Trap counted fourteen men. He wondered how many were left to tend to business around the little town.

The bar was at located at the back, between two peeling cedar posts. A coal-oil lamp, its globe blackened by soot and dust, cast a flickering shadow across two Mexican prostitutes sitting on tall stools and leaning on the rail. Clay and Johannes went straight for the bar. Each ordered a beer and sidled up next to the girls. True to Clay's recent description of his preferences, he struck up a conversation with the chubbier of the two.

Trap and the captain took a table a few feet away so they could observe without being too obtrusive. It didn't really matter; they were the only white people in the place, so there was no doubt they were all together.

To be as young as he was, Clay moved easily around the women. Neither of them appeared to speak English, but the language barrier didn't slow Clay down at all. With a mixture of sign language and facial expressions, he managed to get the heavy girl giggling and flirting back in a matter of moments.

Johannes was more circumspect. He sipped his beer and chatted quietly with the skinny girl. She had a bit of an overbite and a sour look that turned Trap's stomach if he looked at her too long.

Roman cleared his throat and motioned the two men over after a few minutes.

"That's two beers," he said. "Make sure and keep your wits about you."

Webber chuckled and shot a glance at Clay. "I wouldn't worry about us getting drunk," he said. "The stuff they serve here is more water than anything else."

Madsen nodded. He threw a flirting gaze at the chubby prostitute to keep her on the line while he was away.

"Are you finding anything out?" Roman looked down his nose at the two like they were mischievous schoolboys.

Johannes shrugged. "It's all just flirtation and coarse stories so far."

Madsen let out an exasperated sigh. "Beggin' your pardon, Captain, but do you mind if I ask you what thing in this world you consider yourself the best at?"

"Well," Roman blustered, taken aback. "I suppose I'd have to give that some thought."

"Well, I don't, sir," Clay said. "If I'm good at anything it's talkin' to women in general, whores in particular. These sorts of things are touchy. They take a little time, but if anybody in this town knows anything it's these girls. They're the only two sports around for miles. They hear it all, I guarantee it."

"Go on back and talk to them then," Roman said. "But remember, you're working."

Clay grinned and gave Trap a wink. "So are they."

Madsen continued to work his magic on the girls while the bartender brought two hunks of barbecued goat out to Trap and the captain. There were mashed beans on the side and red peppers. It was surprisingly good, and both men dug into the meal with gusto.

"I'm surprised you don't drink," Roman said across his fork. "Is it because your father is a minister?" He'd kept up the familiar tone, and Trap found him an easy man to talk to. In some ways he was like Maggie. There was nothing false about him. His life and his personality were out in the open for everyone to see.

Trap swallowed a mouthful of the tender meat and washed it down with a glass of water. "No, not really," he said. "He takes a drink now and then at the suttler's store. No, I promised my mother when I was still a small boy that I would never touch alcohol. Have you ever met my mother?"

"Chuparosa? I have," Roman said. "She is a fine, temperate woman. I can see her teaching you to stay away from strong drink."

Trap took another bite. "She told me she got really drunk once on *tizwin*—back when she first married my father. Said she almost killed him." Trap stared at his food while he spoke. He'd never told anyone else this story, not even Clay, but he felt like he wanted to tell the captain—to let the man know he trusted him with a confidence. "She's afraid I'd be the same way if I ever drank. I have a bit of a temper, so she's probably right."

"You have fine parents, O'Shannon," the captain sighed. "Heed your mother's counsel. It'll save you a belly-load of grief." He tipped his head toward Webber. "Take our friend Johannes there. I've never met a more intelligent man. His father was a hard drinker. Beat him nearly every day when he was child. My mother and his mother were friends. I promised the beleaguered woman I'd do what I could to look after her son." Roman rubbed both eyes with the palms of his hands. "I suppose it's not a question of deserving—heaven knows I don't deserve all the blessing I have in my own life—but it seems to me that no one deserves the kind of upbringing Webber had. Now, he enjoys his liquor a little too much. I'm afraid it could be his downfall."

"That would account for all the anger wellin' up inside him," Trap said, a hint of melancholy in his quiet voice. He sometimes forgot that not everyone had a kind father and mother like he did.

The girls at the bar suddenly broke into a chorus of oos and ahhs. Trap looked up in time to see Clay give the chubby one a little hand mirror and the one with the overbite a folding paper fan. They tittered and giggled and moved in closer to the beaming Texan.

"I have to hand it to him." Roman shook his head. "He does indeed know women."

It wasn't long before the girls began to speak in hushed tones of broken English. Webber watched as two saddle-weary and sullen Mexican men shouldered their way through the broken door and eyed the sporting women.

Roman followed his gaze to the newcomers.

"I wonder if Madsen realizes he's monopolizing the only other pastime in this little town besides drinking mescal."

"I wonder if he cares," Trap grinned.

A short time later, Johannes helped Clay peel the girls off him and the two took seats at the table with Trap and Roman.

"Those two yahoos that just came in haven't been around for a few days," Clay whispered, stealing a piece of barbecued goat off Trap's plate. "Before they left, they were trying to get Linda, that's the pretty one, to give them a little bounce on credit. Both said they stood to come into a pile of money very soon."

"Neither of them have any job prospects," Johannes chimed in. "At least as far as the girls know. I think these could be two of our kidnappers, Captain."

CHAPTER 39

The girls put up an awful fuss when Clay told them he had to go. Linda clutched her breast as if she'd been shot and broke down in a wailing fit. Esmeralda stuck out her bottom lip in a pout big enough to compensate for her overbite and sobbed until her shoulders shook.

It looked as though the team might have to mount a rescue effort just to drag Madsen away. Trap's jaw fell open when Clay got misty eyed at the parting.

"I just ain't no good at goodbyes," the Texan said, a slight catch in his voice as they left the bawling prostitutes slumped at the bar.

Outside, Roman gathered his Scout Trackers beside their horses. "Saddle up, men," he said, pulling the latigo on his saddle to snug up the girth. He kept his voice low. "We'll move out to the edge of town at a distance, sit back and wait. When those two make a move, we'll follow them. With any luck they'll take us back to where they're keeping the girl."

The plan was straightforward enough and likely would have worked had it not been for Linda.

She was a big girl and the flimsy wooden door flew off its remaining hinge when she hit it and staggered into the street.

"Claymadsen! Claymadsen!" She whimpered his name as if it was all one word. Her yellow peasant blouse hung from one fleshy shoulder. Blood dripped from her swollen nose and splashed across the front of her torn clothing.

When she saw Clay, her eyes brightened and she lumbered straight for him, dimpled arms outstretched in a plea for help.

Madsen gave the captain a sheepish look. "Sorry, sir, I . . ."

A squat Mexican man with a great, twirling mustache that covered most of his wide face crashed out seconds after the girl, his hand on the butt of his pistol. Another followed, shorter than the first, hiding behind a bulbous, troll-like nose. An instant later, a third man ducked his huge head, then turned mountainous shoulders sideways to fit out the doorway. His whiskey-shined face held wild eyes that appeared to look east and west at the same time. He bellowed like an angry bull and beat his chest, tilting his head this way and that to bring the gringos into focus.

"It's the Cyclops," Clay muttered as he tried to peel Linda off him. "And he's brought his two little runts with him."

"Hold on, boys." Roman put up a hand. "We mean you no harm."

"Claymadsen," Linda cried. "These men are murderers. They are the ones you look for. Please help us, Claymadsen."

The giant went straight for Roman. He was at least a head taller than the officer and twice as broad.

The mustachioed bandit went for his gun as the Cyclops made his move. Roman, Webber, and Trap had all retreated from the half-naked prostitute and stood in a tight group by the horses.

Madsen tried to draw, but found it impossible to bring his Peacemaker into action.

"Save me, Claymadsen," Linda bawled like a pestered calf. "They will keeeel us all!"

"I would if you'd turn loose of my arms," Clay spit.

The bandit's first shot went wide and smacked into the adobe building with a loud crack.

At the same time, the giant bowled into the other three members of the team, sending them all flying.

"Leave off hangin' on me, damn it! You're gonna smother me." Clay peeled away one chubby hand, but she grabbed a fistful of sleeve with the other. Her fleshy thighs encircled his leg and she pulled herself in tight, sobbing against his shoulder and enveloping him between her enormous breasts.

"Oh, Claymadsen!"

Another shot split the air. Trap looked up in time to see the giant kick a smoking pistol out of Webber's hand. Señor Mustache pitched headlong into the dirt, mortally wounded.

Johannes went down with a giant fist between his eyes, hitting the ground so hard Trap could hear his teeth rattle.

Roman rushed the big Mexican, plowing into him with his shoulder, while Trap attacked him from the other side. All three collapsed into a squirming pile, kicking and gouging as they fell. Trap's head felt like it exploded when a huge hand caught him in the ear with a strong slap. He heard Roman grunt as he got the wind knocked out of him.

The troll with the wide nose grabbed Linda by the hair and yanked her cruelly back and away from Clay. He held a knife to her throat.

"Much obliged," Madsen panted as he drew his Colt and shot the ugly little man over his left eye. "I thought I'd never get her off me."

The giant knelt over Trap and Roman, who were both addled half out of their senses. He held a bowie knife in his huge fist.

Madsen sent a round into the dirt. *"Sueltalo!"* he snapped, putting another shot inches from the giant's knees. *Drop it!*

Trap regained enough composure to kick the blade out of the big Mexican's hand.

Webber pushed himself up slowly on one arm, rubbing his tender jaw. The front of his shirt and britches was covered in red dust. Roman hadn't fared much better, and he spit to get the dirt out of his mouth.

"Tie him up," the captain said. He was still panting from the fight.

Trap hobbled over to his horse and got a length of stout cord out of his saddlebags while Webber held the giant at gunpoint. Clay tended to a sobbing Linda before he turned her over to Esmeralda, who'd wisely stayed inside and missed the whole brouhaha.

"Glad you had enough sense to take him alive." Roman nodded a short time later at the two dead bandits. "I hope he can tell us something about where they have the girl."

Johannes knelt in front of the sullen giant, questioning him in harsh, rapid-fire Spanish. The big man said little more than an occasional grunt.

Webber stood with a disgusted groan and shook his head. "He's not talking, Captain. He knows where she is, I can tell that much, but he's keeping it to himself."

Roman rubbed his chin in thought for a moment, eyeing the prisoner carefully. "Ask him his name."

"Como se llama?" Webber fired down at the prisoner.

"Tu madre," the man grunted.

"He wants to talk about my mother," Webber scoffed. "He's not going to talk without some encouragement."

"Tell him he'll hang if he doesn't help us. Tell him I can't help him if he doesn't talk to us."

"Aye, sir," Webber said, unconvinced it would do any good. He knelt and looked the drooling giant square in the eye, giving the man's wide face a slap to make sure he was paying attention. *"Escucha!"* Webber said, and translated Roman's threats.

In reply, the giant coughed up the contents of his throat and spit them in Webber's face.

"You son of a bitch!" The trooper drew his knife in less than a heartbeat and slit the Mexican's nose down the middle. With his hands tied behind him, the hulking man could do nothing but wail and thrash in the dirt as blood soaked the front of his shirt.

"Sergeant Webber," Roman snapped. "That is enough."

Johannes glared. The Mexican's spit still dripped from the side of his face. His chest heaved with fury. He wiped his cheek with the back of his forearm and put away his knife.

Trap and Clay stood by, holding their breath.

The anger slowly ebbed from Webber's red face. "I apologize, sir. I don't know what came over me."

"I don't either, son," Roman said. His voice was quiet, but flint-hard. "But I'd better not see it again. I'll not have you mistreating a prisoner while you're under my command. Do I make myself clear?"

"Yes, sir."

"Damn it, man, we don't have time for this. There's a girl out there who needs our help."

Webber swallowed hard, staring at the ground. "Understood, sir."

"Very well." Roman took on his usual relaxed tone again. He drew the Schofield at his hip. "Now, tell the prisoner I'll not let anyone cause him any more pain, but I intend to shoot him dead right now if he doesn't tell us where the girl is."

Webber hesitated. "Captain?"

"Carry on, Sergeant." Roman aimed the pistol at the wide-eyed prisoner. "It is, at times, necessary to kill quickly and as humanely as possible. That is the nature of battle. On the other hand, if we start to mistreat our captives, we're no better than they are. I'll not have it." He thumbed back the hammer. "Tell him the bullet won't hurt him at all, but he'll still be very dead. Tell him he's got ten seconds."

It turned out that the giant outlaw's name was Rafael Fuentes. He had a firm enough grasp of English that he didn't need Johannes to translate a single word. It took him no time to tell Roman and others exactly what they wanted to know.

CHAPTER 40

"This damned antelope's done soured to the bone."
Tug sniffed a piece of meat through a curled nose,
then pitched it out the wide mouth of the overhang.
He picked up his rifle and walked over to the girl.
Hiking up his skin shirt, he rubbed a greasy hand
over the pale belly. "I got me a cravin' for some cat.
You ever ate puma?"

She pressed her face against the sand. Her throat
was so dry she could hardly swallow, let alone speak.
When she tried, it came out as a gurgling, unintelligible croak.

"Brandywine!" the lion hunter shouted over his
shoulder. His hungry gaze never left the girl. "I think
she's gonna die before long. We should take what we
can whilst there's still something left to take."

The Indian agent jumped up from his game and
scurried over to check on his investment. He toed at
her thigh with his boot. She recoiled at his touch and
curled into a tight ball, protecting her swollen hand.
"She'll be all right with a little water," he said. He

dropped a canteen on the ground in front of her. "The Mexicans should have the letter delivered by now. They'll be back with Fuentes and supplies any time."

Pushing herself up on her good arm, she curled her legs around so she could sit against the stone wall. Water. She didn't want them to know it, but she'd have done anything for just one sip. She knew her shredded gown no longer covered her, but she couldn't bring herself to care anymore.

Death was a certainty now; it was only a matter of how painful it would be, how much torment and degradation she would be forced to endure with its coming. Thirst carried with it much more agony than she had imagined it would. Her tongue was swollen and stuck to the roof of her mouth. Crying had plugged her nose, and her breath came in ragged gasps over cracked and bleeding lips. Her vision blurred and the sickening thump in her skull mixed with the white-hot ache of her broken tooth and the dull throb of her stinking hand.

She vaguely remembered a warning—it seemed so long ago in her fevered brain. Someone had warned her that this sort of thing might happen. She pressed the canteen to her lips and let the water slide over her parched tongue. It was warm, but it was wet and she drank greedily until Brandywine jerked it away.

"Go easy, Señorita," the Indian agent snapped. "Too much will make you sick."

The lion hunter chuckled. "And we don't want her sick," he said. "She's sick as a hydrophobic dog as it is, you blind, baldheaded nit. Me and Joe gonna go hunt us up some lion meat. When we come back, if you ain't heard anything about the ransom, I aim to have me a little go with this young'un before she crosses over on us. I don't care what you or anyone else says about it."

Before Brandywine could react, Tug wheeled and shot the Papago in the face with his big-bore rifle. The roar of the gun shook the small rock enclosure. The big Indian's head evaporated and blood sprayed the cave wall behind him.

Brandywine's jaw hung open as he watched his fiercest ally slump in a lifeless heap to the sandy floor.

The girl looked at what was left of the dead Indian and threw up the water she'd just drunk.

Tug prodded her in the rump with the smoking barrel of his gun. "I'll be back, Señorita. You get yourself cleaned up and I'll go get us some fresh cat." He looked up and grinned through blazing eyes at the speechless Indian agent. "Get her some more water. Come on, Joe," he barked to his partner. "I got me a powerful hunger for some cat . . . among other things."

CHAPTER 41

"Son of a bitch!" Madsen snapped as the Scout Trackers picked their way single-file up a rock-strewn trail. It was little more than a goat path out of their fifth canyon of the day. Acacia trees shredded their clothes and jagged rocks threatened to lame the horses every step of the way. A stiff wind picked up bits of dry vegetation and sand, driving them into the men's faces with enough force to blast off a layer of skin.

"This whole place looks like the Good Lord forgot where he buried somethin' important and spent a couple thousand years digging ditches in the rock trying to find it. I've heard some troops say this country's so rough," Clay continued, "you can't get through it without cussing your way up and down these damned gullies and mountains."

"I'm inclined to agree," Roman shouted into the wind. "But from the sounds of things, you're doing enough for the four of us." The captain held his hat down with his free hand and nodded ahead. "Terrain flattens out some after we top this next ridge. I'd rather wait out this wind inside the protection of this canyon, but we don't have the time. Fuentes said the kidnappers are expecting a signal fire on Kill Devil Mesa by this evening. According to him, the cave is supposed to be northeast of there, so we're not far from it now. With any luck, this storm will hide our approach and we can have the girl back by nightfall."

Though it was still early afternoon, dust filled the blowing air and made it difficult to see more than a few hundred yards. Each man's face was caked red above the bandanna he wore to protect his nose and mouth. The horses walked with eyes half shut against the whirling debris, stumbling every other step in the uneven terrain.

Drawn forward by worry for the kidnapped girl, the men pressed doggedly on, braving the cold and biting wind. The howl became too great for conversation, so they rode on in silence.

It was a chance meeting. No war party could have possibly known the men were out on such a bitter afternoon. A dozen Apaches were returning from a hunt, on their way back to camp in the shelter of the slick-rock canyons. The two groups were almost on top of each other before either of them noticed.

It was Trap who realized what was happening first. He caught the hint of cedar smoke on the wind, an instant before he glimpsed a fleck of a painted horse as it ghosted through the dust cloud twenty yards in front of him.

The lead Indian saw him at the same moment and let out a piercing whoop.

Trap spun Skunk back and ripped the bandanna off his face. "Apaches!" he yelled at the group.

"Follow me." Roman shouted his clipped order and turned his horse to the right, spurring it toward a dark outcropping of rocks that was barely visible in the shadowed distance. "Make for those boulders. There's a canyon nearby so watch out."

None of them knew for sure how many Indians there were, but staying around to count heads was not a way to live very long in Apache country.

The four soldiers let their horses have their heads. The animals, half-crazy from the moaning storm, took off at a dead run, jumping cactus and thorn bushes if they saw them, plowing through if they didn't. Hoofbeats and piercing Apache cries carried behind them on the wind.

The sandstorm itself seemed to join in the battle. It grew in intensity, picking up small rocks and hurling them like bird shot at white man and Indian alike. The haven of boulders was invisible in the billowing red curtain, but the troopers pushed for it anyway, knowing it was somewhere out there, somewhere next to a sharp drop into a deep ravine.

Trap saw the rocks off to his left as he sped past. The others were somewhere nearby. Their shouting voices carried on the wind, but he couldn't see them for the blowing dust. It was impossible to tell where he was, and he pulled back on the reins trying to stop.

Skunk squealed as the ground gave way underneath him. Howling wind mixed with the clatter of rock and dirt as the canyon edge turned into a river of rolling gravel and loose dirt. The little horse scrambled to regain its footing, flailing wildly, pawing out at nothing. A sudden sinking sensation pushed Trap's gut into his throat.

They were falling.

He let go of the reins to give his horse the freedom it would need if it ever did get its footing. A jutting branch snapped under them as they half-slid, half-fell to the canyon floor below. The next second, another tree upended the little horse and sent Trap spinning, head over heels, from the saddle. Dirt filled his mouth and nose when he tried to breathe. A harsh wind moaned and whirred in his ears. Then, something slammed against his head. A sharp pain screamed like a banshee behind his ear before the world around him went black and he heard no more.

"I can't find him, Captain." Madsen's voice was tight. His youthful face quivered with anxiety and tension.

The Apaches, equally afraid of an unknown number of enemies, had run the other direction in the blinding storm. They were nowhere to be seen by the time the wind abated an hour later.

When they realized Trap had become separated, Roman and his men began a frantic search. From the rocks above, they saw Skunk, bruised and battered but alive, in the bottom of the canyon fifty yards below them. The wall of the shallow ravine gave way gradually. It wasn't sheer, but it was treacherous nonetheless, and the men had to work their way down cautiously to keep their horses from losing their footing.

The sudden storm had left behind an eerie silence. There was not a breath of a breeze. Even the crows were quiet.

The canyon floor was a labyrinth of sandstone boulders as big as houses, their sculpted sides smoothed over time by water and wind.

"He's vanished." Madsen's frustration poured out in a bitter voice. Two hours of searching had yet to turn up anything but the little black gelding.

"He's around somewhere." Roman put a comforting hand on the Texan's shoulder. "We'll locate. . . ."

"Over here!" Webber shouted from a gap between two sandstone slabs. "I found his pistol."

Webber stood in a narrow side canyon, looking at the ground. He held a Schofield revolver in his left hand.

"The wind didn't get back in this little pocket enough to destroy all the tracks." He pointed the pistol toward the sand at his feet. "Difficult to tell, but I think there were three people here."

Clay dropped to his knees to get a better look. "Wish we had the little runt with us so he could tell us what to look for." He relaxed a notch, just knowing that his friend was alive for the time being. He took his hat off and scratched his head. "It does look like there are three sets of prints here, but it's impossible to tell much else about them."

Webber scanned the rocks above, while Roman took a linen map out of his saddlebag and spread it out on a flat rock.

"According to Fuentes, we're near the cave." He used his forefinger to trace the lines that signified mountains on the map. "We've got about three hours until dark. I'd wanted to make our move then, but if they have O'Shannon, we may not have the luxury of waiting."

Webber took a deep breath. "I hesitate to bring this up, but remember what they did to their last male hostage."

Roman let his fist bounce up and down on the map while he thought. "I know."

"Well," Clay said, slapping his leg with his hat, "I say we just bust in there and shoot everyone who's not Trap or Pilar." He shot a glance at the captain. "One thing's sure. If she's still alive, Trap can keep her company till we get there. She'll be happy to see a friendly face."

Roman took off his hat and held it in front of him. His brow knotted and he rubbed his whiskered jaw with his free hand. "Yes," he said. "About Señorita de la Cruz." His voice was a coarse whisper. "Mount up. I'll fill you in on the details as we ride. There are things I've not been able to tell you until now—things you have a right to know."

CHAPTER 42

A river of fire gushed through Trap O'Shannon's head. He jerked awake from a dream of Maggie, struggling in vain against the thick ropes that bound him hand and foot. Blackness surrounded him. He fought to control his breathing and get his bearings. A familiar smell hung heavy in his nose and stung his eyes. Someone had pulled a coffee sack over his head.

Voices echoed inside his skull, adding to the searing headache.

". . . not as good as a lion, but he'll do," a voice sneered nearby.

"Where did you find him?" This voice was higher, twitching with nervous energy. "He may have something to do with the ransom."

Another, more youthful speaker cackled. "L-Lars s-says we should c-c-cut his head off, like we did the o-other one. He likes to listen to the sss-screamin'."

"Shut up, Hiram," the tense voice snapped. "You boys want your money or not? Let's find out a little more about him, and then you can finish him off however you want to."

"Oh, let the young'uns have their fun," the first voice said. "I only brought him back so they could have a little sport killin' him. Maybe it'll toughen 'em up a little. He don't have our money."

Trap heard shuffling in the sand around him. A girl whimpered somewhere nearby. The pitiful sound made him think of Maggie and filled his belly with anger. He pulled and tugged at the stiff ropes until they cut into his wrists and ankles. At length, he lay back in the dirt panting, waiting.

The soft hiss of footsteps on sand approached from his left. A boot crashed into his ribs before he could protect himself and drove the wind from his lungs. Powerful hands grabbed him by the shoulders, arching his back, while someone yanked the coffee sack off his head.

He blinked to clear his eyes, trying to focus in the scant light of the cave. The gray glow of evening barely spilled in from outside. Inside, the small fire cast more shadow than it did light.

"I know you from somewhere," the small man in front of him said. Trap was able to put a face with the tense voice. "I've seen you before at Camp Apache. You're that preacher's boy. What's your name?"

"Trap O'Shannon." He saw no reason to lie about something the man would surely work out on his own in a short time. Trap recognized him as Payton Brandywine, the Indian agent from San Carlos. His father had had more than a few run-ins with the corrupt official. "I know you too." He had enough of his mother in him that he would never stoop to begging for his life.

"Ohhhh, preacher boy." A greasy man wearing buckskin clothing shook his head back and forth. "Maybe you can say us all a prayer before my compadres cut your guts out and feed 'em to the buzzards."

This brought a chuckle from the other men in the group. Trap counted nine, including the agent.

Brandywine held up a hand to quiet the noise. "What brings you all the way out here?"

"You." Trap kept his face passive, though he seethed inside. It wasn't in his nature to lie or bargain with men like this, but he needed to stall. It would take time for Captain Roman and the others to work out a solid plan now that they were a man short. "We got the note in Agua Caliente. My friends and I have the ransom money. They should be lighting the fire on Kill Devil Mesa any time now."

Brandywine beamed, slapping his fist against an open palm. "What did I tell you boys? I told you it would all work out, but no, none of you believed me. Now, we'll all be rich men. You just have to be patient now." He looked back at Trap.

"Where are your friends now?"

Trap shrugged. "Likely looking for me. Apaches got after us in the middle of a sandstorm and I got separated during the blow. Don't worry, though, they've got your money. As long as the girl is still alive, you'll get paid."

The man dressed in greasy skins jerked Trap's head back by the hair and held a long knife to his throat. "If you got the note, what happened to the two Mexicans? How come they ain't back yet?"

Trap couldn't move. He tried to relax, but found it impossible with the sharp blade already digging into his flesh. "The last time I saw them, they were sidled up next to Esmeralda and Linda back in town."

Brandywine put a hand on the other man's arm. "Hold on for a minute, Tug. We got time to do that later. We're talking thousands and thousands of dollars now. Let's not throw it all away." The Indian agent's eyes gleamed in the firelight. The men around were silent now at the thought of such an enormous payday. "You'd better be telling the truth, O'Shannon. If I so much as smell a whiff of a double cross, I'll let the boys cut your head off like they're itchin' to do already."

"No double crosses," Trap assured him. "As long as the girl is still alive."

"She's fit as a fiddle," Brandywine said. He grabbed Trap by the shoulder, dragged him across the cave floor, and threw him next to the girl. He had no way to catch himself and slammed against the rock wall.

The men jeered.

When his head cleared again, Trap looked over at the girl. She was an awful sight. Naked except for the flimsy remnants of a tattered gown, she lay in a bruised stupor, cowering in her own filth. A young outlaw with a maniacal face and an unruly blond mop stooped down next to her and grabbed a fist of matted black hair. He jerked her head backward, exposing the girl's face and delicate throat.

She moaned, drawing a purple hand close to her chest. Her eyes rolled back in her head, then fluttered open to fall on Trap. They were dark, pleading eyes, void of all but the last shreds of hope.

"Help me," she croaked. "Please help me." Her head lolled to one side.

Trap gasped when he saw her, not so much because of her swollen face, broken teeth, or bleeding lips—but because this girl was not Pilar de la Cruz.

CHAPTER 43

"Inez Hinojosa?" Clay frowned. The men were riding now, working their way along the canyon bottom. "Why all the secrecy? Why not just tell us we weren't coming to rescue the colonel's daughter? We were bound to find out anyway."

Roman looked ahead as he rode, thinking out his answer carefully before he spoke.

"Inez Hinojosa is an American citizen," the captain began. "Have either of you ever heard of the Secret Service?"

"Fake money and such?" Webber asked. He was leading Trap's gelding and urged it to keep up with a cluck.

"Exactly." The trail widened into a dry creek bed, and Roman motioned the two men to ride up next to him. "Treasury has had its hands full since the war. Some people estimate that a full third of the paper money circulating in U.S. border states is counterfeit. Miss Hinojosa is a government agent. She sent word two weeks ago that she and her partner had uncovered a major counterfeiting operation in Mexico. Her partner was murdered and she fled north. She is friendly with the de la Cruz family and knew she could trust him. He agreed to let her pose as his daughter and contacted us to arrange a military escort.

"Unfortunately for Miss Hinojosa, someone in her escort believed the colonel's daughter was worth a substantial ransom. They have no idea who she really is, or that she knows the whereabouts of millions in counterfeit currency." Roman stopped his horse and looked intently at both men. "If they did, she would surely be tortured until she gave up her secret. I don't have to tell you how badly that much money would hurt the government if it was put into circulation.

"Colonel Branchflower put me under strict orders to keep these facts from you until the last moment. The fewer people that knew the better—but our mission hasn't changed."

"We still need to save her," Webber shrugged. "No matter what her name is."

"I don't know about you." Clay urged his horse forward again. "But I'm going to save Trap. I don't give a hoot in hell about any counterfeit money." He eyed Roman warily. "I know you only had to do what you were told, Captain. It just takes a minute to digest all this new information. None of us hold it against you." He paused. "Well, Trap might."

"He might at that." Roman smiled. "And I wouldn't blame him."

The clatter of small stones above them sent every man to his sidearm. Clay relaxed when he saw three desert mule-deer does bounding up the steep slope.

"When they stop," Roman whispered to Clay. "Shoot one."

Clay was already returning his Colt to the holster. "Captain?"

"Shoot the deer, Sergeant!" With that, the captain gave a shrill whistle that echoed off the high rocks.

The does stopped in their tracks and looked back, big ears twitching, curious at the unusual noise.

Clay took careful aim with his Peacemaker and dropped the lead doe thirty yards away. She fell instantly and tumbled down the mountainside, almost at the horses' feet. The other two deer flagged their tails and bounded out of sight in an instant, evaporating from view.

"Wish it was always this easy to retrieve meat," Madsen said as he put his pistol away. "Don't know what you have in mind, Captain, but the kidnappers may have heard that shot. They're likely to know we're here now."

Roman nodded slowly. "Pistol shots don't carry far in all these canyons. I doubt anyone heard it. In any case, they have O'Shannon. I imagine they know we're here already. In fact, I hope they do."

Webber chuckled softly. "I can tell you have a plan—and I want you to know I'm behind you no matter what—but at some point I think you're going to have to tell us what it is."

Roman nodded at the jumble of cliffs and piled rocks ahead. "It's difficult to make a concrete plan when we don't know what's around the next bend. The cave is nearby if Fuentes was honest with us. With a few minor changes to stack the odds a little more in our favor, I'm inclined to proceed with the plan as Sergeant Madsen presented it."

Clay jerked back in surprise, startling his roan. "Me? I don't know what you're talkin' about, Captain Roman. I never laid out any plan."

"Oh, but you did." Roman dismounted and walked over to the dead deer. "We're going to kill everyone who isn't Trap or the girl. Now, let's get this deer gutted and slung over O'Shannon's horse."

By dark, Trap's headache had fallen off to a dull thump behind his left ear. It was bothersome, but he could live with it. One look at the poor girl slumped beside him was enough to make him feel guilty for worrying over his own pitiful pain. It was nothing compared to hers.

She shivered in her fitful sleep, whimpering like an injured pup and pulling her knees up tighter to her chest.

Impotent fury welled in Trap's chest, pressing at his gut, until he thought he might be sick. He couldn't help but think of Maggie lying there in such awful circumstances, and supposed it would always be that way. If he saw a woman in trouble, he would always think of what he would do if it was his sweet Maggie.

Trap shook his head to clear the thought, and attempted to calm himself by taking careful stock of the situation. A cold throbbing in his toes drew his attention to his feet. His boots and socks were gone. A quick glance around the chamber revealed one of the blond twins had himself a new set of Army-issue brogans.

All the men but Brandywine cussed and laughed at each other while they huddled over some kind of game. The Indian agent sat alone, staring out the cave mouth.

Trap wiggled his fingers and found his struggles had loosened the ropes—not enough to escape—but enough to be able to twist his hands some. If given a chance, he might be able to pull his arms under and bring them in front. Roman and the others would be coming soon. Trap wanted to be able to fight when they did.

Five hundred yards away, Hezekiah Roman pulled a dry tuft of bunchgrass, crushed it in his hand, and let it drift away on the night breeze. Only the faintest sliver of a moon cut the night sky, but a white curtain of countless stars provided enough light to navigate.

Once he got a fix on the wind, the captain began to heap dry brush, sticks, and anything else that would burn into a large pile.

Johannes pushed a sharpened cedar stave, as big as his wrist, lengthwise through the skinned mule-deer carcass. Clay took one end and helped him position it over two boulders to one side of the wood.

"This ironwood will burn hot and long," Clay said, pulling a match out of an oilskin bag in his shirt pocket. "We were lucky to find it."

"I don't believe in luck, Mr. Madsen," the captain said. His voice was reverent in the darkness. "Change out of your boots and into moccasins before you light the fire. We'll need to be as stealthy as we can for this to work. We'll leave the horses here. By the time the meat starts cooking good, we should be in position."

Haywood, the whiskey peddler, scooped up the yellowed bone dice and held them in a grimy hand. He slowly turned his head toward the cave mouth and sniffed through his pug nose. His sagging eyes relaxed and he gave a fluttering sigh. "You boys smell what I smell?"

Brandywine tilted his head and drew in a lungful of night air. He could smell something—something sweet and delicious floating on the gentle breeze— just a whiff at first, tickling the nose and pulling the men to their feet. Moment by moment the savory odor grew stronger. Stomachs used to canned goods and stale coffee began to growl. Mouths began to water.

"Venison," Bent Jim moaned, licking his lips. "Who the devil would be cooking venison hereabouts?"

Brandywine slapped his thigh and shot a gleeful look at O'Shannon. "You say your friends have the ransom?"

Trap nodded. The girl flinched in her sleep when he spoke. "They're prepared to meet you tomorrow like you instructed in your note."

A crooked smile spread over the Indian agent's round face. He smoothed his thinning hair and smacked his lips, bouncing with energy, hardly able to contain his excitement.

"What the hell's the matter with you, Brandywine?"

Tug spit a slurry of tobacco juice through the gap in his front teeth. "You look like you're about to catch fire."

"Don't you see?" The agent slapped his knee again. "This is just perfect. Those fools have the money with them. I say if they're stupid enough to cook their meat where we can smell it, we ought to go help ourselves—to dinner and the cash."

Realization rippled slowly over the men, each catching on at different speeds. The twins were the last to figure it out.

"If we go ahead and take the money tonight, we won't need to turn the girl over tomorrow. You can keep her at no extra charge. We win the whole damned pot."

"What about the preacher boy?" Hiram sneered, his voice twitching with anticipation. "C-c-can we go on a-h-head and k-kill him?"

Brandywine held up a hand. "All in time, Hiram. Let's make sure we have the money first, then you can have your fun." He walked to Trap, looking down at him. "How many friends do you have out there?"

"Twenty," Trap said.

Brandywine kicked him hard in the side, doubling him over in pain. "I never expected you to tell me the truth anyway. It doesn't matter. They don't know we're coming.

"Hiram," the agent said, spinning on his heels. For the first time in a week he thought he might live to spend his money. "You and Lars stay here and guard these two. Don't do anything to them until we get back. The rest of you boys get your guns ready. Those men out there have our money and I'm ready to go take it from them."

"Y-you better bring us b-b-back some meat." Hiram stood, unhappy at being left behind.

Tug elbowed the boy in the ribs, hard enough to make him flinch and touch the spot gingerly. "We'll bring you meat back, don't you worry about that. Just do like Brandywine says and take care of the prisoners."

Hiram grinned, showing a mouth packed full of crooked, yellow teeth. "Oh, we'll t-t-take c-care of them all right." He began to cackle and his brother Lars joined in.

Tug grabbed him by the collar and hauled him off his feet with a powerful arm. "Listen, you stutterin' little bastard. I don't care what you do to the runt, but you leave that girl be till I get back, you hear me?"

"I h-hear you, T-Tug." Hiram swallowed hard.

Lars nodded his agreement. "Do what we want to the runt."

Hiram and Lars sat poking the campfire for some time after the others left. They whispered to each other, giggled hysterically, then whispered some more. Every now and then they'd leer at the girl or look at Trap and draw a finger across their throats.

Trap scooted up next to the wall next to the girl. He didn't want to startle her.

"Can you hear me?" he whispered.

She opened her swollen eyes and stared at him. There was a sudden wildness there, as if she'd been awakened from a nightmare, but it subsided when she realized who had spoken to her. She gave a slight nod. "I hear you." Her voice was hoarse and frayed.

"I don't want to frighten you," Trap said. "But those boys are working their courage up to try something any time now."

She sighed. "I know. I've been waiting for this time. Maybe it will all be over." Her head fell sideways, so she looked Trap square in the eye. She was young, not too much older than him. She had the broad-hipped build Clay thought so much of, and could have been pretty if not for her present condition. "I'm Inez Hinojosa. What's your name? Since we're about to die, I think we should at least introduce ourselves."

Trap pulled at the ropes behind him, gritting his teeth at the effort. "Trap O'Shannon, United States Cavalry. I came to rescue a girl named Pilar de la Cruz."

The girl gave a halfhearted chuckle, but winced at the pain it caused her raw throat. "They think I'm her."

"Inez, listen to me," Trap said. "We don't have much time. They'll try for me first. But I'm going to need your help."

"Okay," she said, sounding tired and unconvinced.

"My hands are tied, but yours aren't. They will underestimate us because they believe we are helpless."

Her face was expressionless, but she held up her injured hand. The ring and little fingers jutted out at right angles to the palm. They were purple and swollen to twice their normal size. "I'm afraid I won't be much use to you."

Hiram was already on his feet. He threw another armful of branches on the fire and stood for a minute, staring with gleaming eyes at the prisoners. Lars stood behind him, a little to the left.

Trap watched them carefully out of the corner of his peripheral vision, knowing that if he made eye contact they might sense his determination. He wanted them to believe he'd given up.

When Hiram started to move toward him, creeping in for the kill with a wood-handled butcher knife, Trap let his head fall sideways next to Inez's ear. "Do what you can," he hissed. "I can't do this without you."

"It's good to meet you, Trap O'Shannon," the girl croaked as Hiram made his move.

CHAPTER 44

Trap rolled away on his back, kicking up at Hiram's hand. He connected and felt the white-hot pain as the blade sliced the ball of his foot. Hiram yowled in surprise and the knife spun away, clanking off the cave wall.

Lars moved in to help, but Inez threw herself into him, screaming like a spirit of the damned. All the rage from her long hours of torment and suffering boiled out of her and overflowed onto the startled boy. She wrapped her arms around both legs and pulled him to the ground, sinking her teeth into the tender flesh of his thigh.

"Turn aloose of meeeee!" he squealed, beating her on the top of the head. She held fast.

Trap kicked out again, as Hiram descended on him. He caught the boy a glancing blow in the midsection, knocking him sideways but not doing much damage.

Quickly, Trap pushed his arms down as far as he could and brought them up in front of him. He was still tied hand and foot, but he was far from helpless. He knew Inez wouldn't be able to hold out for long; he had to finish this fast.

When Hiram fell on him again, Trap let him come, rolling to the side at the last possible second. He delivered a powerful haymaker with both fists to the back of the other boy's skull. Reaching over Hiram's head, Trap pulled the cord that bound his wrists tight against the stunned twin's throat. He wrenched back with all his might, feeling the windpipe collapse as he twisted and pulled.

Hiram flailed wildly, both hands clawing at Trap's wrists. It did him little good. In a matter of seconds the gurgling stopped and the boy lay still.

Trap pushed him aside and rolled toward the knife. He had it in an instant.

Lars had been so busy with Inez he'd not noticed his dead brother lying in the sand. When he finally knocked the girl out and wrenched himself free from her grasp, he turned to face Trap and a butcher knife in the belly.

He groaned and slumped forward, his mouth open, gasping for air like a suffocating fish.

Trap pushed him aside and let him finish dying in the dirt beside his filthy brother. He held the knife in his teeth to finish freeing his hands, then bent to cut the cords around his ankles. When he was free, he dropped to his knees to check on the girl.

He put a hand to her neck. She had a pulse, but not much of one. She was a fighter, though, she'd shown that. He carried her to a clean spot by the fire and put her carefully in the soft sand, taking care to watch her injured hand, then took off his shirt and draped it over her shivering, twitching body. He gently brushed a lock of hair out of her face.

One eye was swollen completely shut; the other only opened a crack. She smiled. "I'm glad to meet you, Trap O'Shannon. Could I please have a drink of water?"

"What the hell do you think you're doin', preacher boy?" Tug stood at the mouth of the cave, his rifle in his hands. The lion hunter's chest heaved from anger and the exertion of a long run. His face glistened with sweat in the firelight. "You gone and done it now, haven't you, boy." He nodded at the dead twins. "Well, I don't care about no money. I aim to get me a little of that sweet thing there and there ain't a thing you can do to stop me."

Trap scrambled to his feet, casting his eyes around for a weapon of any kind. In his haste to take care of the girl, he'd left Hiram's knife on the ground beside Lars's body.

"You're an awful brave man," Trap said. He heard Inez moan softly behind him. "Killing an unarmed man and molesting a half-dead girl . . ."

Tug spit and gave a long belly laugh. "Aw," he said. "You're gonna make me get all weepy." He raised the rifle to his shoulder and aimed at Trap's belly. "This'll be slow. That way, you can watch—"

A boom like a clap of thunder rocked the inside of the cave. Trap flinched, knowing he was mortally wounded. When he opened his eyes he saw Tug had fallen to his knees. The lion hunter's face twisted, his jaw hung open in a mixture of shock and outrage. A dark and ugly stain spread across his chest.

"Damn it," he spit and fell face-forward into the sand. His rifle hit the ground an instant before he did.

A moment later, Clay Madsen stepped into the cave. "Bad hombre like that shouldn't stand out in a silhouette if he don't want to get shot."

"What took you boys so long?" Trap suddenly felt heady and collapsed back into the sand next to Inez. "I thought I was going to have to kill all these outlaws myself."

"With what, your teeth?" Madsen knelt down in the sand beside his friend and shook his hand. "I was worried about you, compadre." He grinned, blinking moist eyes. "Most of all, I was afraid you'd get all sad and despondent without me around to tell you stories."

Roman and Webber came in the cave with pistols drawn. Both men relaxed when they saw things were under control.

Webber toed the bodies of the dead men, kicking weapons out of their reach to be on the safe side. "How many were there?"

Trap counted in his head, trying to remember faces. "Nine, I think. You got Brandywine?"

Roman slid the Schofield back in his holster. "Juan Caesar won't have to worry about him cheating the Apache anymore."

"This is all of them then." Webber smiled smugly and nodded his head. "This cave is a fortress. I don't care how determined we were; if we would have attacked this place head-on, we'd have been slaughtered. Captain Roman, I have to hand it to you. Your little plan saved the day."

Clay and Inez had already formed a tight kinship by the time they reached Camp Apache. He didn't seem to mind her broken tooth, and she appeared genuinely interested in hearing lots of stories about Clay Madsen and Bastrop, Texas.

After two days of rest and reuniting with their respective sweethearts, the three sergeants sent a special invitation, penned in Lieutenant Fargo's flamboyant hand, to Captain Hezekiah Roman, asking his presence at a ceremony in the Camp Commander's office. The Reverend and Mrs. O'Shannon, Maggie, Inez, Mariposa, Webber's sweetheart, Lieutenant Fargo, and Colonel Branchflower were all in attendance in the cramped, but tidy room.

Dressed for the first time in the blue kersey uniform of a cavalry trooper, Trap O'Shannon did the honors.

"Sir!" The entire room came to attention when Roman walked in, hand in hand with his beautiful Irene. Trap held a shining saber out in front of him in both hands. He offered it to Roman. "The men—your men—wish to make you this gift."

Irene Roman gave her husband's arm a squeeze. He snapped to attention and accepted the sword. His eyes glistened as he drew it from the metal scabbard and held the polished blade up to the light. "I am deeply honored, men." He coughed to clear the catch in his throat. "I . . . I don't know what to say."

Colonel Branchflower harrumphed from behind Fargo's desk. "Don't keep us in the dark, Captain. Read the blasted thing."

Roman swallowed and took a deep breath. As strong as he was, he leaned against his wife for support and read haltingly the words engraved on the blade.

"TO CAPTAIN HEZEKIAH ROMAN—A MAN WORTH FOLLOWING. THE SCOUT TRACKERS. OCTOBER 1878. SANGUIS FRIGITIS!"

CHAPTER 45

1910
Idaho

"Do you reckon the good captain would mind a little toast of some good hot coffee over his casket?" Madsen sniffed, using a red bandanna to wipe a tear out of his eye. "I miss the straitlaced old son of a bitch." He tipped his hat. "Pardon the language, ladies."

Trap smiled and helped Maggie out of her seat. "I imagine he'd be happy to see us."

It was chilly enough to see their breath in the mail car, and everyone but Maggie buttoned their coats up around their necks.

Clay raised his cup above the simple pine casket. He started to speak, then seemed to think better of it and changed course. "If we haven't said it yet, it's too late, I reckon."

"Forgive me." Hanna Cobb reached up to touch Clay gently on the arm. "I know I'm an outsider, but from what you've told me, Captain Roman knew full well how you felt about him."

"I hope so," Trap said, raising his cup next to Clay's. "I sure hope so."

A muffled grunt from behind a stack of bags interrupted the toast. Clay's eyebrows shot up and he set his cup gently on top of Roman's casket. "If you don't mind holding that for a minute, Captain," he said, drawing his Colt.

Trap followed suit and pulled the Schofield from under his coat. He motioned the ladies back toward the door.

"Who's there?" Clay snapped. He pointed the pistol at the boxes. "Come out and show yourself."

A head full of disheveled black hair poked warily over the top of a steamer trunk. Two eyes as big as pie pans looked back and forth from the Colt to the Smith & Wesson. "What have I done to make you boys so mad?" the man said. He slowly raised two rough hands above his head.

"It's the sick passenger I was telling you about," Hanna said.

"What's your name?"

"Reed," the man said in a hoarse voice. "My friends call me Big Mike."

"You sick, Big Mike Reed?" Clay kept the pistol aimed in.

"No, sir," the wobbly man said. "Leastways, not anymore. Got a hold of some bad whiskey back in St. Regis. Thought it was gonna rot my guts out for a while there. The swayin' of the train nearly did me in, I don't mind tellin' you."

"So you don't have the smallpox?"

The man's mouth fell open. "Smallpox? I don't know what you're talkin' about, mister."

Blake O'Shannon arrived a short time later and after a short conversation with his father through the window, boarded the train with Dr. Bruner from Wallace. The doctor took one look at Reed and declared him hungover, but as of yet not infected with smallpox.

There was a sudden commotion outside the mail car door as the doctor helped the queasy miner to his feet. The portly conductor eased in backward, shoved into the cramped and narrow confines of the mail car by Birdie and Leo Baker.

Leo's eyes were swollen and blue. A bandage crossed his pink nose. Birdie's piled hair had fallen a good six inches. Her black boots were scuffed and the tail of her linen blouse was untucked and trailing behind her. Nostrils flared on her prominent nose. Her squinting eyes burned with revenge.

"Get out of my way, you incompetent imbecile. This is all your fault for letting that filthy Indian woman on the train in the first place." The beefy woman beat at the conductor's raised arm with a rolled-up newspaper.

"Ma'am," the pestered man said. "Please, let's work this out like civilized adults."

Leo weighed in at that. "Are you implying that my wife is uncivilized? Why, she's the most civilized person on this train."

"No." The conductor frowned. "Mr. Baker, I must insist—"

"Insist this, you ignorant bastard." Leo Baker took

a wild swing at the conductor. Maybe it was his lack of spectacles, maybe he was just a poor pugilist, but his punch missed completely.

The conductor stepped to one side and Leo, along with his wife, who'd crowded in behind him, both fell headlong into a wide-eyed Big Mike Reed. The postmaster's balding head hit the queasy miner square in the gut, causing him to throw up all over Birdie's coiffure.

Birdie wailed in outrage.

Leo pushed himself back to his feet and fumed. "I am the postmaster of Dillon, Montana. I deserve a little respect around here."

Clay attempted to step forward, but Blake raised his hand and winked.

"Oh, this is bad, sir," he said. "Very bad."

"And just who might you be?" Leo tried to console his screeching wife. "You look as though you are part of the problem."

"Blake O'Shannon, deputy United States marshal." He plowed ahead before Leo could make any more comments about him looking like an Indian. He turned to the doctor. "Doc Bruner, I believe it would be prudent to quarantine the Bakers for a few days since they've had such close contact with someone who may be infected—for their own safety, that is."

Bruner grinned, then caught himself. His brow creased and a serious look crossed his face. "You are right, Deputy." He found a packing blanket and draped it around Birdie's sobbing shoulders. "This is extremely sensitive. We don't want to start a pandemic. Afraid we'll have to keep you here in Idaho for a while."

Leo looked up at him, suspicious. "How long? I have a conference in Phoenix in a week."

"Not this year, sir." Doc Bruner herded his three patients out the door. "You'll be fine. We just need to watch you a while." He looked over his shoulder as they crowded out the narrow door. "We'll take special care of the postmaster of Dillon, Montana."

"So this is your son," Hanna Cobb said when they were all seated in the dining car again and Blake had a hot coffee in front of him to warm his shivering bones. Trap hadn't had time to notice it before, but the boy was drawn and trail-worn. His clothes were damp from a hard ride and he was soaked to the skin. Dark circles hung under weary eyes.

He downed his steaming coffee like it was water.

Hanna filled his cup again with a porcelain pitcher at the table. "Your father and mother have been telling me so much about their youth—the Scout Trackers and all."

Blake's eyes suddenly widened. He slapped the table. "I almost forgot, Pa. I have news."

"I thought so," Maggie said, giving Blake a sidelong look. "You seemed to be carrying a heavy burden."

"It's about Mr. Webber," Blake went on. "He was recuperating in a hospital in Phoenix under the name of Johannes Fargo. He was in pretty bad shape and wasn't expected to live. One of the local deputies recognized him from a poster I sent down and put a guard on him." Blake took a sip of his coffee. He'd finally stopped shivering.

"There's more, isn't there?" Trap sighed, knowing, sensing what his son was about to say next.

"There is. Webber killed the man guarding him and slipped away last night."

"I knew it was too good to be true." Clay pounded his fist on the table. He fiddled with the end of his mustache while he stared, blank-faced, out the window. The train was moving again. "Johannes is too wily to be cooped up in some hospital."

"I can't believe he murdered the captain." Hanna stirred a spoonful of cream into her coffee. "From the sounds of things, Roman was the one who watched over him the most."

"Some folks fight because they're angry," Maggie said. "Or because they hate Indians or some other such thing. Johannes Webber fights because his brain is on fire. He resents what he was, and he grew to despise Hezekiah for trying to help him."

"I know I wasn't as close to him as Trap or the captain," Madsen said. "And it will likely fall on me to kill him someday. But, there's one thing I know for sure. I would have died for him all those years ago."

"Any one of us would have," Trap said. "Without hesitation—and he would have done the same for me."

Hanna Cobb took a drink of her coffee. "To go from a devoted comrade at arms to hateful killer— that's quite a leap for anyone. There had to be something. Something had to happen to make him hate you all so much."

The train picked up speed now, rocking the dining car gently. Snow-clad firs and spruces rolled by outside in the chilly blue shadows of evening. It was beginning to snow again.

"That, my dear Mrs. Cobb," Clay said, "is a very long story."

Hanna pushed her cup away. She put both hands flat on the table and leaned forward, spellbound with anticipation. "I'll bet it's interesting." Her green eyes sparkled.

Madsen looked at Trap, then at Maggie. They both shrugged. The big Texan sighed. "Oh, darlin', you have no idea."

AUTHOR'S NOTE

On rare occasion, when enlisted men in the United States Cavalry desired to bestow the highest honor on a particular officer, they gave him the gift of a sword. By this token, these leaders were inducted into an exclusive order of fighting men, an order of absolute respect and devotion from their subordinates—the Order of the Saber.

ACKNOWLEDGMENTS

The list of good people who helped me and buoyed me up during this adventure is almost without number. I should take the time to thank my fellow trackers and gun-toters for watching over me when my mind was somewhere else: Holland, Sonny, Kevin, John, and Wanda—and especially Ty Cunningham, a superb comrade at arms and a tracker who knows no equal.

Further, I ought to thank the librarians and teachers in my life: Lou, Al, Julie, Lola, Billie, and Irene— the only people who are sure to read this story and tell me they like it—no matter what they really think.